LONDON LOVERS

THE TAYLORED MEN SERIES

J R GALE

J R GALE PUBLISHING LLC

Editing: Ellie McLove- My Brothers Editor

Proofing: Rosa Sharon- My Brothers Editor

Cover: Bee- Bitter Sage Designs

Photographer: Wander Aguiar

ISBN: 979-8-9885905-2-1

"Two souls are sometimes created together and in love before they're born" - F. Scott Fitzgerald

LONDON LOVERS

1

Sadie

FINALLY! The wheels hit the ground, and I'm instantly bouncing in my seat. Anticipation runs through me, excited for what's to come. But it's taking freaking forever to get off this plane.

It's been eight hours since I've left Manhattan and eight hours since I left my old self behind.

Now, I'm excited to get the hell away from New York and to start my annual girls' trip.

But I'm especially excited to see my best friend, Annabelle—it's been almost one year since I've seen her last, the longest stretch since we have been kids.

Finally, the seat belt light switches off, and all the passengers jump up to grab their carry-on bags. Lining up, eager to head off the plane.

"Bienvenu en France," the stewardess kindly welcomes me as we disembark the plane, and I thank her.

"Merci beaucoup," in what I can only hope sounded French.

I walk out onto the tarmac, waiting for the shuttle to bring us to our terminal, and that's when I'm hit with that familiar feeling I always get when I arrive at my final destination.

It's that buzzing energy and eagerness you feel from other travelers excited to start an adventure.

I take a minute to check out my new surroundings, and almost everyone looks the same. Eyes wide, backs tall, heads high, smiles wide. No matter where you land in the world, everyone does it. It's the magic of traveling.

For some, it's the excitement of starting something new, maybe a honeymoon or a well-deserved holiday they've saved for. But, for others, it's a feeling they've escaped whatever it is they are leaving behind. And, unfortunately for me, it's the latter—the cheater ex-boyfriend and parents who aren't worthy of holding the title.

An hour later, I finally exit the customs area after getting stuck behind the loudest New Yorkers known to man. Not exactly the way I envisioned this starting. But I'm off to retrieve my baggage, where Belle should be waiting for me.

"Sadie, darling, I'm over here!" she screams across the baggage claim, waving her hands like a crazed woman.

She isn't hard to miss. I spotted her instantly, along with half of the airport.

I'll never know if people are staring because she's screaming or because of Belle's looks. She must have been a model in her former life; Tall, blonde, and perfect—inside and out.

Growing up, we spent every summer together, and all the boys fawned over her, giving her the unfortunate nickname of "BB" or "Double *B*" for Bombshell Belle. Luckily the only time she ever hears that now is if my brother is trying to piss her off.

I walk over to where Belle is still waving her arms. I love this girl with all of my heart, but I can already see her enthusiasm is at level one hundred. And, after my long overnight flight, I'm not exactly ready for it.

The saying "opposites attract" is not just about romantic couples. It applies to best friends too.

Annabelle has that larger-than-life attitude. She's a busy bee, Miss Popular, career-driven, and all around good person with a strong backbone. On the other hand, I tend to be more reserved and shy. I probably could use a little of Belle's charisma in some instances.

That's what this trip is all about, breaking all my bad habits of letting everyone walk all over me and finally doing what's best for me. Although I don't love being the center of attention, I am still a strong, independent person. I just lost my way a little, and I am finally set to be back on track with my life.

And, with Belle by my side, I know it will happen. She is the only person in the world I want to be right now, my bestie and sister soul mate. The best support person you'll ever need in your life.

"I've missed you so much," I mumble into her hair.

"Oh, Sadie. I've also missed you so much. I can't believe it's been so long."

"Please, Annabelle, don't start. If you cry, I cry."

I need to go into this trip with good happy vibes.

I've felt terrible that I canceled going to London to see Belle and my brother for Christmas. Instead, I was suckered into staying for my mother's charity luncheon, her charity banquet, her charity cocktail party, and who knows what other event she made me attend for appearances. *But no more.*

"Right, right, well, let's get your bags and make our way to the hotel. Our driver is waiting right out front."

We drive a short distance to our hotel located on the Cote d'Azur in a small town called Antibes, located somewhere between Nice and Saint-Tropez.

Initially, I rented a country home right outside Avignon, where I could reset, think things through, and try to understand how I let myself get steamrolled by my family and Colton, my ex, time and time again.

But unlucky, for me, lucky for Belle, the house caught fire a few months ago, and Annabelle insisted on staying here. Which now isn't looking so bad, after all.

We enter the property down a long, tree-lined driveway, barely making out the hotel in the distance. This place is top notch, I can already tell. But then again, I did not expect anything less from Annabelle.

We might have grown up "upper class," but I try to live a more reserved lifestyle. Belle, on the other hand—not so much.

The bellhops walk out to meet our car while the hotel staff waits with champagne and warm towels.

"Welcome, you must be Ms. Hughes," the one attendant says to Annabelle.

"Yes, and this is my friend, Sadie Peters."

"Welcome, please let us take your luggage while my colleague Jacques escorts you to reception to check in."

I pinch Annabelle's side and raise my eyebrows.

Jacques is gorgeous, and if I know Annabelle, she will jump right on that.

"Jacques," she purrs. "What a beautiful French name. Where are you from?"

Paris pronounced Pa-ree in his beautiful French accent

I walk away to explore the hotel before catching Annabelle go into full flirt mode.

And, wow, I am lost for words. This hotel is beyond gorgeous.

After you pass through the two massive front doors, the reception area is entirely open, greeting you with the most spectacular view of the Mediterranean Sea.

The lobby is done mainly in sleek white marble and glass walls, adorned with huge flower arrangements of orchids, white roses, and I definitely smell jasmine somewhere. White-and-beige linen curtains blow from the sea breeze, giving it a relaxing but romantic feel. This place is perfect.

I make my way over to the beautiful lady waiting for us to check in. *Geez, do they only employ good-looking people here*?

I look down at my overnight flight outfit, realizing I probably should have freshened up and changed at the airport before arriving at the hotel.

After giving our information to the front desk attendant, Annabelle wanders back over.

"Holy shit, Sadie!" she whisper-screams.

"What? What's the matter?"

"Did you see who's here?"

"Who?" I ask, turning my head, looking to see someone familiar.

"Well, knowing you, you probably were more worried about the decor and floral arrangements than paying attention to anyone else."

I roll my eyes. "Oh, shut it, Miss I Need To Flirt With Every Man I See."

"Well, don't look now. But Wills Taylor and three other extremely good-looking, probably also rugby players, are standing over to our right, about to check in."

"I have no idea who Wills Taylor is, Belle," I say in a huff.

She knows everyone and their mother. Why would I expect anything different now that we are in the South of France?

I slowly move my head to check out this Wills Taylor she is talking about, and holy hell, she wasn't lying.

There are four massively huge, very attractive men over on the other side of the hotel check-in area. Usually, the big muscle type is not my cup of tea, but no one can deny how good-looking these men are. They are all dressed perfectly in crisp summer suits and loafers, but one of them is just that much more handsome than the others. He looks like he should be in an old Hollywood movie, the James Dean of our time, but with a very muscular, athletic body. It's hard to move my eyes away. It's like I'm glued to him. But just when I go to turn back to Annabelle, he slowly turns to me, and his eyes catch mine.

Oh god, this is like a bad car crash, where I can't look away. He slowly lifts one side of his mouth with a too-sexy smirk, and I can feel the heat of embarrassment spread through my body.

"What the hell?" Belle snaps me out of my gaze. It's also when I realized I've been holding my breath.

"What's the matter?" I widen my eyes and act surprised.

"I just told you not to look, and you were staring right at Wills. Now he is staring right over at us. Actually…"

"Actually, what?" I snap a little too fast.

She raises her eyebrows slightly and says, "He's staring at you, and he just tapped one of his mates. They are both looking at you right now."

"You need to get your eyes checked, Belle. I'm standing next to you, and I'm in yoga pants and a T-shirt. Let's go. Our room is ready."

I start to head toward the elevator, not waiting for her. I need a shower and a glass of wine to relax in our suite. I can't be thinking of any guys.

"What does that mean? You're standing next to me?" she huffs once she catches up.

I roll my eyes at her. "It meant nothing, just that you're standing here dressed like we're about to go out to a garden party, all perfect and beautiful, and I look like I just did an hour of hot yoga."

I press the elevator for one of the top floors where all the suites are located; we are sharing a two-bedroom suite that Belle says is "to die for."

As the doors are closing, I catch another glimpse of this Wills she keeps going on about, and my stomach drops. He really is strikingly handsome, all serious and mysterious looking. But fortunately, the doors shut before I could think any more about him. I am here to turn over a new leaf, not troll for men.

"Sadie, are you even listening?"

"Huh? No, I zoned out for a minute, sorry. What were you saying?"

"That you need to stop being so hard on yourself—you are your own worst critic. You're beautiful even with yoga pants on. Plus, I would die for your bum." Belle laughs and pinches my behind.

"Okay, okay, enough about me. Our room is here, number 1414."

We walk inside, and again the beauty of this place has me lost for words.

Our bags are already up here, and the porters must have opened all the windows so we could smell the fresh sea breeze. We walk through the white-and-gray marble foyer that leads to the balcony.

Holy crap, this is bigger than some New York apartments. We have a small dipping pool overlooking the sea, a dining room table, lounge chairs, and a small bar area. We could probably stay here the whole vacation and never leave.

"Wow, Belle, you did good. This place is amazing. This is the exact place I need to be right now."

She settles up next to me, leaning over to give me a side hug. "I'm glad you're happy. You deserve this trip more than anyone. But I know you're exhausted, so go jump in the shower, take a power nap, and get ready so we can relax, catch up, have some drinks before dinner. Woo!"

"Take it down fifty notches until I get that nap, crazy!" I laugh as I head toward the shower.

"Love you, too!" she yells.

I find my room, and holy crap, it's filled with multiple bouquets of flowers. Well, there goes the no-crying rule because the tears are already streaming down my face. I know this is Annabelle's doing. I walk over to the small arrangement next to my bed with fresh lavender and read the attached small card.

My darling Sadie,

I think each of our paths is already set for us when we are born. We may not understand the whys and reasoning behind our journeys yet, but we will all go through things in life that set us up for what is meant to be. You have already overcome some obstacles that have only made you stronger. So, please don't let anyone erase your spirit and sparkle that makes you, you.
You are the most selfless, kindhearted person I have ever had the pleasure of knowing in my life. What comes next for you on this life journey will only bring you happiness and love. I know it. So please embrace whatever comes your way next. I am so proud of you. You deserve it all.
I love you.

Your sister soul mate,
Annabelle

Now sobbing, I take the note and store it in my bag to avoid losing it.

Between Belle and I, we have more emotions than a romance novel. But I don't know what I would do without her, always knowing exactly what I need to hear. People could only wish to have an Annabelle in their lives.

After I shower and nap, I stroll out to the balcony where Belle is relaxing, sipping some champagne. I walk over to her and hug her tightly. She kisses my cheek, and I whisper, "I love you."

"I love you, too, Sadie."

We sit there hugging for a minute until Belle decides it's time for more champagne.

"A toast is in order!" she shouts. "Cheers to the almost birthday girl. Let's make this trip the best one yet. Sleep all morning, beach all day, drink, dance, and have sex all night!" She clinks my glass.

I hit my hand to my forehead and laugh. "I am not having sex all night, or sex at all. You're lucky that I'm agreeing to party, *sometimes*."

"Sadie, you need to let loose on this trip. Why can't sex be in order? The way Wills was staring at you made it very clear he would be interested. It just so happens, I think I know one of his friends. I'm going to invite them out tomorrow night if I have the chance."

I ignore her and continue to drink my champagne. I feel a blush creeping up and butterflies in my stomach. The feeling I got when Wills just glanced over was something I am certainly not used to.

But he looked like he would be all too consuming and a little intense for my liking. I practically roll my eyes at myself.

Yeah, right, Sadie, you liked exactly how he was looking at you.

I ignore those thoughts and stare out over the balcony. I take in the view before me, thinking about what this trip means to me. Belle and I take a few weeks' vacation every year, but tomorrow, I turn thirty and I promised myself I would start doing what was best for *me* now.

I am finally going to open my own floral design shop, it's something I've dreamed about my whole life. I want to volunteer more and travel even more.

Belle has been trying to get me to move to London for some time now, and honestly, it isn't the worst idea. A place to start fresh. Plus, my brother, Jackson, lives there, and I miss him a ridiculous amount. So I know it's the right move, I just need to woman up and take the plunge.

Besides being close to Annabelle and Jackson, the other major perk of moving would be to distance myself from my parents and our toxic relationship.

The other reason would be I wouldn't have to see Colton anymore. Since I caught him cheating, he has tried to get back together numerous times, claiming it was only that once.

But little does he know—I know the truth. It's been going on for more than six months, and honestly, I'm not sure I even care. Which tells you… I'm done.

I clearly didn't love him anymore, and it took an unfortunate circumstance to show me that. At the end of the day, I was more embarrassed than heartbroken with what he did.

He was what my parents always wanted, a rich boy from a high society family with strong political ties. We met when we were twenty-four and were good friends first. Both of us were so carefree and enjoyed many of the same interests. I did love him. But he grew to be everything I hate about the social circles our families run in. Caring more about status and appearances than me.

Annabelle tops off my champagne, not saying anything. She knows when I just need to process things by myself.

Maybe it wouldn't hurt if I let loose this trip and lived untroubled like Belle? I know how to go out and have a good time. It's just not my priority like her. Plus, I don't have many friends in Manhattan that I enjoy letting loose with like I do with her. Since she lives over three thousand miles away, it's easier to have quiet weekends with a good book and wine. On occasion, a nice dinner, or if I'm forced, my family drags me to events to be "seen."

So, to let loose and have "Annabelle type of fun" is just not second nature to me.

But maybe it's time to set out and try.

"Let's go shopping tomorrow, Belle. I think I need something sexier and more birthday appropriate if we aim to go out dancing tomorrow night."

She couldn't whip her head faster toward me, clapping her hands like a little kid.

"YES, YES, YES, let's do it! When we head down to dinner, I'll ask the concierge where the best shopping is. And on that note, let's go inside so you can get ready for dinner," she says as she tops us off with even more champagne.

I'm jet-lagged and now tipsy. We better leave soon. Otherwise, I'll be passing out again.

I'm finishing up my makeup when Belle comes into my room looking freaking gorgeous.

"Belle," I moan. She always does this. "You said we were getting drinks and dinner at the bar downstairs—nothing fancy tonight."

She looks down at herself and smirks. "You know me, fancy is my middle name."

"I'm almost done, and to be clear, when we get downstairs, I want no more talk about me. I only want to hear about you—you can catch me up on this new guy you're dating."

"Dating is too serious of a word. I'm not tying myself to anyone right now."

Of course, she's not.

"Done! Let's go."

My stomach rumbles loudly as we leave. It's only now I realize I haven't eaten since the plane ride.

We make our way to the hostess stand to get seated for dinner. I'm still in awe of the decor in this hotel. The beach theme continues throughout but adds different elements as you explore.

The restaurant reminds me of beach meets Paris, all-white flowing linens, but high ceilings and beautiful moldings. The bar is a white marble with brass hardware fitted with mauve-colored velvet chairs. I think I need to recreate this at home somehow. It's classy, simple, yet super sexy all at the same time.

The hostess is an attractive young girl—*shocker*—and not the friendliest. Nevertheless, she's giving Belle the once-over, and I can already tell this will be an issue.

"I am sorry, but we are very backed up tonight. So, you will need to sit at the bar and wait," the hostess says in a short, clipped voice.

"Well, that's not good enough. How long will it be? We traveled all day and have a reservation for right now," Belle explains.

"Madam, I do not know. You need to move to the bar now. I have other customers to help."

"Annabelle, let's just get a drink first, then eat." I hate confrontation.

"Fine." She glares at the hostess. "One drink, then our table better be ready."

We walk off to the lounge area near the bar. "Don't get all worked up," I warn.

"She just hit a nerve. She kept looking me up and down. It was as if she just decided right there and then that they were busy and we couldn't sit."

We switch from champagne to some slightly dirty martinis. I can already predict most of our drink orders—champagne, wine, martinis, and lots of spicy margaritas.

"So… spill the tea, Belle. Starting with this new man of yours."

We may talk every day and get caught up with each other. But it's just not the same as an in-person gossip sesh.

"Ugh. He is not my man. I am still a single woman. But I think there is potential there. I met him through a coworker of mine. His name is Trey."

"Trey?!" I spit my drink out, laughing. God, why am I laughing? That's so mean. But I can't help it, I can't stop. "Trey has to be listed as one of the top ten douchiest names, right?"

I cannot see Miss High Society Annabelle with a "Trey."

She starts laughing now too. "I know it's terrible, isn't it? But he is rather handsome, so it makes up for his name."

I take a deep breath. "Okay, okay. Sorry. Tell me more. Give me the rundown."

"He is older by a few years and very close to his family. Which, by the way—they have a house in the Alps, so now we have a ski house if this works out. He is an only child, lives in Mayfair, has many good-looking friends for you, and he's a barrister." She takes a deep breath. "He's just over six feet, so tall enough for me, which is crucial."

Belle, being probably around five feet ten, needs someone tall, no question about it.

"He has more of a runner's body, but still muscular, dark hair, light eyes, light skin. Proclaimed foodie. No faults so far, except he works a lot. And he lives a lifestyle a little closer to yours." She winks. "Probably better off since I am always out and about at events and openings all around London for work and fun. If we both lived a similar lifestyle, it wouldn't work."

Belle is in public relations, which suits her perfectly.

"Well, even though I will probably never be able to say his name without laughing, I am glad you're happy and giving this guy a try." I smile at her softly.

"You've been killing it at your job, and now you have someone that seems just as successful. Who, hopefully, won't feel threatened like other men in your past."

"Boys, Sadie, not men. Too emasculating to date a woman that's more successful than them."

She chuckles and adds, "Plus, they all had small dicks. I can't work with that."

She is too much. I'm laughing hard again—god, I've missed this girl. At least my abs are getting a workout tonight.

We finish our martinis when I feel someone's eyes on me. I turn to the bar and spot Wills's friends all standing ordering drinks, but I don't see him.

But for some reason, I just know he's here somewhere. I'm getting the same feeling I had when we were in the lobby. So I take another look around when a deep voice whispers in my ear, sending a shiver through my body.

"Looking for me?"

I slowly raise my eyes. Jesus, he is freaking hot. His gorgeous gray eyes bore into mine, and he raises an eyebrow in question.

"Huh?" I hear him chuckle a little. Jesus, I can't even put together a sentence.

"I asked if you were looking for me? I saw you looking over at my friends. Then it seemed like you didn't find what you were looking for."

So smug.

"I, um, no. I was looking for the waiter to order another drink," I say.

Belle's eyes are as wide as saucers right now, and I am trying to telepathically tell her to jump in here and say something.

"Wills Taylor." He reaches his hand out for mine.

I extend my hand to him, and he kisses the back, leaving his lips there a little longer than expected.

"And you are?" he says in his posh British accent.

"Sadie. And this is my friend Annabelle."

He doesn't even glance over at her. This is very intense. *He is very intense.*

"Can I buy you ladies another round?"

"No," "Yes," Belle and I say in unison.

"Yes, please." Belle beats me to it.

"Okay." He chuckles. "I'll be right back." He drops my hand. I hadn't even realized he was still holding it. But the second he lets go, I feel an instant loss.

What the hell is that all about?

"Holy shit, Sadie! That was freaking hot. I told you he wanted to devour you."

What do I even say to her? She's right. He looked like he wanted to eat me alive, right there and then.

I glance back to the bar and catch a glimpse of Wills talking with his friends. He's in the perfect position for me to see him full on now.

He's wearing a different suit than earlier and has undone a few top buttons for a more relaxed feel. His chest is broad, where you can see the outline of his muscles and a dusting of very light-brown hair. But his legs, holy hell! The way they fill out his suit is just, wow.

I think Belle mentioned he played rugby, and I can see it now.

I realize I'm staring, so I slowly turn my eyes back to a very smiley Belle. "Don't start. That was too intense. I could barely form a freaking sentence," I mutter.

"That's because you're turned on. Look at you—you're beet red."

"I am not," I deny. But I know I am. I can feel the heat radiating off me. And I can't help but reach up and touch my face to confirm. "I was just taken by surprise, that's all."

"Well, I don't believe that one bit. Anyway, Wills is coming back over now, with his three friends."

I jolt up and fix my dress and hair quickly.

I think I hear Belle murmur, "That's what I thought." But I ignore her. I can't have her in my head right now.

All four guys make it to our table with our drinks. Wills hands me mine.

"Thank you, Wills," I whisper and look down at my drink. His stare is too intense for me.

"Annabelle Hughes, it's lovely to see you. How are your brothers?" I hear one of Wills's friends ask Annabelle.

Now, I remember she mentioned she may have known one of his friends.

"They are trouble, as usual." She laughs.

"George, this is my best friend, Sadie Peters. We are here on holiday for the next few weeks."

George walks over and kisses both my cheeks.

"It's a pleasure," he says.

Behind him, Wills is staring daggers into the back of his head. What the hell is that about?

"Seems like you met Wills. These are our friends Leo and Declan. Lucky for you girls, we are also here on holiday for a few weeks." He winks, and I shake the other two's hands, introducing myself.

Leo and George seem like fun boys. Declan seems just as intense as Wills but with a gentler side. I'm getting this feeling that there is more to him than meets the eye.

"Anna, it's been so long since I've seen you. I'm surprised I recognized you," George states.

"Ah! Anna, I haven't heard someone call you that in a long time." I laugh, and she glares at me. She would rather be called Double *B* than Anna. Not sure what her hang-up is, but she's hated it for as long as I can remember.

"You've known each other a long time?" George asks.

"Yes." Belle smiles over at me. "We have been best friends for twenty-five years."

Wills still hasn't said a word since walking back here, but I can feel his eyes on me. I don't chance a look because I'm afraid I'll start drooling or do something equally as stupid.

"Why don't you ladies join us for dinner?" Leo chimes in.

"No can do, boys. The first night is always just Sadie and me. No matter where we travel, it's our rule. Just her and I." She grabs my hand and squeezes lightly.

We made that rule when we were teenagers, as our life got too busy. Whenever we saw each other, throughout the years, the first night was always to catch up and just spend time together.

"But I have an even better invitation," she adds. "Tomorrow, it's Sadie's thirtieth birthday, and we are going dancing. Meet us at the club after dinner? I can send you the details, George."

They all nod.

"See you boys tomorrow, then!" Belle giggles and blows kisses to the guys as they walk off like she's known them for years.

Wills is still beside me, so I finally look up as he leans down toward me. "Good night, Sadie, until tomorrow, beautiful," he whispers, then kisses my cheek with a slightly open mouth, lingering there for a second.

I'm speechless. Again.

What the hell was that*? And why did I want to turn my head so my lips could feel his open mouth?*

2

Sadie

"… happy birthday, dear Sadie, happy birthday to you!"

I slowly open one eye, hoping Belle doesn't realize I'm awake because I'm not sure what the hell is going on, but it feels like I'm in some crazy nightmare.

Annabelle is on the bed, standing over me, flowers in hand, and there are a million and one balloons around the room. I turn over and smash my face into the pillow. I am not a morning person.

"Wake up, darling!"

"Belle, thank you for this, but I am so jet-lagged. I need a little more sleep. Please, please, please. It is my birthday, you know?"

"It's noon, Sadie. I think you've slept long enough, birthday or not. Get that cute little bum of yours up."

Noon? What the hell? I never sleep this late. Even when I'm on vacation.

Groaning, annoyed, I still feel so tired, I finally turn over to stretch and finally get out of bed.

"What's on the agenda today?" I begrudgingly ask Annabelle because I already know how she will want to start the day.

"A quick workout, and before you complain, it helps with the jet lag. Then, we won't feel as bad after we eat and drink all day. And after, birthday fun! Shopping, spa, dinner, dancing."

Ugh, I know she is right about working out, but who the hell wants to work out on their birthday? Shouldn't I be stuffing my face with cupcakes and champagne?

I scoot her out of my room so I can have some privacy then get ready without complaint because I know there is no changing her mind. And, of course, there is a brand-new workout outfit laid out for me to wear. Happy birthday to me, a new workout outfit. *Yay*!

But I have to give it to Belle, she always gets the fit perfect even though we have completely opposite bodies. She is tall, lean, with huge boobs. I'm average height, average boobs, but have, as Belle likes to call it, a bubble butt. Even our features are entirely different. I have long, dark hair, olive skin, and green eyes. Belle is a natural platinum blonde, fair skin with crystal-blue eyes.

I rip off the tags once I know it fits. Only Belle would buy Stella McCartney workout clothes. Although, I'll admit these are super cute, trendy, and very comfortable.

I check myself out in the mirror one last time and make my way out to the foyer. Belle is running in place, ready to go. Is this girl on crack? What is with her this trip?

"Okay, you lunatic. Let's go. Don't you think you could have waited five minutes to start your workout?"

She doesn't even acknowledge me and heads to the elevator.

We walk side by side, down the long corridor to the double-wide wooden doors that lead to the outdoor gym. I'm about to step in when the doors fly open, and out walks Wills and Declan.

I stop dead in my tracks, mesmerized by the two Adonises in front of me. I've honestly never seen two such good-looking men side by side like this before. They are both shirtless and holy muscles! I'm desperately trying to keep my eyes from popping out of my head, but it's impossible with them this close.

Declan is covered in tattoos that were hidden by his suit, and Wills is standing there dripping with sweat down his glistening chest, and holy crap, he is h-o-t.

I stand there, stunned. What is it with this guy that makes me mute? *He's insanely gorgeous and domineering, that's what.*

"Ladies." Declan smiles and raises his chin in greeting. I smile up at him and then chance another look at Wills as he takes a step closer to me.

"Happy birthday, Sadie. Will you save me a dance tonight?" I feel his low, gravelly voice deep down in my stomach.

"Okay," I whisper and can't help the smile creeping up my face.

He reaches down, lifts my chin higher, and rubs his thumb gently back and forth. My lips part slightly, goose bumps scatter up my body, and instantly his lips turn up in a smirk. He's no fool, he knows exactly the effect he has on me.

"If you look this good in workout clothes, I can only imagine how sexy you'll look tonight."

"Alright, Casanova, let's go. Leo and George are waiting for us. See you tonight, ladies," Declan says with amusement, and with that, they both turn and stride away.

"Not a word, Annabelle," I warn, but I can see her fanning her face in an exaggerated motion.

How the hell am I going to work out now?

We finished a light workout, or at least that's what I did. Belle, on the other hand, was on another level. We quickly shower, change, and head out for lunch and shopping.

I haven't been able to stop thinking about Wills and the effect he has on me. If I'm being truthful with myself, I'm actually a little nervous for tonight. I haven't felt excited about a guy in a long time, probably since I met Colton five years ago, and even then, I'm not sure it ever felt like this. I've never met a man like Wills, who unashamedly flirts with me like I'm the only one in the room. So confident.

It's also hard for me to understand what he sees in me. I'm not saying I'm ugly—I'm pretty enough with a great body I work hard for. But this hotel is filled with supermodels and women who are literal perfection, Belle included. And, since Wills is on another level, like magazine cover level, I don't understand why he isn't going after girls like Belle.

But on the other hand, I did promise myself some fun this trip, and since Wills definitely doesn't seem the relationship type… a holiday fling may be precisely what the doctor orders.

Heading to lunch, we walk through beautiful cobblestone streets that are lined with different shades of orange, peach, and pink houses. The windows are flanked with shutters and flower boxes that are planted with beautiful flower varietals. This place is a dream—I could see myself easily retiring here one day.

We walk a short distance more, and the scene changes right in front of our eyes. You definitely know you're at the beach now.

People are in bikinis and cover-ups, with sand stuck to their tanned bodies. Tomorrow, after a long night out, I'm going to tell Belle we need to just lie out and tan all day long. I brought several books I want to read, and nothing screams vacation like reading on the beach with a margarita in hand.

Finally, we make it to our destination, and it's just so quintessential Coastal French—

this is breathtaking.

The restaurant is mainly outside, set right on the sand. They use bamboo reeds as a roof, and all the tables are set with white plates and different shades of baby-blue tablecloths with rattan chairs.

The beat of the music is pumping through the air, and people are drinking, dancing, and eating. The rosé is flowing, and it's used almost like a decoration—the soft pink color of the wine blending right in with the light blue. I'm in awe of this place.

Okay, now this is an excellent start to my birthday. The gym, not so much.

"A good stop for a birthday lunch, I gather?"

I realize now I've been taking this all in, not saying a word to Belle until she interrupts me. I've been doing that a lot lately, just daydreaming, thinking about the things going on around me.

"It's perfect. Thank you so much for bringing me here." I kiss her cheek.

We get seated for lunch and order salads, bread, and wine, a balanced French diet, right?

"Have they called?" Belle asks, breaking me out of the blissful bubble I've been in all day.

"No, why even bring it up, Annabelle? They suck. I'm sure they don't even remember the day their only daughter was born. Of course, being a good daughter, I left a message when I landed to let them know I made it, but I haven't heard back. So, it is what it is. That's why I'm here now, on this trip, with you."

I see her flinch slightly. I know I'm getting worked up. My parents don't even deserve the time for us to breathe their names.

My phone rings at that exact moment, and we both look down at it like it's miraculously going to be my parents.

"Ah! Someone who actually loves me. Hi Jackson, honey, how are you?" I answer.

Put it on speaker, Belle mouths.

"Happy birthday, Sades! I miss you."

"You wouldn't miss me if you jumped on a plane to see me while I was in Europe. By the way, you're on speaker. Belle's with me. We're out to lunch."

"Hey B, what's going on, stranger? I've lived in London for over a year now, and I still haven't seen you. What's up with that?"

"Oh, you know, super busy with work," she spits out.

"After our summer holiday, let me know when you're free, and we can put something on the calendar."

Her breathing is labored, and she's doing everything to not look at me.

She normally plays it off well, but she has had a crush on my brother since we were about thirteen years old. We don't keep secrets, but it's the one thing she won't admit to me.

Jackson is oblivious, and probably for the better. He is a fuckboy through and through. I love him, but he has a new woman on his arm every other night.

Jackson invests and starts up high-end restaurants and clubs worldwide, so I guess it fits his lifestyle for now. And as much as I may not exactly condone his playboy ways, he is the best brother in the world and would defend and protect me no matter what—so I don't bother him about it.

"So, Sades, what else do you have planned for your birthday trip?"

"Well, today just some shopping and spa, tonight Belle has set us up to go out dancing, which I'm excited about. Then no plans for the rest of the time. I just want to relax, explore the small little towns around the coast and Provence if we have time."

"A guy she met is meeting us at the club!" Belle quickly yells over me.

Is she freaking kidding me? I kick her hard under the table.

"Ow!"

"I'll kick you again if you don't shut up," I say through my clenched teeth. "Don't listen to her, Jackson. Yes, a guy showed interest, but he's not my type. He's too cocky. I just want to go out dancing and have fun for my birthday."

"Okay, well, don't do something stupid, Sades, don't go home with a stranger. You're not that girl." He continues, "I know you're hurt about Colton and our dumbass parents, but don't jump into something because you get some attention."

Is he kidding? "You know me better than that. I'm the responsible one. I'm not you or Belle." I stick my tongue out at her, and she just shrugs her shoulders and smiles.

Jackson snickers. "Okay, I'm just looking out for you. You know I'll always have your back, no matter what you decide. But, hey, I need to run into a meeting. Have the best time tonight, and I'm so sorry I couldn't get there for the big three zero. I promise I'll make it up to you soon, especially if you move to London. I love you, Sadie. Bye, B."

I ignore his moving comment. I need to figure it out more before I commit and let them know I want to move there for sure. The more and more I think about it, though, I have nothing left in New York. I can easily work as floral designer anywhere in the world. So why would I stay?

"I know you do. You're the best brother I could ever ask for. I love you too."

"Bye, Jack," Belle quickly adds.

"How much longer is this walk, Annabelle?"

"We're here."

The next stop for my birthday is shopping, and Belle says this place has all our favorite designers. A little tipsy now, all that rosé may not have been the best idea for my wallet before a shopping trip. But I guess you only turn thirty once.

We get up to the door. It looks closed. "Shit, Belle, did we even check if it's open?"

"By 'we' you mean me?" She gives me a sideways glance and rings the doorbell.

A petite older lady in a beautiful Chanel suit opens the door.

"Bonjour, Madam Annabelle? Entrez."

"Oui. Parlez-vous Anglais?"

I think Belle asks her if she speaks English. Belle can speak enough French to help us get by, which is always helpful when we travel together.

"Yes, I speak English. Welcome to my shop. Please come upstairs, and I will show you what I have for you." She looks us both up and down quickly, probably assessing our bodies to see what she could pull from the racks.

We make our way upstairs, and I'm shocked *again.* This place is out of this world. I feel like I'm in my favorite movie, *A Midnight in*

Paris, and took a step back into the nineteen twenties. The shop is perfectly glamorous, with black-and-gold art deco motifs. Small spotlights are shining down on pieces throughout the shop. The owner turns on the music, and jazz starts to play throughout the shop. This might be the best day and best birthday I've ever had.

"I knew you would love this place since you're obsessed with the twenties."

It's like she's reading my mind. "This is beyond, Belle! How the hell did you find this place?"

She winks. "I have my secrets."

"Also, anything you pick is on Jack. It's part of his birthday present to you. He closed the shop so you can have the whole place to yourself." She picks up a bottle of champagne and pours us each a glass.

Geez, how am I going to make it until tonight with all this drinking?

"I can't believe Jackson did this. It's too much." I get teary-eyed. I really miss him. And at this exact moment, I see that it should be a no-brainer to move to London. The two people who I love most in this world are there. Maybe the champagne helped me come to this decision, but whatever. I need to get out of New York.

Belle wraps her arms around me. "You're the best person I know in this world, Sadie. You deserve only the best from everyone."

I grin up at her. "I'm going to do it—I'm moving to London."

"What? Are you serious?!" She jumps up and down, then squeezes me tightly.

"Yes. Yes, I'm totally serious," I squeal.

This is going to be good. I can feel it.

After what I would deem the perfect birthday afternoon, we are finally back in the room, and I'm really in need of a quick nap.

We made one more much-needed stop at the spa after shopping, pampering ourselves with a facial, mani-pedis, and I even got my makeup done.

But now, I finally have a second to think about my move to London. I can't even believe I made that decision so spontaneously.

But, hey, maybe I am changing for the better. The old me would have needed to speak to my parents for no reason at all, just for them only to tell me how stupid I'm being. I usually would need to weigh all the pros and cons, figure out financials and have a better game plan overall. But this is exciting.

I feel sad I'm leaving the only life I've ever known behind. But what kind of life was it? I wasn't exactly happy, and I could probably count on one hand the things that made me happy. One is speaking to Belle, and she's in London, not even New York.

I'll miss my tiny little apartment in SoHo, my job working for the floral designer, and most of all volunteering at the animal shelter. But these are all things I can do in London, especially volunteering.

It's such a rewarding job finding these animals forever homes and taking care of them when they have no one else. And I'll get another job and apartment. I can even live with Jackson or Belle for a while, spending time with them would be nice.

This is good! I can finally be with my real family. The two of them have always put me first and make me incredibly happy. I should have made this move a long time ago.

I hear the beats of music getting louder and louder by the second, so I know that means one thing, it's time to get up and get ready for tonight.

My hair is down, set in voluminous waves, and I had the makeup artist do a sexy smoky eye. I decided not to show Belle which dress I picked because I'm positive she's going to lose it when she sees the one I actually bought.

It's simple but definitely makes a statement. I chose an ivory-colored silk slip dress, which works great against my olive skin. It's high in the front with a square neckline and the thinnest, barely there straps to hold it up. The dress is short, and the back is nonexistent. It's opened pretty much all the way down to my backside, which is why Belle is going to freak out.

I also added the most gorgeous pair of gold Jimmy Choo heels. They are simple but bold. One thin strap crosses over my toes, but then another skinny strap ties around my ankle and up my calf, similar to a Grecian sandal, except these are five inches tall.

And after I take one last look in the mirror, I add a bold-red lip for a bit of color. I might as well go all out.

I walk into the living room and see Belle waiting. She's busy with her head in her phone, so she hasn't noticed me yet. I casually walk over to the bar to pour myself a glass of champagne.

"Would you also like a champagne, Belle?" Getting her attention on me now.

"Freaking hell, Sadie!"

"What is it?" I can't help myself but laugh because I knew this would be her reaction.

"You are a smokeshow. I can't believe you picked that dress. It's exactly what I would have wanted to choose for you. And damn, your arse!" She can't pull her eyes away. "Wow, I really can't believe how gorgeous you look. Well, I'm glad I got you this birthday gift now. It will go perfect with the outfit."

She hands me over a beautifully wrapped box. Belle always gives the best gifts, always so generous. I'm maybe just a tad excited.

I unwrap everything, and I see a logo I can't deny that I love. *Chanel.*

It's a gorgeous metallic clutch that's light-colored gold with dark-gold hardware. It's stunning.

"This is beautiful, Belle. Thank you so much. It's, of course, over the top and way overboard for a birthday gift. But I can't deny I love it." I kiss and hug her as thanks.

"I was hoping you would be able to wear it tonight, and it matches perfectly. It looks great with your outfit. Now pour that champagne." She winks.

We had decided to have dinner in our suite tonight, out on the patio. What better way to start your birthday night with dinner from a private French chef, overlooking the Mediterranean Sea.

We say our thanks to the chef as he leaves after serving us our dessert. The meal was to die for. Much to Belle's dismay, he was an older, slightly overweight man.

She had some fantasy with her and chef—not really sure, I zoned out halfway through.

"Let's get this party started!" She gets up to turn up the music and pours us more drinks.

This is going to be a fun night.

"Happy birthday, my beautiful, kind friend. I hope tonight is everything you wish for. And that Wills Taylor fucks your brains out because you need to get laid!"

"Oh my god, Annabelle! Are you freaking serious? What kind of toast is that? And what is wrong with you? I don't even know him."

"Sadie, tonight you're going to let loose, and whatever happens, happens. Promise me. I love my little goody-two-shoes, but you need to get it good. Your dry spell is dryer than the Sahara Desert."

"Seriously, I have nothing to say to that except, what goes on in your head?"

She just shrugs.

"Let's take some birthday shots and get a little tipsy before we head to the club. And don't say no."

Screw it… there is no fighting her. I might as well have fun.

"Cheers!"

We pull up to *Club Argent*—Belle says it means something shiny or silvery. And as you walk inside, you can see why. This club is incredible. It's sexy and black, and all the seating is a beautiful silver velvet. Silver abstract artwork hangs high up on the walls, making it look like it's floating throughout the club and sheer shimmery drapery divides the VIP sections.

"This way, Sadie."

I continue to follow Belle, who is following the manager of the club. I feel like some celebrity the way he is treating us. How does she know someone in France who runs a club?

As we walk to our section, I'm noticing a trend here in the South of France. There are beautiful people everywhere, and both men and women dress to the nines on all occasions.

The manager stops in front of one of the VIP sections, pulls back the curtains, and secures them to stay open.

My eyes go wide, and I gasp, covering my mouth in shock. The back wall is covered in different-sized balloons of all shades of silver and floating on top are more oversized balloons with the numbers 3-0 suspended from them. In addition, there is an array of different-sized candles, making the space feel extra sexy. Multiple buckets of champagne and tequila fill the table. Thank God we have more people coming because we would never be able to finish this.

I look over at Belle, who is smiling widely, while tears sting the back of my eyes.

"This isn't from me, another Jack surprise. He's really laying it on thick since he missed this birthday." She explains how he knows the owner and how he helped to open other clubs of hers.

"Well, I guess we shouldn't let this go to waste!"

"That's the spirit, my darling Sadie."

After a few more shots and a glass of champagne, we were definitely feeling it. So, there was only one thing to do. Dance.

"Ohhhhh shit," Belle suddenly blurts out while we're dancing.

"What?" I look around to see what made her curse out loud, and *oh shit* is right.

Wills, Declan, George, and Leo walk through the doors of the club like they own the place.

Each and every girl in the club turn their head to check them out.

You just can't help but stare, they're like four models on steroids who exude complete dominance.

My eyes go right to Wills, who is dressed in a light-colored linen suit that looks like it was made just to fit his body—which I'm sure it was. He has a white collared shirt unbuttoned, letting his muscular chest peek out, and his hair is styled to perfection. He must have lain out today because his skin is already golden, and his hair has a few streaks going through it.

Belle elbows me. "Holy shit, Wills is a smokeshow! Look at all the girls checking him out."

A feeling of unease passes through me, and my stomach hollows out. What the hell is that all about? I don't even know this guy, but I can't deny he does something to me that I've never felt before.

"Yeah, he's okay."

Belle bends over, dying of laughter.

"I don't know if you're trying to convince you or me, but the way you're flushed and staring definitely makes me believe you think he is a little more than 'Okay.'"

I don't respond and quickly walk back to our table to grab two more champagnes. I'm already a little past buzzed at this point, but I'm thinking I need to take more of the edge off.

The guys were stopped by a few fans, it looks like. So, I quickly pour the drinks before they make it over to our table. And when I see Belle isn't looking, I powder my nose and reapply my red lipstick. I then speedily make my way back out to the dance floor.

Belle is now dancing with a tall, dark, and not to be cliché, handsome man. He looks Spanish or something exotic. I walk up to them, and I pass her the champagne.

"Cheers, my darling girl."

She continues to dance with Mr. Spanish, so I enjoy the music alone. I've had enough drinks to feel confident enough to dance by myself.

Dance music pumps through the speakers, and I sway my hips back and forth, really letting my body feel the music. My face is tipped up, and my long hair falls free down my back. It's now when I realize I am beyond the buzzed point, and very drunk is settling in.

The DJ switches to a slower tempo song, and I take that as my cue to take a breather and grab some water.

I'm not sure how many songs have passed because when I look over at Belle, she's now dancing with George.

I guess the guys know we're here, I sigh to myself as I push through to make my way over to them.

I've been avoiding looking over to our section. It's not that I don't want to see Wills, it's that I'm scared because I want to see Wills *too* much.

When I'm within earshot of Annabelle and George, I stand there frozen, thinking today is the day I kill my best friend because she is repeating to George what she told me earlier.

Earlier today, she informed me that tonight was the night that I popped my one-night stand cherry. "Tonight is the night you let your inner slut be free" were actually her exact words.

I've told her many times how I envy her laissez-faire attitude when it comes to her love life. But just because I admire her openness doesn't mean I want to indulge myself. I can now hear how she tells George every detail of how she will make it happen tonight.

I push my way through the last few people between us, and I am just about to make it to them when someone knocks into me from behind, causing me to stumble forward and crash into a very hard chest.

"I'm sorry," I say just loud enough over the music for him to hear. I try and take a step back, but he grabs my waist to steady me.

"It's okay, bella," he says in the sexiest Italian accent.

"Dance with me?" he asks but doesn't wait for my reply. His hands are still on my hips when he takes a step closer and presses himself into me.

We both start to move to the music, and there is no denying he can dance. His hips are expertly moving side to side, round and round, while his hands move up and down my sides.

I'm awkwardly moving my body, not really dancing, but I think, *screw it.*

I press back into him, and I think I feel, no, it can't be. I think I feel something hard pressed against me.

It couldn't be, already, could it? I look up at him, and he presses harder into me, and I guess that answers my question. What the hell? I just started dancing with this guy—what a creep.

Before I can step away, he spins me around, so we face a new direction on the dance floor. He's really grinding into me, and I'm a little uncomfortable, but the drinks are making it hard to pull away from his grip.

I finally look up, and we are right in front of our VIP section, and what I see is not good.

My eyes connect with Wills's, and he looks like he is going to murder someone. I can practically see the steam coming out of his ears. He slowly rises from his seat and starts to make his way over here.

Shit, shit, shit. I attempt to pull away from this guy I'm dancing with, but he tightens his grip on me. I try and turn to him to ask him to let go. But I guess I'm not fast enough because I can feel him before I see him.

3

Wills

"TAKE A BREATH, MATE," I hear Declan say with laughter in his voice.

"Fuck off. Are you seeing what I'm seeing?"

We arrived at the club no less than an hour ago, and my patience is running thin waiting for Sadie to be done on the dance floor.

I've been sitting in the VIP section that Sadie and Annabelle secured, drinking scotch and staring at her body moving in perfect rhythm to the music.

I've never had an attraction to a woman like this before, and I'm not sure if I love it or hate it. But I do know I can't sit back and watch her grind into that fucking guy for another minute.

"I'm going to kill that guy," I mutter under my breath, but loud enough for Declan to hear.

I slowly start to stand up, rolling my head and neck because I'm tense as hell.

"What are you going to do, Wills? You haven't said more than five words to this girl. You can't tell her who she can and can't dance with."

"Watch me."

"Oh, this is going to be good," Declan replies as I head to the dance floor.

I push my way through the crowd, squeezing through all the people grinding on one another, and

quickly make my way over to Sadie and the douchebag that has his hands all over her.

When I finally make it there, her whole body freezes. She hasn't even lifted her head yet, but she knows I'm here.

Good, I hope I affect her as she affects me.

What happens next is like an out-of-body experience. I'm not sure what comes over me.

I reach out for her slim, delicate wrist and pull her body toward me, making her crash into me.

Her breath catches, and very slowly, she lifts her head to me, looking as shocked as I am, really.

"Hi, having fun?" I sarcastically ask her, not able to help myself.

Before she can respond, the dickhead she was dancing with goes to grab her from me.

"Hands off," I growl.

"I was dancing with her. Who the fuck are you?" He tries to stand taller, appearing bigger than he really is.

I look down at him. "She's mine, now fuck off."

"Wills!" Her head snaps up, and if looks could kill.

Fuck.

She turns to the other guy. "Sorry, I don't want a fight, so I am going to go with him. Thanks for the dance."

She grabs my hand hard and pulls me away, stopping just short of our table. "What. The. Hell. Was. That?" she yells.

"What was what?" I play dumb. I think I might be in slight shock. The shy, quiet girl I met yesterday is not the same girl standing in front of me right now.

"Wills, why did you just pull me away from that guy I was dancing with?"

"Honestly, I'm not sure what came over me, Sadie. I wanted to dance with you, and I couldn't stand watching you with that guy for another minute," I tell her the truth, and I see her face soften slightly.

"Why didn't you just ask? You were acting like a caveman!"

I don't say anything because she's right. I have never acted like this before with a woman.

Have I gotten jealous before? Sure. But possessive over a girl I haven't even had a whole conversation with yet, no, definitely not.

"I would have danced with you." I think I hear her say quietly, but the music is making it hard to hear.

"I'm sorry," I say truthfully. I don't want to scare her off, but she doesn't respond to that.

"I need another drink. Let's go back over to our section."

"Can you dance with me… please?" Now I beg, apparently.

She looks down, taking a second to answer, and starts to wring her hands. Something I noticed yesterday, as well. A nervous habit.

She shakes her head slightly, more to herself than to me. "Let's just get a drink first."

Well, it's not a no.

She walks ahead of me and fuck. Her dress, or lack of it, is killing me. I bite my lip so I don't outwardly groan at her arse swaying back and forth as she walks away.

That arse is going to be mine.

I wait a second to calm myself down but catch up quickly when she looks back to make sure I'm still following. I can't get a read on this girl. She's shy but not, forward but not. I need to know more.

When we make it to the table, Annabelle and George arrive at the same time. Annabelle wraps her arm around Sadie and pulls her in for a quick kiss on the cheek.

I want that kiss.

Annabelle turns her head to me and winks. She knows I can't keep my eyes off Sadie. It's pathetic, really. She's caught me numerous times now.

The guys all wish Sadie a happy birthday, and they start pouring a round of shots for everyone.

I lift my glass of scotch to signal I'm okay without.

Sadie must catch it and passes me one anyway. "It's my birthday, you have to."

I'm not going to argue with that.

"Thank you all for coming to celebrate my thirtieth birthday. We may have made fast friends, but I'm so glad you're all here, and I appreciate it deeply. Cheers to you all!"

Everyone clinks glasses and shouts, "Happy birthday, Sadie!"

Some time passes, a few more shots are taken, and the girls have been laughing over in the corner for the last thirty minutes. I know because I've been waiting for her to dance like a lovesick puppy the whole time.

She's chanced a few looks but would quickly look away, not wanting to get caught. I'm happy to get caught. I'm not trying to hide how much I want this girl anymore.

George settles up next to me after a while.

"Saw you out there with Annabelle." I jut out my chin toward the dance floor, then give him a knowing smirk.

"Nah, it's not like that with her. She's my mate's sister. I wouldn't go there."

"Hmm, fun." George fucks anything that walks, I'm not buying it.

"I did learn something interesting, though, while we were dancing."

"Do tell."

"Annabelle is pushing Sadie to go home with a stranger tonight—fuck a random guy, pop her one-night stand cherry."

"Fuck mate, I get it. Shut the fuck up."

He laughs.

"Well, that's not happening on my watch. If she's going home with anyone, it's me, and only me."

He's still laughing.

"Are you making this up? Why are you laughing?"

"Definitely not making it up. But I do like seeing you all fucked over this girl."

I don't answer. Goddamnit, he's right. I'm not waiting another second. I need to make my move now.

"Here he goes," George yells loud enough for the girls to look up.

I hate all of these guys right now.

Annabelle is the first to make eye contact and has a mischievous sparkle in her eyes.

"Sadie," I say in greeting.

"Wills." She's smiling, which is a good sign. Her smile is big and gorgeous but also contagious. I'm smiling back at her now.

"I was hoping you were ready for that dance now."

She doesn't get a chance to respond because Annabelle pushes her hard to stand up.

Sadie gives her a dirty look, but then they both laugh.

"Sure, I think I'm ready to dance now." She smiles up at me again, and my breath catches.

I'm not sure I've noticed how big and green her eyes were until now, but they are staring deep into me and not looking away.

I reach my hand out, and she takes it willingly, so I pull her close to my side and walk her onto the dance floor. Not wanting to break the eye contact, but I need to get her alone, now.

I find a spot that's not in view of our friends and quickly grab her hips and pull her into my body. I hear her breath catch, even over the music and I know she's just as affected by me as I am her. She's just better at hiding it.

I start to move my body with hers, slowly at first, finding that rhythm together. I might be a big guy, but I've been told I can move pretty well on the dance floor.

I push some of her hair away from her face, so I can see her when I ask, "Are you enjoying your night so far?"

"Yes. I'm having way more fun than I thought I would." She smiles and shrugs a little.

I like this look on her, far more than I probably should.

We start swaying a little more to the music, and I'm running my hands up and down her sides, itching to run them over her back but not wanting to push it yet.

But then she starts to rub her hands up my chest, and I'm about to lose control.

"I love this linen suit."

"Yeah?" I croak.

"Yes, it fits you perfectly and feels even better. I noticed it right when you walked into the club," she confesses.

She's still running her hands around my chest. I feel like my chest is on fire, and her hands are igniting it.

"Tell me, Wills. Are you enjoying your night?"

"I am, Sadie. This, right now, it's perfect."

I hear her sigh and lean in a little closer to me. I take this opportunity to move her hair to the side and glide my hands over her exposed back.

Fuck. Her skin is so soft, even with the slight stickiness from dancing, I can't stop my hands from roaming all over her back. This girl is going to be the death of me.

A few more songs pass now, and we haven't said one word, but this feels good. She feels good in my arms.

She starts to move a little faster now as the song switches to a remix of "**Rendezvous**" By Rüfüs Du Sol, still swaying her hips with the beat and moving her petite hands over my chest. It's time I make my move and transfer my hands over her arse. I've never had so much restraint in my life. She pauses for a second but doesn't stop me and starts to dance again. My hands have a mind of their own now, and they can't decide if they love the feel of her exposed back or her firm, plump arse. In all of my thirty-five years, I never realized what an arse man I was until right this second.

Deciding I want to feel it pressed against me, I grab her hips and spin her around so her back is to my chest.

Sadie groans when she feels my hard cock pressed into her and grinds into it as she continues to dance. I'm so fucking hard, it's painful.

I lean down to press a few kisses down her neck, she stretches to give me full access as her eyes shutter shut. She tastes sweet and salty, and I can't get enough of her. I lick up her neck in between kisses, and she lets out a loud moan when I hit the spot right behind her ear. *Jackpot.*

"Wills," Sadie sighs.

I take her chin to position her just right, and I lean down to kiss her soft lips.

"Fuck, Sadie."

She closes her eyes again, and I go back in. My tongue sweeps over her lips to gain access, and she moans into my mouth. Our tongues are dancing in rhythm with our bodies and I can't get enough.

"You taste amazing," I mumble into her mouth.

She gives me a small smile and reaches up so her arms stretch around my neck. This is no easy task. I'm six-four, but the *come-fuck-me* shoes she has on give her that extra height needed to reach over my shoulders.

I run my hands up and down her arms, all the way down to her slim waist and over her hips.

She feels perfect under my hands—fuck, everything about this girl is perfect.

She leans her face into me, and again, not wanting to make her wait even a second, I crash my lips back into hers.

We are really grinding into each other now, and I can't take it anymore.

"Let's get out of here," I mumble into her mouth.

She stiffens.

Fuck, that's not the response I want from her. "Sorry, I didn't mean to assume." I'm not even sure what else to say.

"It's okay," she whispers.

"I'm going to go to freshen up. I'll be back in a little." She walks off, not looking back.

Fuck, Taylor, you just couldn't help yourself, could you? She felt so good pressed against me, I didn't think.

I head back over to our section, assuming she'll go back there rather than try to find me on the dance floor. *If she even tries to find me at all.* I shake away those thoughts—she'll come back. I could feel she was enjoying herself too.

Annabelle's off somewhere, so at least I don't have to receive the fifth degree from her. I can tell those two are close, but Annabelle seems very protective of Sadie. I wonder what the story is with those two.

The lads are all staring at me with amusement. "Why are you all just standing around here in the same spot as before?" I ask.

"There is literally the crème de la crème of women in this club. Go have fun."

Still, no one says anything.

"What? Why the hell are you all still staring at me?"

Leo's first to respond. "Where's Sadie?" he says with a cocky grin.

"The loo, why?"

George chimes in now. "Sure about that, mate? We saw her run off outside a second ago." They all start laughing.

"Fuck off. What type of mates are you?"

Declan, who has been quiet this whole time, makes his way over to me.

"Wills, I've told you before. Sadie isn't like all the women we're used to. You need to be more delicate with her. Think of her as a flower. Be gentle."

I look at him deadpan. "A flower?" I look down, between his legs.

"Did your cock fall off, and you grow a pussy while I was dancing?"

He rolls his eyes. "You like this girl, I can tell. Find her and make it right, man. But don't be so aggressive. Be you. I don't know when you turned into this crazy asshole but knock it off."

Declan's younger than me, actually, he's Sadie's age. But he is wise beyond his years.

People see this tall, fit rugby player with his upper body covered in tattoos and don't take him seriously. But he's the smartest one out of the bunch.

And, of course, he's right. Declan's always right.

"Alright, mate, I'm going to find her."

I walk off. *I'm coming, Sadie. I'm going to make this right.*

Sadie

I walk as fast as I can without getting the attention of the others and make my way outside.

I froze up back there. I don't know why, but I did. So, I just needed a second to myself.

When Wills suggested what I think he did, I freaked out for a split second.

It's not that I didn't want to take him up on his offer, I did—trust me. If he could make me feel the way he did on the dance floor, I can only imagine what he would feel like in the bedroom.

I just freaked out because I don't know how to do this, and it's embarrassing. I don't know how to do casual or a one-night stand... that's just not me.

I do emotions, feelings, and connections. So even if I'm not looking for a long-term commitment, I don't think I could just do, wham bam thank ya ma'am.

If I go home with Wills, I won't know how to separate myself. I'll want more. If he weren't a stranger, I would have suggested leaving the second his lips touched my mouth.

Those beautiful soft lips. Ugh.

After taking a few calming breaths, I'm wondering what I'm going to do now. I've embarrassed myself. Why didn't I just answer him with some noncommittal response, like "not tonight" or "you wish" and try to laugh it off? Instead, I froze like a freaking loser.

I can't even text Annabelle to help me with my inner freak-out because I came outside with no phone.

I lean against the side of the building and close my eyes for a second. I need to think of a plan.

But, after a few moments in solitude, I feel I'm not alone. I can feel him before I see him. *Again.*

He rubs my arms up and down, this time, it's not in a sexy way—he is reassuring me.

I don't know why, but that almost makes this situation worse.

"Sadie," Will starts with his low, gravelly voice. It somehow sounds even deeper now. "I'm so sorry for asking you to leave with me, it was inappropriate, and I should have never assumed anything."

He continues. "Please come back inside with me and enjoy a drink. We don't even have to dance again."

Why is he sorry? I'm the idiot that freaked out.

"Wills, stop apologizing. You did nothing wrong." I look everywhere but at him. "I was dry humping you like a dog in heat. Of course, you would assume, anyone would… I would!" I add, "Plus, it's not that far off from what I want." *Did I just say that out loud*?

He looks stunned. So, I keep going, my mouth won't shut up, I'm on a roll now.

"I'm very attracted to you, like majorly attracted. But I've never had a one-night stand. That's more Annabelle's thing and my brother, you don't know my brother, so that wouldn't make sense to you. But—"

"Sadie," Wills cuts off my rant.

"Take a breath, beautiful." He's bent down now, so he's at eye level with me.

"You're majorly attracted to me, huh?"

I swat at his chest, and he catches my wrist, keeping my hand pressed against him.

"Sadie, I'm wildly attracted to you too. I'm not even acting myself around you because you've been driving me crazy."

As he talks, he rubs his thumb idly back and forth on the sides of my wrist where he's still holding me.

"I'm sorry if you got the impression I just wanted tonight with you. We're staying at the same hotel for a couple of weeks. How could you think tonight would be enough?" he asks and presses a kiss to my hand.

I look up into his gray eyes, which are staring back down into mine through his long, thick lashes.

I stay silent because I'm not sure how to respond. But it's exactly what I wanted, a companion for this trip, so to speak. But can I really do that without getting attached?

He breaks the silence and adds, "Why don't we leave here and take a walk on the beach? We can get to know each other a little better. I think that would make us more comfortable, right?"

I don't even need a second to think about it. Nodding my head, I say, "Okay, yeah, I would really enjoy that."

"Perfect," Wills huffs out, relieved. "Please stay here. I'll go grab your things and I'll let everyone know we're leaving," he says with vulnerability in his voice. "Don't move, please." He adds as he's already halfway back to the front door. Did he think I was going to run?

This man gives me whiplash. He's broody and intimidating one minute, then sweet and gentle the next.

Within a few minutes, Wills is already back with my bag and his suit jacket that he must have taken off.

"Annabelle wasn't at the table. Declan assured me he would inform her we left, but maybe you want to send a text?"

"Good idea." I'm sure she's going to be jumping with joy when she receives this text.

I grab my phone from my new purse, and I'm shocked.

"Whoa, it's three in the morning."

He chuckles from beside me and grabs my hand to pull me toward the beach. "Time flies when you're having fun, Sadie." He smirks.

He's right about that. I think I might have been having just a little too much fun.

We walk a while in a peaceful silence, which normally would be awkward but feels right. Wills hasn't let go of my hand and gives it a squeeze every few minutes, reassuring me he's here with me in the moment.

We make our way farther from the club, walking along the coast, admiring the beautiful view. Even this late at night, or should I say early morning.

The moon is full and lights up the sky, giving you a perfect outline of the mountains past the coast.

The lights of the houses and hotels are still lit up as if it's not past three in the morning, and the city is very much alive.

Breaking me out of my inner thoughts, Wills picks up his other hand that's holding my heels and points toward some lounge chairs on the beach for us to rest on.

"I don't want to get in trouble if these are for another hotel," I say. I just can't help myself.

I look over to the stunningly handsome man to my side, and he's laughing. *At me*? "What?"

"Something tells me you never break the rules, Sadie," he says, still kind of laughing.

"But this time, I'll let it slide. Take a closer look."

I look up, and I'm stunned that our hotel is in front of us now. How did we make it here so fast? I know we've been walking for a while, but people never walk that fast on the sand.

Like he knows what I'm thinking, Wills adds, "Our hotel wasn't actually all that far away in proximity to the club, just seemed farther taking the small winding streets. This way was a straight shot."

We head toward the loungers and share a double bed that fits us both. Well, Wills barely fits, but that can't be helped when you're his size.

After we get settled, he grabs my hand again. I'm pretty positive he doesn't even realize he keeps doing it, but hey, I'm not complaining.

"You look beautiful tonight, Sadie, stunning, really. I didn't get a chance to tell you earlier."

"Thank you." I can feel my cheeks turning the same shade as my lipstick.

"Don't be shy. I wasn't able to take my eyes off of you all night."

I don't respond, not because I'm shy, but because what does one even say to that? It's also hard to read Wills. He seems pretty serious most of the time, but I also sense there is more to him under some of those big muscles.

"Anyway, why don't we play a game?"

"You don't really strike me as the playful type." I turn and smile at him.

"Mmm, I suppose I'm not. But this game will be beneficial for us both."

"Okay, enlighten me, please." Curiosity getting the better of me. What has he got up his sleeve?

"Let's play something along the lines of twenty-one questions. If at the end of the game you still feel uneasy, I walk you back to your room —no questions asked. But if, in the end, you feel comfortable enough, I would like you to come back to my room tonight."

Say yes, say yes, my head screams.

"Even if it's just to sleep," he continues. "I don't want this night to end, Sadie, but when it does, I want to start tomorrow the same way it ended—with you."

Okay, swoon. I pretend to think about it for a minute. "Okay, deal." I shoot him another smile. This game could be fun. "And since it's my birthday, I go first."

He raises his eyebrows to say, "go ahead."

"Okay, first question… why do you go by *Wills*? I assume your name is William, so why Wills and not Will? I've never heard someone use an *s* at the end." Not the best first question, but it's been annoying me since the second I heard Belle say his name.

"Interesting choice for a first question," he agrees.

"Well, I guess I don't know the answer to that. I know Will is the more common shortened name, but I've heard it both ways in England. And I guess it comes down to not having a choice. When I was a child, my parents never shortened my name, only calling me William. So it wasn't until my younger sister Evelyn started talking that she started to call me Wills. Who knows why, but it caught on, and I would never correct her."

I can see the sparkle in his eye when he speaks about his sister, he's clearly fond of her. I admire that in a person, knowing how close I am with my brother.

"You're close with your sister?" I already know the answer.

"Extremely. Evelyn is one of my best friends, it's hard to trust people. Fame and money come at a cost. Family and very few close friends are the only ones I trust. My sister constantly tells me I've built a wall around me, and I don't come off as approachable. But most of the time, it's the only way I know how to separate myself from the world I live in and the world I want to live in."

I can't relate, but I could imagine it becoming very taxing on someone always in the limelight.

"This isn't exactly a question, but I have a confession," I admit.

"I, uh... so... I had no idea who you were when I first saw you," I spit out.

He looks like I wounded his ego with his hand on his chest.

"I don't follow sports or follow celebrity stuff. Especially people that don't live in New York." I try to defend myself.

"Sadie." He is quiet for a few more moments but then says, "I was kidding. I can't even explain how happy that makes me. I love that you were interested in talking to me for me alone."

I can sense how genuine he's being, and it makes me feel sad for him. How must it feel not knowing if people are trying to talk to you because of you or because you're famous?

So, over the next hour, I try to show him how I want to get to know the real him, asking him so many questions, and he returns most of them. I feel like I almost know him better than I know myself.

I learned his parents are retired teachers and live in the countryside now.

He told me how he wants to adopt a dog now that he's retired. I told him how I work at the shelter. I think that impressed him.

Most people in my social circles say they "volunteer," but what they mean is they sit on the board and donate a crap ton of money. Not me—I take care of all my babies at the shelter.

He tried to explain rugby to me, which was a lost cause because I suck at sports.

But he did win the Rugby League World Cup, which is pretty cool. Even if I've never heard of it before, it still sounds impressive.

He has a love for all things vintage, cars, and watches especially.

We compare things we say in America vs. England. Like when he was calling my ass, arse.

He spoke more about his sister, telling me stories from when they were younger. It makes my heart warm when he talks about how close he is to her. I never really considered it a turn-on, but it makes me want him more because of it.

We're having such a great time, chatting and laughing. I think I'm seeing a different side to Wills, and I like it.

"Okay, my turn again. Why are you on this trip?"

"Well, Annabelle and I go on a yearly trip—"

"No," he interrupts me.

"Tell me why you're 'reinventing yourself.' George filled me in with a little info Annabelle shared. I also overheard you talking when we were back at the table."

What the hell did I say to Annabelle? I was so drunk before I barely remember our conversation at all.

I'm shocked. I'm not sure what to say.

He must sense this, so he lets go of my hand, which I just realized he was still holding, to rub my exposed back. A sheet of goose bumps scatters over my body and looking up to see him staring at me doesn't put me at ease.

He's asking hard questions that I don't want to discuss and is putting a damper on this perfect night. But more than that, he makes me nervous in a way I've never felt before. I've never been so attracted to someone before.

"I'm sorry if I overstepped."

I don't reply but flash a small smile.

He really is beautiful. His gray eyes have tiny specs of hazel running through them, they're quite unique. And he has these long thick eyelashes that women would pay for.

His hair is light brown or very dark blonde. I can't tell. It's slightly waved and styled to perfection, but something tells me he doesn't really take the time to do it. And he's just blessed with perfect hair.

I didn't realize how close we were until now, so I take in more of his whole face since the moonlight gives me the perfect light.

I lift my hand involuntarily and trace his high cheekbones and straight, chiseled jaw. His lips are full, and the only imperfection I can see is a slight curve to his nose. Probably not even noticeable to the human eye. But to my now closely trained Wills Taylor eyes, I'm catching everything. I run my finger down his nose…

"It's from a rugby injury," his voice mumbles, taking on a lower octave now. It's the same tone I heard him use in the club.

He cups my cheek with his large, strong hand, forcing me to look up into his eyes, and that's when he leans down and presses his lips so softly against mine. We stay like this for a moment, relishing in the feeling of one another.

But it's me this time that makes a move. First, I bring my hand up to my cheek and press it on top of his hand. Then, I turn my head for better access and open my mouth slightly.

All questions are forgotten.

Then, all restraint is gone. Wills snaps and groans like a wild animal, opening our mouths more with his tongue.

This kiss that started soft and sweet is now heated and desperate. Something about it feels so familiar, like we've kissed a thousand times before.

"God, Sadie. I've wanted to kiss this sweet mouth of yours again like you couldn't believe."

He delves back in with precise movements that I can now feel between my legs. I'm on fire, and I realize I'm pressing my thighs together so hard to stop the throbbing that's happening. His hand moves from my cheek and starts exploring my backside, rubbing and squeezing.

I break our kiss for a second. I need to calm down before I rip off all his clothes right here, right now.

I'm panting and slightly gasping for air. It's also when I realize the sun is coming up.

"Wow."

"Yeah, wow. You're so fucking sexy, Sadie. I can't stand it."

I chuckle. "No, look, Wills."

He turns his head, and we both stare over at the sea.

He wraps his arms around me, and we stare in awe. The sun is just starting to peek through, a gorgeous array of mixed blues and deep purples that are reflecting from the water. I've never seen anything like this. It's perfect.

"Wills," I whisper. "Take me back to your room."

4

Sadie

Wills and I crash into the elevator, lips locked, and he has me boxed in against the wall with both arms raised beside my head. I've never felt so starved like this before in my whole life. I need more of him *now*.

Wills starts pushing his groin into me, and I'm rubbing right back, trying to create some type of friction between us. He kisses up and down my neck, one hand on my exposed back and one squeezing my backside hard. This may be his favorite thing to do, it's the first place he touches when he has his hands on me.

He continues, licking and sucking. My eyes roll back into my head. The throbbing between my legs is making me burn with a need I never knew I had.

"Wills…" I sigh.

"I know, beautiful girl, I know."

God, why is it even a turn-on when he calls me beautiful?

The elevator pings, and the doors open. Wills can't wait for even a second longer, so he picks me up and throws me over his shoulder, and I squeal in delight.

I'm running my hands along his muscular back, feeling all the ridges as his hand goes under my dress and grabs my butt again.

"God, are you not wearing knickers?" He squeezes again. "I fucking love this arse." He picks up my dress a little and bites hard into my flesh.

I groan, it's painful, but also, why the hell does it turn me on so much?

"Someone might see!" I realize now we barely made it out of the elevator.

He turns his head toward me with a deadly stare. "I'd kill someone before I let them get a look at what's mine."

Oh god, I shouldn't like the way it sounds when he says, *"What's mine."*

We make it into Wills's penthouse, and he's yet to put me down.

I can feel the anticipation in the air, just swirling around the room. He doesn't say a word and continues walking into his master bath, placing me on the countertop. He kisses my forehead and turns to start the shower.

I see him take a deep breath, then slowly turn back toward me. His eyes catch mine, and it's like they went from gray to black. He has a look of intense determination as he strides back over to me.

"I need to slow down, Sadie, otherwise I won't cherish you as you deserve."

I'm squirming now. Who needs to be cherished? *I don't.*

He takes one more purposeful step closer to my body, leaning down, he whispers in my ear. "But what I want to do is rip this dress off your sexy body and fuck you so hard from behind. I want to watch your perfect arse bounce around while I spank it, leaving a handprint on this flawless skin. Then there will be no question you're mine."

"Yes, Wills, that, do that." I don't even know what I'm saying. Do I want him to spank me? Who even knows anymore?

He chuckles. "Soon, beautiful."

Wills leans down, cups both my cheeks for a deep kiss, but breaks away all too soon.

He's freaking killing me here. How does he have so much restraint?

He lowers me to the floor, then slides down my body to take off my shoes one by one, kissing up and down along my legs. Every time he touches my body, in any way, it's like fire exploding over my skin. I'm a freaking inferno now, ready to combust.

His hands, still on my backside for a second, then slide up and take my little slip dress with them. His eyes widen and he curses under his breath when he remembers I'm entirely bare of a bra or panties under the dress.

I reach and fumble, trying to unbutton his shirt. He pushes my hands lower to undo his pants while he does his shirt. I smirk, dirty boy.

I bend over to lift each leg out of his pants and then his briefs. As I make my way back up, I kiss him softly as he did me, stopping to place a quick peck to his exposed hardness. He sucks in his breath, then roughly grabs me and pulls me into the shower.

His eyes are raking me up and down in appreciation. "Let me wash you, beautiful." His voice low and gravelly.

"Okay," I croak.

Wills pours the soap into his hands, then rubs up and down my body, stopping at my breasts, pulling at my already stiff nipples. Shit, this feels too good.

He turns me around and pushes his body flush against mine, my back pressed to his front, and his large cock wedged between my cheeks.

I moan out loud, and he continues to play with my nipples as he leans down, kisses my ear, and then bites down.

"Oh, Wills," I sigh.

One hand continues to play with my nipple, but the other starts to travel south, and two fingers press between my legs.

"Fuck, Sadie, you're soaked." He continues to slowly move his fingers round and round, focusing on my clit.

My body shudders, and he wraps his other arm around me to keep me upright, and without warning, he impales me with one large finger.

"Ah!"

"It's okay, Sadie. You're so fucking tight. But you can take my finger."

He moves his fingers in and out, slowly at first letting me adjust. But he picks up his pace, pushing harder and harder, adding a second finger when he knows I'm ready.

You can hear my arousal over the running water. *I am freaking soaked.*

"I can smell how aroused you are from here, and it's fucking amazing. You like my fingers on your cunt, Sadie? You like my cock pressed against your arse?" He pushes hard into my backside.

"Oh my god," I scream out. I can feel burning deep in my stomach… my orgasm is close.

"Answer me."

"Mmhmm."

"Use your words. Otherwise, I won't let you come." He slows down his movements.

"Yes."

"Yes, what? Sadie," he growls.

"Yes, I like it all!" I shout.

He laughs, that asshole.

He picks up his pace, rubbing back and forth over my clit again. "Next time, you'll tell me in detail what you like. Understood?"

"Yes, Wills, Yessss."

He starts to rub faster. He knows I'm close. I lean my head back on his chest—he's still holding me up with his arm wrapped around me.

"I'm going to come, Wills. Oh god, oh god." My legs start to shake, and I'm holding on to his arm so tight I think my nails are cutting into him.

"That's it, Sadie, let it go, come for me, beautiful." He pushes his fingers back inside of me and finds my nipple, pinching it hard between his fingers.

"Wills, yes baby, yessss!" My eyes roll back, and my whole body is shaking as he keeps going. I don't think I can handle it anymore.

He starts to slow down his movements when he realizes I'm coming down from my high. Holy shit, that was the best orgasm I have ever had, and we haven't even had sex yet.

He turns me back around, and I sink into his arms while he's kissing my forehead a few times, squeezing me in his hold.

Ugh, why does it feel so good to be here with him like this?

I look up at him shyly. "Hi."

"Hi, beautiful girl." He smiles down at me; I really do like when he calls me that. *Too much.*

We stay like this for a few minutes, letting me catch my breath.

"That was hands down the sexiest thing I've ever seen in my life. I can't wait to be inside you and watch your face as you come all over my cock."

Oh god, he's so filthy.

I don't even know what to say back; I hope I can keep up with him because he's intense, like full on.

Oblivious to my thoughts, he rinses me off and quickly washes the sand off of himself. Then he grabs us both towels, drying me first.

"I can dry myself." I smile up at him.

He play growls when I try to grab the towel from him.

"You can't do anything yourself when I'm around."

I roll my eyes and let him continue drying me.

"Would you like water or anything?" he asks.

"No, thank you."

"Good, on the bed. Now."

I obey and crawl on the big bed up to the pillows. I bounce a little because this bed seems better than mine.

"Goddamnit, Sadie!"

I look over, and he's stroking his hard cock, *oh that's hot.*

"You can't crawl like that unless you want me to take that fucking perfect arse of yours."

Ah, he wouldn't!

He shoots me a wicked grin. "Not yet, Sadie, not yet."

Yeah, right, not ever.

Wills walks over to a bag, grabs a few condoms, and throws them on the bed.

"Always prepared, huh?" I ask jokingly, not even sure why I said it.

He turns to me, annoyed. "No, Sadie, I bought them yesterday after I met you. I only wanted to use them with you."

Oh.

He stands at the edge of the bed, slowly stroking his hard-on again. I've never been with a man so sexually confident. It's intimidating but also such a turn-on.

I'm already getting aroused again. I can feel my wetness building between my legs. *God,* it's been way too long.

My eyes greedily look him over, and I realize it's my first time seeing all of him with nothing between us.

Wills's body is unbelievable, his legs are so freaking huge, but his abs, his abs, are goals. He lets me check him out, but when I make it back over to his cock, my breath catches. I watch as he continues to stroke himself, but now I can see how large he really is.

I was in such a sex haze earlier, I hadn't even realized how massive he was. How the hell is that going to fit into me?

"It will fit," he states confidently, always knowing exactly what I'm thinking.

I'm not sure it will, though. Who can actually fit that thing in them?

Finally, he crawls on the bed and leans down for a kiss. He has one hand on my cheek, and the other is stroking my hair. He kisses so good that I probably could just get off from the feel of his tongue on mine.

"I'm going to make you come again and open you up. I won't hurt you, Sadie."

He kisses me a few more moments, then slowly moves down my body, peppering kisses along my chest and the swell of my breasts, giving my nipples a little lick. My whole body is tingling as he continues and teases me around my stomach.

"Don't stop, Wills. Please, go lower," I beg.

This is going to be embarrassing. I'm going to come so quick, again. I can already feel it.

He moves lower and presses his nose against my center.

"You smell so fucking good, Sadie. I can't wait to eat you up."

He opens me up, presses his tongue flat against me, and licks me from bottom to top. Then continues by attacking my clit. I groan out loud. This feels too good.

"Wills," I cry out. "I'm already going to come if you keep that up."

"Fuck yeah, you are!"

"You have such a potty mouth, Wills Taylor." I laugh, trying to catch my breath, and I feel him smile against me.

I reach down, grab hold of his hair and press him into me. My hips start to buck into his face wildly, but Wills loves it. Picking up his pace every time I press down onto him.

He presses two, then three fingers into me and moans so loudly it vibrates on my clit.

"Holy shit, that feels so good, Wills. Don't stop."

"You're so tight. I can feel you contracting around my fingers. Your cunt is leaking all over my hand. You're so fucking wet for me."

He leans back down and starts to move his face and tongue back and forth, up and down, attacking my clit, at the same time pumping me full of his large fingers.

He's moaning again, and I can see him grinding into the bed. He's just as turned on as I am, and that turns me on even more.

"Wills, I'm going to come!" My head is flying back and forth as my back arches up. "Ahhhh," I scream. "That feels so good." My eyes are prickly with tears. Holy shit.

He keeps licking me up until I stop screaming.

I try to catch my breath. "Okay, okay. Wills. It's too sensitive."

He licks one more large swipe and smiles up at me proudly.

He crawls up my body while I lie there lifeless. Leaning over me, he presses a kiss to my lips and I taste my arousal on him.

"My good girl, is not such a good girl in bed after all, is she?"

I am, normally—I don't know who this bitch in bed is right now. I chuckle to myself.

He reaches over and slowly puts on a condom, his eyes never leaving me.

How is it possible that I'm already aching for him? *Is that even physically possible?*

"Sadie, you're so beautiful, your body." He pauses. "It's unreal. Every inch of you is perfect, your soft skin."

Wills reaches down and caresses my neck and collarbone with his fingers. He seems lost for words, and this moment seems way more intimate than it should be. Why don't people have one-night stands more often?

I reach up greedily, moving my fingers in the *give me, give me* motion, wanting Wills closer to me.

"Kiss me," I plead.

He places a soft kiss on my lips, intensifying as the seconds tick by. I feel him at my entrance, slowly pushing in.

"Ow," I whimper.

"I'll go slow, Sadie, don't worry. I won't hurt you."

He pushes in more, and I scrunch my eyes closed and grab at his shoulder.

"Relax, beautiful, open up for me."

I'm struggling to take him fully. Wills reaches down between us and starts to rub my clit, which does the job of relaxing me, so he slips in more. He stills again, waiting for me to adjust around him. Wills pushes one more time, and he's now entirely inside of me.

I take a deep breath. That wasn't as bad as I thought it would be.

"Move, Wills. I'm good," I pant.

His eyes glaze over as he pulls back and then presses into me. God, I'm so full of him. He's so big. After a few unhurried pumps, he reaches down, pulls both my legs out wide, and presses them to the bed. Ahhh, he is so freaking deep now.

He's moving faster and harder, stretching me so wide. Our skin starts slapping together, echoing throughout the room.

His breathing is ragged, and he's looking up at the ceiling, his face strained.

"Fuck Sadie, fuck. This feels too good. My cock is being sucked into your tight cunt. I don't want to come yet."

He looks tortured. But I'm secretly happy I do this to him too. I clench hard.

"Fuuuuck," he roars. Then, grabbing my hips, Wills starts to pound into me with punishing hits. Finally, he sends me over the edge, and we both come in a rush.

Wills falls on top of me. His breathing is erratic.

"Was that even real?" I whisper.

He rolls over and pulls me into his side. "Oh, my beautiful girl, you have no idea how real that was."

That was the last thing I remember before I closed my eyes and passed out from exhaustion.

The light is shining through the window into my eyes, waking me up from my deep sleep. Mmm, I stretch my body, and that's when I realize I'm sore, like ridiculously sore. Oh god, I'm still in Wills's bed. I turn my head quickly, coming face-to-face with the Adonis sleeping next to me.

He's on his back with one arm over his eyes and the other suspiciously somewhere under the covers. He looks good enough to eat, he's so sexy I can barely stand it. I can't believe I'm in bed with someone who looks like him, honestly.

I can feel myself getting wet and my traitorous sex clenches. I look down.

"He's not yours," I whisper to my vagina.

Was I supposed to sleep here last night? I don't know what the protocol is for being a slut? *Okay, maybe not a slut.* But still. I was so tired I just passed out, I think in his arms? Who even knows, it was like eight a.m.

So, what the hell do I do now? I can't face him this morning, that I know. I can't bear to be rejected.

I quietly get up out of bed and find my clothes still in the bathroom. I put them on quickly and make my way toward the front door. I pause quick, shamelessly ogling him one more time—*bye, baby.*

I dash along the hotel's corridor, heading to the elevator bank that leads to the suites. Who knew this hotel was so big?

Thirty, plus one day old, and I experienced my first walk of shame. This shit's for college kids. What am I doing? In the middle of the afternoon, no less!

I guess if you're going to do the walk of shame, you might as well go all out. At least that's what I'm telling myself to ease the embarrassment running through my body right now.

I finally make it to our room, crossing my fingers Belle is still sleeping, but as I open the door quietly, just my luck, she's standing there midsip of water, looking worse for the wear.

I grimace and audibly sigh as I put my head in my hands. My compulsion to flee to my room quickly is high on my list right now, but I know she won't let that slide.

I hear her slippered feet shuffling over to me. "Sadie, what's wrong, darling?" she asks, throwing her arm around me in a side hug.

"Oh god." I throw her arm off of me.

"You smell like a brewery, I may puke." I scrunch up my nose with disgust.

Belle starts to make a gagging sound. "Please, stop it right this instant!"

She's laughing, and I think she may be drunk still. It's now when I notice she's wearing a men's dress shirt.

"Whose shirt is that? Is someone here right now?" I look toward her bedroom, and she looks down at the shirt like she's forgotten she was wearing it.

"Oh, this shirt? It's not what it looks like," she states matter-of-factly.

I raise my eyebrow in question. Would she care to elaborate?

"Well, I probably smell like a bar because a bar was sprayed on me. I can't remember the particulars but let's just say things got a little rowdy once you left last night. My dress was soaked, so I made George give me his shirt."

Ummm… "Let me get this straight? You stayed at the club in just a men's dress shirt, and George, what? Just danced around topless?"

She leans against the doorway to hold herself up because she's laughing so hard now.

Yup, she's definitely still drunk. In between breaths she struggles but says, "When you say it like that, it sounds kind of scandalous, doesn't it?"

I'm just staring at her now because I'm not sure what to say. But that's when I remember something else. "Annabelle Hughes!"

"Yesss?" she slurs. I hit my hand to my forehead, I'm too tired for this shit.

"You were not wearing any underwear under your dress last night! So that means you are wearing a short and loose dress shirt, commando?" We both could see panty lines, so we decided as a team to go without.

She picks up her shirt to check, this is too much for me.

"Okay, drunky, let's get you back to bed."

"Oh no, you don't. Why are you already home? Don't think I didn't notice you trying to slip in unnoticed."

"That's a story for after. Let's go, we can sleep together and snuggle."

"Mmm, sounds good."

I grab some water and follow her to her room for some much-needed rest.

"Beep, beep, beep…"

"Ughhh, what is that god-awful noise? Shut it off. Please just make it stop!"

"Annabelle, it's coming from your side," I grumble.

I barely make out what's going on. What time is it? I hear Belle moaning and grunting, trying to roll over to see where the noise is coming from.

"I'm going to kill my assistant." I hear her mumble under her breath after she shuts off the beeping.

"Since when do you have an assistant?"

"Since I can't juggle anything anymore and I was starting to forget shit, I thought I told you. But I *do* have to tell you about her. Hold on."

When she's doing whatever she's doing, I get up to go to the bathroom. I'm scared to pee, though. It's going to burn, I know it. My arms, legs, and muscles I didn't even know I had down below, all still ache . A good ache, I think as I smile to myself.

Ugh, I have to stop these thoughts. We had a good time, and last night was it, even after what he said. It was just a way for him to get me back to his room. It's usually why I avoid guys like him. *Unless... he's different.*

My thoughts are not helping my hangover, so I quickly grab some Advil and water then make my way back toward the bedroom.

I do chance a quick look in the mirror, and I shut off the light *real* quick. I'm not ready for that sight yet.

Belle is sitting up against the headboard when I make it back, scowling at her phone.

"What's wrong?"

"I forgot I had a quick video call to introduce myself to a potential new client tonight."

"Okay, well, good thing you have time, let's just relax a little longer, then get ready."

"Sadie, It's five o'clock."

She must be joking.

I'm so turned around. The last two days have been such a whirlwind.

Plus, staying up all night and not going to bed until this morning is screwing up my days.

Belle must realize my inner turmoil and assures me it will be fine. She gets up to get ready for her call and leaves me to think again, which is precisely what I don't want to do. I need to keep busy.

"I'm going to order us some food for breakfast, dinner—whatever you want to call it," I yell to Belle.

"Sounds great, darling, thanks."

I order burgers, fries, mashed potatoes, and dessert; we deserve something bad and greasy. I also have some weird obsession with

French mashed potatoes, a.k.a. pomme puree, and order them at every meal.

Plus, I've probably burned off enough calories during my whirlwind night with Wills that I could skip the gym all week. I chuckle a little. *Who am I?*

While I wait for our food, I decide to grab my swimsuit and jump into our heated plunge pool. Relaxing in the water will help my poor achy and hungover body.

I've been out here for just a few minutes, and I can't stop my mind from thinking of Wills. I wish we had met at a different time, gone on some dates, and didn't have sex the first time we had a conversation. Don't get me wrong. Last night was… epic. I've never experienced sex like that.

First, I hadn't realized someone could have that many orgasms in a row. Second, I've been missing something so important with my past partners. Colton was so selfish I would almost always have to finish myself off.

But Wills… Wills put me first all night long. We were so in tune with each other it made for a perfect night.

I can't explain it, but we just clicked. From the second our eyes met across the hotel lobby, I knew I needed to learn more about Wills Taylor.

I also know I'm getting ahead of myself. How could it ever actually turn into something, even if I wanted it to? When do you ever hear, "Oh, this is my husband. He was supposed to be a one-night stand, but he just couldn't live without me?" This isn't some romance novel with a happily ever after. It's my real life.

I know I said I wanted a companion this trip, but Wills is not that.

I can't have a fling with someone I can see myself having a relationship with. Which I still find hysterical. Wills Taylor is exactly the opposite of what I would typically look for in a guy.

But then again, I did see a different side to him on the beach, one I'm not sure many people see.

I usually go for the cute book nerd, Clark Kent type. Fewer complications. *How did that work out for you with Colton?* I think.

Plus, let's not forget Wills lives in London.

I know I told Belle I would move to London, which I will, but who knows when that will be. It takes time to set up jobs, visas, housing, etcetera. You can't commit a long-distance relationship with a mere stranger.

I do hope one thing to be true, that he had as much of a memorable night as I did.

I know I'm nowhere near experienced as Wills, but last night came naturally, I think, for both of us, and I hope I can take that as a good sign.

I lean my head back to rest on the ledge of the pool and look up into the sky.

I wonder what he's doing now. Has he thought of me, as I have him? Or am I trying to kid myself? He's probably elated, basking in happiness that he didn't have to deal with the uncomfortable situation of waking up with a stranger.

"I can see the wheels turning in that head of yours."

I didn't hear Belle come outside, but she's smiling at me when I turn around. A warm, genuine smile. She knows how I can overthink things and drive myself crazy, and she'll be here to comfort me.

"I've been outside what, twenty minutes? You look like you can shoot a cover for a magazine. Your makeup is perfect. But why are you still in George's shirt?"

"I was too lazy to shower just yet, figured it looks like I'm wearing a trendy oversized dress shirt. So I'll just be extra careful not to move the camera anywhere below my top."

She sweeps her arm across her chest and says, "Food is served, princess, let's eat."

I'm starved. I really must have been deep in thought, I didn't hear the staff come in either and deliver the food.

"Alright, spill. How was last night, and why did you come back so early? I figured you would spend the day with him."

I sigh. "That's not what last night was, and you know it. So there is no hanging out again."

"I don't think so, Sadie. I think he's really into you. The way he was with you last night just proves my point."

After a moment of silence, she adds, "Plus, even if it was truly a one-night stand, why did George text me asking for your number? I'm sure Wills was looking for it."

"Oh…" It's all I have to say.

"Yeah, Oh. Well, at least give me the goods. How was it? The way you're walking makes me think it was time well spent." She giggles.

"I'm walking just fine, thank you very much." Even though I think she may be right.

"Last night was honestly perfect. We talked on the beach and got to know…"

"Perfect," Belle cuts me off.

"You chatted, got to know each other, blah blah, how was the sex, chemistry, was he huge, I feel like he would be huge."

This girl is crazy, and it's precisely why I love her.

"Honestly, that part was also perfect. He's like some type of sex god." I giggle and cover my face with my hand.

"I've never experienced anything like last night, it went on for hours. He is just. Wow."

"So, you were thoroughly fucked then?"

This girl.

"I guess you could say I was." I smile up at her.

"It's about damn time, Sadie."

After dinner, I head back to my room to shower and get comfortable. We decided to stay in and watch a movie while eating the dessert I ordered. I needed a night to relax after last night.

I'm about to walk back out into the common area when I hear my phone chime from the side table where it's charging.

Unknown Number: What happened to you this morning? – Wills

No, hello, or how are you feeling? Rude.

Maybe he's annoyed I made a move to leave before he could make it like it was his idea. Who knows? I ignore the text and leave the room to snuggle in with Belle for the movie.

Tonight is girls' night, and I'm not dealing with Wills now.

Three days after my wild night out, we are headed to the pool for some sun and cocktails. I finally feel well enough to consume some type of alcohol without getting sick. It's like I turned thirty and instantly can't hang anymore.

The last few days have been amazing, though. We rented this cute light-blue convertible and drove into the Provence countryside. Since we weren't staying there anymore, I figured we should still experience it. So, we went for hours upon hours, stopping in small villages to eat and shop. I bought some antique trinkets to bring home, and Belle bought this fantastic vintage headscarf she wore during our drive. We decided last minute to stay in an exquisite château near Aix-en-Provence to avoid wasting time driving back to our hotel.

The same family still owns the house, passed down from generation to generation starting in the early 1700s. They had such great stories to tell us about their family's history and the house. This definitely will be a highlight of the trip.

After we woke up, we joined the family and other guests for a picturesque breakfast in their outdoor garden filled with stunning flowers and herbs.

You can see the care and love that went into creating the grounds. I was just surprised that it was a mix of a French and English-style garden. Both are structured but wild at the same time. It was one of a kind, and I can't wait to print all the pictures I took of it.

After departing the house, we headed back toward our hotel, stopping at the famous lavender fields, and they didn't disappoint. Belle was happy she got great content for her social media, and I was just happy to sit and reflect on how lucky we truly are to be on a trip like this.

We finally make it to the pool entrance, and Belle turns to me with a serious face.

"Don't be mad."

"What did you do, Belle?"

She is looking straight into the pool area, avoiding my eyes. "All the guys will be here, and it's time you face the music."

With that, she stomps away, leaving me to trail after her.

I'm going to kill her.

5

Wills

I'VE BEEN ENDURING long days, being busted by my mates, calling me a pussy for acting crazy over a girl. But what the fuck? I'm going out of my mind wondering why the hell Sadie left the morning after and why she hasn't answered my text.

I don't have time to screw around… this is why I don't trust people or open up to them. But I took a chance on Sadie. I thought she was different. So, I opened up to her on the beach, letting her in—something I very rarely do.

And the sex, fuck. I can get a hard-on just thinking about how fucking hot it was. Sadie was so sexy. I know she felt the connection, and that's why it's driving me out of my mind.

This is why I don't do relationships. *This isn't a relationship.*

Sadie, goddamn, Peters is driving me batshit crazy. Her and her fucking magic cunt that sucked me in. *Fuck.*

Like I conjured her, Sadie and Annabelle walk into the pool area, finding a seat on the opposite side of where the lads and I are sitting. I watch her unpack her bag and settle in… she's tense. Good, she knows I'm here.

I watch her, read her book, order a margarita, and talk to Annabelle for the next hour. Not once does she look at me, *not once?*

Fuck this. I'm going to the bar.

"Let's go get drinks," I say to Declan as I walk away.

After ordering, I slam my pint back and then order another for us. Besides my family, Declan is one of the only people I trust. Not only to keep my secrets but to give it to me straight. You wouldn't believe how many people try to kiss my arse, just to be my friends. It gets old real quick

"Alright, mate. I'm losing my mind."

Declan smirks.

Arsehole.

"Same advice as before, just go talk to her. Maybe she was nervous, or something happened. You don't know until you speak with her. Communication is key."

Is it that simple, just talk to her after she walked out on me? A part of me wants to say, screw her. But the other part, the bigger part, wants to run over to her right now.

"Thanks, I'll see." I look back over, and there it is. We finally make eye contact, and I know she's just as affected as I am.

God, she's gorgeous.

Sadie

God, he's sexy. I watch as Wills walks back over to his lounger near the pool. Every head turns to get a look at him, men and women.

"So…" Annabelle continues.

"You'll have to meet her when you move to London!" she yells excitedly. She won't shut up about it, going on and on about how thrilled she is.

"Do you remember the movie *Clueless*?"

"Duh, of course." What girl our age hasn't seen that movie? It was like a rite of passage as a teenage girl.

"Well, my assistant is that teacher, Miss Geist, remember her? She was like all over the place, but a really good person? That's Lola. She's probably in her midtwenties, super sweet, and a total mess. But also could be like a sexy librarian type with her glasses and all."

"Why are you thinking of your assistant as a sexy librarian?" I laugh.

I look over at Wills again, and he's staring at me. This time I give in and don't look away.

He licks his lips as he gives me the once-over and then motions his head for me to go over to him.

I couldn't, could I? *of course I can.* I barely even give it a second thought, I tell Belle I'll be right back as I throw on my cover-up and make my way over to Wills.

He pats his hand on the lounge to sit. My body betrays me, obeys him, and sits right down next to him.

A few seconds pass, and he's just staring at me with a look I can't read.

"Hi, beautiful." His deep voice vibrates through my body, finally breaking the silence.

"How are you?" I ask, wringing my hands. Why does he make me so nervous?

"Honestly, not good."

I lift my head and look him square in the eyes, concerned. I am wondering what could be wrong.

"You see, a couple of days ago, I spent the night with the most amazing woman. I thought she liked me, and I like her. But I woke up the next morning, and she was gone. Poof, disappeared into the morning without a word."

"Oh." I wasn't expecting him to say that.

He reaches out and stops my hands from fidgeting.

"So maybe you can explain to me what happened?" He clenches his jaw, and his face turns serious.

What do I say here? The real reason is that I just couldn't handle it.

But I know I need to go with honesty here. Wills doesn't trust easy, that I know.

"Well…" I pause. This is harder than I thought.

"Look at me, Sadie," he demands.

I look up, not getting a read on him, so I continue. "Well, honestly…" I let out a long breath and then continue. "I told you, I have never done the casual sex thing. I was nervous about when you would wake up and ask me to leave. I didn't want to feel rejected. So I thought maybe if I left, it would be easier."

"Was it easier?" he asks.

"It wasn't," I answer and look down. I thought of him all day and all the days since.

He shakes his head. I can tell he's annoyed. I don't like that look on him.

"I'm sorry."

"Sadie," Wills sighs. He reaches down the lounge, pulls me up between his legs, and wraps his arms around me.

"I'm crazy mad, my beautiful girl. But I'm sorry if I gave you the impression you needed to leave. I thought I was clear that this wasn't just a one-night stand. I wanted to wake up with you in my arms." He squeezes me, leans over, and kisses my forehead, leaving his lips to linger. "Don't ever run from me, Sadie. I won't be happy."

"Okay," I whisper and nuzzle into him. There's the intimacy again, and that's what makes me think that maybe it's not okay. I like Wills more than I should for just meeting someone, and at the end of this trip, I'll be the one getting hurt, not Wills.

But I ask myself… wouldn't it be better to have experienced a Wills Taylor in your life than never have before? And my answer comes quick. Yes, it definitely would.

After a while of lying together, I'm getting hot, so I suggest we go for a swim.

"Any excuse to look at you in that little bikini you have on under this is fine with me," Wills responds.

I'm floating around in the water, taking in the scenery as Wills swims up behind me, bringing me flush to his hard body. And by hard, I mean everything.

"Wills." I laugh and look down and shimmy a little to tease him. "Why are you hard right now?" I whisper, and this time, I discreetly reach down and stroke it once over his swim trunks. This trip is really bringing out my inner minx.

Wills groans. "Because you're so fucking sexy, I bet half the guys here at the pool are hard." He frowns, thinking for a second, and continues, "Which also makes me want to murder everyone."

I laugh, and he tightens his hold around me. "Let me take you to dinner tonight," he asks as he presses his lips to the spot I love below my ear.

"I'd love you to," I say as I throw my arms around his neck and kiss him properly.

"Okay, get a room, you two. It's starting to get nauseating," Belle says.

I look up, and there she is with a smiling Declan.

"So, leave," Wills deadpans. I hit him in the chest.

"Don't be rude to her."

"Well, I don't like my time with you interrupted." He snuggles back into my neck.

How did I get this so wrong? He never insinuated that it would be a one-night stand? So why was I so insistent?

Belle and Declan both make a gagging noise, and all four of us laugh.

I smile up at Belle, and she is beaming down at me. She's happy, I'm happy, and that's exactly why I love her.

I'm standing in the lobby waiting to meet Wills for our date a few hours later, and I have zero chill.

I was a madwoman getting ready, and Belle was probably glad to get rid of me. After trying on fifty outfits, I decided on white high-waisted wide-leg trousers, white strappy heels, and a champagne-colored silk blouse with an open back. My makeup is bare, with just a little mascara to bring out my green eyes and a nude lip. My hair is pulled into a super sleek high ponytail, exposing my open-backed shirt more. Knowing it will drive Wills mad.

I feel him behind me before he speaks. He presses a quick kiss to the back of my neck and whispers, "Ready to go, my beautiful girl?" He doesn't wait for my response but interlocks our fingers and pulls me toward the waiting cars out front.

I notice he's quick to leave and doesn't say another word. It dawns on me that he has his Wills Taylor armor on because we're in public, he doesn't like to give the public one inch of himself.

Wills opens the door of an old-looking Porsche, unique in a maroon color exterior and cognac leather seats. Wills sees me taking in the beautiful car. "I rented the car for the night. It's a 1972 Porsche 911," he explains proudly.

"I don't know what any of that means, but I can appreciate an old car, it's exquisite."

"Vintage," he corrects me. "I have two vintage cars I leave at my parents' place in the countryside that are better than this. I'll have to show you when you're in London."

When I'm in London? What does that mean, he would want to see me again after this trip? I get butterflies doing somersaults in my stomach right now. I try not to show my excitement, but not sure how much I'm hiding it.

He smiles, cups my cheek, and places a quick peck on my lips. "Ready for our date, Sadie?"

"I sure am" I don't need to smile back because one hasn't left my lips since the second he asked me on this date.

We've been driving awhile through small winding countryside roads. Wills had said we would be dining somewhere far from the tourists, and although curious where we are going, I'm enjoying this time with Wills, even if it's sitting here in comfortable silence.

Every so often, when he doesn't have to shift gears, he moves his hand in mine and places it on my thigh or smiles over at me when he catches me staring at him.

It's never uncomfortable—it just feels easy with Wills.

And, what I love most, is he doesn't know Sadie Peters from New York, he knows Sadie Peters living her best life in France.

Wills turns off onto a small dark road, only lit up from the stars and moon. "Are we almost there? I ask Wills, bouncing in my seat a little.

"Almost, patience, beautiful. It's worth the drive, I promise."

A few minutes later, I'm looking out the passenger side window, and even though it's dark out, I realize we are driving through a vineyard.

I turn my attention to the front of the car, and I'm amazed at what I see.

I look over to the man sitting next to me. "Wills," I whisper, reaching over to him, squeezing his forearm. *Is Wills Taylor a romantic*?

There's a circular clearing ahead in the middle of the vines, with hundreds of different-sized candles lighting up the area, with only one table in the center. In between the candles are vases of red poppies and giant sunflowers—a beautiful contrast to the green on the vines.

This isn't a restaurant, he set this up just for us.

Wills parks the car, and we make our way over to the table. When I notice a small stone house in the short distance, I assume it houses the kitchen. The lights from the house light up the adjacent area, which is not a continuation of the vines. It is acres and acres of those beautiful sunflowers. I can't help myself. I walk over to the edge of the garden to take it all in. It's perfection.

I'm brought back to the moment when I hear Wills walk up behind me, I turn, and he is standing there staring at me with an unreadable look on his face.

"Is this okay?" he asks skeptically.

"Wills," I sigh, in awe. "Is this okay? Are you kidding? This is perfect, baby." I look around again. "It's beyond perfection. I can't believe you did this for me." I shake my head and shed the tears that had been sitting there. Is this even real life? This feels special, too special, in a way I'm afraid to think about right now.

He closes the distance and wraps his arms around me as I look up into his eyes. He searches my face and thumbs away the few tears I shed.

"Don't cry," he whispers.

"These are happy tears." I smile. "I'm filled with so much happiness right now because of you, Wills. I will never forget this."

He leans down and kisses my forehead.

"Let's eat, beautiful." He takes my hand and leads me toward the impeccable setup.

Just as we sit, a man comes out of the vines to pour us both a glass of champagne.

"Dom Perignon, 1973 Plenitude P3 vintage," he says, then walks away.

"Wills," I whisper so the waiter can't hear. I'm frowning down at my champagne. "I can't drink this. This is way too expensive for a first date." Or for most occasions.

He just shakes his head. "Tonight is the start of something special, so a special champagne is in order." I'm speechless. "Cheers."

"Cheers, Wills Taylor," I whisper. Cheers to this unexpected handsome man in front of me.

After we toast, we are poured a perfect Bordeaux for the remainder of our meal and start in on our small tasting menu.

First was a mix of shellfish locally sourced, in a beautiful display, of what I can only describe as looking like smoky dry ice covering the fish when it arrived at the table. Followed by an artichoke soup with black truffle, mushroom, and herb brioche.

"This is amazing," I say between sips of my soup. "How did you find this place and do all of this?" I sweep my arms around.

"I know the owner, Pierre, and his wife. I told them I had an extraordinary lady to impress tonight and needed the help to make sure you were blown away." He smiles at me.

"Mission accomplished." I reach over and rub my hand up and down his thigh in appreciation.

"Pierre is the chef tonight. He and his wife bought the property about a year ago and live between here and London. He's not producing wine yet. He just sells the grapes to other wineries. Eventually, he would like to get into the winemaking business when he retires, but he is happy cooking for now. He also makes sunflower oil from those." He points over to the beautiful garden.

"He was a private chef for an event I was lucky enough to attend a few years back, and I was blown away by his skills. It was Michelin star worthy. I'm interested in eventually investing in restaurants and nightlife in London, so I reached out to him, and we have been friends ever since. I plan to have him as a head chef one day at one of my restaurants."

"Wow, that sounds amazing. I think Pierre would do well because his food so far has been some of the best I've ever had. I would absolutely eat at a restaurant he was chef at, he is very talented."

I think for a second. "I should introduce you to my brother. He also lives in London, and that is what he does for a living. He opens and invests in high-end clubs and restaurants."

"That would be amazing, thank you. I have contacts set up, but anything helps." He smiles.

"So, Wills, what is it you do now then if you're not ready to invest? Do you still play rugby?"

"No." He stares at me and gives me a genuine smile.

"What?" Why is he looking at me like that?

"I sometimes forget we just met, and we don't know everything about one another. I feel like I've known you forever."

The things that come out of his mouth continue to shock me. But the thing is, I usually agree with whatever he's saying.

"I am officially a retired rugby player. It's why we sort of took this holiday. But, one year ago, I opened my own sports management company. **The Taylor Group**. We '*Taylor*' to all our athlete's needs, it's a one-stop shop. We will set them up with a manager, publicist, agent, and we just added a law division so that they can get legal representation as well," he states proudly.

"Wow, Wills, that's amazing, congrats and good luck. You must be so proud of yourself to have accomplished so much already by the age of thirty-five." Genuinely impressed by him. I can't help the huge smile spread across my face.

We are interrupted quickly when the waiter brings the main course, but Wills won't take his eyes off me, and I can't get a read on him.

"What's wrong? Is it the food?" I can't take it a second longer. I need to know.

"Nothing's wrong, in fact, everything is perfect," he says, not elaborating, and digs into his food, ending the line of questioning.

After we finish, I see a man walking toward Wills and me, holding two perfect-looking soufflés.

"Bonsoir!" he calls over to us.

"Wills, my boy, it is so nice to see you." This must be Pierre. He is a handsome older gentleman.

He places the dessert down, kisses Wills twice, and turns to me.

"This must be your Sadie," he says in the loveliest French accent, sounding like, 'Saydee.'

He places both hands on my shoulders to give me a good look, then leans down to kiss me twice as well. I smile up at him, but he turns to Wills. "Your belle fille?" And I think I see Wills blush. I don't know much French, but I do know belle is beautiful, and I can only guess *fille* is girl. And those butterflies are back in full force.

I decide to ease his obvious embarrassment and praise Pierre for his fantastic meal and property he let us use for our date. I see Wills scowling over the table, and I chuckle. I know he's jealous of Pierre right now, either because of my praise or that he kissed me again.

"Okay, thank you for dinner. We would like our dessert in peace," Wills rudely interrupts.

"Wills!" I whisper through clenched teeth. He's not even bothered, he just shrugs.

Pierre doesn't seem insulted. He just laughs, leans down, and kisses me once more, lingering longer than appropriate. I think he purposely is trying to get under Wills's skin. Pierre smiles softly at me. "Until next time, Sadie." And then he disappears back into the house.

I turn to Wills to tell him how rude he was being, but he is up out of his seat before I can even say anything. Leaning over me, he picks me up and carries me over to his seat, placing me on his lap.

"What the hell, Wills?" I laugh only because I'm so in shock.

He looks confused as if what he just did was totally normal. "That was very rude how you dismissed Pierre."

He doesn't look apologetic at all, and he almost looks mad.

"Sadie, I told you at the pool. I don't like my time with you being interrupted, and he was flirting with you."

I can't help but laugh at this. "He was not flirting, he's French."

Wills doesn't look any happier, but I ignore him and smile at my big jealous baby. I turn in his lap a little and place a chaste kiss on his lips.

"Let's eat this dessert while it's still warm."

Wills feeds himself and me, switching between both soufflés of chocolate and pistachio.

"Tell me something else about yourself," he asks.

"Like what?"

"How did you meet Annabelle? You seem very close despite living so far away from each other."

I wondered when he would ask. I lean back on him and tell our story.

"Belle's aunt and uncle live in the brownstone next to the one I grew up in, on the Upper East Side of Manhattan. And like most wealthy New Yorkers, they also have a house in Southampton, very close to ours. When Belle was five, she came to visit for the whole summer with her mom, while her dad stayed back with her brothers. I was playing outside when they pulled up, and not much different than how she would act now, she marched right over to me, stuck out her hand in my face, and introduced herself."

Even though I was five, I can remember it like yesterday. "I'm Annabelle Hughes. Who are you? She asked, getting right to the point in her British accent. I asked Belle if she knew the Queen, and she thought it was the funniest thing anyone has ever asked. We became fast friends, which wasn't the easiest for me. I was shy and wasn't like most spoiled kids I grew up with. I wanted to help our housekeeper with the garden and read. That whole summer, Belle and I were inseparable, and when she left, we became pen pals."

My mother once read how I described her to Belle in the letters and flipped out. She would stop the letters from being sent, but our housekeeper, Maria, would never let that happen. She would never let me down.

"Each summer after, Belle would beg her parents to visit New York so we could spend time together. Annabelle quickly became more of a sister than a friend. She was my sounding board and confidant. I didn't…" I pause, unsure how much I want to share. But I think it's only right to tell him the whole truth after he opened up so much with me.

"I didn't have the best family life growing up. My dad pretends my brother and I don't exist, and my mother more or less used us like puppets. Although she acts like the doting mother and wife to the public, she is anything but at home. She never raised her hand to me, but her mouth said enough awful things that it was almost worse. I took this harder than my brother, and even though he tried his best to protect me, he was an older teenage boy and just didn't get it at the time. I never understood how a mother could be so cruel. And even though I know better now, I sometimes still wish she would change. Belle was the one I turned to when I needed comfort. She has never let me down. Nothing changed when I was a teenager either, I still hated most of the girls in my school, making me look forward to my summers with Belle even more." I take a breath.

"I wouldn't have survived the other months without knowing I would get to see her in the summer. The best part was when Annabelle's family started to spend Christmas in New York too. That's also when we decided to start taking trips together outside of New York when we turned eighteen. That's how we started our summer holiday tradition together. And that's pretty much our story. We remain extremely close and never miss a summer trip together. We talk every day, even if it's only one text. Some may say we are codependent, but I'm okay with that. I couldn't live without Annabelle, and I owe her everything."

Shocked, I just gave him so much information about my family life. I planned to tell him a little, but I just couldn't stop once I started.

I turn my head to look at Wills since he hasn't said anything.

He closes his eyes and says, as his lips press against my forehead, "I'm happy you had an Annabelle in your life, Sadie." He looks so sad. I almost want to comfort him after my admissions.

I feel like I put a damper on the night, but I have to admit it was nice to get that all off my chest.

Wills finally stands up and walks us toward the car since it's time to leave. He stops and looks at me with the same sad but now determined look.

He places both hands on my cheeks, bends down, so we are eye level, and whispers, "You are enough, Sadie. Always remember that."

Stunned, I just nod, give him a quick squeeze on his bicep and get in the car. I can't look back at him right now. Otherwise, the tears will come.

What Wills just said was such a small sentiment but packed so much meaning. He will never know how much I appreciate it.

On our way back to the hotel, Wills's phone rings as he drives. It's Declan.

"Can you answer it?" he asks. Surprised, but I do. "Hello, Declan, it's Sadie." Declan chuckles.

"Yes, Sadie, I figured you would be the woman who would answer Wills's phone. Especially since you were just on a date."

"Oh, yes, that makes sense," I say, laughing at myself.

"I called to see if you wanted to meet us at karaoke. Annabelle is joining us as well."

I think a minute, trying to envision this six-foot-four hunk of a man standing up on stage, singing to strangers. I laugh aloud this time, and I can see Wills getting agitated, wondering what we are talking about.

"He would hate it," I say to Declan between my laughing breaths.

"One-hundred-percent correct, Sadie."

"Okay, this could be fun. Can you send us the address? We can meet you there within the hour."

"Sounds good, don't let him talk you out of it. It will be fun, or at least it will be fun watching Leo and George make a fool of themselves. And watching Wills wanting to murder anyone who walks within twenty feet of you." I guess he notices how possessive he is too, and it's not just me.

"See you there, Declan." I hang up. I think I like Declan, it's always the quiet ones who intrigue me.

Wills is waiting for me to fill him in on our conversation.

I smile brightly, trying to break the news to him softly. He won't like this, I already know.

"That was Declan…"

"I know, Sadie, get to the point. What will I hate?"

"We are going to meet them all out at a karaoke bar," I rush out quickly.

I don't know the look he is giving me, but then he says, "Absolutely not. No way in hell are we ending our date doing that."

"No, definitely not," he says again.

Oh, he really doesn't like this idea, more than I thought. I don't want to ruin the date, and it's not like I love karaoke. I wanted just to see Wills squirm a little. I think about it, and he's right. We shouldn't end it like this.

"Okay, we don't have to go." He looks over at me and doesn't say anything.

We pull up to our hotel, and he hands the keys to the valet. I see him take a breath and sigh while taking my hand and pulling me out toward the street, not the hotel.

"Where are we going?" I ask.

"Karaoke," he grumbles. Wills still doesn't look happy about it, but I smile that he is giving in.

"That's okay, let's just head back." I tug at his hand a little.

"No, Sadie, we have to do this." What does that mean? He wants us to go but also doesn't look happy.

"What's wrong, Wills? I don't want to ruin the best date I've ever had by making you unhappy."

That makes him smile.

"Best date?" His mood flipped, and he is giving me that signature Wills smirk I love so much.

"Yes," I whisper.

He stops us on the sidewalk and looks down at me. "Me too, beautiful." Wills cups my cheek, something I notice he does before he kisses me, and sure enough, he leans down and places a kiss on my lips. I try to push for a deeper kiss, but he stops it.

"Sadie, we are too close to that hotel. If this kiss goes any further, we will be heading to the penthouse, not the bar."

"Okay, let's go then," I try and pull him back toward the hotel again.

"No," he says, not letting me lead the way. "Sadie." He sounds like he's tormented.

"We need to go to the bar." He pauses, I know he wants to say more.

"I can't explain it right now without sounding a little crazy, even to me."

"Try," I push, and after a minute, he says, "I have this overwhelming feeling to protect and keep you just to myself. I want to share you with no one, including our friends. I know that is not rational, trust me. When I think about it, I see what you and everyone else must think. But I can't help it. So, we need to socialize. Otherwise, the rest of this trip will just be me and you locked away in the penthouse."

Maybe there is something wrong with me, too, because that doesn't sound half bad. I smirk.

But he is right. If that's how he feels, he needs to get used to me being with Annabelle. I won't leave her.

He leans down, kisses the top of my head, holding me for a second longer before he asks if I'm ready to go.

6

Sadie

We walk into the bar hand in hand, and I can spot our group straight away. They are loud, animated, and drunk. Of course, Wills is going to hate this.

I squeeze his hand and shoot him a big, wide smile to ease his knowing discomfort.

He mumbles something inaudible and pulls me toward our friends.

"We don't have to stay long," I promise him.

"Sades!" Belle screams as we get closer. She is using Jackson's nickname, which only confirms she's drunk. She's trying to reach over Declan on the couch to hug me but falls flat on her face. Oh god, this is going to be good.

She rolls over and smiles up at me. "Hello, my darling."

"Hello, my very drunky friend." I smile, lean down for a hug and kiss, and she pulls me down with her, thinking she's the funniest ever.

I hear Wills grumble behind me, he's not impressed with her antics. He pulls me upright, tugging me to his side.

"What do you want to drink?" Wills asks. I look at the plethora of booze they have on the table.

"Champagne, please." He kisses my forehead then walks off to pour my drink.

I see Declan smiling in my peripheral vision so, I turn and raise my eyebrow to him. Wondering what he's smiling at.

He pats the couch for me to take a seat next to him. "How was your night, lass?"

I enjoy listening to Declan speak. He's Irish but went to school in America and has lived in London a little over ten years now. So, his accent is all over the place.

"The best, it was just perfect" I can't help but get excited as Declan studies my face for a moment.

"You like him." It's not a question.

"Yes." I smile broadly. "A lot. Probably too much for someone I just met, honestly." I look over at Wills, who is talking to Leo. I'm not sure why I'm confiding in Declan, practically a stranger. But Declan puts off good energy. The first night we met, he seemed quiet and reserved, and I think I was wrong about all these guys. Much different from my first impression. Well, at least about Wills and Declan. The verdict's still out on George and Leo, but I think I'm still sure they are similar to Jackson, fuckboys at heart.

And, right on cue, George saunters over with his arms around two pretty brunettes.

Declan rolls his eyes and turns his head back to me, looking a little more serious.

"He feels the same," he says, staring right into my eyes.

"Huh?" I look back over at Wills, he's too distracting.

He wore another linen suit on our date, but since removing his jacket, I can see every outline of his muscles through his shirt. He's standing with his legs spread wide and arms crossed, listening intently to whatever Leo is saying.

"Wills, he feels the same about you, Sadie. I've been friends with him a while, and he's like an older brother to me, a mentor. But I've never seen him like this with anyone. Including Wills's last girlfriend years ago."

The word girlfriend and Wills in the same sentence makes me

murderous. I'm not a jealous person, so this surprises me. But I can feel my blood boiling at the thought of him with another girl.

Declan chuckles.

"What?" I cock my head.

"I was going to finish that statement off with the typical, don't hurt my mate. But I think he's in good hands. Your face when I mentioned a girlfriend would have been the same face Wills would have made if the conversation was reversed."

I chuckle. He's right.

"I like you for him, Sadie."

I don't know why that makes me emotional, but I lean over and hug Declan. I think I surprise him because it takes a second for him to hug back.

"What the hell is going on here?" Wills's voice booms over the terrible karaoke singers.

"Oh, surely you can't be jealous of Declan?" My eyes go wide in question.

Instead of answering, he sits down next to me and pulls me onto his lap. I laugh, and Declan just shakes his head while Wills passes me my champagne.

"Not too much, I don't want you drunk tonight," Wills whispers in my ear.

I wiggle with excitement, and he grips my hips to still me.

"Oops." I exaggeratedly bat my eyelashes and smirk over my champagne glass.

He rolls his eyes and pulls me close to him.

Leo gets our attention to ask if we want to be included in their game of karaoke roulette.

Wills automatically says no, and I usually would never. But, hey, why not? *This is fun, Sadie!*

"Add my name in the mix, Leo."

"What? No way, Sadie. I don't want you getting up in front of all these guys in here."

"Oh, shh, it will be fun!"

He doesn't respond, so Leo walks off after adding my name.

Leo picks the first name, and it's George. He seems excited as he gets on stage and spins the wheel.

We won't know the song until the music starts since we can't see the song wheel from here.

But he looks happy enough with the choice.

Belle moves to sit closer to me and get a better view of George.

"This is going to be epic. I need to video this and send it to my brothers," she says.

The music starts, and I know it instantly and smile down at Belle, and she returns the gesture. I know she's thinking of Jackson right now.

"Why are you smiling like that?" Wills whispers in my ear.

"When we were younger, my brother loved Queen. Since he has dark hair, he would pretend to be Freddie Mercury and dance and sing around the house. He even tried to grow a mustache once. Belle had, or has, a secret crush on my brother that she still won't admit, and she would make us sneak and watch his private concerts when we were kids." I smile at the memory of the one time he caught us. He was so embarrassed. It was then when I realized he might also have a crush on Belle, but neither ever said anything to each other.

"I would love to know more about your relationship with her," Wills says. I love he's taking such an interest.

"I would love to share it when we aren't yelling over George singing 'Another One Bites the Dust.'" I laugh.

I turn to see George ripping up the stage singing his heart out, and he's killing it. I didn't expect him to have such a great voice. He has the whole crowd involved. Whoever goes next is going to have to bring it.

George finishes, and the bar goes crazy as he makes his way back to us.

"Well done, mate," Declan yells and claps him on the back.

Leo picks the next name, looking right at Wills with a smirk. "Wills, your girl's up next."

I freeze, oh god, I'm not sure this is a good idea anymore. I felt confident just for a second, but now my typical shy nature is back in full swing.

I can feel my face pale, and I look up at Wills, and he just knows.

"She's going to pass. Pick someone else." He holds me tightly against him.

"Rules are rules," Leo says at the same time as Belle gets up to tug me off of Wills.

She won't let this slide.

"Help me, baby," I whisper to Wills even though I know he can't do anything without making a scene at this point.

He shrugs. This is it. I guess I'm up.

I quickly walk over to our table, take a tequila shot, and grab Belle's champagne from her hand to down that too.

Then I make my way to the stage, if I'm going to do this, I'm going to do it well. *So, woman up, Sadie, and give these people a show.*

Wills

I watch as my girl gets up on stage with her shoulders pulled back, looking a lot better than she did a minute ago.

Fucking Leo, making her feel like she had to go up there. He's going to pay for that.

I know she's putting on a brave face because she doesn't want to disappoint everyone, and she has to follow George's act.

Who the hell knew the guy could sing so well? I smile, thinking of him trying to dance around the stage.

I look back up at Sadie, I'm nervous for her, I realize.

"She'll be okay," I hear Annabelle say. "Sadie's stronger than she seems. She forgets it sometimes, but if you give her a little push, she'll open up."

"She *is* strong," is all I say, even though I want to say more. I don't know Sadie well enough to defend her to her best friend.

But I can tell she is strong. She reminds me a lot of my sister, and unfortunately, people sometimes mistake her kindness for weakness.

Sadie spins the wheel and quickly looks up, trying to find me in the crowd. We lock eyes, and hers widen.

What song did she get? Why are her eyes wide like that? I try to stand up and get her off that stage, which I didn't even want her on to begin with. But a hand grips my shoulder from behind to stop me.

I look up, it's Declan, and he shakes his head to tell me to stay put.

I look back at Sadie, and she's wringing her hands, she's nervous. I try to stand again, and he won't let me. "Declan, what the fuck? She needs me."

"She's okay, mate." He motions to look back at Sadie. I look up to see her take a deep breath and smile.

"If she has to sing that song that goes, '*I like big butts, and I cannot lie,*' I'm pulling her right down. No one is looking at her fucking bum."

"Okay, calm down. If she sings that, you can get her." He turns toward Sadie shaking his head. *Don't shake your head at me, arsehole.*

The music starts, and it takes me a minute to figure out what it is. *Oooh this may be funny.* Shit, I feel bad even thinking that.

I look over at Annabelle, and she is bent over dying of laughter, tears running down her face as Sadie raps. The guys are all standing around, bobbing their heads to the beat of the music.

My beautiful girl's voice is not that great. I laugh, imagining her face all scrunched up, mad if she heard me say that.

But I'll give it to her, she is growing more confident as the song goes on, getting louder and prouder, and the crowd is loving it. She raps, *"I'm Slim Shady..."*

Sadie, our quiet, prim, and proper good girl, is rapping to Eminem's "The Real Slim Shady."

She's good with the lyrics, I can't believe she can keep up with all the words.

Declan leans down, this even amuses him. "I'm so happy I stopped you from going up there." The whole place is getting into it, and when she sings the chorus again, the entire bar erupts, singing along except for me and Annabelle, who can't stop laughing.

She ends with a bow and runs offstage, embarrassment creeping up, I can see the red spreading from her cheeks down her chest.

She runs right over to me. *I got you, beautiful.* I catch her in my arms and spin her around once.

"You did amazing!" I lean down and give her a big kiss.

"Ohhhhh shit," I hear George yell. Leo and Declan are shouting stuff behind us too.

Sadie gets pulled away by Annabelle, and all the guys cheer her on.

"We have our own *Slim Sadie* in the house, everyone," Declan claims, and they all start cheering. *Since when is he a comedian*?

Sadie rolls her eyes. "Don't even start with the nicknames." Declan throws his arm around her. "Don't worry, Slim, it will only stay between us."

"Alright, hands off," I say, and Sadie smiles up to me, wiggling out of Declan's grip to come over to me. *Good girl.*

"Alright, time to go, Slim Sadie," I whisper in her ear, her eyes widen, shocked I would join in on the teasing.

"Ugh, not you too," she whines.

"What? I think it's quite cute." I tell her but can't keep my laugh in.

"Alright, everyone, we're leaving," I yell over the music. I hear Sadie ask Annabelle if it's okay she leaves. I know she's in a tough spot. I leave the guys, and they all have each other, but Annabelle's alone.

"Yes, Sadie, are you insane? Go get laid, pleeeease," Annabelle yells, and Sadie throws her hand over Annabelle's mouth to quiet her and looks over at me.

Yes, Sadie, let's go home so I can get laid, I think. Sadie rolls her eyes with a smile, knowing exactly what I'm thinking. We walk back to the hotel, holding hands. I'm not sure I've ever wanted to be touching someone as much as Sadie. It should probably scare me a little that this girl I barely know, who lives in America, has such a hold over me. But I can't let it get to me, and I won't ruin my time with her, for however long that is.

We make it to the lobby, and I spot a few people who recognize me. Not sure if they are fans or paparazzi, I straighten my back and keep my head straight. I see Sadie look up at me, she knows I'm not comfortable in public places like this. It's well lit, and we're clearly going back to my room, headed straight toward the private lifts. This is how rumors start in the tabloids, and I never want Sadie to be a part of that.

"Come on, sweetheart, let's go a little faster, so no one has time to stop us."

She scowls. "Don't call me that."

"What, call you sweetheart?"

"Yes! I'm not fragile. You only said sweetheart, because you feel bad putting me in this position." How does she know me so well already?

She continues, "I don't care about those people, or the tabloids, or the bullshit that comes along with it. I'm with you by choice, Wills. I know what that means, so let them bring it."

There's my strong girl, I knew it already. Annabelle didn't have to tell me.

"Did you just curse Ms. Peters?" I try and lighten the conversation, and it works because she giggles and smiles sweetly at me, and now there's my good girl.

"Come on," I say, laughing, pulling her into the lift.

After a while, Sadie asks what I'm thinking about since I'm being quiet.

"The last time we were in this lift." I won't elaborate because she knows and because I wanted to rip her clothes off and fuck her right against the mirror the last time.

But I would never if I knew there was even a chance someone could get a glimpse of Sadie. It drove me mad, having her in a bathing suit this morning, for fuck's sake.

This is how I know I have it bad because this has never crossed my mind with another. Even with Libby, my ex of three years.

Damn, Libby. I never think of her, but she's causing trouble back at home, and I'm doing everything I can do to stay away.

I'm brought back to the moment when I see Sadie's blush, a minute ago, she was about to fight the paparazzi, now she's shy. I love that I get to see all of her, at least she doesn't shy away from that.

We make it back to the room, and although I'm ready to devour her, I want to take tonight slow and end this night right.

"I'm going to freshen up," Sadie says and heads to the loo.

"Meet me out on the balcony when you're done," I yell after her.

I grab us a blanket to set up for us outside, there's a breeze from the sea that adds a chill to the air. I'm about to step out, and I hear a loud thud. What was that?

"Wills, Wills!" I hear Sadie's panicked voice yelling for me.

I rush to the bathroom door and try to open it, but it's locked. "Sadie? What's wrong?"

"I'm stuck," she cries.

"Can you open the door? You locked it."

I'm getting nervous now. Why did she lock the door? How will I help her? I'm panicking.

"No! I can't move," she cries again.

"Sadie, this door is too heavy for me to break down. I can't get to you unless I call for help. Hold on."

"Please, help." I hear her whisper sadly behind the door. I'm feeling frantic right now, I need to get to my girl.

"Hello, Mr. Taylor, how may we assist you tonight?" the front desk asks.

"I need help sent up immediately, I have someone locked in my bathroom. She is stuck on something and can't open the door that's locked."

"I'm so sorry to hear that. I will send someone up shortly to unlock the door."

"Not shortly, right now! I'm paying enough money for the penthouse. I think you can rush this, don't you think?" I yell at the poor girl on the phone. She agrees and promises someone will rush right now.

I run back over to the bathroom to check on Sadie. "Baby, I'm back. Are you okay?"

"No," she whispers and asks, "Why are you calling me baby now?"

"What? I don't know, it just came out?"

"You've never called these names before, though," she says, almost annoyed.

I sigh, she wants to argue about the names I call her when she's stuck behind a locked door, and I can't get to her.

"I called you sweetheart, I agree because I was feeling bad for having you be put in that situation, but… the baby was because I wanted to. I like when you say it to me," I admit.

"Oh, okay."

I can hear the smile in her voice. So at least I'm helping.

"Plus, I feel weird calling you beautiful through a door when I can't see that face of yours."

She's quiet now. Did I say the wrong thing?

"Sadie? Are you okay?"

"Yes." I hear her sniffle. "You always say the right thing and make me feel better."

"So, why are you crying?"

She starts laughing. "I don't know actually, I was feeling bad for myself, I think."

I hear a knock at the door and run to let the maintenance guy in.

"Wills!" I hear Sadie calling me, shit, I didn't tell her I was walking away.

"I'm back, I'm back, sorry, I had to let the maintenance guy in."

"Wait, Wills," she whispers. "My pants are down, don't let him see me."

Good thing she told me because I would have been crazy mad if this guy had just opened the door to a helpless, naked Sadie.

The guy uses his master key to unlock the door. "I've got it from here." I thank the man and tip him generously for coming so quickly.

"Oh, beautiful," I sigh, my poor girl. I walk over to Sadie, bend down to push back hair that's stuck to her face, and rub her back.

"What happened?" I whisper.

She's face down on the tile floor, with her pants down around her ankles caught and twisted on something. The strap of her shirt is stretched and caught on the toilet paper dispenser, and her mascara is running down her face from her tears.

"Maybe you can untangle my pants first. It might be easier, and then I can just pull my shirt off after the tension gives way," she says quietly.

"How did this even happen?" I reach down to figure out her pants, but I can't help but notice the lace knickers she has on, she tries to crane her neck to look at me, and I'm caught. "Sorry, I can't help myself." I cringe. Get it together, Wills. She needs your help.

She ignores me and explains how something is sticking out of the floor by the bottom of the toilet and that the hem of her pants got stuck, making her fly forward when she stood up.

"There was nothing for me to catch myself with, I tried the toilet paper holder, but I couldn't grab it fast enough, it snagged my shirt, and that's, well, how this all happened," she says in a huff.

I lift the bottom of her pants, and sure enough, there is a bolt that holds the base of the toilet down, sticking up. This hotel is going to hear it from me.

I get her untangled as quickly as possible and then help her undress —pants and shirt.

"Come on, let's clean you up." I sit Sadie on the counter to give her the once-over, and she has a small bruise forming on her shoulder where she landed, otherwise she looks okay.

She is shaking her head, and when our eyes meet, we both burst out laughing. What are the odds something like that would happen?

When we finally control ourselves, I grab my face wash and a washcloth. "I'm sorry, I only have this." I show her my products. "But I need to wash your mascara off." She nods and lets me clean her face. I don't think I've ever cared for a woman beside Evelyn, my sister, before. I don't just like doing things for Sadie, it feels natural, like I've been taking care of her forever.

I finish up by drying her face and picking her back up off the counter. "Come on, bedtime." She wraps around my body like a monkey, snuggling into the crook of my neck.

I lay her down in bed, take off her lacy knickers, tuck her in under the covers, and undress quickly to join her.

"Are you okay?" I ask as I pull her back close to me so I can cuddle her skin to skin.

"Yes, just a tad embarrassed." I never want her to feel like that with me.

"It wasn't your fault. The hotel is at fault for not checking the rooms before they let guests stay here." She isn't saying much. She's probably tired too, I hadn't realized how late it was.

"Time for sleep, my beautiful girl." I kiss the back of her neck.

"Give me those sweet lips. I want a proper kiss good night." She turns her head, lifting at the perfect angle to give me what I want.

She moans slightly against my lips, and my cock jumps in appreciation. I need to learn self-control with her. I pull our lips apart and tell her good night, she looks shocked.

"But—" She pushes against my hard-on.

I cut her off, "Not tonight, Sadie, tonight we sleep. It's been a long day."

She huffs, annoyed. I laugh at her frustration. Who would have thought I'd be turning down a naked woman in my arms? I kiss her one last time.

"Wills?"

"Yes, baby?" She laughs at me, calling her baby again.

"Today was… it was just the best day, thank you," she whispers, I can hear the appreciation in her voice. She pulls at my arms so I can cuddle her tighter.

"Anything for you, my beautiful girl." She doesn't hear me, she's already out like a light.

But I mean every word of it.

I feel a lump form in my throat. These feelings are unfamiliar to me, and I'm not sure how to handle them. So, I just hold Sadie tight.

Before I fall asleep, a vision of us leaving France separately hits me. I don't want this to end. Even after just one date, I know it to be true.

Sadie

It's like déjà vu waking up in Wills's bedroom this morning from the sunlight shining into the bedroom. This time I won't be sneaking out, if I am sneaking anywhere, it will be under the sheets to give Wills a wake-up call. I roll my eyes at myself. W*ho am I even*?

I'm lying on my stomach, entirely naked despite keeping last night completely PG. I remember from our first sleepover, Wills said he would only sleep skin to skin with me, no exception.

Wills is lying exactly how he was last time, on his back, one arm covering his eyes and his other suspicious under the sheets, but this time his hand is open, palm spread across my backside. His favorite place, *his words*.

He's given me a couple of quick squeezes in his sleep, and I see his morning wood jump in appreciation each time.

My good girl is not such a good girl in bed. His words ring in my head from our first night together.

I'll show you what happens when I'm a bad girl, Wills.

I slowly lift his hand off my behind and crawl between his legs that are already spread wide.

Damn, I forgot how big he was.

I lean down, and slowly flatten my tongue and lick the underside of his entire hard-on. I wrap my fingers around his base and twirl my tongue around his head, moaning with pleasure as I taste the small amounts of salty come dripping out of him. Already feeling my arousal trickle down my leg.

I suck the tip hard and feel the sheet lifting, my eyes snap up. His eyes are half open, half shocked.

"Good morning, baby," I greet with a cheeky smile as I lean down, open wide, and take him as far as I can.

He inhales sharply. "Fuck!" His gravelly morning voice vibrates through the room.

I continuously bob my head, up and down, building a rhythm, twisting the bottom of his shaft simultaneously.

"Oh god, beautiful, that feels so good, don't stop." I smile with my mouth full of him.

"Eyes up here," he demands, and my eyes instantly rise, meeting Wills's darkened gray ones.

I open my throat, letting his tip hit the back over and over, as my eyes tear and his moans grow louder by the second. He reaches down to grab my ponytail in a punishing grip, guiding me at the speed he wants.

"Touch yourself," he says through clenched teeth.

I look up with wide eyes.

"That wasn't a request."

I've never done this in front of someone else, but I don't hesitate again. Instead, I reach down, rub along my slit, and moan around him.

Hollowing out my cheeks, I suck hard as he starts to fuck my mouth, thrusting his hips up, again and again as I continue to moan around his cock.

"Fuck, fuck, I don't want to come in your mouth." Losing all his control, he pulls me hard and fast to straddle him. He reaches over to grab a condom.

I'm unashamedly grinding down skin to skin. "Oh god, I'm going to come." I'm frantic now.

He grabs my hips. "Not yet!" he barks as he rolls the condom down, holding me in place.

He lifts me, looks down between my legs, smirks, then presses me down, impaling me as I scream out.

"Dripping fucking wet," he growls.

"You like sucking my big cock, Sadie? Does that turn you on?" Wills pants. *Yes, yes, yes*!

I feel a rush of cream below, so I start to move, relentlessly grinding down on him, over and over, rubbing my swollen clit as I go. He grabs my behind and squeezes both cheeks hard.

"Wills," I shout. "It's too much, baby. I'm going to come."

"Fuck yes, Sadie. Come all over my cock."

I scream out in pleasure then he flips me over, pumping fast and deep. He leans down and gives me a punishing kiss, moaning my name continuously as he comes apart.

He stays on top of me, not moving, and we lie there a while kissing and touching. I'm running my hands all over his muscular body, memorizing every inch of him.

"I have to get back to Annabelle at some point this morning," I mumble against his skin. I'd been a shit friend, leaving her again.

He doesn't look happy but doesn't protest. "Let me lie here in happiness a little longer."

He rolls off me, pulling me back on top of him, and we stay intertwined for another hour, relaxing in each other's arms.

"Ok, Wills, it's time, baby."

He growls in my neck, squeezing tighter. "I don't like to share."

"Well, if you want me, Belle is part of the deal. I don't see her often enough, so I need to spend time with her while I can." I haven't told Wills I'm moving to London yet. I don't know what I'm waiting for, but I don't want to jump to conclusions about us.

"Fine." He pauses.

"What is it?"

"I don't want you to misunderstand, Sadie. I will share you today. But you're mine, in every sense. However I can get you. I want you all day, every day."

He doesn't let me respond but plants one last kiss on my lips before I leave.

Help. I'm falling too quick, too fast.

7

Sadie

A LITTLE OVER a week has quickly flown by since our first official date in the vineyards, and it's almost time to say goodbye to Wills and Belle. To say I'm not looking forward to this goodbye is the understatement of the century.

George and Leo flew home earlier today, on their original flight, while Declan and Wills extended to leave Sunday with Belle and me. Although Wills, unexpectedly, has to pop back to London for a meeting later today.

This last week has been utter bliss with Wills and my best friend. These times with Annabelle are always special to me, and although it was hard to give myself to both Wills and Belle, I think I fairly split my time.

Although, I think about how Wills likes to say it doesn't count as "Wills time" when Annabelle is there too, which makes me laugh. He's just a big baby.

We have shared a lot of time with Belle and Declan… dinners, sightseeing, and Wills even rented a yacht for everyone yesterday, stopping for lunch in Saint-Tropez.

I've gotten to know Declan over the past week, he quickly became a friend I genuinely enjoy spending time with. He is a kind soul, and I'm sorry I misjudged him at first.

Wills and I still haven't discussed how we will work after the trip, but I'm confident he wants to try. I couldn't imagine just walking away from what we have. *Could he*?

No, he couldn't. I'm sure of it.

"Show me, darling," Belle says from her sun lounger next to me. We are lying on the beach, taking in the last bit of the Mediterranean sun.

I hand my phone over to Belle to show her the only negative thing to come out of this week. A scathing message from my mother. It landed in my inbox early this morning, very late New York time, which could only mean one thing. She was drunk.

It arrived while I was lying with Wills. He saw how upset I was and didn't like I wouldn't show him what it said, but eventually relented. To my surprise, because Wills is usually not one to back down, I think he realized that I needed to deal with this privately.

It would have been hard for him to understand, only making him angry. He has two lovely parents, whom he has spoken to many times throughout the week.

My parents still haven't even said happy birthday to me.

"You've got to be kidding me," I hear Belle hiss from her chair.

After posting a picture of Wills and me kissing on my *private* social media, the text went something like:

Sadie Marie Peters, I didn't raise a whore, blah blah blah, now Colton will never take you back, blah blah blah... and the kicker, which I quote, "Don't you think you should have sized up in that dress you wore, or maybe ate a few more salads?"

Why am I surprised after all these years? I ask myself that often.

But, living in this mentally abusive relationship I have with my mother will end soon when I break the news. I'm moving in with Jackson come fall. Then her little puppet will be gone, and she won't be able to keep up her mother-dearest appearances.

"Sadie," Belle sighs.

I cut her off before she starts. “You don’t have to tell me, Belle. I had a quick relapse, forgetting how terrible she is. I won’t let it upset me again.”

She reaches over to squeeze my hand for comfort. I turn my head to smile at her and catch a glimpse of Wills and Declan finishing their beach run, making their way over to us.

Damn, they’re hot.

I try to sit up to get a better view and yelp.

“What is it?” Wills rushes over.

“I think a bug just crawled up my vagina!”

“Take it as a compliment, Sadie,” Belle deadpans.

Wills rolls his eyes, and Declan laughs when I hit my hand to my forehead. Where the hell does she come up with these things?

“After all week of fucking this one, that thing is probably one massive opening, inviting that tiny bug right in.” Wiggling her eyebrows toward Wills’s private parts.

My eyes widen, and my mouth gapes open. Wills ignores her and turns to me—he’s already immune to Annabelle’s weird humor.

“I have to leave now, beautiful. My flight leaves soon.” He leans down to kiss me goodbye.

“Don’t forget I’ll be back tomorrow morning for Paris, be ready early.”

Wills is heading back to London for a night to take care of urgent business. He assures me everything is alright, but something has been stressing him out.

When he thinks I’m not listening or occupied, I can hear aggravated whispers. The calls are mostly from his lawyer, that’s about all I could make out from the conversations.

When he broke the news to me last night that he would need to leave, I got this terrible feeling that he wasn’t going to come back to me and I wouldn’t see him again. I know it’s irrational, but I knew this would happen… I knew I would grow too attached.

Wills must have been in tune with my turmoil because I think, or I hope, he feels the same way. That’s when he suggested we go away for the night once he’s back. One night for us, one night for our friends, before we leave and head back to reality.

"Okay, I'm looking forward to it, baby." And with that, he runs back to the hotel to leave.

Wills

"Hello, Charles," I answer my phone.

"William, are you on your way back now? I would like to get this settled, once and for all. I assume you wish to do the same?"

"Yes, I've just landed, and I'm on the way to your office now."

"Very well. I will see you soon." He hangs up.

I lean my head back against the headrest and close my eyes, thinking of Sadie and the past week. We've had fun this trip—more fun than I've had in a while if I'm being honest with myself.

I have never been so comfortable with another person, let alone a woman. I don't know what it is, she puts me at ease with her kind and calm personality.

I love how I've seen her open up so much in the last week. Her sexuality, especially, has grown to new depths. I don't think she knew she even had it in her. But she has opened herself up willingly, and I can't get enough. I feel myself getting hard just thinking about it. *Fuck.*

I can't wait to see her but I need to prepare for this meeting, and I can't be thinking of Sadie and that body of hers right now.

All because of my ex, Libby, and her money-grubbing hands, I needed to leave Sadie behind in France.

I don't know what she has done now, but I booked the next flight out when Charles sent a message saying it was an emergency. I couldn't let her release anything else to the tabloids. It's not just me to think about, it's my parents, sister, and now Sadie. She put us through hell years ago, and I'm not willing to relive that.

"We have arrived, sir." My driver breaks my train of thought, and I get out of the car, ready for whatever is about to come my way.

"Hello, Wills Taylor to see Mr. Whitmore," I announce to the front desk receptionist.

"Yes, Mr. Taylor, Mr. Whitmore has been expecting you. He instructed me to bring you back straight away."

We walk down the corridor to Charles's private office. I'm familiar with the space, I've been here many times. Charles is my personal lawyer, as well as my family's. He is also the father to Poppy and Olivia Whitmore, my sister Evelyn's best friends ever since I could remember.

At the end of the hall, I enter Charles's corner office. He's just finishing up a call and gestures for me to take a seat. I've always enjoyed coming here with my dad when I was a kid. I thought he was so cool having a friend who worked in the city, and now I have an office that overlooks the Shard.

"William, how are you?" Charles comes around his desk to shake my hand.

"Despite this shit with Libby, I'm doing well."

"You look it, let's get this over with you so you can return to your holiday. I'm sorry for pulling you away, but we should square this away."

"I agree." After I broke up with Libby years ago, she accused me of things that were just not true, going to the tabloids with false allegations just to make some cash.

Although inaccurate, my mum and dad's friends and coworkers saw all the lies spewed about me. Women in my mum's yoga class, supposed friends of hers, even started to look at her differently, thinking she raised a son who is anything but a class act.

Once something is put out there in writing, false or not, people don't forget it, and by the time you stop the madness, the damage is done.

"So, let's cut to the chase. What is it this time? How much does she want?"

He shakes his head in disgust. "She wants one million pounds. In return, she won't leak the sex tapes she claims to have of the two of you."

"Are you fucking kidding me right now? Why the hell is she doing this years later?" I roll my neck, trying to relax.

"Does she have sex tapes of you, William?" I know Charles is not judging me, but it's still mortifying having your dad's mate know personal things like this.

"Possibly, yes. We used to tape ourselves on occasion. I thought I had all of them, but I could be wrong." Shit, we dated for three years, and I don't know how I didn't see this side of her.

I think for a minute and know there is only one way out of this.

"Pay her, give her more than what she is asking, have her sign something that she can't come after me ever again, for anything at all."

"William, I highly suggest you think of this before you give in to her demands. We have other options. We can file a police report for blackmail or issue an injunction against her."

"Charles, do as I say please. In the time it would take to process all of that, she will have made her move. She will get paid more in tabloid payments, and I'm not waiting around to see if she is bluffing."

He takes off his glasses and rubs his eyes in frustration.

"Please, William, just take a day to think about it."

"I will not go through this again, Charles, and I will not have my family go through this again. I just chose to be in the public eye, not them. I have someone in my life now I care for, I can't have her seeing these videos, I won't. If the videos are real and Libby doesn't post them, she will find someone who will. So, pay her and do it quickly." I stand up, signally the meeting is over.

"As your lawyer, I highly advise against this. But as a family friend, I commend you for protecting your family."

"Appreciate the help. Let me know when it's done." I shake his hand and head out. I just want to go home, sleep, and fly back to France tomorrow to see my girl.

We need to discuss what will happen when we leave on Sunday, we both have been putting it off, but we need a plan.

My car drops me off in front of my Knightsbridge apartment building, and I make my way inside, greeting the doorman. I'm about to step into the private lift when I hear someone calling after me.

"Wills, hold the lift." Victoria's voice echoes through the lobby. She says to hold the lift as if she would typically take this one to her apartment. However, Victoria lives in an apartment on one of the lower floors, and this lift only goes to the two penthouses in the building, password access required.

"Hello, Love. I thought maybe you didn't hear me." She kisses me hello.

"What is it, Victoria? I've had a long day, and I just want to head upstairs to sleep."

Victoria is one of my sister's friends from university and has become a friend of mine.

My sister, Evelyn, was the lead interior designer on the apartments in the building and had a great relationship with the building developer. In turn, getting us access before they hit the market. Lucky for that, since these apartments sold quickly once they were all listed. The building is located right across the street from Hyde Park, its prime location.

Victoria and I also hook up on occasion, it's easy with her living in the building, and I can trust her to be in my home. I've never brought another woman back here besides her.

"Can I come up for a nightcap? I've had a shit day and wanted to pick your brain about a few things." Victoria is in the process of starting her own public relations company and has asked me for business help in the past. I can't deny her—she's been a good friend.

"Okay, one drink. I have an early flight to catch."

I pour myself a glass of scotch and Victoria a glass of red, and we stand around my kitchen island while I check emails and message Sadie.

"I thought you were supposed to be in the South of France?" Victoria asks.

"I am, came back for a quick meeting, heading back tomorrow morning."

"Oh, I'll be heading there tomorrow night after a few meetings myself. I'm meeting some of the girls from Uni. Maybe we can meet up?"

"Not sure, probably not." *Definitely not.*

"Mhmm," dismissing the blow-off. Although she is in public relations, Victoria is also a model on the side. She knows she's gorgeous and isn't shy about telling you what she wants, so she won't take my dismissal easily.

"How is your lovely sister? I haven't spoken to her in a while. It's too bad she couldn't come on this trip."

"Fine," I grumble. I'm not in the mood for chitchat.

"So, what's up? What did you want to discuss?" I ask, steering the conversation in the right direction.

She shows me her business plan and wants some help structuring it. Easy shit.

"Remind me, and I'll send you an email next week with my suggestions on what to fix. It should be simple enough."

"Thank you, Wills. But, enough about work, let's enjoy this drink for a second. I need to decompress," she says in a seductive voice. But, of course, decompress in Victoria's eyes means only one thing. And usually, I would agree.

I look up, she's moved closer, and I can see the intense desire burning in her eyes.

Not tonight, sweetheart.

I turn around, dismissing her again to clean my glass in the sink, but I can feel Victoria behind me a second later. I turn around to stop whatever she's thinking about doing. She's quicker and presses her body against mine. Her familiar scent awakes something down below, but I won't be tricked. There is only one woman I want.

She catches me off guard and quickly presses her lips against mine. "Oh, baby, I've missed this." *WTF? I'm not her baby. Sadie, I'm Sadie's baby.*

I push Victoria off and away from me.

"Get the fuck off of me, Victoria!" I yell. She's shocked. I've never turned down her advances before, especially with such force.

"W-what's the matter?"

Fuck I shouldn't have pushed her, but I panicked. She has no right to put her hands on me like that. I'm not hers.

But how would she know that?

"Shit, Victoria, I'm sorry, honestly. I'm seeing someone, and I freaked out."

"You're seeing someone? You don't do commitment." She scoffs at the idea.

"Well, it's true, and I think it's time you go home." I'm not comfortable with her being here anymore.

"When did you meet her? Where is she from?" she asks, not that it's any of her business.

"Not long ago. She's from America." Giving her little information, enough to quiet her but not enough to share anything about Sadie.

She laughs. "Long distance? Call me when that fails."

It won't fail. I won't let it. What's with the fucking women in my life today?

I text my assistant to call the pilot and ask them to schedule the first available takeoff time tomorrow morning. I need to get back to France first thing, and I don't care how early it is.

Sadie

It's early morning, but the beach is already crowded, and I'm scrambling around in the heat, trying to find a little Jack Russell terrier. A woman sitting next to me on the beach lost him and is in a state of panic. She has a baby who won't stop crying, adding to the stress. It's not even my dog, and I feel nervous. A storm is coming up the coast, and the sea is not as calm as it typically is. I hope the dog didn't go in the water.

God, why am I starting to cry now? I think I can feel the panic radiating off the woman.

We have been up and down the beach a million times, and there is no sign of the dog. I can't believe how many people just sat here looking at us, not offering any help.

After a while, I offered to stay with the baby to calm her. I think she's upset because her mom's upset. The lady accepts my offer, it will be easier to look for the dog without holding a screaming child.

I'm bouncing the baby up and down, and she is finally starting to calm down.

"Who do we have here?" Goose bumps spread across my body when I hear that deep familiar voice ask behind me.

I turn around so fast the baby whips in my arms, making her giggle. I smile down at her, she's a cute kid.

I can't help the huge smile that's covering my face right now. I'm so happy to see Wills, even though it's only been a day. "This is Brigitte. But she probably doesn't understand English."

"Bonjour, Brigitte." She smiles up at Wills, and he flashes her a genuine wide smile, I have yet to see him give out, other than to me.

Wills Taylor has two smiles for me—his sexy smirk, and one you don't often see, his full-on wide smile.

"You came back." I smile up at Wills too, mesmerized like the baby.

"Of course, I did." His concerned eyes bore into me. "Did you think I could stay away?" I'm too excited to answer, I lean up on my tippy-toes to reach for a quick kiss.

Wills leans down, meeting me, and then takes Brigitte from my arms, placing her on his hip as if he does this every day. He looks hot. A baby looks good on Wills. *Geez, Sadie, get a grip.*

He's playing pretend airplane with her body, and she can't stop laughing. Her laughter is so contagious we both start laughing along with her.

"I saw Annabelle before I came to find you, she told me about the dog. No luck yet?"

"No, I'm starting to get nervous." The tears make an appearance again.

He stops playing with Brigitte and puts his empty arm around me to comfort me.

"I'm sorry, I'm not even sure why I'm crying. I just feel bad for this family. I could never imagine losing a dog."

And, right on cue, Brigitte's mom comes running down the beach with her dog in hand.

"Merci, Merci beaucoup! I couldn't have done it without you. Seriously, if you weren't here, I would have never found him." She takes a breath.

"He was by one of the restaurants, and the waiter was giving him food like a stray! Can you believe it?" I give the little dog some loving pets on his head, and Wills hands Brigitte back to her mom, then takes my hand in his.

"How can I ever repay you?"

"There is nothing to repay, I was happy to help," I say genuinely.

The lady gazes up at Wills and says, "She's a keeper, this one," motioning to me.

His hand tightens around mine and kisses the top of my head.

"Trust me, I know," he says in a warm tone.

He turns his attention down to me, and his striking gray eyes burn with a fire I haven't seen before. It's like he's trying to tell me how much he knows, and I can't deny I freaking love that look.

"Time to go, baby. The plane takes off soon." He kisses my head again, and we walk off, still hand in hand.

Wills sinks into his seat right when we get on the plane, but I'm bouncing around like a little kid.

"I can't believe you booked us a private plane!" I can't even hide my excitement. Forget playing it cool.

"Can I get you something to drink, Mr. and Mrs. Taylor?"

"Oh, I'm not—"

Wills cuts me off. "Two glasses of champagne, please," flashing me a smirk.

"I'm so excited, Wills, thank you for taking me to one of my favorite places."

"Well, my favorite place is in bed with you, can you take me there?" he mumbles under his breath. I hit him playfully in the arm, and he chuckles.

"There *is* a bed back there." He tilts his head toward the back of the plane.

I can feel the heat of my blush on my cheeks, and my eyes widen. I look to the stewardess to make sure she isn't listening.

"Shhh! I'm not going back there with people up here." I can't do that. *Can I?*

"You don't want to join the mile-high club with me?"

I roll my eyes, he's incorrigible. "Have you already joined it?"

"Don't ask questions you don't want the answer to, Sadie."

Oh, I get a knot in my stomach, I was kidding. I sometimes forget how much more experience Wills has than me. I'm not sure what to say, so I turn my head to look out the window.

"Hey," he says, lowering his voice.

I turn my head, he cups my cheek, and he leans in for a kiss. "I'm sorry, beautiful, that was insensitive of me. But you're the only one I want now, and I want to make new memories."

He's right, I'm being immature. I kiss back with more passion than before, and he groans into my mouth.

"I missed these lips yesterday," he says as he starts to kiss down my neck.

This needs to cool down before I jump him like a wild animal and take him up on his offer.

I pull away. "Maybe on the way home." I wink at him.

"I'll hold you to it, Sadie," he says, picking up his champagne glass, giving me that all too delicious come-fuck-me look.

I bite my lip and turn my face away. I can't take Wills when he looks like that. He's too gorgeous for his own good.

"Wow," I whisper in awe as I move slowly into the large room. I clasp onto Wills's forearm and a tingling of warmth runs through my body as

I take in our suite at The Ritz. I slowly release the breath I was holding in. "Wow," I say again.

I don't know where to look first, this is one of the most beautiful rooms I have ever seen. It looks and feels like I have stepped back in time. No attention to detail in this suite has been spared.

"The room is called the F. Scott Fitzgerald suite," Wills explains as we slowly walk deeper into the room.

"I picked this because of your love for the twenties. He and Zelda frequented here often during the Jazz Age, even mentioning it in his novels."

I look up at Wills and have no words for him. He renders me speechless, time and time again. I still don't know how this broody, possessive man can be so romantic and caring at the same time.

My head is on a swivel as the shock wears off, and I take in the room in more detail. It perfectly reflects Parisian charm with mansard ceilings, gilded chairs, decadent drapery, and wallpaper. The subtle hints of the glamour and sophistication of the twenties shine through, sofas upholstered in luxurious velvet, edged in fringed add to the room's decor.

"Let's not waste our day staring at wallpaper." Wills laughs, breaking me out of my daze. "We will have plenty of time to spend here later. So let's get a start on the day."

"Okay, baby… Paris, here we come!"

Wills just shakes his head at me, and hand in hand, we leave to explore my favorite city.

Wills has been a trooper all day, I've made him walk everywhere. We strolled down the Champs-Élysées to the Arc de Triomphe, headed to the Eiffel Tower, and stopped at the Rodin Museum. After that, I gave him a break, and we took a car to Le Marais and had a late lunch in a small French café after we shopped since it's one of my favorite areas of Paris. Then, after a few glasses of champagne, a baguette or two, and a French onion soup, we walked off the calories back toward our hotel. Across the way in the Tuileries, adjacent to the Louvre, I picked up a blanket from the front desk to have a small picnic, with the dessert we bought on our walk home.

The late afternoon sun is shining down on us as we eat our éclairs, the weather has been nothing but spectacular.

We are sitting around, all these beautiful flowers, in shades of blues, purples, and white. I have been taking pictures nonstop.

"What are you going to do with all these flower pictures?" Wills asks.

"When I eventually open my floral design shop, I hope to print and hang all the pictures I've taken from around the world. I've taken pictures of species of flowers I've never heard of in Asia, and flowers like the lavender, here in France that we are all familiar with."

He smiles warmly at me. "That sounds like a great plan, I can't wait." When he says things like this, I can't help but get excited. It seems too good to be true.

"Wills?

"Yes, beautiful?"

"What was your favorite part of today?" He's looking out into the gardens, contemplating his answer.

"You're my favorite part."

"Wills." I smile but chastise, "Give me something real."

He leans over, and his gray eyes stare straight into my soul. He tucks a piece of my hair behind my ear, cups my cheek, and presses his lips softly against mine for a short moment.

"Sadie, this…" He looks around and then back to me. "Couldn't be any more real. *We* couldn't be any more real, my beautiful girl. I knew you were special from the moment I laid eyes on you, and you exceeded all my expectations. I hope this is just our beginning."

A lump forms in my throat as I nod up and down, tears streak down my face. Wills leans over and wipes them away with his thumb.

"Watching you today has made me the happiest man in Paris. I don't know how this will work between us, but I'm determined to do whatever it takes. I can't promise it will be easy, Sadie, but I have never taken the easy route in life, so I don't see why I would start now. You're my girl, Sadie."

I can't wait for a second more, I push him down and tumble on top of him.

"Oh, Wills," I cry. "You make me happier than I've ever known possible. I don't want this to end, ever." I don't give him even a second to respond. Instead, I crash my lips into his, showing him the true meaning of my words.

Our mouths both open instantly, intertwining our tongues with such a deep urgency. Wills's arms wrap around me, and his hands caress my butt. The hard planes of his muscles enfold my body as I lie on top of him. I can't take it a second more, I moan and start to rock into him, in the middle of the freaking Jardin des Tuileries! But I don't care. I'm running my fingers through his hair as we ravage each other.

Wills breaks our kiss. "Up now, Sadie." He pushes me off him.

"What the hell?" I ask as he takes my hand in his, pulls me up then starts to walk back toward the hotel.

"The blanket," I yell.

"I don't give a fuck about the blanket. If we don't get back to the hotel now, I'm going to rip your clothes off and fuck you right on the grass. Is that what you want?" he asks. I roll my eyes, so dramatic. Wills the romantic, long gone.

But I smile to myself because I like crazy possessive Wills just as much.

We burst into the hotel room and immediately start ripping each other's clothes off. I can feel myself growing wet by the second, I'm crazed like I've never wanted anything more. I drop to my knees, and Wills looks down, flashing a devilish smile.

"Good girl," he says and pushes my hair back as I take him in my mouth.

I've never loved giving head before in my life, but it's like I'm an addict to Wills.

"Shit, Sadie, slow down," he hisses, but I can't stop. I'm so turned on right now. I bring my hand down and start to rub my sex to ease the throbbing between my legs.

"Spread those pussy lips, baby. Let me see you touching yourself," he grits out between his teeth.

I moan around his large, engorged penis, rubbing myself faster, taking him in deeper and deeper. It's not an easy task fitting him down my throat, but I've been practicing opening up more for him, taking him deeper for longer.

He grabs my hair and starts to thrust into my mouth. "I'm going to come," I try to say around his cock. I can't help it. I can feel the burn starting in my spine, rushing up my body. I start rocking with his thrusts, riding my fingers to orgasm.

"Fuck, up now!" he growls, picking me up and throwing me on the bed.

He puts on the condom in record time and thrusts right in, no warming me up.

But I love the burn. I'd die for the burn.

"So wet for me, baby." He thrusts with force into me. "I'm going to fuck you so good," he whispers in my ear.

And that's what he does. All. Night. Long.

I wake up, smile, and remember I'm in Paris with Wills. I reach my hand over, and he's not in bed. Hmm, where is he? I've been waking up before him lately, and it's the same every morning. Him on his back and me on my stomach with his hand on my butt. Even in his sleep, he just can't help himself.

I get up and walk over to the balcony, he is standing there in a robe and a coffee in hand, taking in the view of the city.

"Good morning, baby," I say as I wrap my arms around his waist and squeeze.

"Good morning, my beautiful girl." He turns around to kiss me but stops and squints his eyes as he looks me up and down.

"Go put on a robe," he states.

"What, why? We're in our room."

"Do what I say, Sadie. I don't want anyone seeing you naked," he warns, and he points to the open windows on the balcony.

"Whatever, I'm showering now anyway," I say, annoyed. I'm cranky. It's too early.

"Fine, we leave in an hour."

Oh, I didn't realize when our flight was. I don't want to leave. I walk sadly into the bathroom to get ready.

An hour later, I'm done getting ready and packing. So, I stand to take in the room one last time. This was the best twenty-four hours of my life.

"Are you okay?" Wills asks from the other side of the bedroom.

I shrug in response, feeling emotional. I don't know what's up with me lately—such a crybaby.

"Just sad to leave." He walks over, takes me in his arms, and leans down to nuzzle into my neck.

"We'll be back, I promise."

"Yeah?"

"Yes, Sadie. I promised, and I don't plan on breaking my promises to you."

I hope you never do.

8

Sadie

I RUSH through the door of Belle's and my suite. "Hello!" I yell. *Where is she?*

I knock on her door with urgency, and it flies open.

"I just joined the mile-high club," I blurt out. I can't believe I just did that. At the time, it was exhilarating doing something kind of naughty, knowing people could catch us, but now that the high is wearing off, mortification is setting in.

"*You* did what?" she says, widening her eyes.

I return the surprised look and raise my eyebrows. "I know. Who am I?" I cry.

"I would say once again, a thoroughly fucked Sadie is who you are," Belle smirks.

"Will you be serious! Can't you see I'm freaking out? What if staff tell people, and it's all over the internet or something?"

"Wills is not *that* famous, calm down. Plus, I'm sure they all had to sign an NDA to work a private flight with someone who's in the public eye."

"Oh yes, that makes sense. Okay, okay, this makes me feel much better." I take a breath.

"Why are we just standing in front of your bedroom door? Let me in."

"Um, let's go sit on the balcony, it rained here yesterday, and I want some fresh air."

I give her a pointed look. "Why won't you let me in?" I ask but quickly push her to the side and walk into the room.

"Oh. My. God. Why is there a huge pink dildo on the bed? Did you pack that and bring it with you?"

She rolls her eyes. "An orgasm a day keeps the doctor away," she states matter-of-factly.

Who packs sex toys when they are away with another friend?

"No one says that."

"I say that," she deadpans. She grabs the thing, throws it in her suitcase, and it starts vibrating and jumping all over the place.

We both burst out laughing. Is this even real life? "I'm going to pack." I shake my head and head to my room, leaving a still-laughing Belle in her room.

It took a little over an hour, but I'm all packed besides what I need for tonight and tomorrow morning. I'm trying my hardest not to think about leaving Wills and Annabelle tomorrow, and instead, I'm focusing on the future and moving to London.

I haven't even told Wills yet, but I'm going to surprise him tomorrow morning before we leave. I figured it would be an excellent parting gift, you know, something to look forward to.

Annabelle comes into my room. "Finished?" she asks.

"Yeah." I flop onto my bed.

"So, tell me about the trip. You never said where you went to dinner."

I know I have a funny look on my face.

"What?" she asks.

"We never made it to dinner." I scrunch up my face and close my eyes.

A-month-ago Sadie would never believe *now* Sadie existed. But *France* Sadie is here to stay, and when I have an entourage of people like Wills, Sadie, and Jackson in my corner, I know I'll succeed.

"That sounds like a successful trip then." She high-fives me.

I've already filled in Belle about how Wills wants to do the long-distance thing, and she wasn't surprised in the least. I'm glad she's optimistic.

"It was perfect. The whole day was like it was out of a fairy tale." I pause.

"But?"

"It was like it was too good to be true. Nothing in life is that perfect, and I'm waiting for the other shoe to drop." I cringe, knowing she'll be upset with me.

"Sadie, how will you ever achieve happiness in your life if you're only ever looking for the negative?" she scolds.

She's right. I'm so used to an abusive mother, a cheating ex, and so much disappointment that I can't see what's right in front of me. The only thing is, what's right in front of me scares me.

"Come on, let's soak up a little of the sun on the balcony before we need to get ready." She pulls me off the bed, and we head outside.

"Excited to go home to Trey?" I ask.

"Yeah, actually, I kind of am. So that must mean something, right?"

"Definitely, I'm happy for you, and I'm excited to meet him when… wait for it… I move to London!"

"Yes!" Annabelle yells with enthusiasm, and I laugh.

"Okay, time to get ready, darling. I left something on your bed, go take a look," Belle tells me.

I walk into my room, and there is a large white box with the logo of a Paris boutique Wills and I visited yesterday. What the hell?

I open the box and gasp. *He didn't.* While shopping in Paris, I couldn't keep my eyes off this beautiful sequin dress. It would be perfect to go out in tonight, it was just too much money for a random Saturday night. But Wills bought it for me, I can't believe it.

It's a stunning short gunmetal sequin dress with a high neck, small capped sleeves, and of course, Wills's favorite part, I'm sure. It's backless.

I walk over to the side of my bed to grab my phone.

"Hello, my beautiful girl," Wills answers.

"Wills, baby. Thank you so much. I can't believe you bought this dress."

"You're welcome. Do you still love it the same?"

"More! I love it more because you bought it for me. You're very sneaky, Mr. Taylor."

"I bought the dress for both of us. You get a new dress, and I get to look at you all night in it. So that's a win for me." I smile. "Okay, I need to get ready. I love it, thank you again."

"Welcome, baby. See you later."

I finish getting ready, leaving my makeup natural, the way Wills likes it. I add a loose wave and pull it all to one side over my shoulder, so my exposed back is shown. I finish the look off with long drop earrings, Belle's black strappy, sky-high heels she left out for me.

I don't know how she wears such high heels being so tall, she must tower over most people.

I look in the mirror, and I can even admit that I look damn good. Wills is going to love it.

"Ready to go?" Belle pops her head into the room.

"Whoa, Belle, you look sexy as hell." She is wearing a red sleeveless jumpsuit, so low cut the opening reaches her belly button. Showing off her assets, if you know what I mean.

Her platinum-blonde hair is as straight as an arrow, parted down the middle, and rocking the smoky eye, so her blue eyes are shining.

"We look hot, hey?" I bump her hip with mine.

"Hell yeah, we do." And with that, she turns for the door to meet the guys downstairs.

Waiting for Belle to exit the ladies' room, I stand to the side and creep on Wills a little before he can see me. Declan is standing beside him, looking just as handsome, but in more of a cool guy kind of way. He's dressed in a navy blazer and a white T-shirt where his tattoos peek out the top. He has matching casual slacks, white sneakers, and his infamous longer slicked-back hair. He gives off a younger David Beckham vibe, just with darker hair.

But my Wills is always dressed to the nines, in more of a classic look. Wearing brown leather Gucci loafers, no socks—which weirdly turn me on—a white crisp dress shirt showing off his glorious, tanned chest and my favorite linen suit.

Someone like Will's is not rewearing a suit on holiday, so I know he wore it for me, which makes him all the much hotter. Like damn, really hot.

I watch girls one by one walk by and check out Wills and Declan, one brazen enough to stop and flirt. I can feel my blood start to boil, but Wills doesn't even glance in her direction while Declan dismisses her.

When I remember he's mine and only mine, a sense of pride runs through me.

"Come on, stop being such a stalker," Annabelle breaks me out of obsessing.

He senses me walking across the lobby, and his head slowly rises. I can see from here his hooded gray eyes darken as he looks on at me. Like I'm his prey, ready to eat up.

The heat from his stare lights me on fire, and desire burns deep within the pit of my stomach. If my shoes allowed, my body would be running toward him at this very moment.

"Hi," I say in a husky voice, unrecognizable by my own ears.

He takes one step toward me, clasps me around the waist, and brings our bodies flush so even our noses touch.

"Sadie," he croaks out, and his face looks pained. "I think you need to change, beautiful."

I step out of his reach, spin, and give a little shimmy to show off my dress.

"You don't like it?" I ask, knowing full well he loves it and can't stand me dressed like this out in public.

"Wills, stop being a Neanderthal and leave her alone. She looks smoking hot," Annabelle cuts in.

"Yes, that's the issue," he grumbles, and I laugh. He'll just have to get over himself, he bought the freaking dress.

I turn to Declan to say hi and kiss him on the cheek. "Lass, you look stunning."

"Our car is waiting. Let's go," I hear an impatient and cranky Wills say from the front door.

"Let's not upset the beast anymore," Declan says as he playfully shakes his head.

We're pulling up to Club Argent, and it feels like it's been years since we were here last, yet it's only been three weeks. My eyes close, and I smile, thinking how that night turned out. Never in a million years did I think I would be sitting here with Wills, *dating Wills.* I thought he wanted some holiday sex, and that was it. How wrong was I?

We gain access straight away, recognizing the manager that helped us out last time, and he brings us over to a similar but smaller table since it's just the four of us.

"Tonight's going to be fun," I yell over the music to Belle.

"Yes, and don't leave me hanging with Declan all night."

I feel bad when she says that. I thought I was splitting my time evenly between the two of them.

"I'm sorry if I've neglected you. You know I love you, right?"

She puts her arm around me and kisses my cheek. "Darling, I hope you do because you're stuck with me for life."

The cocktail waitress makes her way over with champagne, tequila, and scotch for Wills.

She's pouring everyone's first drinks, and I can see from this side of the table that she keeps looking up at Wills, trying to give him the eye. Bitch, not on my watch.

I saunter over to Wills, plop myself right in his lap, and put my arm around his shoulders, looking right at the girl when I do it.

"Claiming me?" Wills asks as he kisses up my neck, making my whole body shiver.

"Yup." I shrug, not embarrassed in the least.

"Good, I like that you claim me as yours. Because I'll fucking kill someone tonight if they look at you in any way."

I turn in his lap so we are face to face, and I give him a quick kiss on the lips.

"Behave yourself, no fighting anyone tonight. Don't forget it's our last night here, let's make it a good one."

"I won't promise you, but I'll try." He cups my cheek like I love and goes back in for a kiss, coaxing my lips open with his tongue. He runs his hand over my exposed back and down to my behind to give me a squeeze.

"For fuck's sake, this dress is like a fucking weapon." I look down at his hand.

"Don't squeeze so hard next time, and the sequins won't make all those red marks." I give him a pointed look.

"I'll just have to go under." He runs his hand up my legs to get under my dress but inadvertently tickles me instead.

"Wills!" I squeal, and he tries to do it again while holding me down on his lap.

But I'm saved by Annabelle. "Shots, shots, shots." She leans over and hands us all tequila shots.

Then immediately comes back to thrust a champagne glass in my other hand.

Oh, she's sassy tonight.

"Cheers to our last night and lasting friendships," Belle says, short and sweet, and we all clink glasses.

She is staring at me, and I know she wants me to chug my champagne so we can go dance. So, I take a few gulps trying to finish it. But it's hard with all the bubbles. She goes to pour us one more shot. "Sadie, slow down!" Wills warns.

"I'm okay, I just want a little buzz before hitting the dance floor."

"I'd prefer you to remember tonight and not throw up all over the bathroom."

"Don't be dramatic. I'll be fine."

"Sadie." It's another warning but I ignore him and get off his lap.

"We're going dancing for a little," I tell the guys, but Wills clutches my hand and tugs me back to him.

"Kiss me first," he demands, so I lean down and give him a peck, knowing he won't be happy with that, but I shimmy away toward the dance floor. Some of Belle's sass must be rubbing off on me today.

"Here." She gives me another full champagne. "Don't let Dad over there see."

I don't have to look to know she's talking about Wills.

Annabelle doesn't love his demanding, possessive side, but she doesn't say anything because she knows how happy he makes me. She also sees the sweet side of Wills, who always goes out of his way to make me a priority.

The music changes, and the DJ plays a remix, and it sounds like he is mixing two Kygo songs. I freaking love Kygo, and so does Belle. We start dancing like our lives depend on it.

Song after song, we're still going strong. We've only stopped once for another drink when Wills went to the bathroom but ran right back onto the dance floor. This DJ is really good.

I look over to our table, and Wills and Declan are both standing at the edge of the dance floor talking. I see Wills jut his chin out in the opposite direction, so I crane my neck to see what they are looking at. Not what, but who I see is a beautiful, exotic-looking woman. Wills is still talking, and I can read Declan's lips when he says "What?" with a shocked face. Wills shakes his head to confirm, and they both look back over at the girl.

Who is she? Do they know her? Do they want to know her? Ugh, I hate this jealous feeling.

This is exactly what I'm scared will happen when I'm in New York, and Wills is back to being Wills Taylor, the rugby player in London.

"I'm going to the bathroom. Meet you back at the table," I say to

Belle, not giving her a chance to join me.

I stand in a ridiculous bathroom line where I can't do anything but analyze Wills and me, thinking the worst and how it won't work. How he won't want to be with me once he's back to his day-to-day life, or when I finally make the move to London. Damn Belle, for too many drinks—a drunk mind is not a sound mind.

After ten minutes, it's finally my turn, but as I step out of the stall to wash my hands, that woman Wills and Declan were checking out is standing washing her hands as well. This time she's the woman staring at me, or at least I think she is.

I try to wash my hands quickly to get out of there, but she's clearly still staring at me through the mirror, so I ask, "Do I know you?" Drunk Sadie has balls.

She just smirks and walks out. *WTF.*

I don't know what that was, but it felt weird. Like she was laughing at me, and I was the joke.

I need to get back to Wills now.

I push my way back to the table and grab another champagne, and down it. I'm not happy.

Wills, constantly so aware of what's going on, comes over to ask me what's wrong.

I turn to him and ask him straight.

"How will this work, Wills? You're going to forget about me, and you're going to break my heart. I just know it." Oh crap, he does not look happy.

"What. The. Fuck. Sadie? What happened in the last hour that would give you that idea? I've been so good to you. Why would you even fucking say that?" He's raising his voice now.

And I'm on a roll.

"Are you sure we aren't on some holiday high, and that's why this works? What happens when we get home to real life, and the high goes away?"

"Are you seriously asking me this right now? Are these words really coming out of that fucking mouth of yours? You know what, fuck this." And he goes to walk off.

“Wait, Wills, wait,” I cry.

He whips his head around, and he gives me a deadly look.

“I need a goddamn minute, Sadie,” he spits out as he walks away.

“I’m sorry,” I yell after him. And I am sorry, what the hell is wrong with me letting my insecurities get the better of me? This man has been nothing to me but perfect.

This is why people don’t drink!

“What’s going on over here?” Declan asks, and Belle walks up behind him.

“Self-sabotaging,” I answer honestly.

“What did you do?” I don’t answer them and just shake my head. I need a minute.

I chug some water to sober up before he gets back and lean my head back on the back of the chair.

I hear Declan and Belle whispering, but I don’t even care. I just want Wills to come back, I don’t know why I said all that stuff.

It’s been a while since Wills ran off. Declan went to look for him, but no luck.

“Sadie, do you want to go back to the room with me?” Belle asks in a soothing voice. I’m so upset with myself. I’m usually more level-headed but with Wills, all my sensibleness goes out the window.

“I’m going to wait, but you go ahead. I’ll see you bright and early. Unless he still hates me, I’ll see you tonight.”

Belle had already told me she couldn’t stay out too late. She has a very early flight tomorrow, so she doesn’t miss a meeting later that afternoon.

“He doesn’t hate you, darling. You just hurt his feelings. And, because he’s a guy, he doesn’t know how to handle it.”

She’s right. I hope.

“Watch after her, yeah?” she says to Declan, and he answers with a head nod and hugs her goodbye.

“I’ll set my alarm so I can say goodbye in the morning, so just give me a kiss and get on your way," I say as I hug her tightly. "And text me when you get back to the room, okay?"

"Yes, yes, have fun. Just give him a blow job, it will make everything better."

Typical Belle. Declan grunts like he agrees. And then she's off.

Wills never comes back.

"Declan, I'm tired," I sigh. "I'm going to head back and just sleep with Belle for our last night together. Can you maybe stay a little longer just in case he comes back?"

I know he is hesitant to let me go by myself, but he doesn't want to let me down. It's how Declan works, he's too nice.

"Aye, no problem, lass. Call when you get back?"

"Promise."

Before I leave, I decide to use the ladies' room, I'm not sure I'll make it back with my tiny bladder.

As I walk toward the bathroom corridor, I spot Wills with his back to me right away. Thank God! I speed up my pace, as fast as I can in these shoes, but when I get close, I see he's talking to that same woman from before. The same woman he was looking at with Declan and the same one who laughed at me in the bathroom. What's going on?

Instead of approaching, I stand there and stare for a second. Who is this woman? And why is he with her and not me, who's been worried sick?

They continue to talk, and I can't take it anymore. I need to pee and confront them.

As I step up next to them, it's like I'm watching a car crash in slow motion.

She throws her arms over his shoulders and kisses him, full on kisses him.

"WHAT THE HELL?" I scream.

Wills whips his head around. "Sadie! It's not what it looks like," Wills cries.

"It's exactly what it looks like!" I've never screamed so loud in my life, but I'm losing it.

I bend down, take off my shoes, and turn to run the other way. I need to get out of here, now!

"Sadie, wait! Victoria, what the fuck?" is all I hear him say when I run off.

Victoria. A name I will never forget.

I crouched down and run right through the dance floor, knowing he's too big to fit through here. And there is just no way he would be able to catch up. But I don't stop running until I see a sign for the exit, just in case.

I burst through the door and come out into the side alley. Crap, it stinks back here, I look around and spot all the dumpsters. I need to suck up the smell because I can't go back into that club right now.

I lean against the cold brick wall, and think how Colton and now Wills both cheated. *Why is this happening to me?*

But, after a minute of being in a dark alleyway alone, fear sets in. I need to get out of here. I look to the right and see the lights that illuminate the sidewalk and head toward that way.

I take two steps toward the light when a gloved hand comes out and closes around my mouth, muttering something in French.

"I don't know French," I try to mumble around the glove. *Please let me go.*

I try to stay deadly still, and after a second, he slowly takes his hand away, and I instantly scream for help. Recognition that I spoke English must set in because he says, "I said be fucking quiet. Give me your watch and empty your purse."

I try to get a look at him, but he's wearing a mask, and I don't want a fight. So, I give him all the money I have with shaky hands. As I attempt to take off my watch, my hands go from slightly shaky to trembling.

"Faster!" he yells.

When I finally get the watch off, it drops to the ground, and when he bends to pick it up, I take this as my opportunity to try and get away. I run like my life depends on it. But luck is not on my side tonight because he's faster and catches up quickly.

His hand wraps around my throat, lifting me off the ground so we are face to face. Not a second later, he pushes me with all his might, and my head slams against the brick wall, and I collapse to the ground.

The last thing I remember are his soulless, deep-blue eyes staring daggers at me through his mask.

Then the night fades away quickly, and all goes black.

Wills

"Sadie!" I yell one more time in a panic, but my cries fall on deaf ears.

I can hear Victoria's voice behind me, but my brain can't even register what she's saying.

Sadie's too fast, and I know I can't get to her the way she went. So I run around and finally bust through the club's front door. I search up and down the sidewalk, but there are crowds of people everywhere, and I don't see her anywhere.

I turn to the bouncers. "Did you see a girl run out of here? About five foot five, long dark hair, green eyes, beautiful, sequin dress?"

They both just shake their heads no.

She probably jumped in a cab the second she came outside, but I need to talk to her and explain.

I try her phone, no answer.

I throw my hands up and run them down my face as a sudden sensation of dread drifts through my body. This is all fucked up.

Why did she have to walk over right at that second as Victoria threw herself on me *again*?

I don't want anyone but Sadie, but I'm afraid this will break us. She was already nervous about the long-distance relationship to begin with.

"Fuuuck," I roar, and I stand outside for a while until I get my breathing under control. I shake my head, then walk back inside, hoping Declan has a plan because I can't think straight right now and have no clue what to do.

"Declan," I say to get his attention

"Feck you, Wills. Where have you been?" he bellows.

In all my years I've known Declan, he has never raised his voice to me. I'm shocked and take a step back.

"I fucked up, mate."

"You think?" he sneers. "That poor lass sat here berating herself over and over about what she said to you. And you just never come back? Where the hell were you anyway?" He looks away, disgusted. He can't even look at me right now. I drop my head in shame as sudden regret hits me, my poor girl.

"Well, it gets worse." A lump forms in my throat, and I can barely get the words out.

"Sadie just saw Victoria kiss me and ran out."

"What the hell were you thinking, after what she did the other day? You get into an argument with your girl, so you run to another?"

"It wasn't like that! I was outside the whole time, then stopped at the loo, and she was there."

"I swear it, Declan." He just shakes his head.

"The tab's on you tonight. Meet me outside when you're done."

I screwed up big time if Declan can't even look at me.

He's grown a soft spot for Sadie over the last few weeks. Of course, everyone has—she's nothing but perfect, and I royally fucked it up.

It takes forever to get the waitress's attention to pay the bill, but Declan's standing near a cab, still waiting for me once I'm done.

"Let's get out of here quick before traffic starts up, the street's blocked off over there." He points in the opposite direction, where an ambulance and a police car are parked.

"Drunk idiots, the same thing every weekend," the cabbie mutters in a broken English accent.

We walk through the hotel lobby, and Declan starts to head toward our lift, and I go toward Sadie's.

"Where do you think you're going?"

"I have to see her, Declan. I need to make it right."

"You need to let her cool down. Let her be with her friend tonight, who can comfort her. Send her a message or something but respect her and give her some space."

Space? That's not how I do things. I need to talk to her now. I can't let her think I would kiss any other woman than her. We leave tomorrow, it can't end like this.

"I need to, mate." I ignore him and head to Sadie's room. But I knock and knock and knock, and there's no answer. I don't blame her for ignoring me, but it's killing me all the same.

I send a quick text, I'll come back first thing in the morning.

Me: Sadie, my beautiful girl.
Me: Please forgive me for tonight. I'm so sorry.
Me: I should have never walked away from you. NEVER. It will never happen again.
Me: What you saw was a misunderstanding. She kissed me, not the other way around. You're the only one for me, you're my girl, Sadie.
Me: Have tonight with Annabelle, I understand. But we need to talk before we leave tomorrow.
Me: Goodnight, baby. x

Sleep never comes, but regret hits deep. Tomorrow has to be a better day. *It has to.*

"What do you mean, they checked out?" I yell at the front desk clerk.

"I'm so sorry, Mr. Taylor, that is all I have for you. They called early in the morning to check out."

"They didn't leave a message or anything?"

"I'm afraid not, sir."

I have called both Sadie and Annabelle all morning and got no answer. I've called their hotel room and knocked on their door a hundred times. Also, no response, and now I know why… they checked out.

I stalk away from the desk, back to Declan in the lobby. I can't believe this, she just left without letting me explain. How fucking wrong was I about us…

"Anything?" Declan asks.

"Nothing. They checked out very early this morning. Sadie didn't even care to listen to my side of things." I'm mad, I know I screwed up, but we're adults. We should have been able to talk things through.

This is why I don't do relationships. It's too much work, for what? To be let down in the end.

"Maybe she left with Annabelle, her flight was first thing."

"So why is she not answering my text or calls?"

"That I don't know, mate. You messed up last night, maybe she's madder than you think."

"Obviously, Declan! But she could at least have let me explain. Say goodbye, at the very least. She lives in a different country, for fuck's sake!"

I've been driving myself crazy for the last twelve hours, and she didn't even care to say goodbye. So I guess what we had wasn't as important as I thought, and it *was* just a holiday fling.

It's just too bad I didn't get the memo earlier. It would have saved me a lot of stress and heartache last night.

"We're going to miss our flight. Let's go, it's over. I never want to talk about that girl ever again."

"Maybe her phone died?"

"Fuck that, don't make excuses, both of them have been ignoring us all morning and checked out without leaving a note." He goes silent because he knows I'm right. She fucked me over big time.

I look Declan straight in the eyes, so he knows how serious I am.

"Sadie Peters is now dead to me."

I leave France with many regrets and happy memories that turned sour, but for lack of better words. Fuck, France.

9

Sadie

Beep, beep, beep… I try to locate the noise that's making my head feel like it's been run over by a truck, but I can't pry my eyes open. Each lid feels like a hundred pounds.

I can hear whispered voices around me but can't make out who they are. Where am I?

"Hello?" I try to say, but my voice gets stuck, and nothing comes out.

"Hello?" I try again, still nothing. Then, as if just trying to speak drained my energy, I can feel myself slipping back into a deep slumber.

Beep, beep, beep… the distant beeping noise wakes me up again and again. I try to force my eyes open. My vision is flickering in and out, but I'm able to open enough to see two figures sitting next to me.

Beep, beep, beep… I groan at the noise that's pounding through my head.

"She just made a noise," Annabelle says.

At least, I think it's her.

"I didn't hear anything."

Who is that second voice? Wills? Where am I?

"Sadie, darling, it's Annabelle. Open your eyes for me, please," she says just above a whisper, desperation running through her words.

"Belle?" The words barely come out, getting stuck in my throat.

"Water," I croak and try to open my eyes. The harsh artificial light shining above me makes me squint. I slowly turn my head and am greeted with Annabelle's beautiful face streaked with tears.

"Jackson, go get her water and find the doctor."

Jackson, why is Jackson here? Where is here?

I take in the room around me and then look down at where I am lying. I'm in a bed and have an IV in my arm, with monitors set up next to me, I guess that's where the beeping came from.

Jackson comes back in the room with my water, and it's then when I can get a good look at him.

My naturally gorgeous brother looks worn and tired. He has heavy bags under his eyes, and it looks like he hasn't showered in days.

"Here, Sades." He puts the water to my lips and helps me drink a little at a time.

I clear my throat and ask, "Where am I?"

"You're in the hospital, darling. Do you remember what happened?"

I think for a second.

"Ugh, I'm not sure." Where was I last? I don't even know what day it is.

"Jackson, for God's sake, go get the doctor and give us a second alone, please."

"Oh, sorry. Yeah. I'll be right back."

"Why does he seem like someone murdered his dog?" I ask Belle.

Her eyes look over, following Jackson out the door, and when they come back to meet mine, I see mixed emotions lacing through her eyes. Sadness, remorse, and pity.

"Sadie, do you remember anything from our last night out with Wills and Declan?"

My eyes open at the mention of Wills's name.

"Wills? Is he here?" I look around the room. Belle runs her hands empathetically up and down my arms.

"No, love, he isn't. I'm not sure where he is."

What does she mean by that?

"After I left the club, do you remember anything?" she asks.

I think back. I remember that night. Wills bought me that perfect dress from Paris, us going to the club, Wills getting mad at me, me leaving the club, and oh god. My eyes widen when the memories flood back.

"What is it?" Belle whispers.

"I was attacked. In the alley of the club."

"Why were you in that alley, Sadie?" she says, trying to get answers out of me.

I can feel the tears building from the memory that caused me to run out of the club.

"I saw Wills and a woman talking, then they kissed. I freaked out and bolted."

"He kissed someone?" Her voice is shocked. "I-I can't believe he would do that. I thought… I don't know what I thought. But I can't believe he would do that to you."

"Have you tried to call him while I was here?"

"Of course, for the last four days…"

"Four days?" I asked, surprised. "I've been in here four days?"

"Yes, I'll have the doctor explain everything."

"Can I have my phone, please?"

"Your phone was stolen, but you can use mine." She looks up when Jackson is on his way back.

"Sadie, Jack knows you were with someone, but I didn't tell him his name. I didn't know what was going on, and I didn't want him to lose it about Wills."

Good thinking, my brother would kill anyone who hurt me. I smile at her, appreciating her quick thinking.

"The doctor will be right in," Jackson tells Belle. Then his eyes find mine, he looks so broken.

"Sadie." His tears bright in his eyes. I've never seen Jackson cry, ever.

He moves over to the other side of my bed to take my hand and places a kiss on my forehead.

"How are you feeling, Sades?"

"My head hurts, but I'm okay, honey." That's when I realize my head actually hurts a lot. I reach up and feel stitches, and my face must show confusion.

"When you were attacked, you hit your head somehow, and you have a laceration," Belle explains.

Jackson is very quiet. I know he isn't sure what to do in this situation, and it's freaking him out.

An older, sophisticated woman walks into my room with a small but warm smile on her face.

"Hello Sadie, I'm Dr. Laurent. I'm glad you're awake. How are you feeling?" she says in a beautiful French accent.

"I'm doing okay. I'm just tired, and my head hurts."

"That's to be expected," she says as she looks down at my chart and looks over to the monitors. Then she flashes the light in my eyes, asking me to follow her finger.

"Your vitals look good, and in general, you seem to be healing right on track. But I want to go over everything that has gone on in the last few days." I nod my head in agreement, and I see her look over to Jackson.

"It's okay, you can say whatever it is in front of him." Instead of listening, she looks over to Belle, and she also nods her head. What the hell?

"On Sunday morning, you arrived at the hospital unconscious, from what looks like some type of blow to the head, which we stitched up. We found there was some swelling on the brain and decided to put you in a medically induced coma for seventy-two hours." It makes sense why I was confused when Annabelle said it was four days later.

"When a patient comes into the hospital from an unknown attack, it is the protocol to perform a rape kit." What the hell, what is she getting at here? I look over to Belle, who has tears running down her face, and Jackson looks like he's in complete shock.

"Sadie, are you sexually active?"

"I am."

"What type of protection do you use? Are you on any type of contraceptive pill?"

"We only use condoms, I'm not currently on the pill."

She marks something on her clipboard and continues down her list of questions.

"When was the last time you had sexual intercourse?"

I think for a second, I guess it was Paris.

"Friday was the last time."

Jackson closes his eyes. This is probably why the doctor made sure it was okay Jackson was in the room.

"When we performed your rape kit, there was evidence of rape, and semen still present. Therefore, if your last consensual partner was Friday, then what we concluded was correct. I'm very sorry, Sadie."

Jackson makes a sound that I can't understand and paces the room.

I'm in shock. I don't know what to say. I was raped?

Jackson walks back over to me and wipes the tears from my face I hadn't even known had fallen.

The doctor continues, "We will continue to keep you for forty-two hours under observation, but if all is well, you can go home."

I still don't know what else to say.

I was raped.

"There is one more thing to discuss," the doctor says, but I barely hear her.

I was raped, oh god.

"Sades," Jackson whispers. "It's okay. It's going to be okay." He kisses my forehead again. Annabelle is silently crying and is being eerily quiet.

"Sadie, I know this is difficult to take in, and I'm so very sorry for what you have gone through. We will send up a counselor when you're ready. But I still need to go over one other important thing with you."

I hear a squeak from Belle, trying to hold back her tears. She grabs my hand. "I'm so sorry," she whispers.

"What's going on?" I ask, and the doctor shoots Annabelle a look.

"Like I was trying to say, when we discovered you may have been raped, our protocol is to ask if you would like to take an emergency contraceptive pill. You would probably know it as Plan B. Since you were unconscious, we normally would go to the next of kin and ask if they knew of your wishes. But, since Annabelle is not your partner or a blood relative, we couldn't legally ask her. So, we could not administer the pill. If by any chance you get pregnant, there is always termination or adoption if you choose not to keep it. I'm very sorry, Sadie."

I just nod in acceptance, even though I'm in shock. How did this happen?

"A nurse will be in shortly, but in the meantime, the police are here for a statement if you're up to it." I nod again, on autopilot. I don't know what else to say.

When the doctor leaves the room, Annabelle loses it, not keeping her emotions at bay anymore.

"I'm so sorry, Sadie," she cries.

"Belle, why are you sorry?" She didn't do this to me.

"I wish I could have advocated for you. Plus, I wasn't sure when the last time you had sex was. I was almost positive you hadn't with Wills, but what if you had? I wouldn't think you would have wanted the pill then," she whispers the last part, so Jackson can't hear.

"You're right, I wouldn't," I assure her.

She goes on, and I can see the anguish tearing through her body. "Plus, I should have never left you at the club that night. This is all my fault."

"Yeah, B, why the hell did you leave her?" he sneers, shooting daggers at my best friend.

"What the fuck were you even thinking?" He stands tall, arms crossed.

"Jackson!" I say through gritted teeth.

"I'm sorry! I left her with her boyfriend. I didn't think," she cries.

"Enough, both of you. Jackson, I'm a grown woman and don't need Belle to be there to babysit me. It was my fault for running out of the dumb exit by myself. Belle, I will never forgive you if you blame yourself, so don't even go there."

Jackson ignores me. "Ha, boyfriend. So where the fuck is he now, huh? I swear to God, Sadie, if he tries to see you after all this shit, I will kill him."

I look at Belle in question. *Where is he? Why isn't he here sitting by my side?*

After we all cool down, Belle asks Jackson to give us a second alone, but two police officers walk in to take my statement.

The lead detective, I assume since he is asking all the questions, doesn't speak English, so the other officer is translating. "Is there anything else you can remember at all? I know he was wearing a black mask but think hard. Any tattoos, scars?"

I think for a second, was there anything?

"Oh, I know this isn't much, but he did have these very deep-blue eyes. Right before he slammed me to the wall, he looked me square in the eyes. But other than that, I have nothing else. It was just too dark in the alley."

"Thank you, Ms. Peters. We will continue to look and check the CCTV over again. But to be completely honest with you, we don't have much to go on. I think this was a random mugging turned bad, and we may be at a dead end."

"I understand, officers. Thank you." I honestly don't even care. I just want to go home.

I was exhausted after the police left and must have fallen asleep because I could see it's dark out now.

The nurse comes in to check me over. "You're up," she says as a statement rather than a question.

I don't think she speaks much English.

She keeps glancing at Jackson and blushing. She must be early twenties, she looks young and keeps getting tongue-tied when Jackson asks her a question. At least we have a little amusement while we're here. I need the distraction because the first thought I had when I woke up was, *Where is Wills?* He isn't someone who would leave me like this, I don't know what's going on.

"Jack?"

"Yeah, B?" Belle's face falls. Jackson won't even look at her, and I'm sure that's hurting her most of all.

"Would you mind giving Sadie and me a moment alone?"

He doesn't answer her, he just gets up and walks out.

After she watches him walk out of the room. She takes my hand in hers and rubs it with her thumb absentmindedly.

"Why don't you just tell him?"

"Tell who what?" she asks.

"Tell Jackson how you feel about him."

She rolls her eyes. "Sadie, he is like a brother to me. You know that, and it's the only reason why I'm getting so upset. Don't worry about it."

I don't believe her, but I drop it.

"How are you really feeling?"

"I don't know, Belle, like it's all a dream. If my head didn't hurt so much, I would think it's all a bad joke."

She just nods her head.

"It's okay I didn't call your parents, right? Jackson actually agreed with me on that, but I wanted to make sure I did the right thing."

"Oh my god, I do not want them here. I don't even want them to know about this."

She nods again, accepting that answer. I don't want her to blame herself, I can see the chaos in her eyes.

"Belle, why isn't Wills here?" I whisper.

Her face drops, and she shakes her head. "I don't know, Sadie. I promise I called and texted him and Declan."

She goes on to tell me how the events of the last few days went for her. "The hospital called the hotel, the attacker must have dumped what he didn't want because they found your room key and your ID on the ground near where they found you. The hospital called the hotel, who then called the room to inform me and had a car waiting downstairs. I ran out of the room so fast I forgot my phone, so I couldn't call Wills right away. Finally, the hotel sent someone with my stuff. When my phone turned on, I had a bunch of texts from Wills asking where we were. I tried to call him right away, but it went to voice mail each time I tried. I texted him then and every day since, and they all went undelivered. I tried Declan, and on the first day, he responded, saying it's not his place to get involved. I have no clue what he meant by that. He never responded to me after, and all my texts went undelivered to him as well. I called the hotel, and they confirmed they both checked out."

I can't help but cry and wonder what happened. I put my hands over my face to hide my emotions, I know he was mad at me, but this doesn't seem right. I thought he cared for me more than this. He just left after a fight, didn't even check on me? He didn't even say goodbye or apologize for that woman kissing him. The Wills I knew would have stopped at nothing to find me when I wasn't at the hotel anymore.

This is all just too much. My emotions are in overdrive right now, and I don't know how to handle it.

Between my sniffles, I ask Belle if I can just send one text. She looks like she wants to say no, I know she is only trying to protect me but hands it over anyway.

I scroll up to see all her messages.

Wills: Annabelle, where are you and Sadie? I've been calling her cell and your room all morning?!
Wills: WTF? Answer your texts.
Wills: ANNABELLE, ANSWER YOUR DAMN PHONE. Why isn't Sadie answering?
Wills: Please, just answer. ANYTHING. None of my texts are going through to Sadie.
Wills: The hotel just said you checked out. ARE YOU FUCKING KIDDING ME RIGHT NOW?
Annabelle: OMG, Wills. Call me ASAP. It keeps going to voice mail.
Undelivered.
Annabelle: Wills? You need to meet us at the hospital. Sadie has been attacked.
Undelivered.
Annabelle: Hello? WTF. Wills, this is serious.

Undelivered.

Annabelle: Wills, none of my texts are going through. Are you getting any of them? Please confirm, please!!!!!

Undelivered.

Annabelle: Wills! Go fuck yourself, honestly.

Undelivered.

Annabelle: Wills, It's me, baby. What's going on? Why are you not answering? Is everything okay? Please just let me know you're okay.

Undelivered.

Annabelle: I was attacked Saturday night, Wills. I'm in the hospital. I need you. Please, Wills. I really need you right now. I miss you.

Undelivered.

I wait, and I wait, and I wait. Even though it says undelivered, I stare at the phone like something's going to change. I just don't understand, and I wish someone could make sense of this.

Annabelle takes the phone away from me eventually. She's not letting me torcher myself anymore.

She reads the text, closes her eyes for a second, and shakes her head as tears run down her face. I know needing someone I've only known for a few weeks may seem crazy, but he's my person. There should be three people by my side today, I miss him, and I can't help my feelings. But I guess I wasn't his person. My heart hurts, and my head is pounding, so I press the button to receive more pain meds and drift into a dreamless slumber.

I wake up and see Belle, embraced in a hug by Jackson. He pulls back and places his hands on either side of her face and goes in for a kiss on the forehead. I thought he was going to kiss her on the lips at first. Geez.

"I'm sorry, B. I was freaked out, and I should never have blamed you. I know you would never intentionally hurt her. I wasn't coping with it well. I am sorry. Please forgive me."

"I forgive you, Jack," she says as her tears fall, and he moves his thumbs back and forth to wipe them, his hands still placed on her face.

God, we're a bunch of crybabies around here.

Happy that they made up, I close my eyes and fall back to sleep.

"Good morning, Sades," Jackson says as my eyes start to open up.

"Dr. Laurent just left the room. She thinks you can go home tomorrow morning if everything progresses."

"I can fly home?"

"Well, you and I are going to get a hotel room for a few more days to make sure everything is good, then we will fly home after that."

"We?"

He gives me a stern look. "Do you think I would let my baby sister fly home by herself after this? Are you kidding?" He's right. Jackson would never do that. He reminds me of Wills in so many ways. *Wills.* No, I can't think of him.

"You can do that with work? I thought you needed to be in London right now."

"Don't you worry about that, I've got it handled. I also called your boss, and he was very understanding."

God, what kind of employee am I? I forgot about my actual job. I was thinking more of the animal shelter I volunteer at.

"Thank you, Jackson."

"No need to thank me, that's what I'm here for. I also reached out to Maria. She is going to come and check on you after I leave New York because I can't stay long after I drop you off."

"But..."

"No buts, Maria loves you and wouldn't have it any other way, and I would just feel more comfortable, okay?"

"Okay." I'm not going to fight with him. Maria is our family's old housekeeper/nanny, she pretty much raised Jackson and me, and it would be nice to have her with me.

"Once you're better and completely healed, we will set up the move and everything else that comes along with London."

But, of course, what comes along with London is Wills Taylor. He will never leave my thoughts. I know it.

"Where's Annabelle?"

"She went back to the hotel to make sure they have all your belongings together. After that, they will either keep the bags there or transfer them. Do you want to switch hotels or stay?"

"Switch." I feel kind of selfish asking to switch, knowing Jackson would love that hotel. But I don't need memories of Wills to invade my head when I'm already dealing with so much.

"I figured I'll book something now, and we can move over there tomorrow for a few days."

He's quiet for a while, seems deep in thought

"You okay, Jackson?"

"Sades, don't worry about me. I'm more worried about you. I know this is hard to talk about, but have you really thought about everything that went on, that may go on?"

"Yes, the counselor came down yesterday and will be back tomorrow. She's from the UK actually and knows many people in NY to set me up with if I need anyone to talk to."

"What…"

"What, what?" I ask.

"What if you get pregnant, Sadie, what will you do?"

The famous question I've asked myself all day long. I know there is no wrong or right answer, but I think I would keep the baby, honestly. I just can't imagine having an abortion, and I know that If I carry a baby to term, I could never give it up for adoption. I spoke about this all with the counselor and Belle yesterday.

"I think I would keep it, Jackson."

He just nods but doesn't say anything.

"Would you accept the baby if I did? You wouldn't look at it any different because of how it was conceived, would you?"

He looks like I just slapped him in the face. "You must be joking with that question, Sadie."

"I didn't mean it to offend you, but the counselor said If I were to get pregnant, people might have some reservations about me keeping it, and I need your support."

"I would love that child like it was mine. I wouldn't care who the father is, if that baby comes from you, then that's all that matters. Also, there is a big chance you're not pregnant. You said you didn't think you were ovulating."

I nod in agreement. I should be getting my period any day now.

"I'm worried about you, Sades. Are you sure you're okay? You seem like you're totally fine. More a broken heart than anything else.

"I'm sure when I get home, it will hit me. But I also think because I wasn't conscious, it helps. I have no memory of anything besides the mugging."

"Yeah, I guess that makes sense."

"Are you going to explain what happened with this guy you started dating? I thought you said he wasn't even your type. Also, don't you think you should have told me you were in Paris? What if something happened to you?"

"Well, nothing happened, and if something did, he would have told Belle, and Belle would have called you. Just like she did now. So, slow your roll, papa bear. I'm also not ready to talk about what happened, Jackson. I'm really hurt."

I can feel tears creeping up again, and I'm sick of crying, so I change the subject.

"I'm hungry. Do you think you can find me something I'm allowed to eat?" He knows what I'm doing but doesn't push.

"Yeah, I'll be back soon."

I push the button for my pain meds and drift back into another dreamless sleep.

"I'm worried about her B, she's not herself," Jackson says.

"She has a broken heart, Jack. What do you expect?"

"Don't you think it's a little crazy that she is more depressed over some dickhead she just met rather than being upset about being raped in an alleyway and could potentially be pregnant?"

"I know it might seem weird, Jack. But I swear, just from those few weeks, I thought he was it for Sadie. I would have put money on it that they would get married one day. You weren't there, you didn't see them together. To be honest, I'm even sad over it."

Okay, I can't listen to them anymore.

"I'm fine, you don't have to worry."

They both whip their heads toward me, and Belle's eyes look remorseful being caught talking about me. "Sorry, darling. Have you eaten today?"

"It's fine and no."

"Good thing I bought you some pomme puree then, huh?"

"Oh, yes! I love you, give me, give me." They both laugh. This is what I need, a lightened mood.

The following day comes, and I'm sad because Annabelle leaves today. Her boss is already annoyed with her. Of course, she wouldn't dare tell me herself, but I overheard her talking with Jackson about it.

"Okay, my darling Sadie. It's time for me to leave for my flight. Jackson is checking you out now, and then you will head to the hotel. And, once you're ready, I already have some job opportunities for you. I'll send them to you when the time is right."

I ignore all of that. I haven't told her yet, but Jackson and I plan on investing together to start my own company once I get to London. So, I don't need a job anymore.

I take her hands in mine and squeeze. "After everything that has happened, I want to end this trip on a good note, not a sad one. So, I won't get into it, but just know you're the most important person in my life, and I can't thank you enough for just being you."

"Most important person, huh?" I hear Jackson ask with humor when he walks back into the room.

"You're my brother, that doesn't count, it's like automatic." I give him probably my first genuine smile since he's been here.

"Ready to get the hell out of here?"

"You know it!"

These people are my life, and I'm done sitting around thinking about a guy who doesn't want me and what could have or would have been. Screw that. Get me out of this hospital. I'm ready to get the hell home.

10

Three Years Later

Sadie

"Mommy, Mommy, wake up, pwease." A little finger pokes me in the arm repeatedly.

"Ugh, what time is it?" Of course, I ask no one in particular because my two-and-a-half-year-old doesn't know how to tell time.

I open my eyes and look over at my daughter, who is staring at me with her big blue eyes, bouncing on her feet with her arms stretched as far as they can go. I reach out and pull her into bed with me.

"Cuddle Mommy, baby girl." She wiggles her body as close as she can get to me. We do this every morning, without fail. I would hate to start my day any other way.

I stare down at her, and like every other day, I think about how lucky I am to have such a sweet little girl to call mine.

I push her dark unruly bed head away from her face so that I can give her a good morning kiss. Time is flying by, and it feels like she is looking older by the minute.

Charlie and I look similar, but also different. We share my dark hair, but she has big blue eyes and light porcelain skin compared to my olive skin and green eyes.

But what she inherited from me is way more important than looks. Even at such a young age, Charlie has such a kind soul. She is the first kid to share her snacks or toys with her friend.

Just yesterday, I saw her hugging a strange boy on the playground. When I asked her about it, she told me he scraped his knee, and since my hugs make her feel better, she wanted her hugs to make him feel better. After that, there wasn't a dry eye at work when I repeated the story.

She also enjoys helping at the animal shelter as much as I do. We walk the dogs together, but she also helps pour their food in their bowls and pretends to read them books before we leave.

My phone rings on my nightstand next to me and I already know it will be Jackson. He calls almost every morning since his job requires late nights, he usually starts his mornings when we start ours.

I connect the face call, and Jackson's handsome face fills up the screen.

"Where's my precious little angel?"

Charlie's head is wedged into my side, but then pops up quick and yells, "Boo!"

It's October, and Halloween is right around the corner, and her new obsession is ghosts. So naturally, scaring people is her new favorite thing to do.

Jackson puts his hand on his chest and fakes a frightened breath.

"You scared me, angel."

She giggles at Jackson, and it's the sweetest sound I've ever heard. "Hi, Uncle Jack." I've never called Jackson anything other than that in my life. But Belle is God in Charlie's eyes, and what she does, Charlie does.

"Good morning, Charlotte. Are you excited for the big move today?" She shakes her head wildly, trying to show her enthusiasm.

It's only taken me three years, but we are finally making the move to London.

Jackson brings his attention back to me. "You'll be alright by yourself tonight on the flight?"

"Yes, honey. I promise we will be fine. The shipping company already picked up everything last week, so we are only checking a few bags."

"That's not what I mean, Sades." He gives me an unsure look, knowing I won't want to talk about why it's taken me three years to get on that plane.

I dismiss his concern and go on to ask, "Is everything ready at the store?"

"Yep, I just checked last night before work. The last of the furniture was delivered, including the floral refrigerators that were on back order. Lola organized the final IT setup, so the Wi-Fi, phones, and computers will be ready to go once you're ready. The last step is to schedule the flower delivery once you're here."

Since having Charlie, I've become even more of a crybaby, so it's hard now to hold back my tears.

Jackson has exceeded being brother of the year. Not only supporting Charlie and me but taking on the responsibility of getting the floral shop up and running. Annabelle, of course, has also been a critical factor in starting my business. She had Lola, her old assistant, help me with all internal setups and helped to interview potential employees in person. I know how busy Lola is at her actual job. Now that she is head of finance, I will be indebted to her for life.

"I couldn't have done this without you, Jackson. You've made my dreams come true, and I will always be thankful for that. I love you."

"I love you too. No need to ever thank me, Sades."

"Mommy, I hungry," Charlie interrupts.

"Okay, let's eat, sweet pea." I give her a big kiss on her lips, and she giggles that sweet sound against me. I'll never tire of that noise.

"Okay, you two, I'll see you soon. Sades, call me when you get to the airport. I love you both."

"Will do. Love you."

"Wove you, Uncle Jack," she makes a big, exaggerated kiss noise.

We all laugh, and I end the call to make my girl some breakfast.

Today's plan of attack is to drag Charlie to say goodbye to the important people, tiring her out so she will pass out on the flight. Of course, no nap is risky, but I know my kid, and she'll be too excited on the plane to sleep.

"Okay, Charlie. First stop is the animal shelter. Remember what I said, we can't stay all day like normal. Say goodbye to all doggies and kitties quickly, and then we need to go uptown to see Dr. Esposito."

"Otay, Mommy."

Well, I got played, because it's two hours later and we are only just leaving. I couldn't get her out of there. Every time I said it was time to go, she would start to cry and hug Watson, her favorite corgi mix. They have formed a bond, and honestly, if we weren't moving, I would have adopted him for her. So, I felt terrible and couldn't pull her out of there.

"Guess what, sweet pea?"

"What?" She looks up at me with curious eyes.

"When we move to London, we will volunteer at another animal shelter. So, we can walk lots more doggies, and you can meet all the new kitties too."

"More doggies?" she squeals.

"That's the plan." I love how excitable she is.

After we stop quickly at the floral shop I've worked at for the past four years to say goodbye, we head back uptown to Dr. Esposito's office.

"Hi Sadie, come in, come in." I dropped Charlie off in the daycare down the hall while I have my last appointment with my therapist.

"I know today's session is going to be a little less formal since you're short on time, so let's just get right to it."

"Sounds good."

"How are you feeling about today's move, honestly?" she asks, and I knew it would be her first question.

"I think, no, I know, I'm ready. I need to be strong for Charlie, and I'm not letting my past hold me down any longer."

Dr. Esposito smiles proudly at me. "I'm so glad to hear that. I know it took longer than you would have liked to get to this point, but I'm so proud of the work we have done together, and I know this move is exactly what you need to move on."

"You don't think I'll relapse?" I ask her, genuinely concerned.

"Sadie, your PTSD has not affected you in over a year. That's why we picked now for you to move. You're strong, I know you. You know all the exercises to get through the hard times, and you can still always call me."

The last three years haven't been easy on me since my attack. It didn't hit me until I was home in the states that I was raped and that Wills disappeared. I think the two things together were catastrophic for my mental health. I started to have terrible nightmares, and I often had panic attacks at home and in public.

Then shortly after that, I found out I was indeed pregnant. I knew I would never give up that baby, but I found myself in a rabbit hole of worry.

I was nervous that my baby would be a horrible person, then I would immediately feel guilty for thinking such awful thoughts. I was scared I would have no one here to help or that others wouldn't love the baby.

I was also incredibly nervous I would have a panic attack while I was caring for my baby, making me spiral out of control, and that's when Jackson stepped in and set me up with Dr. Esposito.

Once Charlie was born, my parents couldn't handle the idea of her being an illegitimate child and cut us off. They haven't spoken to Jackson or me in two years, and I think that was for the best. I know I had these idealistic ways of how our relationship could change, but I now know I wouldn't dare think of bringing my sweet baby near that cruel woman.

Traveling was a whole other monster to conquer. Since the France incident, Belle and I haven't gone on one of our yearly trips. If we even spoke about planning a trip, I would get horrible flashbacks, and the nightmares would flare up. So, she came to New York, and we would drive somewhere fun for Charlie.

"If you're still worried, I told you I will set you up with someone in London, but I think you've graduated from therapy sessions. If it makes you more comfortable, why don't you and I have a teleconference once every month for a check-in?"

"Yes, just knowing you're willing to do that makes me feel better, thank you."

"We will set one up for after you get settled and then take it from there." She stands and hugs me goodbye.

"I wish you the best of luck, Sadie, in life and business. You deserve it all."

And with that last chapter of my New York life closed, we are off to London.

"Sadie, Charlie, Over here, darlings!" Annabelle yells across the airport.

Wow, déjà vu much?

The last time I saw Belle at an airport, I could have sworn it was in a very similar situation.

I also insisted she *not* pick us up, but Belle can't be stopped.

Charlie pulls out of my hand to run over to Belle. Her little body almost topples over, but Belle is there to catch her, picking her up and twirling her around.

"Auntie Belle, Auntie Belle," Charlie yells in delight. Belle leans down to plant a million kisses all over her face, and Charlie's little arms quickly wrap around Belle's neck, going in for a big hug.

These two have such a special bond already, and it reminds me how lucky I am to have Annabelle in my life every time they are together.

When she looks up to see me standing in front of them, her face softens. "How are you? Are you okay? Everything went well?"

"Yes, we did good, and Charlie was honestly an angel. I was nervous with no nap, but I couldn't have asked for a smoother process. As for me, I think having Charlie with me was a great distraction. I was focusing on her the whole time, not my insecurities. Plus, we both slept most of the flight."

"I'm so glad." Her smile lights up her face. She's been waiting for this moment for me to move to London for a very long time.

"Alright, let's get on our way then."

We drive down a beautiful, quintessential Notting Hill street, filled with row homes of different hues of pastels and bay windows.

Although I would love a fun pink house for Charlie, I know Annabelle would not have picked a house like this. I let her have free rein in choosing a place for Charlie and me. Too busy helping Jackson set up my floral business, I couldn't do both.

I gave her specific directions that it had to have two bedrooms, two bathrooms, an outside area, or at least walking distance to a park.

We make a few more turns until we are driving down a beautifully manicured street and when we start to slow down. I look around to take in the surrounding area.

This can't be it, surely? This will be way out of my price range… I already know it.

The car pulls out front of a beautiful white Victorian period house, attached to a row of perfectly well-kept homes and groomed gardens.

I step out of the cab, lean down to get Charlie, and take a better look around.

"Annabelle, this is… I don't even know. I'm lost for words. But I know we can't afford this." I point to that house we are parked in front of.

"You're wrong there, my friend," she smiles like she knows something I don't know.

Charlie is trying to wiggle free of my hold, but I don't want her running off yet.

"Just a minute, sweet pea." She whines in protest.

"Do you remember I landed that company in Italy? The CEO, Alessia, is half British, and this was her grandmother's house. Before her grandmother passed away, they renovated it into two apartments, so Alessia could stay with her grandmother when she visited. The first apartment consists of floors one and two, the second apartment is on the third floor.

"Alessia will still occupy the third floor when she comes to London, which is only a couple of times a year since her grandmother's passing. So, you have most of the house to yourself."

"This seems too good to be true. And, even if it is true, two floors in a newly renovated Victorian home in Notting Hill must still go for big bucks."

"Also wrong, the grandmother owned this place, it's paid off. You paying a small amount of rent to Alessia is only a gain for her. She didn't even want to rent it out at first because she didn't want the responsibility of being a landlord. But I vouched for you, and voilà, it's now yours!"

"Okay, wow, thank you." I think I'm in shock. I was not expecting this.

"Please pass along Alessia's information, I would like to thank her personally."

I'm staring at the beautiful house in amazement. This is the first step to my new beginning. It took me three years to get here, but I'm here, and I can't wait to be the best person I can be for my little girl.

We take a tour starting upstairs with all the bedrooms. There are actually three and two bathrooms, then make our way downstairs to our living space and the fantastic updated modern kitchen. I wouldn't think a modern kitchen would work in this Victorian home, but the neutral color pallet compliments the rest of the house. Luckily the house had an option of being furnished, so I opted yes for that. I figured I would get settled, then choose what I like and want.

But, my favorite part of the house is the accordion glass door leading to our private backyard area, making it so we can have an indoor/outdoor living space.

As much as I want to stay here, I need to stop by the flower shop to check everything out. Charlie gets a day with her auntie, and I get a day with my brother.

My eyes are as large as saucers, I'm not even sure I've blinked since I walked in here.

I stare at the sign hanging at the entrance when you first walk in.

Sweet Pea Blooms

"This is mine?" I whisper over to Jackson, grabbing his bicep and squeezing in awe and excitement.

"Yeah, Sades, all yours." The warm tone of his voice hits me right in the heart.

"I'm so proud of you, you know that?" I'm feeling so much gratitude for the opportunities coming my way right now that I can't help but cry a few thankful tears.

"Thank you, honey." I give another squeeze in appreciation, and he hands me all the legal paperwork I have to sign still.

I looked over everything and what I see is not correct.

"Jackson, what did you do?" I flip through the papers to see if I'm missing something. I knew I should have been more involved with this part.

"Don't be mad, Sades, I…"

"You what? I told you I didn't want any more handouts. I don't want to sound ungrateful. But we were supposed to do this together," I snap.

After flipping through all the paperwork, it all says the same "Sole ownership, Sadie Peters."

I didn't make much money as a floral designer in New York since I worked part-time. Childcare was more money than I made, so it didn't make sense. Maria helped me initially, but I couldn't ask her to come anymore. She was getting old, and it wasn't fair to her.

Although our parents cut off our trusts, there were still parts that we could touch, but we both refused to use them. Luckily, I had a small amount that my loving grandmother left us, and that's what I used to invest *with Jackson*.

I should be grateful, but I'm mad, so I stay silent. I don't want to say anything I would regret.

"Sadie, you are my sister and the mother of my niece and favorite person. This is for both of you. Don't you see, I'm trying to give you the start of the new life you always wanted to have."

Ugh, I know he's right. But it's not what we agreed on.

"Listen, I don't need or want your money. But, if it makes you feel better and you insist, you can still pay me back, okay? Same plan as last time, no interest and on your own time. But this place is your baby, and my name doesn't belong anywhere on that paperwork."

I don't know where my brother or I came from, because he didn't take after my parents, neither of us did.

"Okay, I'm sorry I freaked out for a second. As long as you will promise to take my money, I'm okay with all of this." I say, happy to come to an agreement.

"Deal. Although you can't pay me back for that, that's your belated birthday gift." Pointing in front of us.

"Jackson, you bought me a designer purse, I don't think you owe me any more gifts." I laugh at the ridiculous notion. But I follow his hand to where he is pointing, and I stop dead in my tracks.

"What? How? That is the table I saw in the antique store in France three years ago, Jackson!"

"I know. You're welcome." His lips turn up in a cocky grin.

I had no use for it then, but I told Annabelle that I wanted a table just like that to display flowers whenever I opened my floral shop.

The craftsmanship is top notch on the light wood table. But what really sold me was the hand-painted detail. Beautiful florals were painted in a light rose pink with gold leaf accents in all the corners. The artist was local to the area in the early 1900s and was famous for his wooden tables.

"How did you get a table to look just like the one I wanted?"

"This *is* the one you wanted."

"How is that possible? They still had it, and you went to France to get it? Are you nuts?"

He's laughing at me now.

"No, dummy, I bought it three years ago. I kept it in storage until you were ready to move here."

He did what? "Oh my god." My eyes close, and I rub both my hands down my face, I really do have the best brother in the world.

"I freaking love you, Jackson. Do you know that?" I'm hugging the crap out of him now. I'm so ridiculously happy.

While we wait for Belle to drop off Charlie, Jackson and I take advantage of the extremely warm October weather and have a glass of wine in my new backyard. I'm thinking I need to invest in some heaters because I'm going to want to be out here all year round.

After we left **Sweet Pea Blooms**, we had a late lunch in my new neighborhood and then interviewed potential nannies for Charlie. Jackson again will be paying for that luxury, he said it's his goddaughter and I can't stop him. Which I wouldn't, when it comes to Charlie's care, I'll let him pay.

But it's just another reason why I didn't want his money as a gift for the floral shop. We narrowed it down to two young women, so we figured we'd meet them both with Charlie and see who gets on with her better.

And when I say *we*, I mean Jackson and myself. Of course, my overbearing brother insisted on staying for all the interviews. They had to pass his questions as well as mine.

Apparently, the mother doesn't actually have the final say. I pity if he has kids himself, he's going to be so damn overprotective. Luckily, we both agreed on the two who are coming over tomorrow.

I also warned him they were off-limits. I don't care if he has some nanny fantasy, he is to keep it in his pants.

"Hey, don't forget about next weekend. Hopefully, one of these nannies will work out so you won't have to stress about a sitter."

"Next weekend?" I play dumb. He's only told me a million times.

"You're joking, right? My new club opening, this is going to be the best one yet."

"You always say that. Literally every time you open a new club or restaurant."

"No, this is different. I told you one of my partners is well known in London. Plus, this club is super exclusive, the price just to join is more than most people make in years."

"Well, I'm honored you're letting little old me step foot inside the place. And Jackson." I wait for him to turn toward me.

"You're always praising me, but I'm the one who is proud of you. I wouldn't be where I am today if it wasn't for you and your hard work. So, all kidding aside, congrats. I can't wait to celebrate with you."

"Thanks, Sades." He can dish out the compliments, but Jackson never took them well.

I'm excited to go out and have some fun, it's been a very long time —since before Charlie. And not because I'm a single mom, but more because of my anxiety. It took a while to even go out to dinner with coworkers, and when I think about that now, I can't believe how much my issues debilitated me. But I think that's all part of the healing process, now that I can recognize what my weaknesses are, I can move on and only get better from here.

And just like I told Dr. Esposito, I'm ready, and I'm done missing out on the important things in my life. There is so much to celebrate next weekend. Jackson's opening being the main event. But Belle opened her own PR company last year, and we never properly celebrated. And on top of all that goodness, I open the doors to my business in two weeks. The three of us are living the best life right now, and I couldn't be happier.

"Charlie, it's time for Mommy to leave. Be good for Miss Kathryn, okay?" Kathryn has been with us for just over a week, and both me and Charlie love her. She has a master's in early education, so she's not just a nanny, she's teaching her too.

"Otay, Mommy. I be good."

"I love you sweet pea, come give me a cuddle." She runs full force into my arms, almost knocking us over. She's strong for a two-and-a-half-year-old. She smashes her head into my neck and starts kissing me there since she can't reach my face.

"Charlie, those kisses tickle," I laugh, which makes her laugh that sweet giggle. God, I don't want to leave her. She stays with Kathryn during the day when I've been at the shop, but this is the first time I'm leaving her at nighttime in London.

Am I ready for this? I squeeze her a little tighter, not wanting to let go.

"Okay, as much as I love this mother-daughter moment right now, we have to go." I try to give Belle a nasty look. She knows what I'm doing. I'm stalling.

"Come on, love, come sit up on the window seat here, and you can watch me and mommy get into the cab." Charlie, of course, follows Belle right away. Belle leans down to kiss her goodbye, and I see Charlie's face all scrunched up.

"What's wrong, sweet pea?"

"That's not a taxi, Mommy." Her little face is still all scrunched up in concern as she peers out the front bay window.

I'm trying not to laugh. "Charlie, in London, that's what their taxis look like. Only in New York are the taxis yellow." Her face is pure confusion, it's hysterical.

I go and kiss her goodbye one more time, I need to leave now before she sucks me back in.

"I'm so full," Belle groans.

"That dinner was delicious, but I shouldn't have worn such a tight dress." I look down at my black minidress, edged with tiny crystals. I couldn't believe it, I fit into one of my dresses pre-Charlie.

Belle took me to some hip and trendy restaurant in Mayfair, which happens to be down the street to Jackson's new club, working out perfectly so we can walk off our food a little.

"Why isn't Trey coming tonight?" Not that I want him here, I would never share this with Belle, but I hate Trey. I don't see what she could possibly see in him.

"Oh, it was too late for him, he has to work early."

I'm not going to press for more, that answer is good enough for me if it's good enough for Belle.

We stop in front of the new exclusive club, the whole front is decorated in autumn decorations, climbing from the sidewalk all the way up the building. As I'm about to make my way to the entrance, I see the sign.

Charlotte's

"Oh my god! I'm going to ruin my makeup. Did you know about this?"

"Guilty," Belle smiles over to me.

"He hasn't told me much at all about the club, but he did tell me that one detail." She explains.

"This is unbelievable, he honestly surprises me, more and more every time he does something. I freaking love my brother."

And on cue, he steps outside to greet us.

"Well, don't just stand there. Come inside. I want you to meet some people."

I run over to him and smash into his body. "I can't thank you right now because I'll start crying, but I love you."

He kisses my forehead and drags me inside.

"Hi, B." He leans over my shoulder to kiss my best friend on the cheek.

"Do you think I can bring Charlie one day during the week before you open? She will just love this."

"Of course, we'll set up a time next week to do an early dinner and stop at the club after."

"I better be invited too!"

"Don't worry, Double *B*, you can come too." I hear Belle grunt her dissatisfaction behind me, she hates when he calls her that, and he knows how much she hates it because I can see the smirk on his face.

"Grow up, Jack."

We make it inside now, and this place is so super chic, I can't believe it.

"Hi, Jackson baby," a voice that makes me cringe says behind us. The girl looks Belle and me up and down.

"Hi, Amanda, come find me later, yeah?" He leans in for a kiss and slaps her ass as she walks away.

"God, Jack, you're such a pig," Belle spits, and he gives her a little wink in response.

We continue walking through two small private rooms with funky wallpaper and sofas before heading into the main room. Here, the ceilings are high, and the space is decorated with emerald, gray, and black. It's masculine but still beautifully feminine.

"This is amazing, Jackson. I'm so proud of you." I kiss him on the cheek and pull away quickly when the hairs on the back of my neck stand straight up.

Something doesn't feel right.

I turn away from Jackson to glance at Belle, and she is wide eyed as she steps forward and grabs my hand in a punishing hold. What's going on?

I feel Jackson move behind me. "Sadie, come here. I want you to meet my business partners."

I turn around quickly, and I gasp out loud.

It's like I'm staring right into my past. Someone I thought I would never see again. Someone who hurt me enough to break me. Someone who hates me because the look he is giving me right now is lethal. It looks like he's about to bolt, but Annabelle beats him to it.

"Sorry, lady emergency, we need to head to the loo." She grabs my arm and practically drags me through the club because I'm in shock. Actually, whatever's past shock, that's me.

She sits me on a couch in one of those rooms we passed on the way in.

"Was, was…"

"Yes, darling. That was Wills."

11

Wills

"Shit, man… I'm sorry, my sister is anything but rude. Must have been some emergency for her to run off like that," Jackson says to Declan and me.

I'm fuming. I can't even look at Jackson. How in the fucking fuck did I not put together that Jackson Peters is Sadie Peter's brother? This has to be a nightmare, and she isn't actually here in the flesh? In my fucking nightclub, that's also her brother's goddamn nightclub. This is a mess, one big fucking mess.

I've tried hard to suppress every memory of Sadie I have, so it's not until now that I remember she said her brother did this all for a living. How did I not remember? What an idiot.

"I can see the smoke coming out of your ears, mate," Declan whispers in my ear.

Jackson, oblivious to my freak-out, keeps talking. Half of which I don't even register until I hear…

"She's been stressed all week over her new business and move, I'm sure that's it."

I just can't help myself. "Move?" I ask, like a drug addict, and my choice of drug is Sadie.

"Yeah, she just moved to London last week. That's why I've been so busy."

She's in London, it's confirmed. She never told me back then that she was moving to London, but I overheard her talking to Annabelle once.

Now thinking how shady it was that she didn't tell me, I should have known then that she wasn't the girl I thought she was.

Even though I wasn't sure if she ever made the big move back then, I tried my best to stay away from where I thought Annabelle would be. Even though London's a big city, it feels like a small town when you run in the same circles. And I knew where Annabelle was, Sadie would have been.

I can't believe it, after all this time and she's now living in London. It's like God is playing a sick joke on me. I've got to get away from Jackson before I give something away. Clearly, she never told her brother about our time together.

"Sorry, mate, I see someone I know. I'll catch up with you in a little."

"Yeah, sure, no worries. Have fun tonight. I see a girl eyeing me up in the corner anyway."

I like Jackson, a fuckboy like Sadie used to call him for sure, but he's good people.

I roll my neck, trying to relieve some of this fucking stress.

"I need a scotch, I need the whole damn bottle," I say to no one and storm off to the bar.

I'm hiding out at the bar because I can't face anyone right now. My sister and her friends are at a table near the back, so they won't need to come near the bar since they have bottle service.

I especially need to avoid Evelyn. I've told her a little about what happened with Sadie when I first came back from France, and since she knows me better than anyone, one look at my face and she'll know something's up.

I'm watching Sadie across the bar. She hasn't seen me yet, I'm in the back corner, lurking like a fucking creep. She's drinking too much tequila. Annabelle better get ready for a long night with Sadie because she will probably get sick.

And then, a thought rushes through me, and I don't like it one bit. But I can't help but wonder, maybe she doesn't need Annabelle tonight because she has someone waiting at home.

Shit.

This is bad. Sadie needs to get out of my life, but how is that going to happen when I'm in business with her goddamn brother?

A good-looking lad walks over to them and naturally flirts with Sadie and Annabelle. My instincts are trying to pull me toward her to get that fucking idiot away from her.

No, I can't do that. My head and body are being pulled in so many directions right now I can't stand it. I should warn the fucking guy that she is as fake as they come and a complete liar. *A beautiful liar.*

No… just a liar. My scotch-induced brain is going to get me in trouble. Because now I'm thinking of her living with someone again, and it's making me want to punch the wall next to me, and that's not a good sign, I need to take a walk.

After making the rounds and saying hello to the right people, I'm back, standing waiting for another scotch at the bar. Jackson and Annabelle are in a heated discussion next to me, and I overhear Jackson asking Annabelle to look after Sadie.

"I don't know why she's drinking so much. She's never like this, especially when Charlie is waiting for her at home."

My anger rises. *Who the fuck is Charlie?*

Annabelle glances in my direction, quickly shooting me a venomous look, then tries to lower her voice but fails. "Don't you dare judge her, Jack! She has her reasons, just leave her be tonight."

He huffs and narrows his eyes at her. "I'm trusting you to take care of her."

"When the fuck have I not?" she practically yells. Annabelle may annoy the shit out of me sometimes, but one thing I know to be true is she will always look out for Sadie.

"How are you doing, mate?" Declan asks from the other side of me.

"Fine," I say under my breath as I take a big gulp of my scotch.

"I don't get it, just go over there and talk to her. Don't you want closure?"

I'm staring at the floor because I can feel the pull to her. I'm sure Sadie is looking at me from somewhere in the crowd if I look up. It's been like this all night; she's followed me to the loo and hasn't stopped staring at me. I know she's trying to talk to me because she's drunk, but I don't want to talk. Not now, not ever.

"I told you once before, Declan. Sadie Peters is fucking dead to me."

"Well, sorry to break it to you, mate, but it seems she has risen."

Funny, I ignore him and walk off because I've had about enough.

Sadie

I'm all out of sorts, I don't know where my brother is, I can't find my phone, but there are two things I do know.

I'm very, very drunk, and Wills Taylor despises me.

Despite Belle yelling at me not to, my drunk self couldn't help it. I went looking for him.

I needed to know why.

I needed to know why he left when I was going through one of the most difficult times in my life.

But he wouldn't look at me. Instead, he would turn the other way or just walk past like I was invisible. And that hurt more than anything. Much to Belle's disappointment, I never got over Wills.

"What the fuck is she doing here?" Belle seethes next to me.

"Who?"

"Victoria Palmer."

"I fucking hate the name Victoria," I grumble under my breath. I hear Belle chuckle. I'm sure because I cursed. It's like I'm a little kid, every time I say the f-word, people go nuts.

"Don't laugh at me, I always say that word. Fuck, fuck, fuckity, fuck." I kid, looking at Belle, but past her, I see *her*.

I point into the crowd, and Belle pushes my hand down.

"That's her, that's the whore Victoria, who kissed my Wills." I slur. *He's not my Wills anymore.* Why is she here? Are they together now? Is that why he never came looking for me?

"What? Victoria Palmer is the one who kissed Wills?"

"Yes! That's what I just said." I stomp my foot to make a point. Drunk me is acting a lot like my two-year-old.

"Well, Victoria is my archnemesis. I hate her. She opened a PR business the year before mine, and she's jealous that I'm pulling clients that she couldn't get. Now I think she's trying to poach my other clients."

"Are you kidding me? What are we going to do about it?" Belle laughs. She actually laughs at me. I'm not kidding… I want to kill her.

"Okay, Rocky Balboa, calm down. Let's take a walk and get out of sight before she recognizes either of us. I don't need you making a scene."

We grab some water and take a lap around the club, I look over and see Belle, deep in thought.

"What is it?"

"Just thinking."

"About?" I goad her.

"I always do the PR for Jack. He told me the deal he signed with his new partners said they had to use their PR company. I didn't think much of it, Jack gives me a lot of business, so I would never complain. But now, knowing Wills is friends with Victoria, they probably used her. This whole operation was on the down low, which also makes sense since Wills is involved, and they probably didn't want it getting leaked to the press."

We turn the corner and walk right into a few people.

"Sorry, excuse us."

"Hey, Slim," a deep familiar voice says, getting my attention.

"Declan!" I lean in and give him a big hug, but his body stiffens, so I pull back, surprised by Declan's coldness toward me. He quickly became a good friend in France, and I missed him along with Wills. I don't understand what I could have done to make these guys hate me so much.

I know tears are pooling in my eyes because I just can't stand the coldness anymore, I did nothing.

Declan comes closer and leans down for another hug. "Sorry, lass." It's in Declan's DNA to be a good person, so this doesn't make me feel better. He just pities me.

"Why do you hate me so much, Declan?"

"I don't hate you, Sadie. I'm sorry, I'm just put in a weird spot. I think you need to talk to Wills."

"I've tried! He just ignores me," I cry.

"Aye, I'll work on him. It seems like you both need some closure."

I shake my head…this is too much.

If it weren't for Jackson's big day, I would have already left to go home. Unfortunately, my big night isn't shaping up to what I thought it would be like.

I walk out of the ladies' room, and Wills is just about to step out of the men's room, and he freezes when he sees me. I swear this time, I didn't plan to run into him. But I have to try one more time. "Can you please talk to me for two minutes?"

He doesn't answer for a few seconds. "Fine! Let's go."

Oh, he's mad. Maybe this isn't a good idea? *But this may be my only chance, I have to take it.*

Wills is pulling me toward the back of the club so that no one can see us. He opens the back door, props it open, and then turns abruptly, shooting daggers at me. His hands drop to his side, fists clenched.

“Why the hell have you been following me around like an annoying fucking shadow all night?” he hisses.

I cover my mouth in shock. Sober Sadie would not be happy… this is so pathetic. If he thinks it’s okay to speak to me like that, I should walk right back into the club. But, instead, I continue to stare at him with wide eyes, all of a sudden uncertain what to say. I can feel the tears building, unsure if they’re from embarrassment or if I’m just saddened by the hatred spewing from someone I fell for so hard and quick and truly never got over.

“What the fuck do you want, Sadie?” he barks like I’m an enemy.

He blows out a frustrated breath, looking up to the sky.

“I only wanted to talk to you for a minute, Wills,” I whisper. “Do you hate me that much that you can’t even give me that?”

“Yes!” he snapped, and I know he means it, I can see it in his eyes.

The tears that were pooling in my eyes fall down my cheeks, I can’t look at him. What have I done to him to hate me so much? He’s the one who left me at the hospital, never looking back.

“Why didn’t you ever text or call me back? I tried so many times!”

“Because it was over, no reason to hash out the past. You checked out of the hotel… I got the hint, Sadie,” he says and shrugs his shoulders like he doesn’t have a care in the world.

What is he going on about? What does checking out of the hotel have to do with anything?

“I don’t even know what that means,” I cry. He doesn’t elaborate, and more silent tears start to fall.

“Why didn’t you ever check on me? You never called.”

“Because we were over! You. Left. Me!”

“W-What? I didn’t leave you, that’s not what happened.” I’m sobbing now.

“Enough with the fucking waterworks, Sadie!” He’s shouting again, which makes me cry more.

“You know what, I’m done with this shit. We were over three years ago. So why don’t you take a hint and stay the fuck away from me?” He turns around and storms back into the club, slamming the door behind him.

What the hell was that? What does he mean, I left him? I was at the freaking hospital after being raped, for God's sake!

I stand there a moment stunned, nothing has been resolved, and I have more questions than before. But I know there is no way I'm getting answers from Wills. I may just have to try Declan one more time, it's my only shot at finally understanding what's going on.

I turn to walk back inside and pull the handle to open the door. It won't open. I try a second time. *Oh god, not again.*

I start frantically banging on the door, but I know no one will hear me over the music.

My breathing starts to pick up, and I can feel the beads of sweat forming on my forehead. What do I do? I back up against the brick wall and slowly slide down to the ground. I pull my knees into my chest and try to take a few calming breaths, but it's not working. My heart is racing, and my body is shivering from the crying, maybe, or from the panic that has set in. I close my eyes tight and rock back and forth to soothe myself. I hope someone finds me.

Before it's too late.

Wills

"She was crying and not making sense. I'm not going back down that road again. Drop it."

"She's drunk, Wills!" Declan declares, annoyed.

"Why are you always sticking up for her? She's the one that left me. Have you forgotten that?" I'm raising my voice now. This is precisely why I don't want to talk about it. There is no use in getting upset over someone who has no right to my emotions anymore.

"I don't think so, mate. I think you have it wrong this time. I tried to ask Annabelle what happened that night, and she said it's not her story to tell." He looks down to gather his thoughts before finishing.

"I praise myself on being a good judge of character, Wills, and Sadie Peters is a good person through and through. She's not like the girls who normally hang around, I've told you that once before. So, I think she deserves a chance to explain when she's sober."

"For the last time, I'm not interested in knowing anything else about Sadie. It's over, I will never put myself through that shit again."

"She isn't Libby," I hear him say as I walk away.

I shake off the chills that run through my body, fuck, I never want to hear that name again. I turn the corner and run directly into Annabelle.

"Where is she?" she snarls at me. *What is it with her today*?

"Whom are you referring to?" I play dumb.

"Don't fuck with me, Wills, where is Sadie?" she asks, as her eyes flash with anger.

My eyebrows shoot up, and eyes widen. "I don't know, probably where I left her, outside?" I say sarcastically as I point toward the back door.

Every muscle in Annabelle's body goes rigid, and her face turns completely white.

"Where does that door lead?" She whispers over the music, but she quickly turns, running toward the door before I can answer.

An uneasy feeling comes over me… why did she just react like that?

"Annabelle," I yell after her. She stops short, but it's not to answer me. Instead, she grabs Jackson and speaks into his ear. His face has almost the exact reaction of Annabelle, and he looks panicked. They both take off running around the corner, toward the back door.

What is going on? Why did they both react like that? Something doesn't feel right.

No, I can't go there. I can't care anymore, goddammit. *But I do care.*

Sadie

I hear the door open beside me, and two people walk out.

"Sades, it's me, Jackson," he whispers so softly to get my attention. I shake my head because I can't look up. *I'm scared, I'm so scared.*

"Don't be scared, you're so strong."

Did I say that out loud, or does he just read me so well?

"Come on, darling, can Jack pick you up so we can get out of here and take you home?"

I slowly raise my face to look my brother in the eyes. He flinches slightly, but I don't miss it. I know what he sees in my eyes, emptiness, that's what I am, a scared but empty person. It's happening all over again, and I can't stop it.

I just nod my head in response to Belle's question.

He places me in the back of the cab, while Belle gets in and pulls me on her lap. Jackson enters through the other side.

He can't leave his party.

"No, Jackson, go back inside," I whisper.

"No fucking chance, Sadie." He picks up my legs and puts them on his lap.

The cab ride is a blur. I'm staring at the back of the black leather seats, not moving, not thinking. Everyone is quiet.

As we pull up to my house, I whisper, "Jackson?"

"Yeah, Sades?"

"What time is it in New York?"

"Around eight at night. Why?"

"Please call Dr. Esposito, please call her when we get inside."

"Of course," he says as he picks me up and carries me through the house. I vaguely remember the nanny looking concerned. But I can't care right now. Jackson will handle that, I have no strength to care, and whatever strength I have, needs to be saved for the morning when my Charlotte Rose wakes up.

12

Wills

IT'S BEEN a few weeks since the opening of **Charlotte's**, and I haven't seen Jackson since dodging all his requests to meet. I've been opting for phone or video calls instead, but I can't put this off any longer, we need to catch up. So, I'm waiting for him at Harry's Restaurant, my favorite in the city, next to my office.

"Hey man, sorry I'm late." He's out of breath and looks stressed as he pulls off his suit jacket.

"What's up?"

"Just came from checking in on my sister. She lives in Notting Hill, so it took me a while to get across town in the traffic."

Why was he checking in on Sadie? Is she okay? After leaving the club that night, I couldn't sleep or stop thinking about her, I had a bad feeling after my confrontation with Annabelle.

"Is everything okay?"

He takes a deep breath and closes his eyes for a second like he's trying to block something out. "It's better now, but it's been a rough couple of weeks, to say the least. Something happened to her at the opening night of **Charlotte's**, actually, and she hasn't been the same since. But luckily, the last few days have been okay. Plus, she just opened a floral business **Sweet Pea Blooms** which just added to the stress."

She finally opened her business, good for her.

"I'm sorry to hear that, mate. Can I ask what happened?" I know I'm playing with fire. If Jackson ever finds out I already know Sadie, he'll lose his shit. And I don't need to lose Jackson as a business partner, he's terrific at what he does.

"It's not my story to tell, but long story short, a little over three years ago, she was on a trip with her best friend when a terrible accident happened. On the night of the club opening, she got stuck outside, and it triggered some type of PTSD in her, and it's taken a while to get over."

Three years ago? Was he talking about France? What happened there? I would have remembered if something happened to her. I'm going to hell, but I need to know more because what could have been so bad?

"I'm sorry to hear. Where was she traveling?" Jackson eyes me for a second, probably wondering why the hell I'm so interested in a person he thinks I don't know. I'm not known for my chatty personality.

"France, but enough about my sister." I nod in agreement, but my mind is going a mile a minute. *What am I missing here?*

The next day, I'm sitting in my office with Declan going over everything.

"He said what?" Declan asks as he sits across from my desk, not as a question per se, but more in shock.

"I know, I don't understand, I don't remember anything happening. If it was so bad, there was no way she hid it, right?"

"Right." He's sitting there in deep thought. "I know you're not going to like what I have to say, but you need to go see her and get to the bottom of this. I know you never truly got over her and having her live in New York was easy. But she's part of your life now, whether you like it or not. Even if you don't see her, you'll be reminded of her every time you see Jackson."

"Fuck, I know you're right, mate." I rub my eyes and think of the best way to do this.

"He mentioned she opened up her floral company here in London, I have the name, and I think I'm going to stop by. Otherwise, I would have to ask Annabelle where she lives, and I don't want to deal with her." I stand to go.

"Like, you're going right now?" His eyes widen.

"When do I ever procrastinate on shit?" And with that, I stroll out of my office and head toward Chelsea to see the woman I thought I never wanted to see again in my life.

I'm standing across the street staring at a shop named **Sweet Pea Blooms**, and an overwhelming feeling of pride hits me right in the chest. I've hated this girl for the last three years, yet being here now, standing in front of her shop, has me feeling things all over again.

I slowly bring myself to cross the street, and I open the door while a small bell signals that I've entered the shop. I take a deep breath, unsure what I'm in for today.

"Good afternoon, sir. We aren't taking walk-ins just yet. May I suggest giving us a call or coming back at a later date?" A young, good-looking lad says in an Italian accent.

Who is this guy? He's dressed in a three-piece gray windowpane suit. And, why the hell is he so dressed up in a floral shop? He and Sadie work here alone, just the two of them?

Fuck. These are the feelings that keep coming up, and I can't stop them.

I eye the guy. "I'm here for Sadie," I say and don't give him anything else.

"Sadie, there is someone here to see you, love," he calls back into an office as he keeps looking back at me.

"Who is it, Marco?"

I shiver, hearing her voice. I never thought we would be here again.

"Umm…" He looks back at me and blushes.

Oh, maybe he's not into Sadie after all.

He whispers, "A really, really big, good-looking guy."

And then it goes completely silent. This Marco guy keeps looking between the two of us, not sure what to do. I hear no movement in the office, so I take charge, walk past Marco and force my way into Sadie's office.

She sits there wide eyed, looking at me like she has seen a ghost. Shit, she's more beautiful than ever. The other night, my anger was at such an all-time high that I didn't get to take her all in.

"Hello, Sadie."

She stays quiet for a second, just staring at me.

"What are you doing here, Wills?" Her face void of emotion.

"I came to talk to you."

"It's too late to talk, I'm swamped, please leave."

Shit, I didn't even think about what I would do if she didn't want to see me.

"Listen, I'm sorry I didn't hear you out the other night. I just needed some time. Please let me take you to dinner so we can talk."

Dinner? What the hell am I thinking?

She's still staring at me, unsure what to say.

"I think we both want some answers, let's just get it out of the way so we can move on."

She quickly tries to mask an expression that I can't make out… hurt or sadness?

"Please?" I beg, knowing she'll understand that I don't typically plead. I usually take.

"Fine," she huffs. "But not dinner. I'll be home in about an hour. You can meet me there. I don't think what we are going to discuss should be at a restaurant." She raises an eyebrow.

I agree, so I take her address and plan to meet her at her house in an hour.

"Do you want a drink?" she asks.

"Water would be great, thanks." I need about ten glasses of scotch, but I think staying sober and levelheaded is a better idea. I watch her walk into the kitchen, she's changed from her work clothes to yoga pants and a tight tank top. I don't need her body to distract me now, we have to have a serious conversation, but shit, that arse gets me every time.

I take a sip of water and eye her over the glass. Why is this so awkward?

"Listen, I'm just going to get right to it."

She nods in agreement.

"I met Jackson for lunch yesterday, and he mentioned you were going through something right now."

I see her body stiffen, so I keep going before I lose her.

"Jackson also mentioned a past accident, he said it wasn't his story to tell, but since he has no idea about our connection, he mentioned it happened in France three years ago." I pause to see her reaction and her face is just stone cold. I've never seen this Sadie before.

"Sadie, I was with you the whole time in France. I don't remember an accident. So, what was he talking about? Is this why you left me?"

"I never left you!" she yells, and then startled by her own voice, she whispers, "I never left you, Wills."

"Well, that's how I remember it, so would you care to explain?" Her face looks so pained right now. All the emotions I've seen in the ten minutes of being here are not putting me at ease.

"Where do I start?"

"The club, the last time I saw you."

"After you kissed Victoria—"

I cut her off so we don't start on the wrong foot. "Sadie, I would have never cheated on you. She kissed me, I promise you that."

"I know," she whispers and takes a breath.

"I saw her kiss you, but in my drunken mind, all I could see was your lips touching hers." I can see the tears welling in her eyes as she replays the memory in her mind. It's taking all my might not to comfort her, but I stay on my side of the sofa because I'm unsure how this story will end.

"After I ran from you, I went through the emergency exit."

"Explains why I didn't see you out front when I ran after you."

She nods slightly. "Let me just finish this part with no interruptions, okay?"

"Okay," I say, and she takes a deep, shaky breath. I can still see her trying to hold back tears.

I'm getting that bad feeling in my gut again.

"When I was outside, I was attacked, mugged."

Wait, what? I can feel my eyes go wide, and she puts up a hand to make sure I don't interrupt.

"I woke up three days later in the hospital, I had swelling on my brain from when the attacker threw me into a wall. They put me in a coma until it went down and the doctor then informed me that I was raped when I was unconscious." She closes her eyes, and the tears finally fall down her face.

I sit here in shock. *Attacked? Raped?*

I can feel my own eyes well up. I got this wrong, so fucking wrong. Sadie didn't leave me, I left her.

"Sadie, I..."

"Why didn't you come to look for me? Belle and I texted you so many times, Wills. I needed you!" Her shaky voice yells.

I lean my elbows on my knees and put my face in my hands and let the tears fall down my face. I can count the number of times I've cried in my whole life on one hand, and this time has never felt like the times before. I'm so ashamed, and completely gutted.

I left my poor girl alone in a foreign country after being raped, someone I thought I was falling in love with. *What kind of man am I?*

"God, Sadie, I'm so, so sorry. I know that doesn't make up for anything, but I thought you left the country."

"Why would you ever think that?" She looks shocked.

"After I left the club, I went back to your room, and I never got an answer. I called and texted a million times. Then finally, the hotel told me you checked out. I thought you were so mad about the kiss that you left me. Then I became so furious, I left because I was mad that you would leave without speaking to me."

"I still don't get why you didn't eventually text back when I specifically said I was attacked."

Fuck.

"I fucked up, Sadie. I blocked both you and Annabelle on my phone. I made Declan do it as well. I was so upset I didn't want to hear any of your excuses once you got back to New York. I know the word sorry will never be enough, but this is all my fault, and I will never forgive myself."

"Why does everyone blame themselves? I'm the one who ran into an alley."

"Because of me! You ran in that alley because of me." I raise my voice, not meaning to but she doesn't notice.

She breathes out a long-winded breath. "This is all so messed up, it was never supposed to be like this for us, Wills. I, I thought…"

I lean over and take her hand in mine, surprised she lets me. This feels so right, her hand in mine.

"What, Sadie?" I know what she wants to say, I feel the same way. She was my person.

She's staring at my hand as I run my thumb back and forth to comfort her, and I see her tears well back up in her eyes. I wipe my other thumb across her cheek just as one falls down her face.

"Just give me a few minutes, okay?" She gets up and walks toward the kitchen.

A minute goes by, and I hear little footsteps walking down the stairs.

A gorgeous little girl rounds the corner and stops dead in her tracks when she sees me.

She looks scared for a second. I'm significantly larger than the average person, I'm sure to her I'm the size of a giant.

"Who, who are you?" she stutters.

"Hi, I'm Wills," I try to say in a soothing voice, not to scare her.

"Where's my mommy?" She looks around, still scared.

Mummy? Maybe she has tenants upstairs?

"What's your name?" I ask, but an upset Sadie cuts me off.

"Charlie! I told you to stay upstairs with Miss Kathryn. Where is she?"

"She went potty, Mommy, and I hungry."

My eyes go wide. *Mummy? Is Sadie her mummy?* I think Sadie realizes when I figure out that she has a kid because she gives me a look of confirmation.

Sadie leans down to kiss her kid.

"I'm sorry I yelled at you, sweet pea. Can you say hi to my friend, Wills?"

The little girl gives me a sweet smile.

"Hi, Charlie." I smile down at her. She seems to have gotten some confidence back since Sadie is here, so she sticks out her hand to shake mine.

"Hello, my name is Charlotte Rose."

I chuckle. This must be a rehearsed line. Then I shake her tiny little hand. "Wow, your name has a flower in it? I bet your mummy named you that because she loves flowers."

Her little blue eyes go as wide as they can, and she starts bouncing on her feet in excitement.

"Yes, yes! How do you know that?"

I smile up at Sadie. "Because I know your mummy very well, and I know she loves flowers." Charlie looks between us a few times, probably very confused by this strange man in her house.

"How old are you, Charlotte?"

"Two and a half," she states proudly.

"Two and a half?" My voice cracks because it's then when I realize that this could be my kid. I slowly look up at Sadie, and she's staring at me and starts to shake her head. How does she always know what I'm thinking?

"She's not, Wills."

For some reason, I feel a loss from that answer. I know I shouldn't, but it's a strange feeling.

"Who?" I ask without thinking, not sure I want to know about the other guys she's been with.

She doesn't answer, so I look up into her eyes, she looks down at Charlotte and then back to me. "From the attack," she whispers.

It takes me a second to comprehend. I look down at the sweet little girl in front of me and back up at Sadie. She got pregnant by a rapist, because of me.

"Charlie, sweetie, where are you?" A younger girl rounds the corner. "I'm sorry, Sadie, I stepped away for a second to use the loo. She said she was going to stay in her room."

"That's okay, Kathryn, not a problem."

"Okay, Charlie, say goodbye to Wills. It's almost time for bed, so I'll be up soon."

"Bye, Wills." She comes over, I think to shake my hand again, but instead, she wraps her arms around my legs and cuddles me. I hear Sadie laugh because Charlotte's arms barely fit around my legs.

After Charlotte is back upstairs, I sit back down. That was a lot of information to take in all at once.

"You know, she must like you," Sadie says, breaking the silence.

I look up, and she's standing in front of me, so I pat the cushion next to me, and she willingly sits.

"Charlotte?"

"Yeah, she's usually timid around strangers, even more than I was." She smiles at me, and the memories of when I first met her run through my mind.

I lean back on the couch and stare up at the ceiling but reach over to put her hand back in mine. I missed this.

"She seems like a special little girl."

"You have no idea, Wills. She's my whole life. She's the kindest, smartest little girl I've ever met. With a side of sass, she gets from her Auntie Belle." She laughs.

"Oh, I do not doubt that." She looks so happy when she talks about Charlotte, so proud to be her mum.

We sit in comfortable silence, when something hits me I forgot about before.

"Fuck, Sadie."

"What is it?" She turns her beautiful face toward me and looks worried. How did I ever think she left me? She would have never done that to anyone.

I never deserved this beautiful human being. I know I always call her beautiful because of her looks. But that's not the only reason… she is beautiful inside and out. And for some reason I forgot that in a time of crisis. I stand abruptly and start pacing her living room.

"What is it, Wills?" She sounds concerned, but this is all my fault.

"I just realized I left you out in that alley at the party. That's why you weren't doing well the past couple of weeks, right?" I already know the answer, it's because I left her again.

"I-I should go. I'm so sorry, Sadie. I'm so fucking sorry." I walk toward the door when her hand wraps around my forearm.

"Wills, wait." I stand there staring straight ahead at the wall. I'm so disappointed with myself, I can't even look at her.

"I was supposed to protect you, Sadie. Not hurt you."

"Don't, don't do this to yourself." She grabs my hand and pulls me outside.

"Come on, let's take a walk around the block before I have to put Charlie to sleep."

"I don't know how this makes sense but talking to you tonight has lifted something off my chest. I feel lighter. I'm going to be completely honest with you. I was having a tough time when I got back to New York. Not just because of the attack, but also because I thought I meant nothing to you. I never understood how you could just leave me in France without so much as a goodbye. But, knowing that we left each other because of a miscommunication has eased something in me. I'm sad for what we both missed out on together, but I feel so much better now. I'm actually feeling so happy, I can't wait to tell my therapist." She laughs, but I don't think any of this is funny.

"I should have…"

"No, don't go there—shoulda, coulda, woulda. Emotions were high that night. You couldn't have known that I got attacked, and I would have never guessed you thought I left you. But, of course, I'm upset,

Wills. I was excited to start a life with you. I was moving to London, I never told you." She smiles sadly up at me.

"I knew you were, I overheard you talking to Annabelle one night. And, again, this is why I'm a terrible person. When I thought you left, I thought you were being sneaky, not telling me."

She shakes her head no. "I was saving telling you for the last day, so we had something to look forward to in the future."

"This is a mess."

After a while, she looks apprehensive about asking something.

"What is it?"

"Are you dating her now?" she whispers, and I see a whole mix of emotions wash over her face, but mostly hurt and sadness. Who is she talking about?

"Am I dating who?"

"Victoria."

"What? Why would you think I would date the woman who single-handedly ruined the best thing to ever happen to me?"

"Me?" She looks genuinely shocked.

"Of course, you, Sadie. I am not dating her. She used to be one of my sister's best friends. But to be honest, they barely talk now, since the whole France incident."

Wait.

"Were you jealous, Sadie?" I shoot her a cocky grin, and she shrugs, embarrassed.

"I saw her at the opening party of **Charlotte's** before you and I had our fight."

Shit. I didn't want Victoria there, but she did the PR for the club opening. She introduced me to an up-and-coming football player that signed with us, and I had to pay it forward.

"I'm sorry, she was there as a favor, I didn't even speak to her." I'm such an asshole.

"Don't blame yourself, Wills. I can see those wheels turning in your head. It's over and done with, I want to move on, okay?"

"Okay, beautiful." I slip with my name for her, not sure how she'll take it, but I see a small smile she tries to hide. We're about to get back to her house, I don't want this walk to end. It feels like the old Wills and Sadie, and I like it too much. I don't realize I'm smiling once we reach her front door.

"Why are you smiling?"

"I did something after France that would make you very happy."

She scrunches up her face, trying to think what I possibly could have done.

"I adopted a dog." I smile widely, probably my first genuine smile in a very long time.

"You did?!" She seems so excited. I love this look on her.

"His name is Buddy, he's a golden retriever, German shepherd mix, and he's the best."

"Oh my god, he's probably the cutest thing ever. Charlie is just as animal crazy as I am. I can't wait to meet him."

And then she goes quiet, and I know she's embarrassed with assuming she would ever meet him. I know exactly how she thinks.

"He would love you both. You know, every weekend we spend a day at the park. Why don't you and Charlotte meet Buddy and me this weekend?"

"Yeah?"

"Of course, Sadie."

"Okay, sure. That sounds great." She's back to shy Sadie, I love her vulnerability toward me.

I reach to cup her face and kiss her on the cheek.

"See you this weekend, Sadie," I whisper in her ear and see all the goose bumps rise on her body.

"Bye, Wills," she whispers huskily.

Good, I still affect her, the way she affects me.

"Make sure to lock up," I tell her.

"I will." I stand there a second, and then she rolls her eyes when she realizes I mean now. I want to make sure she's safe for the night.

I wave one last time as she watches me from her front window, and she smiles brightly. I can't believe today's events went in a direction I would have never guessed, but I'm happy with the place we're at now. I hope we can only move forward from here.

Sadie

I've been in a good mood all week, and I won't play dumb. I know it's because of Wills.

"Your happiness is kind of sickening," Marco says from across the table as he bites into a piece of lettuce, and I laugh.

When I hired Marco as my design assistant, I was deep into a depressed episode. Alessia, my landlord, is cousins with Marco, and as a thank you to her, I hired him. But he is like a saint sent down to me from heaven. He is so talented and helpful and has quickly become a friend. I can't remember ever clicking with someone so quick, other than Belle.

And Wills.

"So, dish."

"I'm not sure what you're talking about. I'm the same Sadie I always am." He eyes me suspiciously, so I change the subject.

"Do we have all the flowers ordered for next week?"

"Yes, love, for the one hundredth time." He laughs.

Okay, I can't help it, I'm nervous about my first event in London. Although down the line, we will open the flower boutique for walk-ins during the day. Now, we are focused only on events and design pieces—think flower Avant-Garde.

Belle represents many fashion houses and submitted my portfolio for a pre-holiday fashion event in Covent Garden. I couldn't be more excited and prouder that they picked my company over the many who applied. But I also want to throw up from nervousness.

"They invited us both with a plus-one to the after-party if you want to bring Henry." He shrugs. "What's wrong now? You guys give me whiplash."

"Oh no, no, no, we are not talking about my love life until you give me the goods about what's going on with yours. Who was that Adonis who stopped by the other day?"

"What Adonis?" I hear a familiar voice say behind me and peek over my shoulder to see Belle standing there with Trey. I cringe slightly, not sure how she's going to react about me seeing Wills tomorrow.

"Some huge, beautiful man stopped by the store a few days ago, and I could feel the sexual tension just radiating through the air."

"You know I'm your boss, right? So you can't say things like that."

Marco just rolls his eyes.

Belle leans down to kiss me, and I see her elbow Trey a little for him to kiss and say hello to me.

What is with this guy?

"Well, from Marco's description, I can only imagine it to be Wills or Declan. So, which one was it, and I'm hoping the name starts with a D."

"Not exactly," I say and turn to take another bite of my lunch.

"What the hell did he have to say, Sadie?"

"Annabelle," Trey chastises through clenched teeth. "I think you should keep your voice down."

Ugh, he's such a tool. We both ignore him.

I give her the rundown as fast as I can, and I'm not sure what she thinks because I think I've shocked her speechless, which I've never done before.

"This is crazy, Sadie. It's like some fucked-up love story you would see in a movie."

"Belle," Trey warns after she curses. She's good at ignoring his pompous attitude, but I'm not, so I shoot him a look.

"I'm coming over tomorrow to chat more about this."

"Well, actually… Charlotte and I are meeting Wills in the park so she can meet his dog," I spit out as quickly as I can.

"Sadie," she sighs.

"Are you sure this is a good idea? You've only been in London a little over a month, and a lot has happened."

"There is only one way to find out, Belle. It was so nice to be with him the other night after we cleared the air. I know it's different this time, but you know he's the only one I've ever felt *more* for."

I look around our table and forget that Marco and Trey are still here. Of course, Trey has no interest in anything but himself. But

Marco has wide eyes, and I know he will bug the crap out of me for more information later. This is going to be a long day.

"Belle, let's just chat later. Call me after work."

"Yeah, okay, good idea."

She pulls me in close for a heartwarming hug goodbye, while Trey just gives a head nod and storms out.

"That's Belle's boyfriend?" Marco asked, shocked.

"Yeah, for the last three years."

"What the hell is up his arse if he has a woman like Belle on his arm? God, I'm gayer than gay, and I'd still do Belle."

We both laugh.

"I think… Trey thinks Belle is lucky to have him on her arm."

Marco scoffs in disgust. *Tell me about it, Marco.* I don't wish bad things upon my friend, but I wish she would see Trey for who he truly is.

"Charlie, you ready to meet Wills at the park?" I yell into the other room from the kitchen, where I'm preparing us all a lunch.

"And Buddy?" she asks. She was excited for a park day with her new friend Wills until she heard Buddy the dog was coming. I've listened to the name "Buddy" over five hundred times today.

"Yes, sweet pea, he's going to be so excited to meet you."

"Woo-hoo," she yells and pumps her hand in the air, no clue where she learned this.

I explained that it's now November, and the ghosts went home until next October. I couldn't hear the word "boo" one more time. So now, her new thing is "woo-hoo."

I pack up our bag, and we quickly head to Hyde Park.

I need to slow my roll, just last week, I thought I would never see Wills again, and now the butterflies in my stomach are back in full effect like they were all those years ago.

13

Sadie

We enter Hyde Park, and I'm pushing Charlie in her stroller, heading toward Kensington Palace, our agreed-upon meeting spot with Wills. Her feet are kicking back and forth in anticipation. I can just feel her excitement from here.

"Mommy, we in London?"

I smile, a month later and she's still so excited about the move.

"Yes, sweet pea. We're in London. Right now, we are walking through Hyde Park."

Today's another warm autumn day. Neither of us is wearing a jacket, so it's a perfect day for a picnic. I think due to the unusually warm weather for this time of the year, the trees are only just starting to change, making for some beautiful scenery.

I take a look around the park, at my new home. It is such a beautiful city—*when it's not raining.*

But before I can even make it halfway into the park, my phone goes off, and I see it's Belle. *Shit.* I've been dodging her calls all morning, knowing she would want to talk about today.

"Hello?" I answer my phone and take a seat on the bench.

"You've got to be kidding me, right? I've been calling you since last night!"

"Ahh, sorry, I've been so busy with the shop and the new house. I was going to call you later."

"Sadie Marie Peters, don't you dare lie to me! Let's just cut to the chase. You're ignoring me because you're afraid of what I have to say about Wills."

Yeah, no crap.

"I already know what you're going to say."

"No, you don't, and I would have preferred to say this in person, but since you never answered me, I didn't come by your place."

I cringe. "Sorry."

"You think I'm going to tell you this is a bad idea, and at first, I thought that it was. And you can't blame me for worrying, Sadie. A few weeks ago, you had a panic attack after fighting with him. I know… I know it wasn't his fault the door locked behind him, and he didn't know about the attack to begin with. But it's still my duty as your sister soul mate to always have your best interest as my priority."

"I know, Annabelle, and I love you for that."

"Sadie, darling, I thought about this long and hard last night. I want you happy, and I know Wills is your happiness. Besides, when Charlie is around, it was probably one of the first times I've seen a genuine smile on your face since… I don't know, probably since the last time you saw Wills. So, I'm going to back off a little, life has changed, and you're stronger than all of us, and I should have trust in that, but…"

"I knew there would be a but," I grumble under my breath.

"But please be careful. Don't be mad at me for caring, okay? Your breakup with Wills was not ordinary, and I want you to protect your heart and Charlie's heart. When the nanny was home, I called yesterday to speak to her, and she mentioned Wills *twice* in her story. She's only met him once, you know. I'm nervous she will get attached, and if something happens, she will get hurt too."

I know she's right, but we haven't seen Wills yet. She doesn't know what will happen.

"I know you care. I'm sorry. And thank you for trusting me on this.

I don't know what it is about Wills, and I never did. But I need to see him today and see how it goes between us."

"I understand, darling. I love you. Have fun today."

"I love you too."

I'm about to put my phone away when it rings again.

"What now? I promise everything will be fine today."

"What are you talking about, what's today?" Jackson's voice asks through the phone.

"Oh, nothing, nothing. I thought you were Belle. Don't worry about it."

Crap, I don't want him to know that I'm with Wills today for so many reasons.

Neither of us has told Jackson we know each other. I never lie to my brother, so I'm going to have to figure the best way to break the news. I'm most scared of when he finds out who Wills is to me. And, although I know now it was all some screwed-up misunderstanding, I'm not sure Jackson will be able to see that. He will just remember the girl in the hospital bed, devastated that her person wasn't there for her.

"Why don't I believe you?"

"It's just girl stuff, don't worry about it. What's going on?"

"Well, I wanted to see If I could come to hang out with you guys today, maybe go to **Charlotte's**, then have lunch."

Shit, shit, shit. Think fast, Sadie.

"We are actually having a mother-daughter day today, but maybe tomorrow?"

He pauses for a second, probably because I'm the worst liar on the face of the earth, and he can see right through my lie.

"Okay, I'll call you tomorrow, have fun," he finally says.

That was close.

After my calls, we eventually make it to Kensington Palace. I'm glad I left early, otherwise, I would have been late. Charlie unbuckles herself so fast, practically falling out of the stroller when she sees Wills walking up to us.

"Buddy!"

"Hey, hey, Charlie, what do you ask?"

"Can I pet Buddy?" Not giving Wills a chance to answer. "Pwease, Wills?"

He laughs. "Of course, and you know what? He happens to love little girls with dark hair and blue eyes."

"He does? I have bwue eyes." She walks up closer to Buddy. "Wook, Buddy, bwue eyes." She blinks fast for effect.

I look lovingly and smile down to my very overexcited daughter, then look up at Wills.

"Hi," I say, all of a sudden nervous and trying not to wring my hands for him to see.

"Hello, Sadie." His deep voice vibrates through my whole body as he leans in, cups my cheek, and kisses the other.

I missed that hand on my face.

I can feel the blush in my cheeks creeping down my neck, and he smirks… knowing the exact effect he's always had on me.

"No need to be nervous," he whispers. I think he gets a kick out of this.

"I'm not nervous." My voice squeaks. "Okay, I am a little. My emotions are just all over the place today, and I'm still confused. It's taking me a little to wrap my head around years of wrong information, you know?"

His face drops, and I can see the sadness in his eyes. "Yeah, Sadie. I know exactly what you mean."

We walk a while in silence, watching Charlie take charge, holding Buddy's leash, thinking she's walking him, although Wills has the end. Buddy's the cutest, he looks just like a golden retriever with German shepherd ears. He's being so patient with Charlie, knowing full well he wants to walk faster than a toddler's pace.

She keeps looking up at me, smiling, making sure I'm watching her the whole time. If I'm not, she dramatically says, "Moooommy, wook at me," occasionally adding, "I woooove Buddy."

She tells me every day how she wants a puppy. And we will, eventually, but after we settle in.

Finally, getting to a good open spot that's not too crowded, I suggest we pick a spot to set up lunch.

"Otay, Mommy. Wills, come." She grabs his large hand that can easily crush hers and pulls him toward the grass. I'm still in awe of how she opened right up to him. Only because she's always known Jackson her whole life is she so close with him. But in general, she takes a long time to warm up to men.

Not sure if it's because I just never had them around or what it could be, but it's been like that for a while now.

But, with Wills, there was this instant connection between them, like they've been best buds forever.

I know this may be strange, but it's kind of the way I felt when I first met Wills. I just had this instant pull toward him. Back then, I tried to play it off like I didn't like him, but who was I trying to kid? Everyone could see right through me.

So, maybe it's like that old saying, "the apple doesn't fall from the tree."

I lay out the extra-large picnic blanket and put out the food I prepared for lunch and a small vase for flowers just to round off the whole decor.

I know this is just a picnic in the park, but I want to make sure today goes off without a hitch.

"Buddy, sit," Charlie bosses him as she takes her spot between Wills and me.

I made some gourmet finger sandwiches, two different salads, and a chocolate mousse for dessert. Charlie is the first to dig in, grabbing a sandwich, then handing one to Wills.

He takes it from her and looks over, flashing his signature smirk. I think he's enjoying Charlie's attention, especially because she never handed me a freaking sandwich.

"Thank you, Charlotte. Your mummy did a great job, this all looks quite delicious."

She nods since her mouth is full of food, chewing fast, trying to say something.

"Mmmmm cheese!"

Wills throws his head back, dying of laughter. I'm so used to this kid that I sometimes forget how funny and dramatic she can be.

"I love cheese too, sweet pea. Mommy just tries not to eat it too much."

"Why?" She looks at me so confused.

"When you're older, you'll understand." I laugh but cut it short when I look over at Wills shooting daggers at me.

"What?" I ask self-consciously.

"I don't want to hear how you try not to eat cheese, you're perfect."

He looks down at my body, letting his gaze drift back up to my face to confirm his statement, but I ignore his words. I could fall for the Wills Taylor charm again, real quick, if I let myself.

Or maybe I won't fall since I never got up to begin with.

"You know she might have gotten your looks, but she's very similar to your brother, personality-wise."

I laugh. "Don't remind me because he often does. I certainly don't have her wit, and I can only imagine what she's going to be like as a teenager."

"She's going to be a real heartbreaker, that one."

I smile at Charlie. I can't wait to watch her grow and see the person she turns into.

"Mommy, I all done. I pway with Buddy?"

I look to Wills to see if it's okay, and he nods in confirmation.

"Sure, sweet pea, but just run right in front of us, okay? And, be gentle with Buddy," I yell as she runs off before I can even get my whole thought out, too excited to play with her new pal.

It's just Wills and me now, and I can feel the tension in the air.

"Sweet Pea? It's the name of your shop too, right?"

I smile, liking that he remembered, but again, Wills was always like that. He remembered every little detail.

"Yeah, it's her birth month flower, and it just kind of fell into place as a nickname."

"That's a thing?" His brows furrow, like he thinks I made that up or something.

"Yeah, mine is a flower called the larkspur, and yours would be a chrysanthemum."

The second it comes out of my mouth, I instantly regret it because after three years, why do I remember his birthday is in November? I know he's looking at me right now. I can always sense when he is. He's probably wondering what kind of stalker he's having lunch with right now.

I can't look his way, desperately trying to think of something to change the subject.

"You know, we both own businesses named after my daughter."

"Yeah, that's right." He laughs. "It was in our contract. Jackson could name the place if Declan and I agreed. He never mentioned it was for his niece, though, until after. So I thought maybe it was his secret lover or a girl he had always loved. Not his baby niece. But, after meeting Charlotte, I can't say I'm mad." After a few seconds, he adds, "And Sadie?"

"Yeah?" I look up into those gray eyes I love so much.

"I remember your birthday is July fourteenth. So, it's okay to know mine too." He smirks again.

Ugh, he's so freaking cocky. I just shake my head and ignore him.

We lie on the blanket in silence for a while, watching Charlie and Buddy playing in front of us. I sneak a few glances at Wills, and he's still the same Wills to me. He grew some tidy scruff on his face, which is sexy as hell. But besides that, he doesn't look much different or older. He must still work out like a maniac because he's still fit as hell.

"You know I've never seen you in jeans before," I say, looking him up and down. He's in dark jeans, Chelsea boots, a cable-knit sweater with a white collared shirt underneath.

He looks well dressed and ready to go out for most, but I know Wills—this is his casual wear.

"I've been trying to be more laid back on the weekends."

I'm not sure if he's joking with me, knowing full well he is anything but laid back, or if he's being dead serious.

"Laid back, Wills? You don't know the meaning."

"I can be laid back," he deadpans.

"You can't even relax on the beach, so if you can't be laid back there, where can you be?"

"I'm laid back right now, sitting on this picnic blanket."

I can't help but laugh out loud, and he smirks.

"I've just watched you tense up ten times as men walked by our blanket. Or how about the old man who handed me back my napkin that flew away?"

"He was trying to hit on you."

"He was not, and he was like ninety! I'm not even your girlfriend anymore, and you're still a lunatic." I'm laughing again, just thinking about Wills trying to be "chill."

But he's gone quiet, and he's not looking at me anymore. What did I say? Is he annoyed I'm making fun of him? *That can't be it.*

I rack my brain with what it could be. Is it because I pointed out we aren't dating anymore? I was just trying to prove a point, not stir up any old feelings.

I can see he's deep in thought while he subconsciously reaches over for my hand. *Some things never change.*

"I'm sorry, Wills. Tell me what you're thinking?" I ask, but he doesn't answer, and whatever it is, he doesn't want to share. "Tell me," I push.

"I don't know how."

He was always so good at expressing his feelings to me, so I'm wondering what could be so hard.

"No holding back. That's what you used to always tell me."

He nods his head as he remembers.

"I'm nervous about what's going to happen."

"I don't understand?"

"I've always been honest with you, Sadie, and I always will be, so I'm going to give it to you straight."

I'm not sure if this will be good or bad, so I brace for impact.

"I was going to cancel today."

I wince a little, I try to hide it, but I know I don't. Why would he cancel? Did he not want to see me?

"Don't start thinking crazy things in that head of yours. It's not because I didn't want to see you, trust me, Sadie, I did. But, by the time I got home from your house the other night, I was a mess. I know you'll say differently, but I was supposed to protect you, and I'm afraid I'll always think about how I failed you. I thought maybe you were better off without me."

"No, Wills. You didn't fail me. It was just a bad twist of fate."

He shakes his head but continues.

"But now, sitting here with you, and even Charlotte, feels so natural to me, like I belong here with both of you. I know it's been three years, but it's almost as if no time has passed. I thought I hated you during those years, I'm so sorry for that, but now it's like all of that has been wiped clean, and we are just back to us again. I'm not a religious man, but maybe, somewhere, somehow, someone's looking down on us, giving us another chance, giving me another chance to prove I'm worthy. Hanging out with you for the last couple of hours has been, I don't even know if I can put it into words, that's how amazing it's been. But it's also brought back so many memories and feelings that make me already afraid to lose you again."

Oh, I'm shocked and rooted in my place because I don't know what to say. I wasn't expecting that switch of thought from him.

"Why would you think you would lose me again?"

"Well, Sadie, what are we doing? You've pointed out we aren't dating. But I already know I want to see you again and again. I want to hang out with Charlotte again too, I might even want to hang out with her more," he jokes. "What did you think when you agreed to today? Did you just want to catch up with an old boyfriend, did you want to be friends, or do you feel the pull that I do, just like when we first met?"

Of course, I feel it—excitement bursts through my stomach, good but nervous energy burning through my body. I don't answer, and I feel Wills's eyes glaring at me.

"Sadie, I can tell you right now, I won't do the friend thing with you. I can't. We were put on this earth to be lovers, not friends. Or at least not friends, without being lovers. The way my body reacts to yours, even from across a room, some people would say it's unnatural. I'm not saying we need to rush into anything but knowing what I know now about our prior relationship, I won't be able to give you up. Tell me you feel the same, beautiful."

I turn to look at him right in the eyes, squeeze his hand that's still holding mine, and open my heart to him. "I feel the same as you, Wills, I always have, I probably always will. I've never gotten over you and have never felt for anyone else what I feel for you. But I'm also scared. I'm too broken to go through something horrific again, and I won't survive it."

He looks over, checking on Charlie and Buddy, and then pulls me closer to him. Cupping my cheek, he presses a quick kiss to my lips, and a spark of fire ignites in my body—I missed his lips, I missed us so much.

"You are not broken, Sadie Peters. Those words are never to come out of your pretty little mouth again. Do you understand me?"

I nod.

"Use your words, beautiful, so I know you mean it."

"I'm not broken, I won't repeat it."

"Damn right. You're a survivor, and you're my strongest girl. You. Are. Not. Broken."

"I missed you," I whisper to him, wanting to give him a truth of mine too.

"I'm so glad you're back in my life, Sadie."

"Is this crazy, Wills? We had a horrific ending, and now we are just jumping back in. What will people think?"

He looks at me, like, *really*?

"You think I give two shits what people think, Sadie?"

I know he doesn't.

"Is it crazy? Maybe. But I love crazy, baby, and when I want something, I go for it. Doesn't this feel so good, you and me together again?"

"It does, it really does." I sigh happily.

I look up again to check on Charlie and Buddy, and the moment's broken when I see a soccer ball come flying over toward Charlie, but before it hits her, it bounces once, then when it hits her in the leg, the blow is lessened, barely hitting her. That could have been bad.

But she still screams, "Owie!" and within a millisecond, Wills is running toward Charlie, picking her up in one swift motion.

"Are you okay, princess?"

Swoon—*princess*.

She nods her head, and I know she's fine, but then she looks up at Wills's concerned face, and the waterworks start.

Oh, she's definitely tired. I know that cry, it's past her nap time.

He stalks back over to me, hands me Charlie, and is off again.

I rub Charlie's back as she cries into my shoulder. "It's okay, sweet pea. You'll be okay. Close your eyes and take a nap." I look at her face, and her eyes are already starting to close. But her hand reaches out for Buddy, who nuzzles his way between my legs to be close to Charlie.

"It's okay, he's not going anywhere. Close your eyes." I look up and see the soccer ball being flung across the field in the opposite direction it came from, where no one is sitting.

"What the hell?" one of the teenage boys yells.

"Next time, watch where you're playing. She could have gotten fucking hurt." Wills's face is deadly, pointing over to Charlie. "If I see you in the park being careless again, you'll be sorry."

The kids cower back from Wills, who doubles them in size.

I hear one of the kids whisper Wills Taylor, so I'm sure he'll be in the tabloids tomorrow.

He's such a freaking bully. He walks back over, and I'm shaking my head at him.

"So laid back," I tease. "She was fine, and she doesn't even have a mark on her."

"Oh yeah, then why was she crying?"

"Because she's tired and cranky, it's past her nap time."

"Those kids were idiots. I'll kill them if they are reckless near her again," he says as he leans down and takes an already sleeping Charlie from my arms like it's the most natural thing to do.

She opens her eyes to see who picked her up and then closes them when she sees its Wills.

What the hell? I'm shocked again. She usually only wants me when she's tired—not even letting Belle or Jackson near her.

We sit there in silence for a little, letting Wills calm down.

"So, what now?" I ask, unsure how to ask what I want to know. But what are the next steps for us?

I'm lying down now with my head on his thigh, and Charlie's still spread across his chest, so I look up to see him when he answers.

"We can take it as slow as you want, get to know each other again. But I feel like I still know you, and it was just yesterday we were in France."

I know what he means, but it wasn't yesterday.

"Okay, that sounds good." I give in response because I don't know the correct answer. "But Wills, just remember, that little one on your chest is involved now, so if it's not working or you start feeling differently, you let me know, okay? I'd rather my heart break over and over again before anyone breaks hers."

He glances down at his chest, takes in a sleeping Charlie, and kisses the top of her head. Then, while still looking at her, he says, "I will never break her heart. That's a promise I will always keep no matter what happens. So if you believe anything I say today, make it that because I've never meant anything more in my life."

I nod my head, willing the tears to stay at bay. I'm such a crybaby around him, but he makes it hard when he says things like that.

I feel the energy bouncing between the two of us again. It feels so natural but also so surreal to be here with him. I'm happy, like scream it from the rooftop happy right now.

But I would be lying if I said I wasn't a little nervous that this feels too easy. Like no time has ever passed, and I'm scared I'm letting him in again so quickly. We haven't finished today, and I'm already wondering when I will see him again. Back in France, I used to eat, sleep, and breathe Wills, but that kind of intensity got me hurt, and I need to protect my heart. *Or at least try.*

We sit there a while longer, eating dessert and catching up on random things in our life.

"That's a lucky dog I've got there,"

"Huh?" I look down at Buddy.

"He's in my favorite spot."

Shrugging, like I should know what he's talking about. "Your favorite spot?"

"Between your legs, beautiful. It was always my favorite spot."

I close my eyes, knowing full well I'm beet red when I hear him chuckle. Although his dirty words always turned me on, I also can't help to be embarrassed.

Charlie's finally waking up from her nap an hour later, I told him he could lay her down on the blanket, but he refused, only wanting to hold her.

She reaches over for me. Even though it's not the morning, she still wants her cuddle.

"Hello, sweet pea. Did you have a good nap?" I whisper in her ear, and she nods her little head slightly, still drowsy and half sleeping.

While we wait for Charlie to wake up fully, he asks, "I don't want to push it, and I know I said we could take this slow, but I also don't want to leave you two. So would you want to come over? We can order an early dinner and hang out at my place."

"Yes!" Well, I guess she's awake now. Charlie looks up to me for confirmation. "Pwease, Mommy?"

"Can't deny the kid." He smirks at me, knowing he has me trapped.

But I was going to say yes anyway. *I don't want this day to end either.*

It's taking a while to get back to Wills. We had to stop for a potty break, and Charlie's refusing to sit in her stroller so she could walk with Buddy and only finally agreeing to let Wills carry her once we're halfway there.

Not sure if Wills having a dog will suppress her want for one or ramp it up, but we start to volunteer again soon, so hopefully, she will have her fill of all things dog.

We walk hand in hand into Wills's chic building. I missed the feeling of always being touched by Wills. It was always like that, he always wants to have a hand on me or touch me somehow, no matter where we are. Half the time, I'm not even sure he knows he's doing it, it's just second nature.

We quickly stop at the front desk before we head toward the elevator.

"Good afternoon, Mr. Taylor."

"Good afternoon. Can you please add Sadie Peters to my list of approved visitors? She should also have access if I am not home."

"Certainly, sir."

I pass him my identification like a robot, I know when Wills is in, he's all in, but this took me by surprise.

We make it over to the elevator.

"This only goes to my floor and one other floor, the penthouse below mine. The code for my floor is 2414."

I nod, still overwhelmed because this is probably going slow for Wills.

"Put it in your phone, you'll forget."

He's right. I will.

I've always wanted to see Wills's place. He had just moved in right before France and told me how much he loved it, so when the elevator doors open, I can see why.

14

Wills

"Oh my god, this is amazing, Wills," Sadie says as she makes her way over to the floor-to-ceiling windows.

The sun is just starting to go down, giving us a perfect view of the park and part of the city. I've always loved my place, but I was nervous about bringing Sadie here, I value her approval and want her to love it here as much as I do.

"What's that?" She points out toward the park.

"They're setting up London's Winter Wonderland. Every year it's in Hyde Park with ice skating, games, rides, stuff like that. We can bring Charlotte when it opens."

"She would love that, wouldn't you, sweet pea? You want to go on some rides?"

Charlie doesn't answer. She's enamored with the large windows and views, smashing her face right into the window. Every time I look at that little girl, it makes me feel things I don't understand. I think it's because she's Sadie's… she made that sweet little girl.

"Don't touch the glass, Charlie, you're getting your handprints all over the place."

I smile, thinking how I won't have my housekeeper wash them, though, I want the memory of Charlotte here tonight on their first visit.

She loses interest fast and starts to chase Buddy around the apartment, and it's a good thing he still has some puppy energy because she's nonstop.

"Come, let me give you the tour, beautiful." Reaching out my hand to take hers.

"This is all pretty simple since it's a completely open floor plan, living room, dining room, and kitchen."

"It's beautiful, I remember you said your sister designed it, right? She did an amazing job."

Sadie is a fantastic listener and was always genuinely interested in every detail about people's lives and interests. It's one of the things I love about her.

"She did, actually, did you know she also designed **Charlotte's**? She'll be excited to meet the club's namesake."

"She did? Wow, I loved it there. She has a great eye for design."

She does, my sister is very talented at her job.

I pull her toward the long hallway. "The rest is just this way, pretty standard guest room." I open the door to show her, this designed slightly more feminine, for when my sister or mum stay over.

"Library and office."

Her eyes widen in shock.

"Wow, does Declan ever come here? He would love it here." She's looking around at all the books in amazement.

I smile down and kiss her forehead. I love that she has a soft spot for him.

"Well, to be honest, most of these are his. He doesn't have the room at his place right now, and since we do business here sometimes, I let him keep his books here." She nods, still taking it all in, but I drag her along for the rest of the tour.

"This is the gym, then here at the end is my room."

I push open the double-wide doors, and if I thought she was in awe of the library, that's nothing from what her face says now.

My bedroom is at the end of the building, so the whole thing is glass, with both views of the park and the city since it's so high up. Most people are shocked when they see the view from my living room, but this is the money shot.

"Aren't you afraid someone can see in? Especially you, you're so private."

"I can see out, but they can't see in."

"That makes more sense." She walks around, taking it all in.

"I remember you telling me about your place right after you bought it, you didn't do it justice. It's spectacular."

I walk up behind her as she peers out over the park. "Thank you, beautiful," I whisper in her ear. I've been dying to get my lips on her all day.

I spin her around, and she gasps, surprised. Pushing back her long dark hair so I can get a good look at my girl up close—*my girl*, that word is heaven on my lips.

"Hi," she whispers, her eyes hooded.

"I've never wanted something more than those luscious lips in my life."

She licks them in response.

I lean down and press my lips to hers, letting them linger for a second.

"I missed these." I give her another peck. "I've missed this arse," I say while giving her a good squeeze.

She smiles up at me.

"But I've especially just missed you, Sadie." And before I become a total pussy, I go back for another kiss, this time coaxing her mouth open, letting my tongue slide against hers. *Fuck.*

One hand still on her arse, I wrap the other around her back and pull her body tighter against mine. She moans into my mouth as her hands explore my body, pulling my hair, craving me. But she has no idea, I'm like a wild beast ready to attack.

"Wills," she whimpers as I press my thigh between her legs. I can feel the heat radiating off her, and fuck, I need her in my bed *now*.

She rocks back and forth on my leg. "Does that feel good, baby? Did that greedy cunt miss me?"

"Yes, yes," she pants, and I can feel her body tensing. Shit, that was fast, my girl needed it bad.

"Oh, my god," she whispers, "I'm going to come." She's still rocking back and forth, pressing harder and harder into my thigh as I kiss up and down her neck, lingering on her favorite spot.

"Yes, beautiful, come for me, come now, Sadie."

That's when she bears down on my quad, and her orgasm rips through her as she screams my name into my mouth.

She tries to catch her breath as I kiss her all over her face and neck. I missed her smooth, soft skin.

Fuck, I'm going crazy. I feel deprived. How did I not realize how much I missed this girl?

"Well, that was embarrassing," she says, trying to hide her face in my chest.

"Are you crazy? Seeing you let go like that makes me so turned on." I grab her hand and press it against my hard-on, but simultaneously we both freeze when we hear the pitter-patter of little feet coming down the hallway.

"Oh my god, Charlie," Sadie whispers.

"Mommy?" Charlotte says, sounding a little frightened, never being at my house probably has her confused.

Sadie is just standing there, wide eyes, looking a little shocked. I chuckle and pat her arse.

"Go freshen up. I'll take care of her."

"Good idea." She runs into my en suite.

Charlotte finally makes it to my bedroom, and she looks around, still a little scared. "Where's Mommy?" she whispers.

I go to her quickly and pick her up before she gets too upset. "She's in the loo, princess."

She scrunches up her face, just like Sadie does. "Loo?"

I laugh. "The bathroom, we have to teach you a few new words since you live in London now."

She doesn't say anything while she stares at the door that Sadie's behind.

"How about we go put on a movie, and you can lie on the couch with Buddy?"

"Otay!" she squeals, changing her mood right around.

"What do you want to watch?"

"*Wittle Mermaid.*"

Luckily, I have a smart television to buy movies because I would be screwed otherwise. "Okay, you got it."

I put the movie on and then give Charlotte her water cup and a snack. Buddy jumps right on the couch to lie next to her, and I cover them with a blanket.

"Tank you, Wills." Her little voice hits me right in the heart.

"You're welcome, princess."

As I walk away, I see Sadie standing there watching us, and she's wearing my rugby sweatshirt, looking sexy as hell.

"You're good with her, you know?"

I shrug. It always surprises people I'm good with kids.

"Remember in France on the beach when I was going nuts trying to find that lost dog? You were so good with that little girl. I remember thinking it was such a turn-on that this big, muscular broody man had such a soft spot for her."

She meets me in the kitchen, and I pull her into me.

"Oh yeah, do you still think it's a turn-on?"

"A little," she whispers, pressing up on her tippy-toes, trying to kiss me, but she can't reach me until I bend down. She gives me a chaste kiss before she moves away and gives me a cheeky wink over her shoulder.

"Would you want a glass of wine or something else?"

"Wine and water, if you don't mind." She sits down at one of the barstools around my kitchen island, checking her phone. I look around my apartment. A pram, my dog, my girl, and a baby. Why isn't this scaring the shit out of me? Because it should be.

She just came back into my life a few weeks ago, and only days ago did we reconcile. Meanwhile, this life with her seems to be exactly what I want.

"I hope it's okay. I stole your sweatshirt. I didn't plan to be out later, and I was just getting a little cold."

"Take whatever you want. I've always told you what's mine is yours, Sadie."

And fuck, do I mean it. I can hear Declan making fun of me in the back of my head, but I don't care, I'd do anything for this girl. After what she went through, I'd give her the whole fucking world.

Shit, I can't think of that right now. The last couple of nights have been entirely sleepless, lying in bed imagining the attack and the aftermath Sadie went through in France.

How I didn't protect her and left her there, never looking for her. What if Annabelle had left already? She would have been all alone.

I will do everything in my power now to make sure she is protected at all costs—her and Charlotte. Because I know deep down, I will regret what happened at the end of that trip for the rest of my life.

"Hey, where'd you go?"

I shake my head. "Sorry, I remembered something about work that I need to do."

She narrows her eyes, not sure if she should believe me. I want to talk to her more about that night when we are both ready. I have some questions. But tonight is not the time or the place.

We ordered Chinese for dinner, and Charlotte was the star of dinner, telling animated stories and trying but failing to secretly give some of her food to Buddy. I caught Sadie up on how business is going and how we just signed a few new tennis pros. But, most importantly, how Declan and I are in the middle of starting an after-school rugby program for children less fortunate. I can see the pride in her eyes, she has always been a supporter of mine.

When dinner was over, Charlotte begged to watch one more movie at my house, Sadie wanting to say no, but I said yes too quickly. I wasn't ready for them to leave. So that's how we all ended up on my, thankfully, extra-large couch watching *Finding Nemo*.

Charlotte and Buddy are both passed out. So, I take advantage, wanting to know the answer to something I've been thinking about all night.

We are both lying on our sides, her back to my front. I run my nose up and down the side of her neck, watching as the goose bumps slowly appear over her skin. We have a blanket over us, so I run my fingers softly over her stomach, making little circles, letting her squirm underneath my touch.

"I have a question for you, beautiful."

"Yes?" she answers, throaty and turned on from my slight touches.

I know again, this isn't taking it slow, but I ask, "Are you going to let me fuck you soon?" I push my hard-on into her arse.

"God, yes," she whispers.

"So, tell me, when was the last time you had sex?"

Her whole body freezes, and she doesn't have to answer anymore. I can tell by that response it's been a while. When I thought about it earlier, she came within a minute, she was starving for my touch. It may have been three years, but I remember everything about her. Even though I know the answer, I'm not going to let her off that easy.

"So?"

Still no answer.

"This is the last time I'm going to ask, and I want the truth."

"A long time," she whispers.

"What's a long time, Sadie?" I have zero patience for this game.

She turns her head slightly to look at me quickly, closes her eyes, and turns back around.

"The last time I had sex was when the rapist took it from me," she finally spits out.

What? That was three years ago. *Fuck.* Why did I force her to answer that?

I turn her around, so we are face to face, and she has tears in her eyes. *I'm a bastard.*

"You listen to me, Sadie, that's not fucking true. He took, you didn't give. That doesn't count, do you understand me?"

"Yes," she whispers, and I wrap my arms around her so tight.

I wish she could just stay here forever, so I never have to worry about her again.

After a while, I realize something. That means, the last time…

I lean back and smile at her. I can't help the big fucking smile covering my face right now.

"What?" She's looking at me like I'm nuts. Because I am nuts for her, this news needs to be celebrated. If that sweet little girl weren't across the couch, I would have already had Sadie naked and under me.

"So, it seems… I was the last person you had sex with. Three years and this is still mine, all fucking mine." I reach down and run my fingers over her trousers.

"You're such a man!" she groans into my chest, laughing.

I pick Sadie's chin up to look her in the eyes, so she knows I mean what will come out of my mouth next.

"Sadie, you were mine then and mine now. But what that means is you were just always mine. *Always* my beautiful girl. And always will be, do you understand? No one will touch this body besides me ever again."

Her breath hitches, and her eyes go wide at my confession. I will never let this girl go ever again.

"It's time for us to go, it's getting late."

"Just stay here."

But she shakes her head no. "I want to get Charlie more comfortable being here before I have her sleeping over, plus Jackson texted me that he will be at my house early with breakfast."

Shit, Jackson.

"Which reminds me. Please don't say anything to Jackson about us yet. I need to explain to him how I know you, and I need to do it on my own time."

I'm not sure I like the sound of that. Hiding will be challenging, and she knows I don't want to hold back when it comes to her. But I have no choice but to agree for now.

"Come, I'll drive you home."

"We can just get a cab. It's fine."

"Sadie, I said I'll drive you, end of story. It's late, and I don't want you both out there alone."

She looks at me for a second and nods her head. *Like she had a choice.*

Sadie grabs a sleeping Charlotte, keeping her wrapped up tight in my blanket, and I take down her bags and pram, Buddy tags along so I can take him for his bedtime walk.

I like a vintage sports car, but I'm thankful for my G-Wagon right about now with all this shit. We load up the car, and I make our way to Notting Hill.

"Let me know what type of car seat she needs, and I'll have one installed in the car," I say through the rearview mirror. Sadie's still holding a sleeping Charlotte in the back.

"Do you always think of everything?"

"Pretty much." I shrug. What can I say?

"You can just take mine. I don't have a car yet."

"What do you mean, you don't have a car? You need a car, Sadie."

She rolls her eyes at me.

"Don't roll your fucking eyes at me."

"Shh! And stop cursing."

"Oh please, she sleeps like you. She's out like a light." Sadie tries to hold back a smile while she looks down at Charlotte and kisses her cheek.

"Sadie, public transportation is not safe, so unless you're taking cabs everywhere, I don't like the idea of you not having a car."

"Well, I did perfectly fine in New York without one, and they are too expensive. Plus, the tube is fine, don't be a snob."

"New York is different, no one has cars. Here, you have a garage attached to your house!"

"Again, it's not a priority financially right now."

Yeah, we'll see about that. I'm getting her a goddamn car.

"Don't you dare."

Of course, she knows what I'm thinking.

"I know you. Don't you dare get me a car. That's a crazy gift I won't accept. What is it with all the men in my life?" she huffs.

"What does that mean?" *What men?*

"Jackson, he's just as bad as you."

"As he should be, he's your brother. He should take care of you."

"Or wait… I have an idea I can take care of myself. Is that so crazy?"

"I don't care if you think it's crazy or not, Sadie. I will get you a car if I think you will be safer with one and don't fight me on this. You won't win."

"We'll see."

"Yeah, we'll fucking see, Sadie. I didn't protect you once, and I won't let that happen again. So, if this is something I can do to keep you safer, I'm doing it, end of story."

I see her face soften in the mirror and reach to rub up and down my arm.

"Don't do it to yourself, Wills. Don't let it consume you. I told you, it's in the past."

I have no answer.

"Wills, baby. I appreciate you trying to help, but I only have one parking spot at work, and we have a company van for the flowers that takes it up. I won't have time in the mornings to look for another spot. I promise I will take cabs. I won't take the tube."

"I will hire you a driver then."

She huffs and leans back against the seat, knowing I won't back down. I don't care if I'm being overbearing, she'll get over it.

We pull up to Sadie's house, and I unload the car when she brings Charlotte upstairs to her bed.

A few minutes later, Sadie walks downstairs right into my arms and pulls me tight to her.

"Thank you for today, I had the best day. I'm so happy you're in my life again, Wills."

"Me too, beautiful. Me too."

"Give me a kiss goodbye before you leave." She smiles against my lips.

She tries to deepen the kiss, but I step back. I really won't leave if that happens.

"When will I see you again?"

"Well, actually, I forgot to tell you I got my first big gig here in London. I'm doing the florals for a fashion party."

"That's amazing, Sadie. I'm so proud of you." And I am, I'm beyond proud of her. She's finally making it happen.

"Well, I have to attend the after-party, and I need a date. Would you come?"

She looks unsure, like I would let her bring anyone else.

"Of course, when is it?"

"Saturday night. But I think there will be a lot of press there. So, I understand If you don't want to be there."

"I wouldn't miss it, Sadie. And you must be on drugs if you think I'm waiting until Saturday to see you again. Come to my office for lunch Monday. We can go over our schedules and make plans for the rest of the week."

She seems pleased with that.

"Okay." She gives me one more quick peck before I turn around to leave.

Reluctantly.

Sadie

It's Monday morning, and I'm standing in my closet, trying to pick out the perfect outfit for work today. I usually dress for comfort if I'm not seeing clients, but I'm going to Wills's office for the first time, and I want to make a good impression without looking like I tried too hard.

If Charlie sees me this morning, it will be impossible to leave her. So, I'm trying to go as quickly as possible, but I'm not accomplishing anything. Mondays I'm usually out of the house bright and early, our flower shipment comes in before the crack of dawn, but today Marco is taking care of it.

My room looks like a bomb went off. I have clothes everywhere. Wills has seen me dressed in everything under the sun, but today I feel like I have to look good not only for him but for everyone in his office. They will all be looking, wondering who the hell I am, and I want him to be proud.

"Need help?"

"Oh my god, Kathryn. Please!"

She strolls through my room, right through to my closet. Her brown curly hair is piled on her head, still in her morning comfortable clothes. Since I leave so early, she usually doesn't get ready for the day until she's here at the house.

Over the last few weeks, Kathryn has become a friend and not just an employee. I know some people don't do business like that, but I think if everyone's getting their job done, it's essential to have a good relationship with your staff, and if you make a friend in the process, great.

Look at Marco and me, we are already becoming fast friends.

"What do I wear? Do I go for business attire, sexy, comfort? I don't know!"

"Okay, take a breath, sit down and let me look through your clothes." She eyes me a few times as she looks through the disaster.

"What is it?"

"So, this is serious? Because you're freaking out."

"Well, the freak-out isn't really about Wills, it's more of the impression I want to make when I walk through his office. I want to be good enough for Wills, and I want people to see it."

"Sadie, maybe I'm overstepping here since you're my boss and I've just met you not long ago. But seriously? Do you think you're not good enough? You're better than good, you're a freaking rock star. You're an amazing mum, sister, friend, and business owner. You make everyone around you want to do better, with your generosity and do-good attitude."

"Kathryn…"

"Call me Kate." Her giant smile is contagious.

"Kate, thank you so much for your kind words. From someone who doesn't know me all that well, it means more than you know." I lean to give her a quick, thankful hug.

"And to answer your other question, it's always serious with Wills and me, there is no in-between. It's hard for me to explain because you won't get it if you don't know us. But Wills and I are very full on, all the time. Not because I'm like that, I've never been like that, and I'm still not. But Wills, he's like another breed, he's so, I don't know, possessive."

She stays quiet. Maybe I'm not explaining it well.

"We met three years ago, and unfortunately, we ended because of a mistake neither of us can take back, but we are moving forward now. The second we met, we had this instant connection that we both felt all those years ago. And now that he's back in my life, it's like we're right back where we started. Wills is hard to describe, but when he cares about something or someone, there's no turning back—he's all in. He doesn't do relationships, so if he's in, that means something." Not sure how else to explain it.

"You just have to get to know us, to understand," I add, throwing my hands up in frustration. Who the hell can explain our dynamic? Obviously, I can't.

"So, what you're saying is you're soul mates?"

"What? No, that's not what I mean."

"Well, Sadie, you're telling me from the second you met, you both had an unstoppable connection. And today, you still feel the same, after not seeing each other for what, three years? He doesn't do relationships, but the two of you were serious from the start and still feel crazy about each other? Am I getting this right?"

"Well yeah, but…" I've got nothing. Because when she says it like that, it's exactly what we sound like.

"Do you love him?"

I just stare at her with wide eyes. How do I answer this?

"I thought I was falling in love with him all those years ago, yeah."

"But now, how do you feel?"

"That I could quickly fall in love with him all over again." I haven't admitted that to anyone, not Belle, and not even myself. But it's true. *It is so freaking true.*

"Ughh, I can't believe you're falling in love with Wills Taylor!"

I throw my pillow at her, thankful she broke the serious conversation.

"I almost word vomited when I came into the kitchen the other day, and you were all standing there. Would you be freaked out to know I used to have a poster of him in my room when I was a teenager?"

I forget Wills was this famous rugby player everyone loved and adored in England.

"Please, don't ever say that when he's around, I don't need his head getting any bigger."

"You got it, boss, now let's pick out your outfit!"

"Daaaamn." Marco whistles from his chair when I walk into **Sweet Pea Blooms.**

I do a little twirl for him. "You think this is okay for his office?"

"Love, you look freaking amazing. He's going to want to eat you right up."

So, Kathryn and I decided to go for a cool chic look, as she called it. Kate said I don't work in an office building, and I don't need to dress as if I do. So, I went with something trendier but still appropriate.

Channeling my inner New Yorker, I'm mainly wearing all black.

I'm wearing black leather pants, which make my butt look fantastic, knowing Wills will love it. An emerald-green silk camisole that brings out my green eyes, showing just the right amount of daytime cleavage, and a fitted black blazer. Paired with blade suede Prada pumps, diamond studs, and a classic black Chanel purse.

Marco called me yesterday to vent about his on-again, off-again boyfriend, Henry. So I filled him in on all things Wills.

"Okay, can we get right down to business? This week is going to be crazy."

"Now she wants to work." He fake looks at his watch.

"Again, you forget, I'm the boss, and you're the employee."

He ignores me like usual and takes out our planner. After lunch today, I can't skip out on any more work hours, it's going to be crunch time to get everything ready for this Saturday. I don't want one detail unturned.

"What did the event space say about bringing props over early?"

"Depending on the cleanup from their previous event, we can bring it Thursday night or Friday morning, which is good. It will be one less trip on the day of the event. We can even install some of the structures Friday night."

We have a lot to do. We'll be hanging different structures to hold the flowers floating from the tall ceilings in addition to the tall stands and glass vases to bring over. For large-scale events like this, it's easier to make all the arrangements at the event space.

The fashion event will showcase their resort wear launch this December, so we need to be creative and blend both winter and summer into one event.

"Have you double-checked with the event planner that nothing has changed? You know how they can be."

"All good on that front."

I nod my head. So far, so good. Since this is our first big account, we are ahead of schedule, but I'm hoping we will be getting more calls once this event takes place, which reminds me.

"Can you make sure we have enough business cards printed today? I want to make sure we have enough to give out to every single person at the event if we need to."

I walk back to my office to check my emails, and I have an unread text message.

Wills: I can't wait to see you today, beautiful. Salad and grilled chicken wrap okay?
Me: That sounds great, thank you! I can't wait to see you too. I'm so nervous about Saturday, though, so I may be a little stressed.
Wills: You will be incredible on Saturday. I'll say it a million times, I'm so proud of you. But, if you need de-stressing, I know exactly how to help.

Me: You better behave. NOTHING will happen in your office, but nice try.
Wills: Maybe, maybe not. See you later xx

He's insane. After catching up on emails, I send my portfolio to a few potential clients and grab my stuff to head to Wills's office.

As I step out of the shop onto Sloane Street across from Sloane Square, I notice a new black Mercedes parked there with an older gentleman standing alongside the car.

"Ms. Peters?"

"Yes?" He sticks his hand out to shake mine.

"I'm John, and I will be your driver. I'm very pleased to meet you."

"You've got to be kidding me." I practically growl, and John looks taken aback. The poor guy didn't do anything wrong.

"Sorry, John, nothing against you. My boyfriend is just crazy."

Boyfriend, god that sounds so foreign on my tongue.

As I get in the back seat, John just shoots me a polite smile, closing the door behind me.

Wills is in big, big trouble.

15

Sadie

John drives me from my shop in Chelsea toward the city, and it's like my own personal London tour. I haven't gotten out to see the city since I moved here, and after this weekend, I'm making a note to explore London with Charlie.

We pass Buckingham Palace, Big Ben, and St. Paul's Cathedral, trying our best to stay out of the traffic. Then, finally, we head back toward the river Thames, where Wills's office is located between London and Tower Bridge.

"Ms. Peters, we have arrived," John informs as he steps out of the car to open my door.

"Thank you, John. I'm so sorry about earlier, I was just shocked to see you. I promise I'm not usually that rude. And please, call me Sadie."

"Very well, Sadie. Mr. Taylor had already informed me you would be displeased with my services today. So don't worry about it, and I take no offense," he tells me with a warm smile.

I think I'll like John. He reaches into his pocket and passes me two cards—one with Wills's company name on it. **The Taylor Group**

"Just use this at the turnstiles, and then again at the lift. It will bring you straight to the twentieth floor. No need to stop at security. When you arrive at Mr. Taylor's office, the front desk can help you from there."

"Sounds good. I'm assuming you will be driving me back?"

He points to the second card that has a number on it. "Just give me a call when you're done, and I'll make sure I'm out front to pick you up when ready."

"Okay, thank you, John. See you soon."

I swing around and gaze up at the modern building in front of me. So, this is where he works. Trying to ignore the nervous flutters in my stomach, I strut into the building, acting confident.

The glass elevators bring me to the twentieth floor in no time, opening up to a large office space. It's an open floor plan with tons of natural light shining over the dark modern furniture. I walk up to the front desk, and a young, attractive woman eyes me up and down, probably wondering who the hell I am.

"Good afternoon, I'm here to see Wills Taylor, please." She eyes me suspiciously.

"I'm sorry, how did you get onto this floor without security calling me from downstairs?" She doesn't wait for me to answer. "And he doesn't seem to have anything scheduled for this time, Ms…"

"Ms. Peters, and that's because I'm not a meeting. I'm his girlfriend. So, if you can call him and let him know I'm here, that would be great, thanks. Oh, and I got up here with this little thing called a key." I wiggle it in front of her face.

Don't be snarky with me, sweetie. I hate confrontation, but when it comes to Wills, my inner B-I-T-C-H comes out in full force.

"Girlfriend?" Her eyebrows rise, and her voice rises an octave.

"That's what she said, right?" a deep voice answers behind me, and I turn my head to see my friend Declan. A smile slowly covers my face, it's so good to see him again. He places one of his large, tattooed arms around my shoulders and squeezes with affection.

"Come, Slim," he says with a smile, and he takes me through the office, never letting me go.

I can see all the eyes on me as I walk through. Probably wondering who the girl with the leather pants is, with Declan Buckley's arm around her.

We stop at an office and I instantly know it isn't Wills's. It's covered in bookcases, overflowing with books of all genres. This is probably why Declan needs to use Wills's personal library too.

"Sadie, I wanted to apologize."

I can see the remorse shining in his eyes, and I just shake my head back and forth. "No, No, you don't." He grabs my hand and looks so sincere that I stay quiet and let him have this. I sometimes forget I had three years to process what I went through and others didn't.

"Yes, I do. I was so cold toward you the other night. You became my friend, a friend I missed quite a bit after France. I should have given you a chance to explain or to push Wills to find out more."

I know Declan knows my story now. Wills asked if it was okay to share.

"Declan, you couldn't have known what happened, I've tried to tell this to Wills a million times. For all you knew, I really could have been some crazy psycho who up and left." I laugh, trying to lighten the mood.

I see Declan trying to hold back his emotions, he is like me and wears his heart on his sleeve.

"I didn't want you to leave that night by yourself, I knew I should have gone with you. What kind of man lets his best friend's girl leave by herself?"

"A man who did a favor for his other friend, who was hurting."

He's just staring at the floor, so I walk over and wrap my arms around him.

"Declan, for me, forgive yourself because I don't blame you or anyone else. I don't want to relive that night anymore, and I certainly don't want pity. So instead, let's all move forward together and start this new chapter of our friendship, yeah?"

I can see he's struggling, so he doesn't say anything but nods his head in confirmation.

"One thing good did come out of that night, my Charlotte Rose, and I'd love for you to meet her."

"I'd love to, Slim," he says in a sad, gruff voice. I know my ultra-sensitive and caring friend will take a while to get over this, but at least he'll try for me.

"Let's plan a day together. She'll love you, but be prepared for a lot of questions about your tattoos."

That gets a smile out of him, and I give him another hug to let him know I appreciate him trying.

"What the fuck is going on in here?"

"Do you always curse in the workplace? I think Declan should complain to Human Resources." I laugh and give Declan another big squeeze just to piss off Wills.

I hear a growl escape, so I look over my shoulder, and he's shooting Declan a furious glance.

So, I shoot him a venomous look right back. Wills's hand wraps around my stomach and drags me back against his chest. Shit, why does he have to feel so good against me?

Wills reaches down and brushes a lock of my long hair away from my neck, giving him access for a kiss. "Mine."

"I thought we were taking things slow?"

Declan barks out a laugh at the insinuation. Of course, we both know Wills doesn't know the meaning of slow.

"Some things never change. Can you two take this lovefest out of here?" Declan's voice is laced with humor.

We make it to Wills's large corner office. It's decorated differently than his apartment, but I can still see his sister's touch on it. There is a large glass desk in the middle but the rest of the office is done in dark, rich colors. Manly modern is what I'm calling it.

In a nanosecond, he's in front of me, going in for a kiss, and I can't deny how much I've missed this. Wills's lips are soft, sexual pillows.

"I missed you yesterday, beautiful. I quite liked having you and Charlotte at the penthouse on Saturday."

"Oh, please, you and Charlotte both. She wouldn't stop talking about it. I was so nervous when Jackson came over that she would accidentally let it slip."

"Speaking of Jackson, we need a plan." He releases me from his grasp and pulls out a chair for me to take a seat at a round table in the corner of his office.

He has our lunch and water waiting for us, and my stomach growls, remembering I never ate breakfast.

"Jackson will forgive you for keeping this a secret because you're his sister, but it's different for me, we're business partners. We have trust in each other that shouldn't be broken. It wouldn't work otherwise."

That makes sense, I never thought about it, and I hate putting him in this situation.

"I understand, Wills. Give me just a little more time, okay? After the stress of my first event calms down, we will tell him, okay?"

He looks hesitant, but he'll agree.

"Sunday after your event, I have a business trip, when I get home, I want to tell him. No more stalling."

I gulp down some water, peering around his office, trying to think about anything but telling Jackson.

"Sadie, he doesn't know this, but I was going to offer him a job the night of **Charlotte's** opening, and I would still like to, so I don't want to screw up his trust."

"A job? What could he do here at a sports management business?"

"I want to expand again and open a division to help our clients and former athletes learn to invest. When most athletes invest, we're lucky that if our name is attached to something, it will probably succeed. But that can only last for so long. Jackson is the master of investing in restaurants, bars, nightclubs, and he could even excel in more. I would like him to run this division for me."

"Wow, I think he would be great at that."

Wills nods in agreement. I want to get off the Jackson topic, so I do my best to distract him.

"And you know." I lower my voice to a seductive tone. "All this success of yours is a turn-on too, I love a hardworking man."

I pull off my blazer to add to the effect of seduction, I'm complete shit at trying to be sexy. But the way his eyes instantly glaze over, I think I may be doing something right.

"Sadie, don't fucking play with me right now. Otherwise, I'll bend you right over this table, and that's not how I want to have you for the first time again in three and a half years."

I'm torturing myself, as much as him, because reminding me I haven't had him in that long has the temperature of my body turned on to full freaking heat.

These feelings have my mind turned to full-on mush, and I have nothing else to say to him, so I lean down to take a bite of my salad.

I chance a look up through my lashes, and Wills is unable to peel his gaze off me as he palms his cock through his pants.

Why is that so hot?

"My good girl likes what she sees. Do you like watching me touch my cock, beautiful? You always did."

I swallow my food and draw in a sharp breath, he knows I like that. *He knows I love it.*

"Enough," I whisper through my heavy breathing. "We're in your office."

"And I locked the door."

Of course he did, he probably planned this all along. I look back toward the door, could I do something? No, no, I can't.

"Wills..."

But I quickly angle another glance down toward his privates and watch him continue to touch himself over his pants. I throw my head back and groan so loudly, I might as well announce to the office what's going on in here. I pick my head up, and Wills is standing right there in front of me now, the outline of his huge hard-on right there in front of me. I lick my lips, and if I want, I could just reach out... no, god, this man makes me think like a freaking sex-crazed animal.

He slowly unzips his pants, and I watch, captivated by the movements, not stopping him.

"Take it out, beautiful."

I look back toward the door and check.

"Now, Sadie, take it out now."

Fine. I'll do this for him, I'll do anything he asks right about now. I'm so hot for him, I can't turn him down.

I lean toward him and push his pants and briefs down together. I can feel my heart pounding through my chest, and I watch as his large erection springs out right in front of my face.

God, I forgot how big it is.

I look up at him, bite the bottom of my lip, and wait for my next command. I know he loves it when I play submissive.

"Wrap your hand around it, and tug hard. I need it rough, baby."

I do as I'm asked and squeeze him while I jerk him up and down. My other hand reaches to massage his balls as I pump him hard and fast.

"Yes, Sadie. Just like that, baby. That feels so fucking good. I missed your delicate, pretty little hands wrapped around my big cock."

"Did you miss it, baby?" he grits out through his teeth, and he starts to rock his hips, fucking my hand.

"Yes, I missed it so much," I say as I run my thumb over his head and spread the come that's leaking out all over his cock.

"Wills, baby, do you want my mouth around it? I'm so hungry." I bat my eyelashes and play innocent.

"Fuck, Sadie. Yes, be a good girl and wrap those lips around me. I want you to suck so hard you suck the come right out of me."

I used to be so shy in the bedroom, but he taught me how to play in France. After that, I guess I never lost it.

I lean over, open as wide as I can, and take him in my mouth, and I instantly moan around him.

Giving head was never a turn-on, but it's everything with Wills. I can almost come without touching myself.

I continue to jerk the base as my mouth glides up and down his shaft.

I pull back. "Does that feel good, baby?"

"You fucking know it does. You give me the best fucking head ever."

I tease and place small kisses up and down his swollen, angry cock, it's ready to burst.

"In your mouth now, Sadie."

I flatten my tongue and give him one last lick from the bottom to the top of his shaft, twirling it around his head and then sink as far down as I can go, never losing eye contact.

"Motherfucker!" he yells.

My eyes water from the thickness of his cock entering the back of my throat but I continue to suck hard and fast, knowing he's ready to blow.

"Sadie, I'm going to come, baby."

A useless warning, he knows I'm craving this just as much as him.

He palms the back of my head and starts to fuck my mouth, and within a second, hot, salty come shoots in the back of my throat. It's so much I'm barely able to swallow, and some leaks out the side of my mouth as he slowly pulls out.

His hooded eyes bore into me as he leans down and wipes the leaking come from the side of my mouth. He presses his thumb through my parted lips and I suck the wetness right off of him. *Fuck, that's hot.*

"Thank you, beautiful," he whispers against my lips. "That might have been one of the hottest blow jobs you've ever given me."

I'm still so turned on right now, as I watch him walk back over to his side of the table and tuck himself away.

What the hell? And then he smirks and shrugs his shoulders.

"Don't tease me, and maybe next time I'll let you get off too."

I sit there in shock.

"And don't you dare touch yourself," Wills warns, sounding deadly.

But I'm about to freaking kill him first.

"Mr. Taylor, your sister is on line one."

When the voice comes through, I practically jump out of my seat—shit, I forgot where I was.

He reaches over to the phone in the middle of the table to press a button to respond.

Trying to suppress his laugh, he gets out, "Have her hold one minute, please."

"Wills!" My eyes are so wide, they start to tear from not blinking, then I lean all the way over into my lap and put my arms around myself in a protective hug. I'm so freaking embarrassed right now, how will I leave this office?

Wills comes around the table and crouches down in front of me, and he's laughing. He's freaking laughing!

"Sadie, look at me."

I release my arms to sit up and look him in the eyes.

"My office is soundproofed, baby."

WHAT?

"Wills." I want to scream, but also my whole body relaxes in relief. "You think you could have led with that!"

"How well do you know me, Sadie? Do you think I would have ever let that happen if there was even a chance someone could hear us?"

I think for a second, he's right. He's too jealous to share even the sounds of me.

He leans over to answer the phone and places a kiss on my forehead in the process.

"Wills Taylor," he answers as he stands in front of me, stroking my hair.

"I bloody know who you are, idiot. I called you."

"What do you want, Evelyn?"

"Just calling to say hi to my big brother."

I don't know her, but I can hear the smile in her voice.

"And that happens to just be now, at lunchtime?"

"Oh, is it lunchtime? I've been so busy I lost track of time. Am I interrupting something?"

"For fuck's sake, Evelyn, you know you are." She laughs, and it sounds like a warm, playful laugh I would use with Jackson. I remember Wills telling me they are also very close.

"And you're on speakerphone, you fool."

I straight up and pull back my shoulders as if she could see me. Why did he tell her?

"Oh, well shit," she says, seeming embarrassed now.

"Well, this is not how I wanted to introduce you both, but Sadie, Evelyn, Evelyn, Sadie."

"Hi!" we both say at the same time and laugh.

"Sadie, I'm sorry, I was just messing with my brother. I didn't know he would answer on speaker. But it's nice to meet you, I've heard great things about you."

"Don't worry about it, and likewise, Wills speaks very highly of you."

"I doubt that." We both laugh.

"Evelyn, I've seen so many of your projects, and I have to say your work is astounding, but I especially love **Charlotte's**."

"Thank you, Sadie. That means a lot. **Charlotte's** was so fun to design because the guys were so laid back about it, letting me run with my own ideas," she states proudly.

"I can't believe Jackson is your brother, by the way! Do you look alike? Wills never showed me a picture of you."

"Yeah, I guess some people would say we do."

"Ah! So, you are gorgeous then. Because your brother is a smokeshow." I hear Wills grumble.

"Sorry, my sister has no filter, and yes, Ev… she is gorgeous," he says in a warm, loving voice as he looks down at me and kisses me.

Hmm, Ev. He doesn't shorten anyone's name, I wonder why hers. I'll have to ask him later.

I hear Evelyn sigh. "In all seriousness, I can't wait to meet you in person, Sadie. I'm so happy you both found your way back to each other."

Of course, I start to tear up at that, it's so lovely to hear that people are happy for us because I'm so happy. I smile up at my guy, my big, loving, possessive, handsome man.

"Same here, Evelyn, same here."

"Oh Evelyn, aren't you going to that same fashion event I told you about this weekend?"

"Oh yes, I nearly forgot. I can't wait to see your flower designs, Sadie. Wills told me all about it, but I especially can't wait to meet you. This is so exciting, I can't believe I completely forgot."

I love how much he shares with his sister, and that he told her about me again, already.

"I can't wait either, Evelyn. But I'll apologize now in advance if I seem like a lunatic, it's my first event in London, and you know how it goes."

"Just have lots of champagne, and you'll feel fine." She laughs, and I already know I'll like her, a girl after my own heart.

It's interesting because it sounds like Wills and she couldn't be any more different, yet they are still so close.

"Bye, both of you, see you Saturday."

"Bye, Evelyn," we say in unison.

"I have a feeling… I'm going to like your sister."

"I hope so, because besides you and Charlotte, she's my other favorite girl. Not including my mum, obviously."

I love how he always includes Charlie. I think that's why it was so easy for me to jump back into this, most men don't want to take on someone else's kid.

We finish our lunch, and I'm getting ready to leave.

"We didn't even discuss our schedules, that was the whole point of this lunch."

I look at him deadpan. "Really? I wonder why?" I continue.

"Well, I can just tell you quickly, I can't go out this week at all because I have too much to prepare for the event. But you're more than welcome to come by my place any night. I just might have to work some. So let me know."

"Okay, I'll be there tonight."

Of course he will be. Give an inch, take a mile.

"Fine, either come before seven or after eight. I don't want Charlie all worked up around bedtime tonight, she didn't have much sleep this weekend."

"I'll aim for before, but don't tell her in case work gets crazy, I don't want to upset her."

He gets it.

I give him a quick kiss before he walks me back toward the elevator to head back to **Sweet Pea Blooms**.

It's Friday, and tomorrow is my first big event. I feel like I want to throw up everywhere. My nerves are on an all-time high. I thought having Wills around all week would keep me calm until I realized he didn't want to have sex. *What the actual* F *is that all about?*

He came over most nights with Buddy before Charlie's bedtime. Then we both worked way into the night. I was hoping maybe something more would happen between us, you know, for pleasure and relaxation. I needed a natural relaxant, and ever since he mentioned it'd been three years, it's like my body is going into overdrive, wanting more.

Wills is usually a sex fiend, but he never tried once, *not once*, since his office blow job this week. What's that about? He even told me he knew how to destress me, yet—Nothing.

So, I'm a little on edge, because of tomorrow *and* because of Wills.

"Marco?!"

"Yes, love?"

"How the hell are you so calm right now, we need to leave in five minutes to the venue, and where the hell is my brother?"

We needed an extra hand setting up, I was going to hire someone, but both Jackson and Wills volunteered. Jackson has been sniffing around, wondering why I haven't been able to hang out all week, so I thought it was best to go with him.

"I'm about to slip you a Xanax in your tea. You need to breathe and calm down. We have everything under control."

He's right. I close my eyes and breathe. I'm never stressed like this. But I guess I've never had an opportunity like this before, and I need this to go off without a hitch. I need the client to love it, and I need this for Charlie and me. I need to be a good role model—I need her to know I'm strong and will always be able to take care of us.

"Hello?"

"In the back!"

Jackson walks through, coming over to hug and kiss me. He keeps a hold of me, taking a good look at me. "Hey, Sades, you okay?"

"Trying to be. Let's just get everything over to the venue."

And that's what we do for the next few hours, many trips back and forth, lifting and setting up equipment. Prepping as much as we can before the actual installation of flowers tomorrow.

The following day, the flowers are delivered right to the event space, and Marco and I start the installation. There are thousands of flowers to set up, so we've been here since four in the morning. Kathryn has been my savior, with flexible hours. Otherwise, I wouldn't be able to do any of this.

"Talk to me about Henry. Distract me while we work. It will go faster."

"Henry who?"

"Marco, don't be cheeky. What's going on?"

"You've lived in London like a month, and you're throwing around the word *cheeky*?"

"Just testing it out to see how it feels on my tongue." I smile and stick mine out at him.

"There's nothing to tell. One day, he loves me, one day, he hates me. I don't know what to do. When it's good, it's so good. So, is there something wrong with him or me?"

"Marco," I sigh.

"There is nothing wrong with you, babe, unless you're someone completely different at home. There is no way you're the one causing this."

"Did you invite him tonight?" I ask and see him cringe a little in the corner of my eye.

"What is it?"

"Saying this out loud will make it sound so much worse than it already is."

He's silent for a while, and I can't take it.

"Spit it out already."

"I invited him, and he said no. But then he found out it was for this up-and-coming fashion designer, all of a sudden, he wasn't busy anymore." Marco physically deflates after saying this. I know it's killing him because he truly loves Henry.

I'm stuck on what to say because if I tell the truth, it may hurt his feelings. If I don't, I'm not sure I'm being a good friend. So, I go with something neutral.

"Marco, you're a great catch, and you deserve better. However, I don't think Henry is treating you right, and I think you should uninvite him tonight."

"How could I possibly do that now? Plus, you have Wills. I'll be all alone."

"Well, first off, Belle and Lola are coming alone, so they will be your sidekicks. Second, it's time to do better and stick up for yourself. Say I gave his ticket away, and since I'm the boss, you couldn't do anything about it."

"That's a good idea, but this is where it's screwed up, I want him there to support me. Even though I'll know that's not why he's actually there."

"You're right, he's not. You'll be sad, but would you rather someone want you or use you?" I hand him his phone and make him send the text.

I'm glad we still have a shit ton to do, he needs to get his mind off of Henry, and I shoot Annabelle a text.

Me: Hey, you're on Marco duty tonight. Henry's not coming, long story I'll explain later, but he's down about it and needs a friend while I try to get new clients.
Sister soul mate: On it!

Simple and to the point, I love this girl.

A few hours later, and we are done. We freaking did it, and I can't believe it's over—I can't believe we did this. I grab Marco to bring him in for a hug.

"We did it, babe. We freaking pulled it off."

"Sadie, I never doubted us once. It looks amazing. Better than I thought." His eyes are wide, taking in the whole room.

It's November now, which means London is full force with the Christmas decorations, and we were told we needed to come up with a floral theme that suited a party for the Christmas season but could also reflect the warm weather clothing they would be selling. Whatever that means.

But it means that we use the designer as our inspiration, we use Australia! The designer was born and raised in Sydney but moved to London to pursue her fashion career. When it's the holiday season in Sydney, it's the summer, Christmas in warm weather.

So, we brought Sydney to London. Flying in flowers native to Australia, that are red, white, and green. Representing Christmas. Using flowers like the waratah flower and Sturt's desert pea, tropical enough to feel like summer, but color matching Christmas.

I'm not someone who pats myself on the back, but today might be the first because I'm proud of myself, I really am.

Marco and I make our way to the back of the venue to get ready for the party. And, when we are done, it's time to face the music because, at the end of the day, it doesn't matter if I love the flowers, it's if the client does.

I grab Marco's hand, and we strut into the event space to face our judge and jury.

It's showtime.

16

Sadie

A happy client, *check*, four new clients booked, *check*, a successful event, *check*. The client couldn't get over how I brought Australia Christmas to London. Usually, I'm the crybaby, so I was happy she was the one crying happy tears this time.

My dream has come true, and I'm damn proud of myself. It's been so hard over the last few years to imagine how this would eventually come to fruition, but I did it, and I owe it all to Charlie.

When I became a mom, who I wanted to be in life became clear. At first, I thought going on that France trip with Annabelle would be my fresh start, but instead, Charlie was.

She became my reason to live, to succeed, and to conquer. And I did it, I freaking did it—and it's only the beginning.

"This is so impressive, I'm in awe of you," Belle says from beside me. I already have my arm wrapped around her shoulders, so I give her a little squeeze in appreciation.

"You inspired me."

We are standing off to the side, waiting for Wills to get back with our drinks, taking it all in. The fashion show went off without a hitch, and we're now celebrating at the after-party. I was even interviewed for a prominent fashion magazine that wanted all the event details. I can't believe this is freaking real life.

"It is, Sadie. You've wowed a lot of people here tonight." Evelyn says from my other side. I'm glad I forgot she was coming tonight, otherwise, it would have been just another thing to stress about. But meeting Evelyn couldn't have gone any smoother. She is the complete opposite of Wills in the personality department. She's laid back, fun and I think we will get along just great. The one thing they share is their looks, she's stunning, which I wasn't surprised about if she has the same genes as Wills. They both share those big gray eyes, along with long thick eyelashes, which pop her eyes out even more than Wills since she has darker hair like mine.

But what I loved most of all was she never once pitied me. Every single person who has ever heard what happened to me in France has felt sorry, and I'm so over it. I know she knows what happened, and she never once looked at me with those sad eyes everyone else gives me.

"Thank you, Evelyn." I smile up at her. It's been a month, and London has been so kind to me. I've reconnected with Wills, I live near my two other favorite people, and now I've made more friends than I've ever had in New York.

Marco and Lola are headed toward us now.

"Are you all free tomorrow?" I ask, and they all say yes.

"I'd like to take you all to lunch tomorrow to celebrate and thank you for making this all happen."

"It was no trouble, Sadie. It was a pleasure working with you. Better than this one." Lola points to Belle, laughing. Lola's done helping me now that everything's up and running, and she's back full time with Belle, who I heard could sometimes be a little crazy at work.

And it makes me wonder how they work well together, maybe it's a little like our relationship, where opposites attract.

"Evelyn, why don't you join us at lunch?"

"Oh lovely, I would have enjoyed that, but I leave for Dubai tomorrow to visit a client, and of course, I still haven't packed."

"That must be such a glamorous job, jet setting around the world, designing people's homes," Marco says, with a sparkle in his eye.

"It is. I think once I get a little older, I'll stick to one place or only travel on occasion. But, for now, it's definitely fun." Evelyn has become quite a sought-after interior designer at such a young age. Wills showed me her portfolio online, and it's beyond impressive.

"Belle, can you pick somewhere good? You know all the spots."

"Of course, darling."

"And make sure to add a seat for Charlie, she's going to join us if you all don't mind."

"Charlotte's going to join you where?" I turn to see Wills, back with our drinks.

He's been so supportive all night, standing by and letting me take the spotlight, but also never taking a hand off of me, so everyone knows I'm his.

Reporters and photographers have been hounding him since he arrived, and he blows them off every time, saying, "I'm here to support my girlfriend. If you have any questions about the florals, I'm happy to talk." Most walked away, but some took our picture and asked a few questions.

At first, I freaked out, I didn't want Jackson to open up *UK Daily Mail* and see a picture of us.

Wills reminded me Jackson's in New York at one of his best friend's weddings, and he's not worried about tabloids this weekend. *Let's hope*.

"Charlie's celebrating with the grownups tomorrow, I'm taking everyone out to lunch to say thank you."

"Oh, she'll have so much fun out with everyone, prepare to have your ear talked off, though." He laughs, as well as everyone else. They all love my little girl, but she sure loves to be the center of attention when she's comfortable with everyone.

"After this drink, are you ready to head out? I think the party is winding down, and I have an early flight tomorrow." I nod my head and take a look around. Today is a day I'll remember for the rest of my life, the night that jump-started my career.

"Sadie, the venue said we don't have to come back until Monday to collect everything, just FYI." Marco breaks my train of thought.

"Okay, we can check out all the new venues, then collect our things on the way back."

"Sounds like a plan, and with that, I'm going to head out of here. I'm exhausted and need my beauty sleep—see you tomorrow."

Marco is the male version of Belle, there is no beauty sleep needed, he's like a perfectly sculpted Italian man.

"Congrats again, love. Thank you for letting me be a part of this, I had a great time tonight." He kisses both my cheeks.

"It's you I need to thank, I couldn't have done it without you, see you tomorrow."

"I think we should all get out of here and grab cabs before the party officially ends," Lola adds, and we all agree and head out.

"When will you be back from your business trip?" I ask as we drive toward my place. His arm is wrapped over my shoulders, while my head is leaning against his chest, and my legs are draped over his.

"I'm hoping I can come back tomorrow night, just a one-day trip."

"You're trying to acquire a new player?"

"We are trying to save an existing one. I'm not too happy about it, but he's good for business."

"Why wouldn't you be happy about it?" I might not understand the world of sports, but I try to ask as many questions as possible. I want to understand what Wills does and have him talk to me about his day when we are together.

"He signed with **The Taylor Group** when he first started playing, now he's some big shot and thinks he can get a better representation with one of our competitors. Which is a joke since we're the best."

I laugh into his chest. "Of course you are, baby."

"It's the truth. He'll see his mistake if he leaves."

My eyelids are getting heavy, and my eyes start to close just as we are about to pull up to my house. So, I sit up straight to wake myself up.

Wills opens the door and then leans back into the taxi and asks the driver to wait a minute so he can walk me to the door.

"You don't want to stay?" He hasn't slept here yet, but it's the weekend, and I thought maybe he would finally stay over.

"My flight is early, beautiful." He cups my cheek and goes in for a kiss, but I pull back.

"So can't you just leave from here or stop by your place in the morning?" I know I'm being needy, but I want him to stay over tonight. I thought we could finally celebrate in bed, you know—him and me.

"Sadie, baby, I'm sorry. Next time." I turn to walk away. I'm too tired and cranky now.

"Hey, don't walk away from me, Sadie. I'm sorry, I just need to get home tonight. But I'll see you Monday." I nod, and he pulls me back toward him. He cups my one cheek again, and the other hand presses into my lower back to bring me closer to him.

His lips slightly touch mine, and he whispers, "I'm so proud of you, I hope you know that." I just nod again, not wanting my emotions to get the better of me.

He presses his lips to me, steps back, and walks toward the taxi. "Talk to you tomorrow, beautiful girl."

"Bye, Wills."

"Then… Buddy wicked my face!" Charlie throws herself back in the booth, hysterically laughing, after telling her tenth *funny story*.

"Let's just get this kid a dog already," Annabelle whispers.

"Don't you dare, I'm not ready. Plus, Wills brought Buddy over almost every day this past week. We don't need another dog, we are barely settled."

"You guys looked good last night; it was nice being with you both again."

I turn my head to get a good look at her, to see if she means it. It was the first time she's been around us since we reconnected. "Yeah?"

"Yes, you both seemed so happy. It was nice to see. I never doubted Wills's love for you, I just wanted you to take it slow. But I guess that's just not you guys, slow was never your thing."

"Love? He doesn't love me." My voice goes up about three octaves. *Could he? Do I?*

I love him and care for him, of course. But am I *in* love with him? *Stupid question.*

"Oh, don't be daft, Sadie. He is head over heels in love with you, he always has been."

I wiggle back and forth in my seat as the excitement runs through my body. Is this a possibility? He's never said it, but I guess neither have I.

"Oh, he definitely is. You are that man's everything. You should have seen the way he was looking at you yesterday," Marco adds in.

"How does he look at me?"

"Like you are the only one in the room, like you're his world," Lola adds, without looking up while she cuts Charlie's food for her.

"It's a good thing, love, be happy," Marco says.

"Oh, I am, trust me." I smile brightly over at him, and that's how my face stays for the rest of our lunch.

"Excuse me, miss, we are ready for the check," I tell our waitress.

She smiles and pulls out a card from her apron. "The bill has already been paid for," she says and then walks off.

What the hell? I open the card, maybe it's from Jackson? He does things like this all the time.

Sadie,
My beautiful girl, congratulations on your first job as a business owner.

Your drive and determination to be successful in life and business are qualities I respect and love about you. This week, I have woken up every day thinking how proud I am that I get to call you mine. You're accomplishing such big things in life at such a young age, and I can't wait to see what else you have in store for this world.
But, of all the things in life ***you*** *should be most proud of, it's what an amazing mum and role model you are for Charlotte.*
There will be a day when she looks up to you and realizes what a strong, beautiful person you are, and I can't wait to be there to see it.
You deserve infinite happiness in your life, baby.
Congratulations again,
Wills xx

I don't know how I hold back my tears, but I do—Belle doesn't. Marco and Lola are waiting for me to share, so I pass them the card, and Lola's eyes instantly fill with tears.

"Auntie Belle?" Charlie's concerned voice breaks the silence. She crawls over me in the booth to get to Belle, and she snuggles up to her side.

"I'm okay, baby girl, these are happy tears." Charlie scrunches up her face in confusion that someone would cry when they are happy.

"He's a keeper," Marco says after reading the card a second time.

"He really is," I whisper in a dreamy state. *He really is.*

Me, Belle, and Lola decide to walk the hour's trip toward home to work off some lunch calories since we all live in the same direction. Marco lives in Shoreditch, east of where we are, so he jumped in the tube to head home.

Charlie passed out in her stroller two minutes into the walk, and I wish I could join her. Or I wish I told John to pick us up instead of walking, because I'm beat after yesterday.

We're just cutting through Holland Park when I see Henry.

"Oh no…" I say, and my eyes go wide and I quickly try to duck behind Belle.

"Oh, boy, this is not good," Lola adds.

"What the hell are you two talking about?"

"See that guy over there on the bench, sucking face with the other guy?"

"Yeah?" She drags out in question. "Well, that's Henry, Marco's boyfriend."

"Oh, fuck off, come on, really?" Belle yells. "Quiet! I don't want him to see us. Crap, what do we do?"

"This is making me very nervous. I don't like to be in these types of situations," Lola says.

"Who the hell does, Lola?" I whisper. "Should I go over there and call him out?" Belle asks.

"Oh my god, I don't know, should you?" What the hell do we do? Marco is going to be devastated.

"Maybe take a picture first, so we have proof, and he can't deny it," Lola adds, just as she trips and falls over the stroller.

"Oh, for fuck's sake, Lola, you might as well have just screamed his name," Belle says with an eye roll. I love Lola, she is a klutz, but luckily, Henry is too occupied even to notice.

"Okay, I got a bunch of pictures. Now what?" Annabelle asks. How the hell do I know? Should we just walk away and show Marco tomorrow?

"I don't know," I whisper. "Screw it. I'm going over there. I hate cheaters, and I love Marco." Annabelle marches right over there without a care in the world.

"The scary thing is, I don't know if she is just that crazy or if it's the four glasses of champagne talking."

"Shit, Lola. You're right. It's too late now. Come on, let's get closer."

We watch Belle walk right up to the two making out like teenagers, she taps Henry on the shoulder, and he doesn't even move. They are too engrossed in each other, he doesn't even realize. God, this is so bad. She taps harder now.

"What the…" He looks up at a furious Belle. She thrusts her phone in his face. "You're lucky I only poked you in your shoulder, you cheating piece of shit! These are being sent to Marco right now." Henry's face pales, but he quickly regains some of his confidence.

"Who the hell are you? You know nothing about Marco and me. We have an open relationship."

Oh, that creep! They do not, he's lying. I push the stroller to Lola and step toward Belle.

"That's a lie, Henry, and we both know it." He snaps his eyes toward me, and they widen with surprise.

"Sadie, it's not what it looks like."

"Really? Because I just watched you play tonsil hockey with this guy here, not even coming up for air. Not only are you a cheat, but you're a lying piece of crap too. I feel sorry that Marco fell for your lies, but not anymore, my friend, not anymore."

"Come on, Belle, he's not worth our time."

"Wait, Sadie," Henry yells as we walk away.

"Don't utter my name out of your dirty mouth again."

Belle turns, and we high-five and walk away. Now I'm left to think of a plan to tell my good friend his love is a cheat.

"What do you want to watch, sweet pea?" After today and yesterday, I just want to be with my girl, so I'm letting her sleep with me tonight, and we are doing a Sunday movie night in my bed.

"Wittle Mermaid."

"Charlie, that's what we always watch. Should we try another princess movie?"

"No, pwease. Wittle Mermaid."

How can I say no to that cute little face of hers? I lean down and squish her face with both my hands and plant a million kisses on her until she can barely breathe she's laughing so hard.

"You silly, Mommy."

My phone rings, and Wills's face lights up on the phone.

"Wills!" Charlie screams in my ear.

"Hi, baby," I answer.

"Hi, beautiful. How are you?"

"Wills!" Charlie is still yelling in the background, so I place the phone on speaker.

"Wills!" she says again, and I can't help but laugh. She's so excited her little body is vibrating the bed.

"Hi, princess. How are you?"

"I watch Wittle Mermaid."

"Oh yeah, you and Mum are having a movie night?"

"Yes! You come?"

"I'm sorry, Charlotte, I'm working. Next time, okay?"

"Otay." She looks sad, and I place a kiss on her head. The second the movie starts, Wills will be forgotten.

"Wills."

"Yes, beautiful?"

"Thank you so much for that beautiful card you wrote me. I will cherish it forever. I already have it locked away somewhere safe."

"I meant every word. You're a special person, Sadie. I'm so glad you're in my life again."

"You too, Wills. I can't wait to see you."

"I was hoping to get home early to surprise you, but it's not great weather leaving Switzerland, so I won't be home for a few hours. But I'll see you tomorrow."

"Sounds good. I'm going to drop off your blanket and sweatshirt at the front desk tomorrow, I'll be right near your building."

"You can bring it up if you want. You have the code. I'm going to be working from home tomorrow, you can come say hi."

"Okay, sounds good. Have a safe flight. I'll be sleeping but just text me when you land so I know when I wake up, you're safe."

"I will, good night, my beautiful girl."

I wake up the following day, with no text from Wills.

Me: Wills, you didn't text me when you landed. Are you home?

Wills: Yes, baby, sorry. My phone died. I must have fallen asleep before it even turned back on.
Me: Okay, just making sure you're okay. Have a great day xx
Wills: You too, look forward to seeing you later.

Marco and I have been all over this city for meetings, we have so much new exciting stuff ahead, I can't wait. And after a very long morning and afternoon, we just finished our last in-person meeting, which happens to be next door to Wills's penthouse.

"I'm going to just run these up quick, do you want to come up and say hi?"

"No, it's okay. I have to give Alessia a call quickly."

I haven't told Marco about Henry yet. Lola and Marco have also become good friends, so we decided we will meet at Belle's after work and break the news to him together.

I walk into the building foyer and stop at the front desk. "Hi, I'm here to see William Taylor, penthouse 1A, I should be on the approved list, and I hand him over my identification."

"Yes, Ms. Peters. You have preapproval, I don't need to call, you can go right up."

"Thank…" My words get stuck in my throat when I see Victoria walking through the lobby to exit the building. What the actual hell? What is she doing here? I stand there in shock, not sure what to do. Wills knows how much I hate her, why is she here?

"Ms. Peters, is everything alright?"

"Uh, I'm sorry. Can I just leave these here with you? Something came up, and I need to leave immediately." I hand him the bag with Wills's belongings in them and get the hell out of there.

I run away from his building as fast as I can. "Taxi!"

Marco is still on the phone, but whips his head around to see me run past him. I just don't understand what's happening. Why was she there? I just don't understand. Did he get home late last night, or was that a lie? Maybe he wanted her to come over.

"The Savoy Hotel please." I pull Marco down into the taxi with me, and he gives me a questionable look. I can't even talk to him right now.

"Um, Alessia, I'll call you back," he says at the same time I call Belle.

"Hello?" Belle answers her phone.

"Can we come over? I need to talk to you."

"Are you okay, darling? You don't sound yourself."

"I'll explain when I get there. See you soon."

We head to The Savoy, a luxurious hotel Belle is staying at while her flat is being remodeled, which makes me think—why is she not moving in with Trey? They've been together for three years. *Weird.*

I could have moved in with Wills tomorrow, I was so sure. So, freaking sure this was it for us, our happy ending. But now… I don't know.

Belle answers the door in a rush, I push right past her and start pacing back and forth around her room.

"What the hell is going on?"

"Beats me. She's been mute the whole taxi ride."

"I saw Victoria coming out of Wills's building," I cry. "She walked right past me in the lobby!"

"What? Why was she there?" Belle asks.

"If I knew I wouldn't be here right now, would I?" I throw my hands up in frustration.

"Okay, calm down. How do you know Victoria was there to see Wills?"

"Oh, come on, what are the chances in all of London, the woman who ruined us would be coming out of his building?"

I'm screaming now, it's like I'm having an out-of-body experience, and I can't wrap my head around any of this. I need answers, but I also don't want to talk to Wills right now. The door opens to one of the rooms Belle uses as an at-home office.

"Oh hi, are you okay?" Lola asks, looking a bit concerned but also scared.

"I don't know, honestly."

"Okay, let's all sit down and talk over the facts. Have you called Wills?" Belle asks.

"No way. I don't want to even hear his voice right now."

"Okay, so Victoria comes out of Wills's building, and you think what? He's cheating on you?"

"Well, why else is she coming out of there in the middle of the afternoon?"

It's not like I've never been cheated on before.

"Maybe she knows someone else living in the building?" Lola asks.

"I already suggested that, but Sadie thinks it can't be a coincidence," Belle answers.

"I guess, yeah, I can see where you're coming from, Sadie. Like, of all the buildings in all of London."

"Yes! That's what I said. Where is Marco, by the way?"

"He's taking a call." She points over to the room Lola just came out of. Shit, I forgot about our four o'clock call.

"Sadie, there is no way Wills is cheating on you. Like zero percent."

"Annabelle, how would you explain this? And oh my god, this makes so much sense now."

This is why he hasn't slept over… he has another woman. I just moved from New York, and we started a relationship. We never even spoke about exclusivity.

No, that's not right either, Wills is an all-or-nothing kind of guy with me. My mind is going round and round right now, and I'm losing control.

"What makes sense?"

"Why we haven't had sex!"

"You haven't had sex?" Belle blurts out in shock. She knows how Wills and I are. This would be a shock to her as much as to me.

"Maybe he's trying to take things slow," Lola suggests.

"So why did he have me give him a blow job in his office the other day? Doesn't seem very slow to me." I'm getting snippy now, saying things without a filter. I need to take it down a notch.

"Okay. This is getting out of hand. A blowie is different than sex, and you know it. The rest, I don't know what to make of it. But guess what? There's someone who could help us out with that."

Yeah, no kidding. I just don't want to talk to him right now. I don't know how to handle this if my suspicions are correct. I lean back in the chair and close my eyes while taking a deep breath. What are the odds Victoria was visiting someone else in that building? I feel my heart sink in my stomach. I want to believe in Wills, I do, but I have such a terrible feeling.

"Hello, Kathryn? This is Annabelle… Yes, I'm well, thank you. Would you please bring Charlotte over to The Savoy Hotel?… That's fine, let her enjoy the library, and then you can drop her off here. Thank you."

I open my eyes to send a warm smile toward Belle. "Thank you," I mouth.

She puckers her lips and blows me a kiss.

We all stay quiet for a while. Lola is working on her laptop, Belle on her phone, and I'm trying to remain calm. Maybe I am overreacting, but I think I still need a little space from Wills tonight, just in case.

"Oh, god…"

"What is it, darling?"

"What kind of mother am I, introducing Wills so early on? What if he is cheating? Charlie will be heartbroken. This is why they say to wait to introduce kids to your new partners."

Belle looks at me, annoyed. "Oh, don't even go there. You're the best mum I've ever met, besides my own. And he's not freaking cheating on you, Sadie!"

"How can you be so sure?" I yell back at her.

Lola breaks up our yelling. "Okay, enough, you two. Sadie, I hope your assumptions are wrong but imagine that both of you were cheated on, now that would be bad."

"Both of who?" Marco says as he exits the office.

Oh, come on, Lola. I close my eyes in defeat. I have no patience or energy to deal with this right now.

Belle smacks Lola's arm. "Really, Lola?"

“Oops, sorry.” Her face crinkles up in regret. I give her a look, like, now you have to tell him.

Lola explains the whole story to Marco, and his whole body goes slack with defeat. The thing with Marco is, he knows it’s true. Henry is not a good person. His forehead creases and I see the pain in his eyes as they well with tears. I get up to comfort him, and he shakes me off.

“You knew about this all day?”

Shit. “I’m sorry, babe, I thought it was better if we all told you together, so you had a support system.”

He nods his head as he understands.

“What can we do, Marco?”

“Nothing. I knew this would happen. But I just hoped things would change.” He slumps into the chair next to me, and I reach over to link our fingers together.

“Well, how about we all stay here tonight? Charlotte’s on her way here, we will have a slumber party. You know all the girls.” Belle winks over to Marco, which gets a slight grin from him.

“You going to be okay?” I whisper.

“I don’t feel it right now, but I’ll figure it out.”

“And I’ll be there every step of the way. I have the extra bedroom you can stay in if you’re feeling down, okay?”

“Thanks, love,” he says as Belle hands us all a glass of wine—Marco’s filled to the top.

A couple of hours later, my suspicions about Wills may have changed a beat. After talking it over with Marco again, I realized that Wills isn’t Henry. Perhaps seeing Henry yesterday with that other man, then seeing Victoria, while having a past of being cheated on, made me jump to some conclusions that aren’t fair to Wills.

“Hey, do you think you can put Charlie to sleep?”

Belle looks over to me from her spot in her bedroom. “Of course, you’re going to go talk to Wills?”

"Yeah, I think you're right. I need to talk to him before I accuse him."

Her eyes sparkle as her lips tilt up in a playful smirk. "Obviously, I'm right."

I roll my eyes and tell Lola and Marco I'll be back in an hour or two.

I need to sort this out like an adult, then everything will be okay. *I hope.*

17

Wills

"SORRY, MATE, BAD NEWS." Declan comes into my home office, shaking his head, annoyed as he walks over to one of the bookshelves.

"He didn't re-sign with us, did he?"

"He did not, and he went to Acler Management. Those feckers."

"Well, then he can fuck off. I hope he comes back groveling, and we turn him away. That's the problem with young kids now, they have no loyalty." I throw my phone on my desk, annoyed at everything today.

"What's going on?" He eyes my phone as I let out a sigh.

"It's probably nothing—Sadie dropped off something for me earlier, she was supposed to come up but left it at the front desk in a rush. Now she's not answering her phone."

"Ah, I guess you guys are still working through everything."

"What are you talking about? Everything is fine," I snap, not sure what the hell he's trying to insinuate here.

"Chill out. I'm just saying you seem worried. Even though we know now she didn't run three years ago, it's hard to forget."

Shit, he's right. It's exactly what I was thinking earlier. It's going to take some time to kick that feeling.

I change the conversation direction, not in the mood to talk about it right now. "So, what's going on with you lately? When are you going to settle down?"

He continues going through all his books on my shelves, ignoring me. It's the same as he always does, evades the question. I wouldn't ask any of my other mates if they were settling down, or honestly, I'm not sure I care. But Declan is like a brother to me and it worries me that he's lonely at times.

He's never had a girlfriend in all the time I've known him. I mean, I've only had one serious girlfriend, Libby, besides Sadie—but I've dated plenty of women.

Declan barely seems interested. I know he has one-off hookups, but that's it. One-night stands and nothing more. He won't even bring a date to an event or party. And he definitely won't talk about any girls, ever.

The only thing I got out of him years ago, when we were drunk, was that he thought he was in love with a girl who used to visit her granny near his home in Ireland. But that was when they were kids. Since then, he's never mentioned anyone. I was never against a relationship, but I wasn't interested after Libby. He has no excuse.

"Hey, in about a month's time, my parents' annual Christmas gala for cerebral palsy will be taking place. You and Sadie will be attending, right?" Declan's younger sister was diagnosed with cerebral palsy when she was an infant, and Declan is exceptionally close with her. I haven't missed the event since I've known Declan.

"I wouldn't miss it for the world, mate, and why don't we invite Jackson this year? And, I'll have Sadie invite Annabelle."

"Yeah, let's do it. We can all rent a house for the night and you better tell Jackson about Sadie and you soon then. He's going to flip that you've been keeping it a secret this long." Shit, he's going to be fucking pissed. I've wanted to talk to him about it, but I promised Sadie I would wait. I'm just not sure how much longer we can hide this.

My phone vibrates across my desk, and I see it's the front desk.

"Hello, Wills Taylor speaking."

"Hello, Mr. Taylor, I have a Ms. Sadie Peter for you. May I send her up?"

"Yes, please," I told her always to use the code, but I don't even care right now. I'm just happy she's here, and we're okay.

The lift dings. "Hello?" Sadie calls from the foyer as Declan and I make our way out of my office. Buddy already jumped off the couch and is between her legs begging for pets.

She's a sight for sore eyes, let me tell you. I missed her yesterday, not that I would tell anyone but her that, since it's been only a little over twenty-four hours. But I really can't stand to be away from her since she's been back in my life.

"Hi, beautiful, I told you not to call up." I lean down to give her a kiss hello, wanting nothing more than to grab her and pull her into me, to feel her skin pressed against mine. But I'll spare Declan and wait until he leaves.

She kisses me back and gives me a quick smile that doesn't reach her eyes.

"I didn't want to walk into anything, just in case."

What the hell does that mean? Walk into what?

"Hi, lass." Declan leans down to kiss Sadie after me, and her smile is much brighter for him. *What the fuck*?

"Declan, the library is doing an interactive music class incorporating poetry for children this Wednesday at lunchtime, and I thought you could join us. I know you said if you weren't busy during lunch, a weekday would be okay."

Declan opens his calendar to check for, I guess, whatever they are talking about for Wednesday.

"Yeah, Wednesday sounds great. I can't wait to meet Charlie."

"Wednesday, I'm in Manchester for the day," I add.

"You weren't invited," Sadie answers quickly and shrugs her shoulders. I look at Declan, and he seems to agree with Sadie.

"What? Why are you two hanging out, just the two of you?"

"Because we're friends. That's usually what friends do, hang out, right?" Sadie with the smart mouth tonight. Declan raises his eyebrows, a little shocked by Sadie's sharp tone.

"Well, I'm heading home. See you Wednesday, Slim."

The second Declan is on the elevator. I turn to Sadie. "What's going on?"

She walks into the living room without saying a word and sits on the sofa.

"Sadie, spit it out already." She lifts her head, and her green eyes are boring right into me, trying to mask all her emotions.

"I need you to tell me the truth. Was Victoria here today?"

"Victoria?" What is she talking about?

"Yes, Wills. Answer me."

"No, she was not here today or any day in the last three years. Why the hell would she be at my house?"

Sadie's staring at me again, I can tell she's trying to read me.

"What's this about, Sadie?"

She keeps staring for another beat, then says, "I saw her walking out of the building today. What are the odds at the exact moment I'm at your place, Victoria is walking out of your building?"

Oh fuck. She is not going to like the answer to this. I honestly never talk to Victoria anymore since the France incident, with the exception of a handful of times for work. But I know Sadie is not going to understand. *Shit.*

"Okay, I didn't think of this until now, so don't freak out."

"Wills, when someone says, don't freak out, it means I'm going to fucking freak out!"

Oh, for fuck's sake, she's cursing. This is not good.

"She lives in the building," I blurt out. *Smooth, Wills, real smooth.*

"She what?" Sadie yells.

"Stop fucking yelling, Sadie."

"Don't tell me to stop yelling! So, the woman you cheated on me with lives in the same building as you, is what you're telling me?" She looks ready to burst. She. Is. Mad.

"First of all, I never cheated on you."

"Semantics, Wills."

I cut her off before she could add more. "Second of all, I never see her."

"Funny, the first time I come to your apartment. *I* see her."

Well, I guess she has a point there.

"This is worse than cheating, she is going to be here all the time. I hate her!"

Cheating?

"Wait a fucking second. You thought I was cheating on you?" I bellow, and it echoes through the house. Sadie flinches, but I'm angry, and I don't care if I'm being a dick right now. Now it makes sense what she said when she first walked in, *she didn't want to interrupt anything*. "After everything we've been through, Sadie. You thought I was cheating on you?"

I walk into the kitchen to grab a glass of water, I needed to step away for a second. "This is so messed up," I mutter to myself.

"Tell me about it," Sadie says from beside me, who I didn't see walked over. "I'm sorry, Wills, I trust you. I do. I think I just had some flashbacks to that night, of her lips on you, and I freaked out."

Of course she did, if the roles were reversed, I would have killed someone. She wraps her arms around me and buries her head in my chest. I don't even hesitate, my arms wrap around her, and I press her to me. *Where she belongs.*

Sadie whispers something inaudible into my shirt. I pick her chin up with my fingers, and she has a few unshed tears in her eyes. I can't even imagine how she felt today. I know I'm mad she thought I was a cheater, but I get it. I do.

"What's that, baby?"

"I don't want to have to see her, Wills, ever again. And now she's going to be here all the time. Even if she's not here, I'm going to think she's here somewhere in the building or that I'm going to run into her in the lobby."

Again, I get it. But this is my home—I don't want her to feel uncomfortable.

"Look at me, Sadie," I demand, and she tilts her head up, her green eyes meeting mine. I'm immediately captivated by her beauty. Before I speak again, I take a second to look at her and soak her in and that's when it hits me, I love this girl. *Shit, I do, I love this girl.*

I don't know why I'm acting surprised. I'm almost thirty-nine years old, and I've never felt this for a woman in my life. She's it for me, I know it, and I want her to know it. I never want her to have to doubt me again. I push back her hair that's covering part of her face so I can see her fully.

"Don't ever doubt us again, beautiful. We have a bond that can't be broken."

She nods in agreement.

"You had me then, you have me now, and you'll have me forever. Do you understand? No one will ever get between us, I forbid it."

"You forbid it?" She chuckles.

"Yes," I say and give her a strong one-nod confirmation.

She reaches up, places her hand around my neck, and presses down so I can reach her for a kiss. She doesn't deepen it but just presses her lips lightly against mine.

"You had me then, you have me now, and you'll have me forever, Wills," she whispers against my lips and then deepens the kiss. *Then, now, and forever.*

"You're sure you can't stay longer?" I ask her as she's getting ready to leave.

"I wish. I really should get back to the hotel for Charlie."

"What hotel? I thought she was at Annabelle's?"

She rolls her eyes. "The hotel *is* Annabelle's home right now. She's living there for a little. Long story. Oh, hey! What do you want to do for your birthday this coming weekend, birthday boy?"

"You," I deadpan, and she giggles. I know we haven't had sex yet, but I'm losing the battle with my mind, soon it will happen.

"I can't say no to that, but what else? Do you want to go out to dinner, I can set up something with our friends?"

"To be honest, I just want to spend time with you, Charlotte, and Buddy."

Her smile widens when I mention Charlotte.

"As much as I love my daughter, we need some time, just the two of us, Wills."

"Fine, Friday we stay in the four of us. Then Saturday, just the two of us go out. Can you maybe ask Katherine to stay overnight with Charlotte?"

"I can't, she has off, and Belle is going away with Trey."

"Jackson?"

"Yeah, if he can stay home from work. Charlie can stay at Jacksons."

"And then in the morning, we pick her up together and tell him."

"What?" she shrieks. "What are you talking about?"

"It's time, Sadie, we can't hold off any longer. I'm not hiding anymore. So, you have the rest of the week to wrap that pretty little head around the idea, but it's happening. End of story."

"Fine." She huffs. I lean in for a kiss, and she turns her head.

"Aw, baby, are you upset now?"

She narrows her eyes at me and pretends to be mad.

"Give me a kiss goodbye, John's waiting for you downstairs already."

"Fine," she says, still trying to act mad, but I can hear the smile in her voice. I kiss her goodbye, and I can't wait until tomorrow to see her again.

Sadie

Work has been crazy for Wills and me, only seeing each other once since Monday. Unfortunately, Wills had a last-minute business trip, leaving right from Manchester, so I'm excited to see him tonight for his first birthday celebration.

I've been cooking up a storm, and now Charlie and I are decorating his birthday cake. We have Christmas music blasting, dancing around the kitchen together in between overdosing the cake with sprinkles.

I hear my front door open and shut over the music and look at my kitchen clock. It's too early for Wills to be here, maybe his meeting ended early.

We continue dancing, Charlie is shimming her little behind around the kitchen, it's the sweetest thing to watch in her pink tutu.

"*Rocking around the Christmas tree…*" my brother sings into a pretend microphone as he glides *Risky Business* style into the kitchen, looking sharp in his fitted black suit.

"Uncle Jack!" Charlie runs over to him. He picks her up, spins her around, and continues to dance around the kitchen. I look on at them, and it's moments like this when I'm reminded that I'm so much happier here with him in London. I really wasn't strong enough for the move back then, but I'm glad I finally built the strength and courage because Charlie would have missed out on growing up with her family around, it would have only been a disservice to her.

"Look at those moves, Mr. Suave, no wonder why the ladies love you." He laughs, and I kiss him on the cheek hello.

"You look beautiful, angel. Why are you all dressed up?" he asks Charlie.

No, no, no, don't blow it, Charlie.

"It's a party!"

"Charlie, can you try and find Mommy's phone inside? It's missing."

It's not. I need to get her out of here.

"What brought you over tonight?" I ask Jackson, and I instantly hear the accusatory tone in my voice. *Calm down and act cool, Sadie.*

"I'm on the way to work, but wanted to stop over and say hi, I miss you. Why are you guys all dressed up, and is that a birthday cake?"

"I miss you too. You would think I would see more of you now that I'm in London." I ignore his other question and babble on. "We have a busy day tomorrow, but I'll drop Charlie off to you before my dinner if that's okay. She may even be sleeping, so you'll have an easy night."

"Yeah, whatever you want, Sadie, it's no problem. But I have to get to work. I was just stopping by really quick."

"Okay, honey, I'll see you tomorrow."

"Bye, my precious little angel, I'll see you tomorrow."

"Woo-hoo!" she yells in response, and Jackson looks at me.

"She's excited."

"It's her new thing, she says it in response to everything." He smiles back at her and then leaves.

That was close, Wills was right. We need to tell him, but it's not going to be good. It's going to be really freaking bad.

"Come on, Charlie, let's finish Wills's cake and put up some decorations."

Not long after I hear a knock on the door, Buddy comes flying into the house right to Charlie. "Buddy! Mommy wook."

"I see, sweet pea, it's your best friend."

"Woo-hoo!" Well, that's two for the night so far, let's see how many we can get tonight.

Wills walks in closely behind, straight to me, doesn't say a word, and pulls me into him as he leans down and brings our mouths together.

"I missed you this week, Sadie. So much."

I smile against his lips. I missed him too. The two of us are a pair of saps, it's embarrassing.

"Happy birthday, baby." I run my hands up and down his chest. I love feeling his body under my touch. I took off my heels after work, so I barely make it up to his shoulders, he's so tall. I lean in to press my head against his chest and he wraps his arms around me in a tight hug. I really did miss him.

We both look down, and Charlie is wrapped around Wills's leg, so he leans down and picks her up to join us in one big family hug. *Family.* He's not our family, but it feels like he could be. We told each other we'd have each other now and forever, so is it wrong to think of us as a family? I know it's soon, *so soon*. But when have Wills and I ever taken our time with anything?

Charlie tries to wrap her arm around me in a hug like Wills and me, but her arm doesn't reach since she's so tall in Wills's arms.

"What do you say to Wills, Charlie?" She looks at me, confused; we've been practicing all day.

"Happy…"

"Happy birthday! Woo-hoo!" And that's three.

"Thank you, princess."

She wiggles to get down, then takes his hand and pulls him toward the kitchen

"Wook."

"Did you make that cake for me, Charlotte?"

Her mouth and eyes are smiling when she nods her head yes. She was so excited to help today.

"I love it, it's perfect. Thank you."

She leans down to open the cabinet she calls "hers" and pulls out his present, thrusting it into his hands excitedly.

When I told Charlie it was Wills's birthday, his present was all she could talk about. I guess when you're a kid that's really what birthdays are about, lots of cake and presents.

He picks her up again and sits her on the counter, so they are level with each other or at least more than they were before. He takes his time opening his present, and Charlie swings her feet back and forth against the cabinets in anticipation.

I watch his smile widen, reaching far across his face when he sees all her artwork that she made him. "Charlotte, you're a great artist. I'm going to hang them all up in my office."

"I draw them."

"I know, princess, you're very talented. I can't wait to show everyone at work." She's getting so excited that Wills loves her drawings. Her little body is squirming all over the place. I'm afraid she might fall off the counter.

"More," she tells him and points to the bag.

He goes back in and pulls out the real gift. "Oh, princess, I love it," Wills says, then silently stares down at his gift. His eyes slide over to me, and I think they may be slightly glassy. I wouldn't have guessed he would be this emotional over a picture in a frame. I had a photograph of Charlotte and Buddy—lying in his dog bed cuddled up together—printed and put in a nice frame for him.

He picks her up again, and gives her a big hug, then reaches over for me to join them again. He kisses both of our heads and thanks us.

"She also dressed up for you," I whisper in his ear.

He looks down at her tutu. "Look at you, Charlotte, you look beautiful. You and Mummy both." He places her back down, and she does a spin to show off her outfit. *She's too much, this kid.*

"Okay, you two, out of the kitchen, I have to finish dinner," I announce.

An hour later, I'm finally done with dinner, and when I look over at Wills and Charlie, it warms my heart so much.

She's sitting on his lap, and they are both watching rugby. He's explaining how he used to be on that very team that's on television, and he played a position called a kicker. She's so enamored with him. She's hanging on to every word he says.

"Do you want me to bring you to a game one day? Maybe when the weather is a little nicer."

I can't hear her response, but she looks pretty excited. Watching them right now also reminds me of how this might not go so well with Jackson. In the short time Charlie and Wills have known each other, they've grown to have a special relationship.

I'm not sure she's even this close with Jackson, and it's not something I can change. Wills and Charlie just had an insta-bond, as we had insta-lust.

"Alright, dinner's ready, guys."

I made an Italian feast since that's Wills's favorite cuisine, but I think I may have overfed us. We are all stuffed—even Charlie looks like she's in a food coma.

"So, how were your work trips? You never really did say," I ask Wills.

"Well, the one to Manchester wasn't for **The Taylor Group.** I was meeting with some of my old teammates for advice for the foundation that Declan and I are starting. Thank you for inspiring me."

"What could I possibly inspire you to do in rugby?"

"Not in rugby, but your altruist ways. I know I started to tell you a little the other day, but I've decided to open an after-school program for kids who have nowhere to go in the afternoon. It will be rugby focused, but I'm hoping we can make it a full sports program."

This man, he's always surprising me.

"I think that's a wonderful idea, Wills. I'll help in any way I can as well. We stopped by the animal shelter quickly yesterday. I'm feeling guilty that we aren't going as much as we did in New York, but I still haven't found the balance with my new job."

"I think you need to relax and let things fall into place. You've been here not even two months yet. You need to settle in, then things will come easier."

"That makes a lot of sense, thanks." I can't help myself, I'm always go, go, go. But Wills is right, I need to remember I just moved to a different country, and it's okay to take some time.

"Mommy, cake."

Of course, how could I forget? We sing "Happy Birthday" and eat the cake that Charlie and I made, but I see her now in the living room looking through the movies on the television. How does she even know how to use a remote to scan movies? Kids these days are so advanced, or just seem like it with all this technology at their fingertips.

"Sweet pea, it's almost time for bed. No movie tonight." She looks at me, and her eyes fill with tears, and her little bottom lip starts to quiver.

"Pwease, Mommy."

"Charlotte Rose, it's already past your bedtime." I never use her full name unless I'm trying to make a point. This time she doesn't listen because Wills speaks over me.

"How about we change into your pajamas, and you can watch just a little with me? It is my birthday, so I say what goes, right?" he says to Charlie as he looks at me.

I shake my head at him, he spoils her. He can never say no.

"Fine, Wills can change you when I clean up. And only a little bit of a movie. Not the whole thing," I warn.

"Otay, Mommy."

"Yeah, otay, Mummy." Wills smiles at me.

"You need to stop being the yes-man every time she wants something. You'd be in big trouble if it weren't your birthday." He's already walking up the steps with Charlie, totally ignoring me.

I can't hear what they're saying from the kitchen, but I can hear them moving around and lots of sweet giggles coming from my girl. It really does make me so happy that they get on so well.

I look over, and Wills looks exhausted, and I'm right there with him, I can barely keep my eyes open. Charlie passed out five minutes into her movie, and Buddy is sleeping right on Charlie's legs. "Are you going to stay here tonight?"

"Not tonight, beautiful. We will be together tomorrow night."

"So? That's not tonight." I sound whiny, but I don't care. When I was with him years ago, we never spent a night apart. Even if I hung out with Belle, I would always go back to his room.

So, I don't know why it's different now. I have a bed and extra food here for Buddy, and I know it can't be because of Charlie. So, what's the issue? We still haven't had sex since we got back together, and he won't sleep over.

"I know baby, I just have a lot of work to catch up on in the morning, and I want to be able to get it done so we have no interruptions tomorrow night."

Of course, he has an excuse, and I have a feeling he's lying. I don't know why, I just do. I'm not going to start a fight, it's his birthday. But something seems off.

"Fine." We both get up, and he carries Charlie up to her room while I put on Buddy's leash.

"Don't be mad. We will have all night tomorrow." I am mad, but since I can't be a bitch on his birthday, I'll pretend for today. But tomorrow, he's not getting away with shit.

"It's okay, we have tomorrow, you're right." I smile, and he eyes me suspiciously. He knows I'm putting on an act.

"Okay," he draws out. "I'll talk to you tomorrow." He leans down for a goodbye kiss. I don't deepen it, nor does he. *This is weird.*

"Happy birthday, Wills," I say and step back.

"Thank you for everything tonight, and I love my present. Now lock up behind me, and I'm going to stand here until you do it."

Of course he is.

"Yes, sir." His eyebrow rises in amusement after I call him sir. "Don't get any ideas, you. Good night." And I shut the door, of course locking it right away.

I guess we'll see tomorrow if he really will sleep over.

18

Sadie

"PRETTY, MOMMY!" Charlie claps her hands as I try on lingerie.

"I'm going to hell, right? Letting my toddler pick out the color of my lingerie so I can finally get laid is probably not okay," I whisper to Marco and Lola. Lola blushes, and Marco is in another world. He is not doing well… I'm worried for him. I know we have become close in the time we've started to work together, but I still don't know him that well, which makes it harder to help.

I thought maybe this shopping trip *would* help since it's his favorite thing to do. But he seems so down on himself, I feel terrible.

"Parents do a lot worse, and she has no clue what you're doing," Lola says.

"I guess you're right. Which one should I get?" I narrowed it down to two, and I love them both.

Wills doesn't care about lingerie either way, and to be honest, I'm not the most comfortable in it either. But I have to pull out the big guns tonight. I'm not giving him a chance to pull away from me.

"Both," Marco mutters.

"They cost a fortune. I'm not sure that's smart." Lingerie is something you can't skimp on. When Belle and I were teenagers, we thought it would be fun to pretend we were sophisticated women, and we wore these sexy lace corsets under our dresses. It was not a good idea, the lace was so cheap it gave us both a rash that we couldn't stop scratching.

I shake my head, pushing the memory away. It's not a time I want to remember.

"Christmas sales have started. You'll get both the *Agent Provocateur* and the *Fleur Du Mal* practically for the price of one. It's not like you can't use one another time."

I guess he has a point.

"Okay, you sold me. I will have to put one of them on once I get back to the house. Unfortunately, my dress is backless, so I can't wear either of these to dinner."

"What does your dress look like?" Lola asks, curiosity shining in her eyes. She might not know how to dress herself, but she loves to go through Belle's and my closet. I think Belle's right, it's time we give Lola a makeover instead of her living vicariously through our closets.

"Well, I'm wearing a beautiful sequined dress Wills bought me three years ago. I haven't worn it since; it just brought back memories of him. But now I think he would enjoy seeing me in it. It meant something back then, and it was a shame I could never wear it."

"Do you have any pictures?"

"I do, I have some saved on my phone." I have a saved folder of that trip on my phone, I never told Belle, but I would go through them when I was sad and lonely. Of course, Dr. Esposito was unhappy about it, but it comforted me.

"Oh, wow, Sadie, you look gorgeous." Lola can't take her eyes off of me.

"You guys make the perfect couple, you two are perfect specimens," Marco adds dryly.

"Look who's talking, you could have been a model," I tell him, as Lola, and I laugh—he pretends to walk down the catwalk. It's the first thing to bring a smile to his face.

"Mommy, I see." I lean down to show her, but of course, she

doesn't see me. Instead, she points to Wills and smiles up at me. "Wills," she whispers.

"Oh my, he has her under his spell too," Lola says with a smile.

"He sure does. I think she likes him more than me." We all smile down at Charlie, still smiling at Wills in the photo.

"Okay, let's get out of here. I have to feed Charlie, and I want her to see the lights before I have to bring her over to Jackson's."

We did our shopping at Selfridges, a department store on Oxford Street that is lined with fun Christmas decor and lights. She's going to love it.

"Marco, do you want to come over for dinner and a movie? I'm staying in tonight," Lola asks him. It's sweet she is thinking of him. He needs support. Marco has lived in London most of his life, but he went to boarding school with kids from all over the world, and he went to University in Italy, so his friend population here in London is small. It doesn't help that most of his recent friends were Henry's.

"Yeah, let's do it."

I feel better he's not alone tonight.

"Did you enjoy your shopping trip?" John asks us from the front seat.

"I saw wights and Santa." She was so excited, it's a good thing I had the strap buckling in the stroller, or I think she would have fallen out from all her bouncing around.

"Oh yeah, Santa. Are you going to be a good girl so he can bring you lots of presents?"

"Mmmhmm," Charlie responds, lost to the outside, watching as the city goes by through our car window. I'm hoping she'll be asleep in no time. I may or may not have planned it so she would pass out, I was scared she would slip tonight about Wills to Jackson.

"Okay, we will be back in the morning to pick her up," I say as I lay her down in her portable crib, which Jackson bought for his apartment.

"We?"

Oh shit. "I mean, like, Charlie and me, *we* will be back together." *What the hell?* I have no idea what I'm saying, and now Jackson is looking at me funny.

"Okay, I need to go home and change, so I'll be off." He follows close behind me, and I can feel his stare burning the back of my head, so I just keep moving fast out of his place and into the car with John. *A car Jackson thinks is an Uber.*

I finally turn and give a wave goodbye, and he's still glaring at me. Maybe this is a good idea that we are telling him tomorrow because I'd never be able to keep up the facade.

"Let's go, John, I'm already behind."

I hear the front door open as I'm walking down the steps, and I see Wills standing at the bottom of the stairs, dressed all in black. A look I've never seen him in, but he's smoking hot. Black blazer, black turtleneck, black dress pants, and suede black Chelsea boots. It's pretty stylish for Wills, different from his proper suit and button-down he usually wears. He's holding a bouquet of white, pink, and purple sweet pea flowers—sweet *peas.*

I almost melt into a puddle right on the steps.

"Hi, baby," he says in a low gravelly voice that hits me low in the stomach. He's staring at me, and I can't read his reaction. After I put the dress on, I wasn't sure if it would bring back bad memories of that night or not. But I never want to associate that trip with bad memories again. I met Wills on that trip, and I couldn't be more thankful for that.

"Sadie, my beautiful girl." He takes my hand and helps me down the last few steps.

"You look just as perfect as the day I got this dress for you." He leans down for a quick hello kiss, then spins me around so he can get the full view. He stands there staring and shakes his head a little like he's trying to get rid of the image of me in the dress.

"Here, baby. These are for you." He hands me the flowers.

"It's your birthday, I shouldn't be getting flowers," I say as we walk toward the kitchen to put them in water.

"It is, but it's our second first official date," he replies.

Oh, I guess it is. I didn't think of that. It's a good thing we sent Charlie off with Jackson then, we need this alone time.

Speaking of Charlie, I look over at the couch, and Buddy is already lying with his head snuggled up into one of Charlie's blankets. He didn't even say hi to me, he misses Charlie, and it melts my heart.

Wills is staring at me when I turn back. "What is it?" he takes my hand in his and pulls me toward the front door.

"Wills." I laugh. "What are you doing?"

"Bye Buddy, see you later! I need to get out of this house, otherwise, we will never leave," he says as we are already outside.

"Why is John here? I told him to go home for the night."

"I haven't gotten a new driver yet, so I asked him to stay."

"Are you sure that's okay? He's been with me all day, and how will we fit with the car seat?" He points to his car parked in front.

"It's just for tonight. I brought my car for tomorrow since he has off, and he removed the car seat already, it's in the boot." I guess that's okay. I still haven't gotten used to being driven around everywhere.

When we pull up to the restaurant, there are a ton of paparazzi outside, it's not for Wills. He doesn't get hounded anymore unless he's at an event, unlike he did a few years ago, right after he retired.

Someone famous must be here, but just because they don't follow Wills around anymore doesn't mean they won't take this as a chance to get some pictures tonight.

"Sorry, sweetheart." I hear the remorse in his voice, and he doesn't look happy to put me through this. But I hate when he does that. I don't love getting my picture taken. But I can suck it up for a night out with him, he used to deal with this daily.

"Don't call me sweetheart, Wills."

He laughs and cups my face for a kiss. "Sorry, I forgot. Are you okay with still going in, or should we pick somewhere else?"

"No, this is where you picked, I would like to go in. It will be over in a minute."

I take a deep breath and get ready for the camera flashes and all the questions they will throw at us.

John opens the door for Wills, and then Wills comes around to open mine. He takes my hand to help me out of the car but releases it instantly, and I feel a sudden loss. But then he places his arm around my midsection, settling his hand on my hip to keep me close.

This is better. I needed his touch to comfort me. I thought maybe he didn't want to touch in public when the cameras were flashing, but I should have known better.

"Look straight and keep walking," he whispers in my ear.

He pulls me along in a crisp but steady walk, so I don't fall on my heels.

"Wills Taylor, over here!"

"Wills, Sadie—smile!" I'm not surprised they know my name, especially after my floral debut. But it still comes as a slight shock. They never figured out who I was back in France, but now I guess it's all out in the open.

"Wills, Sadie... Wills... Wills... Wills..." For the extremely short walk to the restaurant, it sounds like his name was called over a hundred times.

"Sadie, did you ever find your attacker?"

I freeze. What the hell? Wills turns so fast, you wouldn't even think a body his size could move like that and charges at the paparazzi.

"What did you just say? What the fuck did you just say?" he screams. He has the guy by his neck, almost using his shirt as a noose.

"Wills, baby. Stop, let's go inside." But he can't hear me. Security from the restaurant is walking over now, and luckily John never left, and he's out of the car already running toward Wills. John used to be part of Wills's security team when he needed it, so this comes second nature.

"Inside, now, Wills!" *Whoa, go, John.* "Please escort Mr. Taylor and Ms. Peters into the restaurant," John asks the security guard, but Wills is hesitant. "I will take care of this, Wills. Trust me."

Wills nods and lets go of the man as John switches places with him.

The security guard must be a fan because his face lights up when he sees Wills.

"Yes, sir. This way, Mr. Taylor. I'm sorry about the paparazzi. We can't stop them when they are far enough from the restaurant."

"I understand." His voice is short and clipped.

I smile up to the guard in an apology. But I'm sure he gets it, that was a lot to take in for Wills. He usually only has to worry about himself, but now he has to look out for me too. He interlocks our fingers.

"Are you okay, baby?" I ask.

"I'm so sorry, Sadie. That shouldn't have happened." I can see his emotions written all over his face. He's furious right now, but there is a lot of remorse hidden behind that anger.

After we step into the restaurant, Wills shakes the security guy's hand and thanks him.

"Sadie, let's just stand here a second. I need to cool down before we start dinner."

"How did he know, Wills?" He closes his eyes for a second and rolls his neck.

"I don't know. I'm assuming when they found out your name, they went digging. And if there was a police report, it would be public. It's their job to find out everything. I fucking hate them."

I nod. I get it. I don't like it, but I get it.

"Let's just enjoy tonight, I'm not mad. Okay?" He closes his eyes again for a while.

When he opens them, I can see the pain and torture running through his eyes. He thinks he's letting me down, not protecting me. But he will always be my savior, even in times of duress.

I lean my body flush against his, hoping to calm him and press my lips against his wildly beating heart.

He wants to protect the outsiders, but I want to protect his insides—when they are crumbling down with emotions he can't handle.

He takes a deep breath. "You're stronger than I am, Sadie."

I am strong. Something I wouldn't have agreed with years ago.

I place his hand in mine, and we walk toward the hostess stand. It's time to move on and not give that guy another second of our thoughts.

"Mr. Taylor, we've been expecting you, right this way, please." My calm just turned up a notch when the hostess looks Wills up and down. I'm standing right here. Do people have no shame?

She walks us through the restaurant, and I look around and love the decor. It's so different than what you would typically see in London.

The mood feels romantic and sexy, even with tons of sunflowers everywhere. And I mean everywhere. Some painted, some fresh, some even dead and dried. On the wall ahead of me, there is a glass box filled with cut flowers, with paint dripping down them. Some type of art installation, and it just hit me. The restaurant's name is *Tournesol* which I remember means sunflower in French. Sunflowers will always remind me of our first date, I wonder if he did this on purpose or was it just a coincidence?

"Where are we going?" Most patrons turn their heads to look at us, *or Wills*, as we walk by. I never know if it's because he's a professional athlete or because he just holds a presence in a room.

We bypass the main dining room and walk through the kitchen into a small private room filled with tons of candles, more sunflowers, and even some poppies.

He remembered.

I place my hand over my heart and press it into my chest to settle my emotions. Then, I look up, and Wills has a smile on his face when he sees how tonight has affected me.

"Some memories from France I hope we lose forever, but most I hope live in our hearts for the rest of time." He always knows exactly what to say.

I nod and keep nodding because I can't use my words yet. Wills pulls out my chair when I continue to take it all in.

"You did this for me?" I whisper.

"Everything I do now is for you, Sadie. Don't you know that?"

"Why are you so perfect?" He laughs aloud, a boisterous laugh.

"Sadie, you may be the only person to think that." I don't deny it because he's right, he's not perfect. He's grumpy, demanding, possessive, but he's perfect for me, and that's what matters.

"Ah, look who has made it back to me." I turn my head toward the voice. *Pierre*. It all makes so much sense now with all the sunflowers.

"Pierre. It's so nice to see you." I get up from my seat to greet him. He kisses me twice, and we hug until Wills clears his throat.

"Okay, that's enough of the hugging," he warns. We both ignore him.

"Is this your restaurant?" Pierre looks toward Wills. "He didn't tell you?"

I look between the two of them. What are they talking about?

"We opened this together, it's mine and Pierre's, but I'm a silent partner, so no one knows I'm associated. I was afraid if my name were attached, they would only see that and not appreciate Pierre's talent," Will explains.

He's right, that's precisely what would have happened.

"Wow, congratulations to both of you. It's beautiful. Did Evelyn design this place?"

"She did, it was out of her comfort zone, but she did well, right?"

"It's amazing. The concept of the design and flowers is so unique. Your sister is very talented." Wills gives me an appreciative smile. This would not work if I didn't get along with his sister.

"One more thing, Sadie." I just love how he says my name in his French accent.

Pierre places his hand on my back to guide me toward the table, and I see Wills tense. But I'm sitting back in my seat quick enough for him not to react, although he still has a deadly glare aimed at Pierre that doesn't falter.

What does he think will happen with him sitting right there in front of us?

Pierre opens the menu and places it in my hands. At first, I think he is being polite opening my menu. But then I notice the food items on the menu.

"I change the menu, usually weekly, depending on what I can get in fresh. But these always stay… since the day we opened." He points to the top four that are in their own category.

Wills isn't looking at us, he's embarrassed. I'm not sure I've ever seen this look on him before.

Pierre takes this as his cue to leave, and he says goodbye.

"Wills, baby. Look at me." He turns his head partly, giving me half his face.

"When did you open this restaurant?" It's a simple question, but his answer has so much meaning behind it.

"Two and a half years ago." I feel my eyes go wide, but I try to mask my reaction quickly.

"I guess I wasn't over you after all." He chuckles dryly. I reach for his hand over the table, and I have just one of the biggest smiles on my face.

"Oh, get over yourself, Sadie," he says, but there is humor behind his words.

When Pierre showed me the menu, a small list of items were in bold and separate from the main menu. Listed as "Always a Specialty," those listed were the exact menu from Wills's and my first date.

"You really are a romantic, Wills Taylor."

And he huffs like he's annoyed, I guess I'm messing up his toughness with the truth. So I give him a smug smile and ship the champagne they poured, *the same one from our first date*.

Dinner's over, but we're feeling really good after plenty of wine and champagne. Wills leans over and presents his hand to me like a gentleman, I kindly accept, and he pulls me in close, and we start dancing to the soft music playing. I wonder what the people in front of the restaurant would think if they saw us right now. Wills is beginning to get a little handsy, and I can feel him growing where he's pressed against my stomach. But I'm not letting this slide. I need to ask him.

"Wills?"

"Yeah, baby?" Sometimes I still can't help but smile when he calls me that.

"Ummm." In my head, this seemed a lot easier. He's looking at me, wondering what the hell I'm doing.

"Why haven't we had sex yet?" I spit it out so fast, I'm not even sure it makes sense.

But when he tense's slightly in my arms, I know he hears me, and I'm not sure I want to know the answer if that was his reaction.

I try to pull back from him, but he tugs me back against him and continues to dance.

"It's nothing bad, Sadie. Of course, you won't like it, but it's nothing bad." He sighs in defeat. I'm getting the feeling he doesn't want to tell me.

"If it's nothing bad, then forget it. You don't have to tell me," I say, although I really do want to know.

He shakes his head. "Don't let me win that easy, Sadie." He presses his lips on the top of my head for what seems like a full minute.

"The first reason was, I needed to try and take this slow. I know we had a slipup in the beginning. But I wanted to show you it wasn't all about sex."

"Wills, I never thought that even way back when."

He gives me a tense smile. "But the other reason is why I think you will be mad. I was nervous… I was nervous because I would be the first person since the attack, and I was afraid of hurting you."

I take a deep breath, I'm not mad. But why does everyone keep bringing this up?

"I get it, I do. But please, please, please, can this be the last we bring up the attack? It's making me crazy."

"Okay, beautiful. I'm sorry."

"And, next time, can you please just talk to me? We can work things out together. I was driving myself crazy thinking you didn't want me anymore, or I don't know. But, something was off, and I didn't know what was going on."

"I promise, Sadie. And I promise I still want you. All of you," he says, and he leans down for a passionate kiss. His hand lands on the back of my thigh, and then he trails his fingers up slowly until he hits my behind and squeezes with meaning, then continues to caress me.

"I've missed this almost as much as I've missed you." Giving me another squeeze as he whispers against my lips.

"I'm so sorry, Mr. Taylor!" a young man says, and his eyes go so wide, they look almost comical.

"What do you want?" Wills growls.

"Wills!" I'm going to kill him. This kid looks like a ghost.

"No need to be sorry. Was there something we can help you with?" I try to say in the kindest, most gentle voice I have.

"The chef asked me to bring these to you, treats for your daughter." He passes me a bag with a shaky hand. I see his name Alex embroidered on his jacket when he gets close. He must be a sous chef or a line cook, perhaps.

"Oh, thank you so much, Alex. She will love whatever this is. She eats almost anything. We had such a lovely meal, thank you for everything."

He gives me a quick smile and retreats into the kitchen.

"Do you have to be such a jerk?" I ask so quickly I can barely turn all the way around.

"Yes, I do. What do I always say, Sadie?"

I roll my eyes so far back into my head. "That you don't like your time with me interrupted."

"Correct." He doesn't look remorseful at all.

"Come on. Let's go home and rectify our little problem."

"Sadie." He pretends to be affronted. "You've gotten so brazen in your older years. What has happened to my shy, good girl?"

"Oh, wipe that smirk off your face, and let's go." I can't help but smile right back at him.

Wills tries to pull me over his lap to straddle him when we get in the car, but I won't budge. John is in the front seat, is he nuts?

He pulls me flush against him in an annoyed huff and places a protective arm around me.

My phone starts to vibrate from my purse a million times in a row. *What the?*

We both look down at my phone, and there are about ten messages from Jackson. I can feel Wills stiffen next to me, and my heart drops in my stomach, I don't even read any of them. I call him straight away.

"What's wrong?" I say, panicked when he picks up.

"Nothing, nothing, calm down. Did you read any of my messages? I said it's all good now."

"I didn't, I didn't have service, and I freaked out when I saw your name so many times."

Wills is staring at me. I know he wants to know what's going on.

"It's okay, Sades, take a breath. She woke up a little frightened, she forgot she was sleeping over at my place, but everything is okay. She's okay."

"Are you sure? You know this is the first time I've ever left her overnight."

"Yes, I know. She's fine. I'll see you in the morning." And he hangs up without letting me even say goodbye.

"You've never left Charlotte overnight before?" Wills's worried voice echoes through the car.

"No," I whisper. I know she's okay with Jackson, but now I'm feeling sad, I miss her.

"Are you okay? Is she okay?"

"Yes, she woke up scared because she didn't know she was at Jackson's. She was already sleeping when she got there."

"Did she have her favorite blanket?" I nod a yes.

"And how about her purple elephant?"

Oh god, did I put Ellie with her? No wonder she was freaking out. "I don't remember, Wills!" I'm starting to freak out.

"Okay, let's go get her." Now Wills sounds like he's freaking out. I take a breath—I think we are worse than Charlie. She's sleeping, she's fine.

"No, it's okay. Let's calm down. We need a night alone, just us. I think we are both overreacting a little." I take another deep breath. She's fine, she's with Jackson, and Wills and I need this.

Both of us are quiet for the rest of the trip home. Wills rubs my arm in comfort, placing small kisses on the top of my head.

As we are about to pull up to my house, Wills blurts out, "No... No, I can't do it. John, we need to go pick up Charlotte."

"Oh, thank God!" I cry in relief, who the hell was I trying to kid? I need my baby girl home with me now.

Wills

"Just pull up front, I'll run in and get her," Sadie says. I wish I could go with her, it's late, but Jackson doesn't know about us yet. So, I can't.

"Should we park here so he doesn't see the car?" John asks. This must be something that's a regular occurrence. Of course, Jackson would want to know why Sadie has a driver otherwise.

"It's late and dark. Right in front, I think is okay. I can say you're an Uber."

Sadie runs into Jackson's place and comes back quickly, she called ahead so Charlotte's things would be ready to go.

Charlotte is asleep, with her head pressed against Sadie's shoulder. This kid could sleep through anything. I see Jackson watching Sadie walk to the car to ensure she's okay. When Sadie gets to the car, she opens the door, and the light turns on. I look up and make direct eye contact with Jackson. *Shit.*

"Sadie, in the car now," I say as I step out. Judging by Jackson's face, this will not be good.

"What the fuck is going on here?" Jackson screams, and Sadie's body goes completely stiff. Her back was to him, and she never saw him coming.

19

Wills

"I REPEAT, what the fuck is going on here?" Jackson yells.

"We… we were going to tell you tomorrow," Sadie stutters, and her face falls in horror. She presses a still sleeping Charlotte against her as I move closer to her for comfort.

"We? What do you mean we? There is no fucking *we* between the two of you."

"Stop cursing when your niece is a few feet from you, Jackson!"

"Sadie, you better explain yourself soon, or I'm going to lose my shit. Are you telling me you're dating Wills and the both of you kept it a secret?"

"I have had countless meetings with you, and you lied to my face." He directs himself to me now.

"It wasn't my place, mate. Sadie wanted time to tell you." I've wanted to tell him for weeks now, but I had to respect Sadie's wishes. And I might be pushy as hell but overstepping with her brother isn't something I plan on doing.

"How did you even meet? You barely talked at the opening."

I look over to Sadie, and her face pales to a concerning color. This was the part she was most worried about, disappointing her brother and her brother not approving,

"I've known your sister for three and a half years. We didn't just meet." I keep my answer vague, again it's not my place to tell him. I'm not sure how much Sadie wants to say to him, or how much he already knows about our past.

He looks between the two of us, and confusion crosses his face. All three of us are silent, looking at each other, waiting for the next one to say something.

"Again, how did you meet? And why did you act like you didn't know each other when you met at the club that night?" Jackson asks, his voice skeptical, he's unsure what to make of this. Neither of us speaks up and we continue to be quiet for what feels to be like forever.

I look down at Sadie, she has her head buried against Charlotte. I rub her arm to get her attention, and without speaking, she knows what I'm asking.

She nods her head to give me the go-ahead to tell Jackson.

"I met your sister in France over three years ago. We dated but unfortunately—"

I'm cut off and taken off guard when Jackson swings his fist hard into my face. I moved last minute, so he only hit the side of my mouth, but fuck. Sadie's high-pitched scream echoes through the night, followed by Charlotte's cries.

"Fuck!" I look down and blood is dripping on the ground. I see John moving fast around the car, but I wave him off. This is between Jackson and me. I'll let him get in his one shot to stand up for Sadie, but that's it. John hands me a towel and gets back in the car.

"You fucking piece of shit! It was you… it was fucking you who left my sister alone in the hospital after she was raped. What kind of scum on earth are you? I'm going to fucking kill you with my bare hands. You're lucky my niece is here, and I only hit you because I'm not done with you. You will pay for what you did to her, do you understand?" Jackson bellows, the vein in his forehead bulging and his breath labored.

"Enough!" Sadie interrupts, and Jackson moves closer to her.

"How stupid can you be, Sadie? I thought you were smarter than this. You just let this piece of shit back in your life after everything he put you through? Do you have that little respect for yourself?" he spits out.

"Don't you dare talk to her like that, do you understand? You want to be mad at me, fine, but don't fucking talk down to your sister like that ever again, or we will have bigger problems than you think," I snarl right into his face, keeping my voice down in front of Charlotte.

Jackson pushes me hard in the chest, but he's messing with the wrong guy, I'm twice his size. So, I don't even move. "You touch me again, Jackson, and see what happens. I let you have one free shot. But I will end you if you even lay a fucking pinkie on me, and there is no one here to stop me."

"Enough, both of you!" Sadie sobs, and Charlotte's cries break the moment. I look over and she's reaching out over Sadie's arms. Jackson is still standing right on top of me, so he leans in to take Charlotte from Sadie, but she shakes her head no.

"Wills," she cries. So, I reach over for my princess, and I see a glimpse of Jackson's face. He is fuming. He thinks I took his sister, now his niece.

But I'm too furious to give him any sympathy after how he just spoke to Sadie. If Charlotte weren't here, I wouldn't have let him get away with it. I shoot him a smug smirk, and he turns back to Sadie. *Dick move, but I couldn't help it.*

"I don't understand you, Sadie. I'm so disappointed in you." Jackson shakes his head in disgust.

"Jackson," I say through my clenched jaw. "You can't be that stupid after I just warned you, can you? I will go put Charlotte back in your house, and we will have it out right here on the lawn if you can't cut your shit."

"Go fuck yourself, Wills. I'll do what I want with my sister. You're a nobody. Stop acting like you care when all you did was hurt our family. Don't act like her protector now, when you left her and never cared before."

"Fuck you, Jackson. Your sister is one of the only people I *do care* for, I love your sister, more than life itself, and I always have." I growl, trying not to upset Charlotte, holding her close to me.

Sadie gasps behind me. "You love me?"

I turn to face her, palm her cheek, and look right into those magical green eyes of hers. This girl is my life.

"Of course, I love you, my beautiful girl. I'm sorry this is the first time I'm saying it." I shake my head with annoyance, this isn't how she deserves to be told. I can't believe I'm letting Jackson get to me like this.

"Oh my god, I love you too," Sadie cries, wrapping her arms tightly around both of us, startling Charlotte.

"Mommy," Charlotte's sleepy voice cuts in. She leans over to put her hand on Sadie's cheek, picking the gesture up from me. Charlotte loves to mimic everything I do, and the hand-on-the-cheek thing is particularly Sadie's favorite.

Sadie squeezes me to get my attention. "We both do, Wills. We both love you so much."

"This is a joke, right?" Jackson interrupts our moment.

Sadie vigorously shakes her head. "No, no, no, you will not ruin this moment for me. Let's go, Wills. We will talk to you another time, Jackson." Sadie grabs my free hand and pulls me toward the car. John is already holding the door open for us, giving Sadie a sympathetic look.

I pat him on the back and we all get in the car and look out the window. Jackson didn't stop us from leaving, but he's standing there with his arms crossed, shooting a death stare through the window.

Sadie

The car ride home was silent, even Charlotte didn't make a peep. I sat in Wills's lap so he could hold me tightly against him.

And, even though things didn't go as planned with Jackson, I am the happiest woman in the world right now. I have my baby girl and my love with me—*my family.* I couldn't ask for anything more.

We walk into the house, I let Buddy out in the backyard and try to clean up Wills's lip, but Charlie won't let him put her down. I figured she would have fallen back to sleep in the car but, I think she was a little frightened from the fighting. It was not my finest parenting moment, but at least she was sleeping for most of it and didn't see Jackson hit Wills.

"It's fine, Sadie. It's a small scrape. I'll wash up after I put her to sleep. I've had way worse things happen playing rugby." *After he puts her to sleep*, he says. I know Wills is a doer, but it still surprises me how he just jumped into the caretaker role for both of us.

"Okay, meet me in my room after she falls asleep," I whisper seductively in his ear. He looks down and flashes a smirk, and practically runs Charlie upstairs.

I can't wait to celebrate our love together, so I lock up and run upstairs behind them to get ready in my room.

I light some candles, turn on some soft music that Charlie won't hear from her room, and then decide on my lingerie. After going back and forth, I finally picked the black set I bought with the floral lace motif. It's a two-piece lace bra and garter, with cheeky bottoms, that has an opening slit. So, if he wanted, he could leave them on the whole time—beautiful yet super sexy.

I freshen up in the bathroom and then fix my hair and makeup. I look myself over in the mirror for a minute and realize this is the first time I've ever worn lingerie for a guy. What a prude I've been. Wills really does bring out my inner minx.

I know Wills doesn't care about all the fuss I'm putting into my appearance, but I want everything to be perfect tonight, even after the show Jackson put on.

I need us to both forget about it right now. I know hell will rain down tomorrow, but tonight I will put it behind me, and I hope Wills does too.

I slowly open the door after I'm done, but Wills is not back yet. What do I do now? I envisioned walking out of the bathroom and him seeing me. Now, I feel awkward and nervous.

I turn the baby monitor on before I forget, and I can see Wills reading Charlie a story, then stop midsentence. She must have fallen asleep. He leans down, kisses her forehead, and tells her he loves her. My heart nearly explodes, I wonder if he always tells her that when he puts her to sleep or if tonight's the first night.

Still standing awkwardly, I finally decide to wait for him on the bed. I prop myself up on a few pillows, cross my legs, one slightly bent so he can get a good view as he walks in. I take a few calming breaths. I'm more than ready for him now, but I'm nervous.

It's been almost three and a half years since I had sex, but I'm more nervous because tonight feels different for us. We hit another milestone in our relationship and I'm happy we waited now. It feels so much more intimate and memorable this way.

The door slowly opens and when Wills finds me on the bed, his eyes instantly darken. He hesitates, but then slowly walks over to the bed without saying a word as he takes off his shirt. My body tingles with anticipation, and the ache for him gets stronger and stronger as he steps closer. He traces one finger up my leg, along my rib cage, up and over my arm, leaving a trail of goose bumps in his wake.

Wills is still silent, but his eyes tell me he wants this just as I do. I lie there as still as I can and won't move until he instructs me on what to do. There is something extremely sexy about waiting for his instructions.

His hand leaves my body, and I feel a sudden loss as he walks back over to the end of the bed, still inspecting every part of me. I'm trying to be patient and contain my excitement for what comes next.

He leans down in front of me, places his hands on my thighs and aggressively spreads my legs wide. A loud moan slips through my lips, just from his touch on my skin.

"Did you buy this outfit for me, my beautiful girl?"

"Uh-huh, I did. Do you like it?" I ask shyly. But he doesn't answer.

He continues staring at me through the opening of my panties, looking lost in thought. My baby is ready. I look down. Yeah, he definitely is.

Why is he torturing us? Doesn't he know how much I need him right now, how much I always need him?

He reaches over and spreads the opening of my panties wider and traces his finger up and down through my center. I close my eyes in pleasure, just this one touch feels, ugh. I'm good to go.

"So fucking sexy," he whispers to himself. "My sexy Sadie."

He leans in. "Mine," he growls, then licks through my sex in one slow motion.

"Tell me, Sadie," he growls again.

"Yours, Wills. It was always yours." He nods his head, then steps away, not looking back, and closes the bathroom door behind him. *What the hell?*

I hear the faucet turn on. What is he doing in there? I didn't even notice if he was still bleeding or not.

I lie there, my body is on fire with anticipation and knowing Wills, he did this on purpose. He likes to get me all worked up. Delayed gratification. For someone so sexually charged, he was always so good at prolonging the inevitable.

If I were more daring, I would reach down right now and take care of the ache between my legs myself. But I won't.

I do throw my head back in frustration and rub my thighs together to ease some of the tension building. I can hear the wetness below when I move my legs back and forth. God, he makes me so hot. Wills has been the only person to get me like this. I'm going crazy.

"Stop," Wills growls. I didn't even hear him step out of the bathroom. But I obey, and instantly stop moving my legs while opening my eyes.

Wills is now standing at the end of the bed, completely naked. We give each other the once-over, I missed his hot freaking body and his long thick erection that's pressed up against his stomach.

"Get off the bed, Sadie," he says in a dark, gravelly tone that shoots straight through my body. I get up and walk slowly over to him, taking in his exposed, perfect muscular chest, wondering what he has in store for us.

He prowls around me a few times, again with no words, and eventually stops behind me. He gets down on his knees and places small kisses along my back as he caresses my behind. His lips press and cover over my right cheek, then he bites down hard, then bites the other.

"Ah."

He bites again. *Oh.* The initial pain subsides, and I feel a rush of cream below.

He licks over where he most definitely left a mark and kisses it lightly, soothing the pain he inflicted.

"Mine."

"Yours."

"All of you, Sadie?"

"Yes, of course, always."

"Even this?" he says as he spreads my cheeks apart and licks along my tightness.

I tense and try to pull away. He's never done that before, and I don't know how I feel about it, it's too much, too intimate.

"No Wills, not that," I whisper. He is so big, he will never fit. It can't happen.

"So, you lied to me? You said I had all of you," he asks.

"Not that, Wills."

"One day?"

"Maybe, one day?" I don't know. He has always asked for my butt, but I just don't know.

He slowly stands up, tracing his hands up my body, unlatches my bra, and then spins me around.

Wills reaches down and rubs his hands along the curves of my breasts, cupping both in his large muscular hands.

It hits me now. He's reacquainting himself with my body. I reach to do the same, and he swats my hand away. "No."

He continues his exploration, then leans down, twirls his tongue around my nipple, and bites down. My eyes close as he goes to the other side. "God, that feels so good, Wills." But I need more, and that's when he stops. I huff, and he laughs as he straightens and walks toward the bed, leaving me in my spot. He knows I won't move until I'm told what to do, I'm not sure if this is normal, being obedient with your partner like this. But, for some reason, in the bedroom, we both love it, so I don't care if it's normal or not—it's normal for us.

Wills looks straight into my eyes as he starts to stroke himself. Once, twice, three times, and a growl slips through my lips in frustration. He smirks, that cocky bastard. "You always did love watching me touch my cock, beautiful. Now walk toward me slowly so I can take in the view that's mine." He continues to jerk himself, his strokes getting harder as I walk closer.

"Stop," he says right before I make it to him. Far enough away, he can reach me, but I can't reach him. *Damnit.*

"Good girl, Sadie. Do you want me to reward you for your good listening?"

"Yes, please," I breathe out as his fingers reach forward to touch me. He glides two fingers down my clavicle, over my stomach, and into my panties, right through the opening. He pushes me apart slightly and rubs his fingers through my flesh. He's been working me up this whole time with his touches, I'm ready to freaking go.

He continues to rub his fingers up and down, focusing a few seconds each time on my clit. "I'm going to come soon," I say as he impales me with two fingers stretching me out. It's tight, but he fills me up so well. "Oh, Wills! This feels too good."

He continues to pump me full of his fingers, then changes to a come-hither motion, hitting my G-spot perfectly. *Shit.* My eyes roll back, I'm about to collapse on the floor.

"Come here," he says as he presses forward, using the fingers still inside of me to pull me toward him. My eyes are wide with pleasure, then shock as he picks me up, spins me around, and puts me on the bed under him.

"I need to taste you, baby. I need you to come on my tongue. I want you to experience all the pleasure I can give you," he says. Head deep already in my privates. It's about freaking time.

His fingers enter me again, slowly adding a third, I feel a slight burn, but it's easily forgotten when he swipes through my center.

His tongue licks with long deep strokes, starting at my behind again, up to my clit. Why is that feeling so good?

"Feels good, right, baby?" I whimper in response. "You're so fucking hot, Sadie, shit I can't get enough." He delves back in. The tip of his tongue swirls around my clit, while switching back and forth with powerful suction, lapping me up like I'm his last meal.

"You taste better than anything that has touched my lips. I'll be eating this pussy for the rest of my life," he says while keeping his lips against me, and the vibration of his voice sets me off.

"I'm going to come, Wills!" My head thrashes side to side, I arch my back, and my legs go straight out, shaking uncontrollably as the orgasm rips through me like a tornado. *Shit.* This man always makes me feel so good, this is heaven.

Wills crawls up over me and places a kiss on my lips, giving me a second to regain some strength. Then he pulls back slightly to speak against my lips.

"Sadie. I want to be gentle, but I'm losing my mind, beautiful. So, I'm going to fuck you, then love you. You good with that, baby?"

"Yes, yes, yes. I'm so good with that. Please, Wills, I need you." I'm desperate, I already need him inside me.

"Turn over, Sadie. On your knees and elbows." His voice drops down. I know that voice. I'm in for it now.

I flip over, and he slaps my ass hard. I look over my shoulder with a wide grin, and he's stroking himself again while his eyes are fixated on my ass. He runs his fingers down and inserts two, then three.

"I need to stretch you out more, baby. Otherwise, I'm going to hurt you." He pumps hard and tries to add a fourth. I tense. "Easy, relax, Sadie. Let me in." He kisses the back of my neck, his body pressed against me. That's what I need. I need to feel his body pressed against me and for his heat to radiate through my body. I need it all.

"I'm ready, let's go," I whine. He slaps my ass again.

"You're ready when I say you're ready." But he pulls his fingers out and reaches for a condom, but I shake my head.

"I'm on the pill now, we don't need that."

His grin is evil, I knew he would like that.

And in an instant, I can feel the head of his cock against my entrance. His hands move to my waist, and he pushes in. I scrunch up my eyes and press my head into the pillow. Shit, he's so big.

"Sadie, you're still too tight," he hisses, in pleasure, pain—who knows.

He moves in and out halfway, loosening me up. Then, he reaches around and rubs my clit to relax me, which does the job because he pushes and slides right in.

"Just give me a second, I whisper." I can hear him trying to control his breathing, we've been waiting three and half years for this. We're both good to go.

The pain turns to pleasure as he slowly rocks in and out, trying to open me up more, but I'm open, and I need more. I look behind me. "Wills?"

"Yes?"

"Give it to me, baby. I'm nice and open for you." He doesn't need to be told twice, he pulls out and slams into me, and I scream out loud.

"Shit, Sadie, is this a good idea? You're too tight to fuck. I'll go slow." He breathes.

"You better move and move hard, or I'll kill you." He chuckles and thrusts deep.

"Fuck. Having my bare cock in your tight cunt…" He can't finish his thought. He's breathing so fast as he leans over and kisses me hard against my throat. He moves his hands to my shoulders for a better hold, and he continuously slams into me over and over again. The headboard is slamming against the wall, surely making a dent, but who the hell cares?

I can already feel pleasure radiating through my body… how does he make me feel so good, so fast?

Wills leans back up, moves both hands to my ass cheeks, and lifts one of his legs, placing his foot on the bed. Shit, this position has him so deep, he feels like he's going to bust right through my body.

He's in his own world, thrusting over and over lost to his own pleasure. He swivels his hips in a way a man his size shouldn't be able to move, and he hits that spot, that all too good feeling of a spot, and I cry out in pleasure. I lean my head back, he grabs my hair and pulls it hard.

I forgot how much I freaking loved that. He hasn't stopped his thrusts. He's going to make me come any second, and I know he's close, he can barely catch his breath. His thumb moves over my behind. I barely register him pressing it against the forbidden spot at first, then I try to pull away a little, but he has my hair in a viselike grip and I'm stuck.

"Please, baby, just some pressure. You'll love it," he pants.

I hate to admit it, but I already don't mind it.

"Fine," I cry while he applies more pressure at the same time hitting my G-spot, and oh my god, that does feel good. Why does that feel so good?

I can feel myself clenching around Wills, and he hisses, trying to hold back his release. He knows I'm there and ready, so he slams into me one more time, at the same time he pushes his thumb inside and I scream out in ecstasy as one of the most powerful orgasms rips through me. Wills picks up his already unforgiving pace and comes right alongside me.

He drops down and lies across my back, both of us sweaty and hot. We are sticking together, but I wouldn't have it any other way.

"That was so fucking perfect, the best birthday sex ever. I could die a happy man right now."

"Please don't." I giggle. I feel the same freaking way.

After a few minutes, he rolls so I can breathe, and we both face each other. What is he thinking right now as he stares so deep into my eyes?

This is a different man than a few minutes ago, my romantic Wills is back. I smile to myself, thinking how he switches it on and off so easily.

"Why are you smiling, baby?"

"I'm just so incredibly happy, Wills." I rub my hands through his hair, over his shoulders and chest. It's the first time touching his naked body, I missed this connection between us.

"I love you, Wills," I whisper and kiss him softly. He pulls back with one hand on my cheek, and the other is stroking my hair away from my face. He's staring longingly at me, and his thumb caresses the apple of my cheek lightly. I have a stupid grin on my face, I can feel it.

"I love you too, my beautiful girl." He hesitates to say something else.

"What is it?" I ask.

He frowns, and his eyebrows scrunch together, but not in sadness. Wills is embarrassed. My baby gets so vulnerable when he thinks deep. He lifts his head, and his eyes search mine.

"You're the only one to have ever touched my heart, Sadie Marie Peters, and the only one who ever will. Something has been missing the last few years, and I know deep down it was you, and even though I didn't know Charlotte existed, it was her too. Both of you are such an important part of my life, I could never live a day without either of you, again."

I hold back my tears, lean forward and press my lips to his. "*Then, now, and forever*," I whisper against his mouth. Our lips stay pressed as one, then slowly, in tandem, our mouths open and our tongues collide.

One of Wills's hands stays pressed between the pillow and my cheek, and the other moves to the back of my head to manipulate how he wants me and pushes our mouth even closer together, fusing us as one, making love to my mouth. His tongue entangles with mine with slow, deep movements. Wills groans as he removes his hand and lets it slowly slide down my body, over my ass, and down the back of my thigh. He lifts my leg high to wrap around his waist, and he arranges his erection and slowly slides in, and we both moan with pleasure.

His hand returns to my behind, and his forearm is pressed into my thigh to keep me in place as he moves with a slow but forceful pace. He's moving his hips, so his body grinds into me, giving me penetration and friction.

I feel the flutters in my stomach building, and if it were anyone but Wills, I would never believe I could have three orgasms back to back, but I've learned anything is possible in bed with him.

We pull back from a kiss, our faces still so close that I can feel his breath on me. His gorgeous face is radiating with so much happiness and love, I hope he sees the same in mine.

My hips start to move in sync with his slow thrusts, our mouths are open wide in awe.

"How do you feel, beautiful," Wills croaks.

"So good," I cry.

He starts to pick up the pace, and now the friction rubbing between my legs is too much, I'm not going to make it much longer. I press my heel into his back, so Wills keeps up with that rhythm as a warm sensation spreads through me, and another orgasm hits hard. "Oh god, Wills. I love you," I scream into his mouth, and I can feel my muscles contracting hard around his shaft.

He picks up his pace, not able to hold back anymore as he moans my name and pumps me hard a few times, then releases and comes inside of me, yelling, "Fuuuuck."

He deflates and presses his head into the crook of my neck as I rub my hand up and down his back. I can feel as his come drips out of me, and I have no strength to care, and a sick part of me loves it.

"That's the first time we've ever made love together," I whisper. He picks up his head and looks offended.

"I hope you know, even when we fuck, I'm always loving you, Sadie. As long as our bodies are one, we are making love." He kisses my lips and then buries his head back into my neck.

Why is it that this man always knows exactly what to say? If it's possible, I love him even more than I did before.

My leg is still wrapped around him, and we are pressed tightly together. I don't want to let him go tonight, feeling extra needy after our lovemaking. So, we don't move, and eventually, Wills's breathing evens out. I lean over, kiss his forehead, and close my eyes.

Good night, baby, happy birthday.

20

Wills

“MOMMY!” Charlie screams through the baby monitor, and we both sit up in a rush, hitting our heads together.

“Ow, Jesus, that hurt,” Sadie cries.

I rub my head. *Shit*. “Sorry, baby.”

She grumbles something incoherent in response—it’s too early for my girl.

“Mommy!” she screams again. We can see her on the monitor, nothing’s wrong. What could cause this kid to be yelling so early?

Sadie gets up and groans. “Ugh, gross,” she says as she puts on her robe. I look down, we are both drenched, covered in perspiration. We slept holding each other all night, never moving.

I watch Sadie through the baby monitor. “What is it, Charlie? It’s very early.” Charlotte’s eyes are as big as a little girl can make them, in shock.

“Wook!” She points to Buddy, who must have snuck into her tiny bed last night.

I smile at my princess. This makes sense, now. It’s like Christmas morning for Charlotte. Waking up with Buddy in her bed is probably one of the best days ever.

Sadie is also smiling, thinking the same thing as me, I'm sure of it. I see her glance at the clock in Charlotte's room, and then I glance at the one here. Shit, it's only five in the morning, we have only slept for three hours.

"Charlie, it's very early, sweet pea. Do you see how Buddy is still sleepy?" She nods her head. "Well, if you want to sleep with Buddy another night, we have to go back to sleep. He needs to be nice and rested. Otherwise, he won't want to sleep with you again." Her eyes widen in horror, and she plops her little body back into bed so fast. I laugh out loud—the horror of not sleeping with Buddy.

"Otay Mommy, night, night." Now, Sadie laughs, walks over, and leans down to kiss Charlotte, and *fuck*, I feel my cock instantly harden. Sadie's robe rides up in the back, and her arse and pussy are on full display. She lingers there for a second. If only she knew what I was looking at right now. I lightly stroke myself—I can watch this all day. *Come on, baby, move a little.*

I must be a sick fuck. Charlotte is right there.

Maybe we should try some video play where she puts on a show because watching Sadie right now is turning me on like next-level shit.

She walks back into the room, and her eyes widen when she sees I'm fully awake and ready to go.

"Not happening," she deadpans and heads for the bathroom. *That's what she thinks.*

I know she's tired, but I can make her feel so good. Who wouldn't want that?

I lean against the bathroom door and watch through the mirror as she brushes her teeth. Her long brown hair is wild, her makeup she forgot to remove smudged around her eyes, yet she still is the most beautiful woman in the world. I can stand here all day and watch her. She leans over to rinse her mouth, and her nipple slips out of her robe. I can't help myself, I walk over behind her to wrap my arm around her and cup her breast in my hand and tweak her nipple. I slowly rub it back and forth between my thumb and index finger. Her mouth is ajar as she turns her head and drops her eyes down my body. She can try to fake it all she wants, but she can't hide the shiver of excitement I see pass through her body.

"It's too early," she whispers, heavy with arousal. I cup her cheek and dip my tongue through her swollen lips. She urges my tongue to move faster, and I know I have her now.

"Are you sore?" I ask as I run my hand down her body, through her sex, not surprised I find her sopping wet.

She smirks. "A good sore, a really good sore," I growl and bite her neck; she whimpers in response. She's going to drive me insane if I don't get inside her soon. This need to be inside her at all times is fucking consuming.

"Good, the only way this isn't happening is if you are too sore," I say as I plunge two fingers inside, and her loud moan of approval echoes through the bathroom. Her juices, combined with my come still inside her, make it easy for my fingers to slide in and out with no problem.

Her head is pressed against my chest, and her body is weighing down on my fingers. She can barely stand—*and she didn't want this to happen.* I pull my fingers out and slip them up and over her swollen clit once and listen to her breath catch. I bring them up to my nose, without losing eye contact through the mirror, I inhale deeply. "Your scent is fucking intoxicating, Sadie. Especially mixed with me." Goose bumps scatter over her body, my beautiful, good girl loves some dirty talk.

"Open," I growl as I press my fingers to her mouth. She doesn't hesitate, she goes deep on the first pass. Sucking both my fingers down her throat. *She's one hot fuck. Shit.*

She twirls her tongue around, then slowly licks up my fingers as her eyes penetrate mine.

"If I didn't want to fuck you so bad, I would have my cock so far down your throat you would be fucking gaggin', baby," I say as I pick her up by her waist, set her on the counter, and impale her in one fast move.

"Wills, shit," she cries. I give her a second to adjust, she should be good to go. We only stopped not too long ago.

"You ready, baby? Because it's go time." Her hands instantly rise to my shoulders as I pull out and slam back in. This is going to be fast and rough. I don't know what she is doing to me this morning, but I need it all *now*.

I continue to give it to her hard, and she's loving it. My baby needs it rough today too. Her legs are wrapped around me tightly, encouraging the brutal pace I set.

"Don't stop Wills, I'm so close already!" she screams out.

"Never, baby. Clench that pussy and take what's yours," I shout back.

We both look down and watch as my very engorged cock slams into her.

In and out, in and out, slowing pulling out and plunging back in. Faster and harder as her sweet moans fill the room.

"That's so hot, Wills." I nod my head; words escape me right now. I'm holding back waiting for her, I can't fucking last with this girl.

I feel her tense. "That's it beautiful, give it to me, give me all you got." I lean down, bite her nipple and rub her clit with my thumb, and her scream is so loud the goddamn neighbors will be up now, and that does me in. The knowing burn reaches up my spine, and as her orgasm rips through her and strangles my cock, I explode into her tight pussy. We are both breathing heavily, trying to catch our breaths.

"Shit, beautiful, you really fucking let it go."

She giggles against my shoulder. "What are you doing to me, Wills Taylor?"

"Nothing you're not doing to me, baby." I pull out slowly, still with a semi. You would think being almost forty years old, my body would slow down. But Sadie is trying to kill me. My body needs her like my lungs need air.

I pick up her robe, put it back on her and carry her to the bed, snuggling in behind her.

She puts her head in her hands and shakes it back and forth. "What is it, baby?"

"What is wrong with me? I forgot about Charlie. I was screaming like a freaking lunatic."

I kiss her softly on the back of her neck and rub her stomach for comfort. Charlie didn't hear. Otherwise, she would be in this room right now.

"Sadie," I sigh. "You know better than anyone that kid can sleep through anything, and people have sex all the time when their kids go to bed."

"We don't know she actually went back to bed, do we? And those people probably try to be quiet, not wake up the whole block." Alright, she was a little louder than normal, and the bathroom's acoustics certainly didn't help.

"We'll be more careful next time, okay?" Not likely knowing us, but I say it anyway to appease her. She nods her head and snuggles in closer as my leg wraps around her, engulfing her whole body.

"Wills, are you up?"

"Mmhmm."

"Do you believe in soul mates?"

Ughh what? What is she talking about? "I don't know, Sadie. I never really thought about it."

"Kathryn thinks we're soul mates. I think I believe her," she whispers so low I barely hear.

"Turn around, baby." She turns slowly to face me, and I lean up on my elbow to look down at that gorgeous face of hers. "Why do you believe we are soul mates?" She shrugs her shoulders, clearly embarrassed. "Tell me," I urge. I'm curious about her take on this, guys don't think of this shit.

"Don't you ever think about our story? What are the odds that I would ever run into you again? That you would be *my* brother's business partner?" Yeah, that is some crazy coincidence, of all the people and places in the world, my girl found me again. I guess if that's the definition of a soul mate, she is mine. "And think about how different we are, yet we click so well. From the second we met, I felt it. We were always meant to be together." She holds my eyes.

"I felt it too, my beautiful girl." She leans in and kisses me slowly, different than before. This is an I-love-you kiss.

I wake up, reach my hand over to the other side, Sadie is not here, and the sheets are cold. I frown. Where is she? I didn't hear Charlotte wake up.

I stretch my body, and herein lies the problem. My cock thinks he's nineteen, but my body feels like it's fifty-five. Today's a workout day with Declan, too—my body is going to hate me tomorrow.

I dress quickly, check Charlotte's room first, but Buddy and her are missing as well. So, I head downstairs to see where everyone is and as I round the corner, I can hear the sound of giggles coming from my two favorite girls in the kitchen. I walk forward a bit to see them without them seeing me. Sadie turns on music to her favorite jazz station, so I can't hear what they are saying clearly, but they both look so happy.

I watch as Sadie cooks breakfast in her yoga pants with her perfectly rounded arse on display. Charlotte, still in pajamas, is lying on the floor with her head resting on Buddy and her little feet bouncing along the kitchen tiles as she laughs at Sadie.

I've known for a while now that Sadie was it for me, but this overwhelming feeling of clarity and happiness hits me as I watch them in the kitchen. These people here are my family, my life, and I'm going to spend the rest of my days with them, making them happy—the three of us and Buddy.

"I not a baby," Charlotte yells, then gets up and stomps her foot on the ground. This kid has so much attitude for such a tiny human, she definitely doesn't get it from Sadie.

"Oh yes, you are. You'll always be my baby girl, sweet pea." Sadie leans down and peppers her face with kisses.

"Hey, those lips are mine," I interrupt. I lean over, kiss Sadie, then pick up Charlotte as she squeals in delight.

"I have to say, it is nice to have someone always this happy to see you."

Sadie rolls her eyes. "Idiot."

"What are you girls doing today?"

"Today, we are going to be tourists with Annabelle. First, we will stop by the shelter, then we have a whole day planned for Charlie."

"Woo-hoo!" Charlotte yells. Really, where does this kid pick up these things? I haven't met many kids her age before, but the ones I have were nothing like her.

"You're working out with Declan?"

"Yes, after I go see Jackson." She stops mid pancake pour and turns to me, her face ashen.

"Is that a good idea? Should I come with you?"

Over my dead body is that fucking happening. I'll kill him if he even looks at Sadie the wrong way. I need to speak to him calmly, and that won't happen if she's there.

I shake my head no. "We need to speak man to man, and I need to make him understand. I may take Declan as a peacekeeper. Declan and Jackson get on well, and he will take Declan's word as truth." She smiles widely at the mention of her friend's name. I'm going to kill Declan one day. "What are you laughing at?"

"You, why are you jealous of Declan? I can see it in your eyes." She shakes her head with amusement.

Whatever. "Declan has nothing on me, you're all mine." I grab her and tickle her.

"Yes, yes, all yours, caveman. Let me go." She pants between her laughs. "Go sit down, crazy, and put Charlie in her high chair, please."

We enjoyed a delicious breakfast, took Buddy for a walk, and now we're relaxing on the sofa before our day starts.

"Oh god, this is great." Sadie chuckles to herself and lifts her eyes over her phone to look at me.

"What is it?" I ask skeptically, what is this look she's giving me? Sadie laughs again and passes her phone over. What's so freaking funny?

"You're a Scorpio, right?"

"Yes? So what?"

"If I didn't believe in horoscopes, I do now. It's like they thought, *let's write today's horoscope for Wills Taylor.*" Her eyes go wide, saying, "*go ahead, challenge me.*" The app on her phone reads:

Scorpio

Scorpios can out-alpha almost anyone. They're strong, intense, and have very domineering personalities. Scorpios like to be in charge, and if that's impossible, they'll aggressively make it happen.
No isn't a word that has any power over Scorpios, except to make them work harder to get whatever they were told they couldn't have. They don't shy away from conflict and confrontation; they thrive on it, and it energizes them.

Alright, this is funny. What, did they go inside my head and pull out everything about me?

"They clearly modeled their app based on someone very, very good-looking, strong and smart." I shrug.

"You've got to be kidding me, you're too much." She is laughing so hard right now, I love seeing her this happy.

Her phone pings with an email, so I hand it back while I continue reading the news on my phone.

"Holy crap, oh my god, is this real?" Her hand flies to her mouth, and tears immediately fill her eyes.

"What's the matter, Sadie?" She's making me nervous until I see her smile.

"Is this real life?" she whispers.

"Sadie!" I snap. I have no patience. What the hell is she reading?

She looks at me, and her face lights up as she speaks.

"The head events manager from Harrods was at the fashion show and wants me to do their florals for their Christmas event! They had someone already booked, and she backed out due to a family emergency, it says." She looks like the happiest woman alive right now.

"Can you believe it, Wills, freaking Harrods!" I smile at her. I'm so proud of her. She has come so far from when we first met. It didn't sound like she had an easy life with her family. But she conquered both her parents, and her success is a freaking turn-on. I grab her hand and give it a squeeze.

"Yes, baby, I one-hundred-percent believe it. You are so talented and hardworking. Someone was bound to see it at the event." She smiles softly back at me as the tears still streak down her face. "And you're a freaking crybaby, but I love you." Her smile brightens more.

"Yes, yes I am, and I own it proudly."

I pull on Sadie's leg that's lying across my lap.

"What's up?" she asks.

"I want you and Charlotte to move in with me." Shock crosses her face. I know she wasn't expecting that at all. But I've been thinking it for a while, since we spend all our time together anyway. And, when I saw them in the kitchen this morning, I knew that's how I want to wake up every day.

She doesn't say anything, and I can see the wheels turning in her head.

"We already spend our time together when we're not working. We love each other, and I don't see myself being with anyone else—ever. Do you?"

"No," she whispers.

"So why are you hesitating?" I ask annoyed, this should be an easy answer.

"I think I'm just taken aback."

"What's the point waiting? When do we do things in halves? We are always full steam ahead."

"Wills, you don't know what it's like to live with a toddler. You've seen her at her best, most of the time, because she's excited to see you.

But it's not like that usually. There are tantrums and crying, and we are in the middle of potty training. It's a hard time."

I don't care about all that, I already know living with a toddler will change my life completely, but it's the life I want.

"Beautiful, don't try to talk yourself out of it. I know how kids are. Don't you want to start our future together as a family?"

"Family," she whispers and nods her head, agreeing with the sentiment of calling them family. "Yes, baby, you two are my family. So, what do you say?"

"I can't move in with you—"

"What? Why the hell not?" I cut her off and push her feet off me, annoyed, and go to stand. She said she loved me, and now she doesn't want to be with me?

She slams her feet back into my lap hard, before I stand—*fuck, that hurt.*

"Calm down, you freaking lunatic, you know you're going to give yourself a heart attack one day." She shakes her head, annoyed.

"*I was going to say* we can't move in with you to *your apartment*. But maybe I should take it back." She narrows her eyes at me.

"Don't even kid like that," I growl and lean down to playfully bite her toe. This girl makes me crazy, I can't help how I respond sometimes.

"We would love to live with you. But I just moved Charlie away from the only home she has ever known. It's not fair to uproot her again so soon. And, unless you want to take care of Charlie by yourself, when I'm in jail for murder. I will not be moving into a building with Victoria."

"Murder?"

"Yes, murder," she deadpans. I fucking love this girl.

"So Buddy and I can move in here?" She nods. "Tonight?"

"Do I have a choice?" she snarks, obviously she doesn't.

"Hello, darlings," we hear as the door slams shut. Annabelle walks around the corner like she owns the place.

"Don't you knock?" I snap and narrow my eyes at her. Sadie pats my leg.

"No, I don't, so get over it. And hi to you too." She leans for a kiss and twists my nipple. Goddamn her. I rub my pec as she smirks in delight and pats my cheek. This is what you call a love-hate relationship. I love Annabelle, honestly, but I also want someone to smack her on the arse at the same time.

She leans down to kiss Sadie next, and Sadie immediately hands Annabelle her phone with a delighted face.

"Bloody hell, Sadie, this is fantastic. Having Harrods in your portfolio is going to be so good for business."

There is a knock at the front door, and then the doorbell goes off. At least someone knows how to use it.

"I'll get it," Annabelle declares. I roll my eyes. This girl really does think she lives here.

"Hello, everyone," Declan says as he enters the room. Sadie stands up to greet Declan with a hug.

"Hi, Dec."

"Hey, Slim." He kisses her hello and gives her an extra little cuddle. Yeah, it's decided. I am going to kill him.

"Hey, can we get a dinner on the calendar for this week or next, so the guys can meet Trey?" Annabelle looks around for confirmation.

"Sure," Sadie says and buries her face in her phone, she's a shit liar. She hates Trey. I haven't met the bloke yet, but if Saint Sadie doesn't like him, then I sure as hell won't either.

"You ready to go, mate?" Declan asks. I didn't even realize how late it was.

"Yeah, let me grab my gym bag from upstairs."

"Where are they going, and what the hell happened to Wills's lip?" I hear Annabelle ask Sadie. "They are going to Jackson's to talk. But, Belle, you wouldn't believe it. Jackson caught us last night, and he went apeshit! He tried to punch Wills."

"What? Are you kidding me? It doesn't look like he tried, it looks like he did."

"I'll give you all the details later."

Thanks, Annabelle, for pointing that out. I walk into the bedroom, and the bed is a fucking mess. What the hell did we do last night?

I shake my head and grab my bag to head back downstairs.

"Did you call my contact in the states? Did you find her?" I hear Sadie whisper to Declan.

"Aye, Lass. But no word back yet."

"Okay, keep me posted."

That sounded shady as hell. What was that about? And who is he trying to get a hold of? I make a mental note to ask Sadie later since he apparently didn't want me to help with whatever they were talking about.

"I'm ready," I announce. I kiss Sadie and Charlotte goodbye and promise to see them later.

"Call me, text me, update me!" Sadie yells from the front door. She's nervous, rightfully so, and I can only hope Jackson is in a reasonable mood today—for Sadie's sake alone.

Jackson swings open his front door, looking as murderous as I figured he would be.

"What the fuck are you doing here?"

"I came to talk, mate, I think I have some explaining to do."

Jackson looks over at Declan. "What type of pussy needs to bring back up, afraid I'm going to hit you again?"

"No offense, Dec." Declan just shrugs.

"Jackson, baby, come back to bed and untie me." An annoying whine comes from inside Jackson's place. Declan snickers behind me. You've got to be fucking kidding me right now. He better have invited whatever whore he has in his bed after Charlotte left last night. Otherwise, today's conversation is going to go a lot different.

"Right now is not a good time." He tries to slam the door in my face, but I'm quicker and stop it before it shuts.

"I think the time is perfect, and you need to ask whoever that is to leave now. We are doing this for Sadie, Jackson. So, we should make it a priority, yes?" I know I sound like a condescending prick, but I couldn't care less.

He's pissed but opens the door wider for us to come in and points to his sofa. "Just go in there, and I'll be out in a minute."

"He better not be having a fucking quickie in there while we are waiting out here," I say to Declan as he rummages through Jackson's refrigerator.

"You need to tone it down and not be such a dick. Why would he ever believe you if you're already trying to start a fight?"

I take a deep breath, because fuck, Declan's right. I like Jackson, a lot actually—he's good people. I'm not sure why I'm on the defense, other than him socking me one last night. But I gave him a pass.

We watch his flavor of the night walk out, not before she made a point to check out Declan and me first. I'm so fucking happy those days are over now. We're too old for that shit.

"Alright, time to talk, Taylor. Tell me why you and my sister have been lying to my face. Why you let my sister leave a club by herself in the middle of the night, which got her raped? Explain why she cried for months, devastated you left her. Please, I want to know it all," he spits out in disgust.

Deep breaths, Wills, deep breaths. This is not going to be easy, and I don't blame him because if this was Evelyn, god, I don't even want to think if this all happened to her.

"Jackson, I'm sick to my stomach every fucking day I think about what happened in France. That I wasn't by her side every second she was hurting in that hospital. A day doesn't go by that I don't wonder if we didn't fight. Would this have happened? I will punish myself for what Sadie went through for the rest of my life. I don't deserve a second chance for not protecting her, for not being there for her. But by some miracle, I have been given one anyway, and I swear to you I won't let her down. I will protect her and Charlotte until the day I die."

I continue to explain what happened in France three and a half years ago and what a tragic misunderstanding it was. I didn't mean to pour my heart out to him, but I think he is one of the only people who may truly understand what I have been living through since Sadie came back into my life. The regret runs through my veins, residing within me, and I won't ever live without it. I won't let myself forget for one second.

"I was there. What he says is all true. If you want to blame anyone for Sadie leaving by herself. Blame me. I let her leave while I was waiting for Wills. I should have known better. Why the hell would I ever let her leave that club by herself?" Declan shakes his head into his hands and curses. He's been having a really hard since he found out about Sadie too, he beats himself up just as much as I do.

Everyone is quiet. I think Jackson is shocked and wasn't expecting any of that. I'm staying quiet until he decides he's ready to talk, he's going to need time to process this all, I sure as fuck did.

"I just don't know, fuck! I owe Sadie a massive apology. What the hell was wrong with me last night? I don't even know what to think right now. Why did this have to happen to her? This was never supposed to happen to her, I couldn't protect her," he says to himself. I never thought he would blame himself. He wasn't even in the country.

"I should have been there, Wills. She's my only sister. Why didn't I go away with her for her thirtieth birthday after she begged me? Why did I choose work over her?"

"You can't think of it like that, and I know Sadie would be devastated if she heard you say that. I won't let myself forget, ever. But I am learning to move on for Sadie. She deserves us to be strong and supportive—she's sick of pity and regret from everyone."

Jackson looks up, stares me right in the eye. "I'm sorry for last night. I should have heard you guys out. Although I'm not sorry for your face, now I get to say I punched the infamous Wills Taylor," he teases. The tension and sadness pass, and we are able to put this behind us.

"Just don't lie again. I hate fucking liars."

"I'll let you take that one out on Sadie." Yeah, I'm throwing her under the bus. "Jackson, honestly, I think you're a good guy. Before I even knew Sadie was back, I was going to offer you a job. I don't make it a habit to lie to people. We just needed time to work it out ourselves." He nods in understanding, then his eyes shoot to me with interest.

"A job?"

"Yeah, I am going to be starting a new division, and I want you to run it."

"What, are you serious? What are you thinking about starting up?"

"I want to extend our services to ex-athletes and help them invest. Most well-known athletes just hand over their money, put their name on a restaurant or club here or there, and know nothing else about it. I want you to advise them." His eyes are wide and definitely intrigued. I nod for Declan to pass over his phone and show him the offer. He would be making seven figures with a bonus, plus any extra commissions. He still has money invested in clubs and restaurants around the world, so I would think Jackson is doing pretty fucking good for himself.

"I was going to offer you this the night of **Charlotte's** opening, but then obviously, that night turned out a lot different than I thought."

"I accept." Well then, I guess someone was eager for a new job. "I'm sick of the hours now, and you two aren't too bad yourself. But, for real, send me the official offer, and I'll have a look. But I think we're in business again, boys!" We all shake hands.

"Welcome to **The Taylor Group**, unofficially," I say. Before we leave, Jackson calls me back, but before he speaks, I beat him to it. "You'll apologize to your sister after I leave. I'm sure she's awaiting your call." He shakes his head. I know he is disgusted with how he spoke to her. I can see it written all over his face, so I won't beat him up about it.

"You're good for her, but treat them right, okay?" a warning I understand from a brother, but I wouldn't think of treating them any other way than fucking perfect.

21

Sadie

"To the birthday girl." I raise my glass toward Annabelle. "To my sister soul mate and one bad bitch!" We all laugh and dramatically clink our glasses together, champagne sloshing everywhere.

"Can someone get them off that table? How much has Sadie had to drink?" Jackson yells at Marco, not impressed at our antics… we are all wasted.

Annabelle, Marco, Lola, and I are at **Charlotte's** celebrating so many things tonight, Marco and I have just finished the floral design for Harrods Christmas party, which was a huge success. Lola is about to leave for her first date with a hottie she met on a dating app. Wills and I have officially been living together for one month, with no issues. But, most importantly, it is Belle's thirty-fourth birthday tomorrow. Since we all leave for Ireland tomorrow morning for Declan's family gala, we are pre-celebrating Annabelle tonight.

Annabelle throws her arm around my brother and kisses his cheek. "Don't worry, Jack, we will behave." She winks at him and takes another tequila shot.

He shakes his head in frustration.

"You need to slow down, B. We have an early flight tomorrow."

"You only live once, Jack. You, of all people, should know that you have to enjoy the happy times in our lives."

He stares at her unimpressed, but what does that mean, "you of all people"?

"Hey, what are you doing here anyway? This is a girls' night out!" I ask, and Jackson looks over to the man by my side that I have my arm draped over.

"Girls and gays, Jackson. Get with the program." I can tell he's getting annoyed at our outward drunkenness, but he can deal. I haven't had this much fun with friends in a long time. Three and a half years, to be exact. I think I deserve one night out while Wills watches Charlie.

"I'm working, Sades. Now get off the table before you break your neck!" He's cranky pants tonight.

"You don't work here anymore." I pout.

"Oh, help me, god, I'm going to kill my own sister," he says, looking up to the ceiling, frustrated.

"I still am one of the owners! Now get down, I need to handle an issue with a manager, and since Wills is home with Charlotte obviously and Declan already left for Ireland, I need to deal with it."

I get off the table, so I don't have to hear him complain anymore. He kisses us all goodbye and heads to do his boss things, I guess. I shimmy up to my best friend, who has been looking a little sad lately, and grab my phone to check my messages. *Oh no.*

Freaking Jackson, the tattletale, must have texted Wills that I'm drunk. I let him know I won't be home late, midnight at the latest, and to stop worrying.

"Who's that? Wills?"

"Yeah, he's just being lunatic, as usual. Too overprotective." I roll my eyes. I've told him a million times he will give himself a heart attack, but I love him despite his craziness.

"At least he cares, Sadie. He annoys the shit out of me half the time, but I love him nonetheless." I smile. *That's exactly what I was thinking.* Wills and Belle do love each other, but they are both too type

A in their own way. Belle could never deal with a Wills in her life, she needs to be the dominant, or at least someone less than Wills.

"Trey cares about you too. He's coming tomorrow, right?"

"Does he, though?" She shrugs, annoyed. "If this were your birthday weekend, I would have had to fight Wills tooth and nail to get a night alone with you. Trey has nothing planned. I'm not even sure he would have remembered if I hadn't mentioned it would be my birthday in Ireland." I frown, sad for her. She deserved so much more than what Trey gives her. She must also be drunk because she never talks about Trey to me.

"Maybe he will surprise you tomorrow with something or take you out when we get home?" I know he won't, he's a jerk, a colossal one. The more I think about it, it just pisses me off. But what the hell is she doing with him?

The guys met him once at a dinner, and they all refuse to hang out with him again—even Declan, who likes everyone. I think Belle sensed it because she never brought him up again, which also breaks my heart. I want us to share our lives together, not hide behind closed doors.

At the end of the day, I want my best friend to be happy. And the only thing I can do tonight is get us drunker, to forget about it. So, I pour us another drink and cheers her.

"I love you," I kiss her cheek, and she smiles sadly back at me. I need to fix this for her. I want my happy-go-lucky Belle back. It's time I repay her for the years of being my rock. She needs my shoulder now.

"Hey, let us in on that cheers, and then let's dance," Marco screams over the music while he shakes his booty and runs his hand through his dark, wavy, thick hair. He's so chic tonight, I can't take it. He's tall and lean but super fit. He skipped his formal wear for a different look, and I'm loving it. He's wearing tight black jeans, black boots, and a silk maroon dress shirt tucked in and unbuttoned almost all the way down, with a leather Hermes belt. Something only Marco could pull off with his beautiful tanned Italian skin glistening from dancing for the last hour. The next guy he finds is going to be so lucky. Marco is handsome, kind, selfless and needs to meet the right guy who won't trample him.

"You guys have fun, I'm off. Wish me luck!" Lola looks smokin' tonight, she finally let Belle dress her and get her ready for her date. I hope it works for her; she deserves the best. All my friends do, I have freaking kick-ass friends.

We've had the best night… it feels like we've danced for hours. I can't even feel my feet. I'm going to be hurting tomorrow, but it was worth it. Belle and Marco were laughing all night, and that's all I wanted—them both happy.

Belle is lying face-first on the couch near our table, and Marco is sitting with his eyes closed, rubbing Belle's head.

"I think I'm going to throw up," Marco mumbles. I look down, and all the bottles are finished. Shit, did we drink all that? What time is it? I sit next to Marco and put my head on his shoulder and close my eyes too. I know we have to get up soon, we can't be sitting here at the club sleeping, but I just need to rest my eyes for a second.

I feel large hands wrap around me and pick me up. What the hell is going on? Where am I?

"Wills?" Is that him?

"You're in so much trouble, Sadie, you might not make it to tomorrow," he says through clenched teeth. I giggle. I've had two death threats tonight, ironically both by my two favorite men,

"This is not fucking funny, Sadie. I'm so mad at you right now, I can't even put it into words. So, I suggest you shut the fuck up before I say something I regret." I frown. Oh, he is mad.

Suddenly, cold air hits my back, sending my whole body into a shiver. I look up and see the sign for **Charlotte's** disappearing as we walk away. Wait! We were still at the club, what the hell is Wills doing here?

"What time is it?"

"Three," he deadpans. *WHAT?*

"In the morning?" I shriek.

"No, in the fucking afternoon." I roll my eyes, but crap, how did it get so late?

"Why am I still here? Why are you here?" He ignores me, puts me in the passenger seat, buckles me, and walks over to the driver's side.

"Where are Belle and Marco?" I whisper. Shit, did we just leave them there? I look over to Wills, and his jaw is clenched. He takes a large breath and runs his hands over his face.

"I put them in a cab before I carried you out." He won't look at me. He puts the car in gear and speeds off toward home.

"Who has Charlotte?" I ask.

"I had to wake up Jackson to come over so I could get your drunk arse from the club." Oh, great. Now I have to deal with Jackson too.

"Can you just talk to me about this?"

"No, I can't. So just shut up, for now, Sadie. I'm being serious. Now that I know you're alive, I'm going home and going to sleep, and I'm not talking to you tonight."

"Please," I beg. My voice cracks, and the tears start to pool in my eyes. He looks over at me and shakes his head in frustration.

"Don't start with the fucking waterworks, they won't work tonight. I'm telling you right now."

"Okay, you don't have to be so mean."

"Mean?" he roars. "I am holding back so much right now that you're lucky I'm fucking exhausted and don't want to deal with you."

"I just don't understand what I did." I fell asleep by accident. So what?

"You want to get into this now, fine. But I warned you. Let's start with how my girlfriend told me she would be home by midnight, so I stupidly fell asleep on the couch waiting for her. To my fucking surprise, when I woke up two hours later, she wasn't home. Of course, it sent me to have a full fucking panic attack, thinking something happened to her. Especially when she doesn't answer her phone or texts." I looked down at my phone. Shit, it's dead. That's why I didn't get any of his calls.

"I looked like a fucking fool that I had the club manager looking for you, especially when he tells me you're all fucking piss drunk, dancing like animals on the dance floor. Then when I get there, you're passed out like a fucking teenager. And worst of all, you put yourself in danger. You will never act like that again. Do you understand me? You're lucky if I even let you out of the house again," he yells. His face is beet red from screaming. I've never seen him this mad.

"And," he continues, "let's hope you don't end up all over the tabloids tomorrow. You're a mum Sadie, start fucking acting like it." My face falls. That's a low blow. I never ever go out, and I'm a good mom, a great mom.

He reaches over for my hand, and I pull it away and wipe my tears. He pulls it back over to him again and kisses the back of it.

"I'm sorry, that was uncalled for, Sadie. I didn't mean it. You're the best mum. I'm just so mad with you. Why would you get that drunk? You passed out at the club, for God's sake. Anything could have happened, and I wasn't there with you. I don't want you drinking like that if I'm not around."

"Wills," I sigh. "You can't tell me I can't drink. We were having a good time for Belle's birthday. We just drank a little too much, plus I passed out more from exhaustion—I worked all day and then went right after."

Finally, we pull up to the house, and he drops my hand in a rush. Great, he's annoyed again. "Oh, you can bet your arse I'll tell you what to do. Don't even try me, Sadie," he snaps as he gets out of the car and slams the door shut. I take a breath and follow him inside. There is no winning this tonight.

When I get to the top of the stairs, Jackson is not looking too impressed. "What were you thinking, Sades?" I just shrug, embarrassed, and I know if I talk, my emotions will get the better of me. He pulls me in for a hug and kisses my forehead. "You scared us, but you scared him the most," Jackson whispers so Wills can't hear.

"I know, I'm sorry." The tears break free again. Jackson squeezes tighter.

"It's not me you need to apologize to." I nod, I know. It's hitting me now—Wills, not knowing if I was okay, probably brought some bad memories.

I don't know why, but time and time again I forget that I've had a long time working out my PTSD and the events of that night, but it's still fresh for Wills.

"Inside now, Sadie," Wills snaps.

Jackson rubs my back in support. "In you get, we don't want to upset Mr. Grumpy anymore." I smile sadly up at him and follow Wills inside and right upstairs to the bedroom. I check on Charlie first, and she's snuggled in her bed with Buddy. Both of them on their back, lying on her pillow. I wish my phone weren't dead, this would be a good picture.

I head to our bedroom, and Wills is already in bed, with his eyes closed and turned the wrong way. I don't even care about getting ready. I just strip down and go right in bed and cuddle his back, skin to skin like he loves. He doesn't push me away, so that's a good sign. But he doesn't cuddle me back either.

"I'm sorry, Wills," I whisper.

"Don't," he snaps. "Not tonight."

"Okay, good night. I love you," I say to my grumpy man. I don't want him to be mad at me anymore. He doesn't answer, so I give him a squeeze but still nothing, so I give up and turn away—the way we usually sleep.

He sighs, rolls over, and pulls me into him. "I love you too."

Ugh, I wake up and put my hand on my head. I can't open my eyes, and my head is pounding. Last night was so stupid. I think we all just needed to let loose, but it got out of hand.

I turn over and finally open my eyes and see that Wills put some ibuprofen, water, and juice next to the bed for me with a note attached

*—You don't deserve this but take it anyway—*I laugh and shake my head, typical. I lie in bed for a while longer, willing myself to get up, but I'm not ready to face the wrath of Wills. Luckily Charlie will be downstairs, and he can't be that mad when she's there.

I take a quick shower, which helps slightly with my hangover. I think I just need some food in me, and I'll be okay. So I quietly make my way into the kitchen where Charlie and Wills are eating without me.

"Good morning," I say, ashamed I'm hungover. I should be up eating with everyone.

"Mommy!" Charlie runs over, and I lean down to pick her up for a cuddle, her love is like instant medicine.

"Wills said you in time-out." He did, did he? I look over at him, and he hasn't lifted his eyes from his newspaper. I walk over and kiss the top of his head and greet him good morning.

"I made you breakfast, it's on the counter. You need to eat and get ready. We are leaving soon." He still doesn't look up, but it's in his nature to take care of me. Of course, he made me food.

"I'm already packed. I just need to dress and put on some makeup." He still doesn't acknowledge me.

"Charlie, can you go inside and play with Buddy while Mommy and Wills talk?" She runs into the living room, no questions asked. She's a good kid.

"Wills, this is going to be a long weekend if we can't talk about it."

"You should have thought about that before last night," he says, uninterested in this conversation.

"It was a mistake to get that drunk, and I'm sorry my phone died. It was irresponsible." I'm apologizing for everything, even though I'm not sorry for going out and having a good time, just the way we acted at the end. But he still says nothing, and now I'm getting annoyed. "Fine, stay mad. I'm trying to apologize!" I snap. If he wants to be grumpy and have a terrible time in Ireland, that's on him. I push my chair back and go back upstairs to get ready.

I'm just about finished when Wills comes into the room. He walks over to me, takes me in his arms, and kisses my forehead. "You scared me, Sadie. It's not like you to act like that." I nod into his chest. I know it's not.

"I'm sorry, Wills."

"I know you are. Don't let it happen again. I'm not kidding, Sadie. I will lose my shit if I ever find you like that ever again." I nod again in agreement. I'm not promising not to go out and have fun, but to get that drunk was irresponsible. And I definitely don't plan on embarrassing myself like that again. I've been checking the tabloids like crazy this morning… I would just die if something like that got out.

"I'm also sorry for insinuating you weren't acting like a good mum. I'm not just saying this, but I think you're one of the best mums out there. I regretted it the second it came out of my mouth." I nod, although the words hurt. I knew he didn't mean them. I could see the remorse on his face even last night. "Okay, fresh start then this morning. Let's have a good time in Ireland, beautiful." He leans down and gives me a real kiss, I sigh and lean into him. I missed him. It's been one day without a kiss, but it feels like years.

"I've never been to Ireland. I'm excited. It's too bad Christmas is next weekend. I would have liked to spend more time there."

"Next time. Let's go before we are late."

We make it downstairs. Kathryn is here, and she's holding a crying Charlie who is leaning over trying to get into Wills's arms.

He puts down our bags and takes her, and she cries into his shoulder. "I go too, Wills?"

"No, princess. Just me and Mummy."

"Pwease, I go too." She's really crying, the tears are running down her face. I turn around, I don't want to see her crying, otherwise, we will never leave.

"Pwease," she scream-cries. *Oh, god.* I scrunch my face up. Stay strong, Sadie.

"Okay, princess, you can come."

I whip around. "What? Wills, no, we can't just say yes every time. It's one night." He's shaking his head like he doesn't care. Why can't he be a softy like this with me? I look over at Charlie, and she's still crying, even though Wills said she could come.

She's distraught. I reach over for her, and she flings her little body into mine. How do parents handle this? I never want to see my kid like this, but we can't keep saying yes every time we leave and she's upset. She's developing serious attachment issues. We will never have alone time, and she's only getting worse since Wills is around. She's extremely attached to him.

Now the mom guilt is setting in. She got herself so worked up she's not calming down and is still so upset.

"Kathryn, do you fancy a night in Ireland? You can have all day to yourself, then you can pick up Charlie from the event midway through." I know there are plenty of rooms in the house we rented, so it shouldn't be a problem.

"Of course, I would have been here anyway. Ireland sounds amazing."

Wills rubs Charlie's back to get her attention while her head is still buried in the crook of my neck. "Princess, do you want to go upstairs and pick a fancy dress for tonight with Kathryn?"

She just nods and goes off with Kate. My poor baby.

"We need to figure this out, Wills. I don't want her upset. But we need to start to transition her somehow."

"We will," he says, dismissing me. He doesn't care. He would have Charlie all day at work with him if I let him.

"Wow!"

"Pretty cool, Charlie, huh?" Her eyes are sparkling with excitement as she stares at the plane in front of us.

"I've never been on a private plane," Kate whispers next to me. I smile. Of course she hasn't. *Who has?*

"The only times I've been were with Wills when he took me to Paris." He looks back and gives me that smirk I love. I think that was the weekend I officially fell hard for him. Even though it was just one night, that was one of the best trips I've ever taken. We had the best time.

"Ahh!" Charlie yells as she goes running down the aisle with Buddy by her side, giving high fives to Lola and Marco, then runs straight for Belle and Jackson, who are sitting together. Where's Trey?

Belle looks at me with questioning eyes. "We couldn't leave her. It was a mess." I roll my eyes, lean down and kiss her hello.

"Happy birthday, my lovely Belle." I kiss her again, and she smiles up at me, looking a lot happier today.

"Charlie, sit on someone's lap, we are going to go up in the air now, and you need to be buckled in." She is currently with Jackson behind us, and I see her look up at Wills, and it's a relief when she jumps in Jackson's lap.

Jackson and Wills are great friends now, but I know Jackson is jealous of how close Wills and Charlie are. He holds his tongue, but I see the hurt on his face.

I lean my head on Wills's shoulder. He takes my hand and interlocks our fingers as he leans down to place a kiss on my lips.

"I love you," he whispers.

"Me too, baby." My Wills is back, I know he's not mad at me anymore. His other hand cups my cheek, and he deepens our kiss. The feeling of his tongue gliding against mine shoots tingles right down me, and I clench in response. God, am I really this horny because we didn't have sex one night?

Wills's hand runs down my neck, over my breast, then back up. He rubs his thumb over the sensitive part behind my ear, his touch awakening my whole body.

"Do you remember the last time we were on a private plane?"

"Yes," I moan into his mouth.

"Do you remember how good I made you feel? How we fucked the whole flight. You were such a good girl, letting me gag you, so no one on the plane could hear?"

"Yes," I moan again. If he touches me, I think I may come on the spot.

"Are you guys freaking kidding? We can all hear you," Belle snaps at us. Wills and I both laugh, and I put my head into his chest. I forgot where we were for a hot second. How the hell does he get me to act like this in public? Luckily our friends are used to us by now and Jackson was too occupied with Charlie.

"Holy crap, is this where we are staying?" I ask Wills.

"This place is insane," Kate adds.

"Look, Charlie, we are staying in a castle," Kate tells her.

"Woo-hoo! Like a pwincess."

"We need to give her something new to say. The woo-hoos are going to drive me insane," Wills grumbles next to me. Yeah, him and me both.

This place is gorgeous. We are somewhere right outside of Belfast in Northern Ireland. It's a huge castle, sitting on a large lot of land that looks like it goes on forever. Buddy is going to be living his best life today.

We all get out of our cars and head toward the house. Next year, we have to stay here longer. Today and tomorrow are not enough.

I catch up to Belle and put my arm around her. "How do you look so good right now?"

"You too, Marco." Belle smirks in response, brat.

"I drank seven hundred bottles of water and ate so much greasy food, I refused to let my body get hungover," Marco replies. "I barely remember how we got home last night."

"Wills put you in a cab," I whisper. I don't want to talk about this in front of him.

"What? Why was he there?" Marco asks, shocked. "We will chat about it later, when we get ready." He looks over at Wills and nods like he gets it.

We walk into the house, and I'm awestruck. It's like we are on the set of *Downton Abbey*.

"Hello, welcome," a cheery older woman greets us in a lovely Irish accent.

"I'm Millie and will help you with anything you need today or tomorrow. I have set a light lunch for you in the formal dining area if you would like to follow me."

"Thank you, Millie," we all say in unison.

"Oh my god!" Kate and I are like two little kids. Why doesn't anyone else look as impressed? The dining table seats like a hundred people. It's long, dark wood with beautifully carved wooden chairs, and this is what they call a light lunch. It looks like it's a feast set out for Louis XIV.

"Kathryn, you're more than welcome to stay with us. But if you want to take one of the cars and explore. You can do that as well. We just need you back around eight tonight to pick up Charlotte," Wills tells her from across the table.

"Thank you. I'd like to explore the castle a bit. Then perhaps I'll drive around." I'm sure Millie can give her some places to go, it sounds like fun, actually.

"Hey B, I thought Trey was coming?" Jackson asks.

"He'll be here later," she snaps. What the hell is going on with her?

"Touchy, Double *B*," he mocks.

"Don't, Jack." He must hear something in her voice because he stops his teasing and leans over to put his arm around her.

"Sorry, B. Are you okay?" he whispers, but I can hear since I'm sitting so close.

"Mhmm."

"Annabelle, look at me, babe." He never calls her Annabelle unless it's serious. I wish I could look over at them, but I feel like I would be intruding on their little moment.

"I don't want to talk about it, please, Jack." I see him nod and kiss her head from the corner of my eye.

"You can talk to me whenever you're ready. You know that, right?"

"I know." Her voice is muffled in his shirt. Why is she so upset? I know it's wrong of me to take it personally, that she won't ever talk to me about what's going on with her and Trey. But I can't help it, I do.

A few moments later, we all turn our heads because we hear

laughter coming from the hallway. "Hello, everyone," Declan announces as he steps into the dining room, followed by a girl in a motorized wheelchair, who is practically Declan's twin.

"This is my sister, Maeve," he says proudly, introducing her as he smiles down so lovingly at her. I know Declan adores his sister, like many of the men in our group. He speaks about her often to me. It kills him to be so far from her, but he tries to fly back often to see her.

"Hello," a computerized voice projects through the room. Declan shakes his head.

"No, Mo Stoirín. These people are like family to me. Don't be shy." She smiles up at him with the same love in her eyes. I feel like I'm looking in on something so intimate, but it's just that Declan's love for his sister is so strong.

"Hello," Maeve struggles and stutters, but Declan rubs her back in encouragement at using her words, then looks back at all of us.

"We wanted to stop by to say—"

"Uncle Dec," Charlie interrupts with her arms stretched out. Everyone laughs around the table as Declan bends over to pick up Charlie.

"Charlie, I'm so happy to see you here. Are you going to come to the party tonight?"

"Yes! I have a pwetty dress," she says as she traces her finger around his tattoo peeking out of his collar.

"Anyway, we just wanted to thank you all for coming today. I hope you all enjoy the gala tonight but remember it's not just about a party. We are here to raise money and awareness about cerebral palsy. This foundation my parents started means so much to both myself and obviously Maeve. I truly appreciate all the donations each and every one of you has kindly given, they were all more than generous." He looks at Wills and Jackson for a few extra seconds when he says that. I don't know how much Jackson donated, but Wills gave enough for someone to practically attend college.

Declan clears his throat and looks down for a second.

"My sister is fortunate enough to have the resources and funds to get things like a motorized wheelchair or this speech tablet she greeted you with. But a lot of families here aren't as lucky. They barely have the funds to send their children to the doctor or the much-needed physical, occupational, and speech therapy. We try our best to help as many as we can, and I can proudly say, just from you all sitting at the table here, we will be able to make a real dent this year. So, from the bottom of my heart. I love you all, and thank you, you'll never know how much this means to us." I squeeze my hand that is locked with Wills as Declan walks around the table to thank everyone again personally. Finally, he gets to Wills, and he hugs him a few extra seconds, a silent thanks.

"You're a good egg, Wills Taylor." I lean over and kiss my man.

"I know," he deadpans. "My mum would agree." I roll my eyes, so conceited. I keep his eye contact and something changes and a mischievous look sparkles in his eyes.

"You want to go to our room? I've been waiting to have make-up sex all day." His deep voice vibrates through my body as he whispers in my ear.

"I thought we made up already?" I tease.

"I'm not sure I'm fully over it anymore. But I can think of a few things that would make it better."

"What's that?" I barely recognized my lust-filled voice. He leans over as close as possible, then kisses and licks behind my ear. I have to suppress a moan, otherwise I'll be giving this whole room a show.

"I think if my good girl wraps her luscious lips around my cock, as she does so well. I could forgive her. Then maybe if she's really sorry, she'll ride me until I'm screaming her name and coming inside of that tight cunt of hers." I can't even answer. I smash my lips into his and thrust my tongue inside. He pulls back quickly, leans down, and picks me up from my seat, carrying me out of the room without a word to anyone. *Good thing Charlie is with her uncle again.*

22

Sadie

"So, then he just carried you out of the club?" Lola asks, affronted.

"Yes, does that surprise any of you?" I ask, and everyone laughs, except Belle.

"He is a possessive control freak *most of the time*. But this time, I'm with Wills. You should make sure your phone is always charged, or at the very least, check in with someone else's phone. Every time you go out, that man is worried something will happen to you. It's not just you who was affected by that night," Belle snaps, and everyone goes silent.

My eyes cast down. *Shit.* "I'm sorry, Belle," I truly am.

But I also don't mention how she was face-planted into the lounge and wouldn't be able to call anyone either.

I know my actions affect others. I was just more upset about how Wills handled himself.

Not that I didn't understand his concerns.

"Don't worry about it, and I'm sorry I snapped. I need a nap alongside Charlie there." I smile at her through the mirror.

While lying on the bed relaxing with Marco, Lola, and a sleeping Charlie, we watch Belle get ready for the gala.

She is going to look stunning tonight. Her birthday/gala gown is out of this world, probably even a little risqué for the event, but she's the birthday girl and could give two craps what anyone thinks.

It's an iridescent gown with a perfect gold shimmer as she moves. The top is see-through with a gold petal design that seamlessly snakes around her stomach, over her belly button, around her back then back around to cross over her chest.

It also has a slit as high as her hip, accentuating her long legs. And this, of course, is why it pays to be supermodel tall, so you can wear dresses like that.

As I continue to watch my friend in the mirror, I can see the sadness in her eyes. Although she won't talk to me, I even tried again after Trey arrived a few hours ago.

He's been in their room or walking around the property on his phone the whole time.

Belle said he has business to deal with, but it's a lie.

I know it.

I was upset she wouldn't confide in me, but Wills told me if she's not ready, she's not ready. And just letting her know I'm there for her is enough support for some people.

So, I'm going to be the best freaking support system she has. It's the least I can do for her.

"Alright, spill it. Tell us about your date, woman," Marco says to Lola, who's lying with her head on his chest.

"Nothing much to tell. He just wasn't for me." Belle narrows her eyes at Lola through the mirror, not convinced with that answer.

"Lola," she warns. I love watching these two interact. It's like having a front-row seat to a comedy act.

"Fine, ughhh," she groans in frustration.

"Well, he got drunk and asked me to come back to have a ménage with his ex, whom he still lives with!" She spits out then buries her face under Marco's sweater.

We all look at each other and burst out laughing. Is that for real?

"Only you, Lola, only you," Belle says through her laughter.

What is wrong with guys these days? Why can't anyone just go out on a regular date?

None of us can stop laughing, poor Lola. She has terrible luck with guys. Last month she met a guy in the park for a stroll, and he brought his pet turtle along for the walk. You can't make this shit up.

After we have our laugh, Charlie wakes up, and we all finish getting ready. With one last spritz of perfume and one last powder of the nose we head downstairs to meet the guys.

I bend down and pick up Charlie once we get to the stairs. "You look like a princess, sweet pea." She smiles brightly at me and then leans her gorgeous little head against my shoulder. I love when she's in this mood, all mushy, and wants to be cuddled and carried by me all day.

She's my best accessory tonight.

We are wearing matching emerald-green dresses, with our hair half up, half down. Belle curled our hair and tied Charlie's back with a black velvet ribbon, and I have a pearl clip in mine. Charlie has sparkly black tights Lola bought her and black patent leather Mary Janes. My gown is floor length, and I'm wearing tall black patent leather stilettos. I need as much height as I can get next to Wills.

The smile on Charlie's face when she saw us next to one another in the mirror is one I will never, ever forget. Marco took hundreds of pictures because I know, one day, she won't want to match me anymore, and I need to have as many memories as possible.

When we all walk down the stairs, whistles and hoots are coming our way from the guys. Wills, Jackson, and Declan are all decked out in their tuxedos. Standing tall and broad, in the exact same position. Their legs are spread wide, arms are crossed, and each has a scotch in hand. They are portraying complete dominance.

"Look at the three of you in your perfectly tailored tuxedos. You guys look super sexy," Belle says.

"You guys really are *The Taylored Men* of **The Taylor Group**," I add, and Belle high-fives me. "Good one." I shrug. "I try."

I make my way closer to Wills, who hasn't said a word. His eyes slowly roam over my body, from head to toe. Then with a slight shake of his head, he finally leans down to give Charlie and me a kiss, pulling us into a tight embrace.

"I'm the luckiest man on the planet, do you know that?" he asks as he locks eyes with me.

"We are just as lucky." I smile up at him and then see a flash from the corner of my eye. I turn to see Marco capturing candid moments of us.

"Let me get a formal one of the three of you. Go stand by the tree," Marco says.

Wills whistles and Buddy comes running into the room and sits by my feet. I move Charlie to my other hip, so she is between both of us, Wills puts his arm around my waist to hold us close, and we stand there as Marco snaps away.

When he's done, I see him staring at his phone—so many emotions cross his face. I walk over, and he passes me his phone.

I look down at the picture and then smile so brightly up at Wills. "I love you," I say, and he bends down to steal another kiss. There is so much love in the last picture he took, I can't take it. Buddy has his head leaning on my leg, and my free hand is reaching down to give him a pet. Charlie and I are staring up at Wills with hearts in our eyes and Wills is looking down at me with such passion. This is my favorite picture to date.

We walk back over, and Trey has joined the group and has his arm draped over Annabelle. They both look uncomfortable and forced. He isn't saying much, just adding in bits here and there.

I see Jackson staring at him with such hatred—I'm glad I'm not the only one.

I love that my brother cares for Belle as much as I do.

Maybe this would be an excellent time to give Annabelle her present since we are about to leave.

Wills and I walk over to the side and call for Belle. He takes a box out of his jacket pocket and hands it over.

She gently unwraps it, and when she sees the name of her favorite jewelry designer, she looks up with wide eyes and smiles at both of us. Then, she slowly opens the box and gasps when she sees the earrings we bought her. I lean over to kiss her. "Happy birthday, Belle. I love you."

"This is too much, guys." She shakes her head in shock. We bought her beautiful, elongated diamond earrings, in a unique shape the designer is known for.

I couldn't afford them, but Wills insisted. She's like family to him too, and "she's taken such good care of my girls" was his reasoning.

She hugs me and then holds on to Wills for a few moments longer. *See, they do love each other.*

"Oh god, I got makeup on you," she cries. Wills smiles and kisses the top of her head. "It's okay, Annabelle. I already took the important pictures," he says, grinning at me.

"Our cars are here," Jackson yells over. Belle quickly puts on her new earrings and hands Wills her old ones to hold in his pocket, then we all head out.

This event was more significant than I ever expected it to be. When we first arrived, there were press and even local news crews from Belfast and Dublin.

Both Declan's parents were professors at Trinity College in Dublin and well-known scholars and philanthropists in the area.

Together, they ran the physics department and were advanced in their field, known for breaking strides in nanotechnology—traveling all over the world giving lectures until Declan's sister was born. Both also have double PhDs, which explains why Declan's a brainiac, and why his parents weren't happy when he became a professional rugby player.

I'm getting used to the interviews and paparazzi. But luckily, since

Wills isn't the only famous athlete here, we didn't have to indulge them for long.

Charlie had the time of her life, of course, the center of everyone's attention. She danced the night away with Wills and Jackson. Even George, who I haven't seen since France, was smitten with her. To my surprise, Leo's here somewhere too, and he's married with two little girls. He looks very much in love—it's nice to see him settled down. George is still a ladies' man in London, living life to the fullest, he says.

The night is winding down, and we are having one last dance with a sleeping Charlie before she heads back with Kathryn, who just arrived.

Wills has Charlie in one arm and the other around me. "What is this song?" I ask. We are swaying a little faster than you would to a slow song, but it's still not too fast.

"I don't know, but I like it." He listens more closely. "This is my song for you," he states.

"No, no. This is my song for you. That's why I asked." I smile up at him.

I lean over to Marco and Lola, who are dancing together. "Hey, do you know this song?"

Lola nods her head and tells me it's called "**You Are The Best Thing**" By Ray LaMontagne.

I need to download this song because it's my new favorite.

"You *are* the best thing; do you know that?" I ask Wills. He smiles and leans down to kiss me.

"I love you, Sadie."

"I love you more, baby."

"I promise you. You don't," he says with so much conviction he almost convinces me. He leans back down for another kiss. And that's how we stay until Kate pulls Charlie away from us, and our friends inform us it's time to head to the local pub.

Wills

I watch a happy Sadie walk arm in arm with Belle into the pub. We all had a great night… the best. Maeve's foundation raised over eight million pounds, and Declan is on cloud nine. So, we are here at the pub for a nightcap to celebrate the last minutes of Annabelle's birthday and a very successful night.

"Can't take your eyes off her, even after all this time, can you? It's nice to see you guys back together," George says from beside me.

"Yeah, who would've thought after all this time, right?"

"Me. You guys were always it."

"Really?" I ask, surprised George, Mister Anti-Relationship, would think something so romantic.

"Yeah, you just clicked. If anyone is supposed to be together, it's you two." I look over at Sadie, and he's right. I think the same exact thing.

"Okay, enough of this sappy shit. How is everything going with you? Tell me more about this after-school program."

"Everything is going well. I have no complaints at the moment. The program has been taking a lot of work to start up, but we are finally on our way. The guys from the old team have already volunteered their time, and the new players and coach are set to put aside time to make appearances. We aim to start after the holidays, and we've selected a few low-income areas to start. Mostly one's a few of our players came from. We have transportation, picking kids up after school and then dropping them off at the end of the day. I hope to extend it over time and add more sports than just rugby."

"That's amazing, mate. I want to help. Let me know how."

"Appreciate it, thank you. I will hold you to it."

We're lucky a big group was just leaving as we walked into the pub, and we're able to sit all together.

I grab a chair with an excellent view of the Irish folk band that's playing, and Sadie puts her arms out for me, and I pull her onto my lap. My girl's tired. It's my favorite time of the day when she's like this.

Charlotte must take after her because when they both get tired at night, they like to crawl onto my lap and cuddle me.

Her face goes to my neck, and I can feel her smile against my skin.

"Why are you smiling, beautiful?"

"Do you even realize the first place you put your hands is always on my behind?"

I lean and nip her ear. "That's because it's my oasis. I want to spend all my time lost in it."

"Are you saying my butt is big enough to get lost in, Mr. Taylor?"

"Bigger is better, baby."

She giggles into my neck and cuddles in closer.

We've all had a couple of rounds of drinks, and it's almost time to head back to the house.

Jackson is still making out with two girls in the corner. Sadie was losing her mind before. She couldn't even stand to look. Belle and Trey are quietly fighting. I don't know what's up with that fucker, but I don't like or trust him one bit.

I saw him a little too chatty with a girl before, and the bloke didn't even have the decency to pretend to look sorry when I called him out on it.

"What happened to your good mood, mate?" I ask Declan, as he's looking a little glum next to me.

"Earth to Declan," I call over, and when he turns his head, he looks like he just saw a ghost.

"What's going on? Everything okay?" I ask.

"Nothing's wrong, sorry. Long day."

I agree. It was. I'll be happy when we get back to the house. I look down at Sadie, and she is sound asleep on my shoulder.

"Hey, you guys ready to leave?" I ask Marco.

"Yeah, I've been ready for the last hour. Let's get out of here."

"I'm going to stay here and finish my beer and head back to my parents' house. I told Maeve I would be there when she woke up."

"Okay, you're flying back with us tomorrow?" I ask.

"I'll see how Maeve is, and I'll let you know in the morning."

"Sounds good." I pat him on the back, then cradle Sadie in my arms as I walk out and head to the cars waiting for all of us.

"We're leaving?" a groggy Sadie asks as she lifts her head to look around.

"Yes, beautiful. Time to get you home, you're exhausted." She nods and puts her head back down on my shoulder. I get in the SUV and strap us in together.

I undress Sadie when we get back in the room, and she lies there lifeless, her dark hair spread across the pillow.

She really is done tonight.

I tuck her under the covers and make my way to my side of the bed when I hear yelling from the room next to us. *Annabelle's room.*

I stand there a minute, listening. I have a bad feeling about this fucking guy, and I don't trust her with him. I don't know how she's been with him so long; Sadie especially is bothered by it.

People fight, couples fight. It's okay, but this is getting out of control. He's been a dick all night, and his voice is getting louder as the seconds pass. I look over at Sadie, and she hasn't moved an inch, sleeping through anything. Another thing Charlotte got from her mum.

I hear a crash, and that's my breaking point. Marco and I both fling our doors open at the same time, having the same idea.

I bang on the door, and Trey whips open the door.

"What the fuck do you two want?" he sneers.

Oh, don't fuck with me, pretty boy.

I look into the room. Annabelle is hysterical and seems so broken. I put out my arms for her.

"Come here, sweetheart." She stands to move forward.

"Don't you fucking dare, Belle," he bellows.

She freezes in her spot, looking at me with scared eyes. I'm not waiting another second. I push him back, and he flies into the door as I storm their room to get Annabelle. I put my arm around her and lead her back to Marco.

"Take her downstairs or back to your room," I say, and I turn back to Trey.

"Get your shit and get out of here. You're not welcome anymore."

"I'm Belle's fucking guest, and I'll stay if I want to."

"I paid for the fucking house, and I'm telling you, you have five seconds to move your arse and get your shit, or I'll pick you up and throw you out of that fucking window."

"You know what, fuck all of you, I'm out of here." He grabs his wallet and phone then storms off through the house.

He pauses at the front door, turning back to Annabelle, who's crying on the sofa in Marco's arms.

"Have a nice life, Belle, and just so you know, I did fuck her. I have been for the last year, and I fucked her last night. That's why I didn't go out for your birthday." Belle wails out loud, and this dickhead smirks. I will kill him; I lunge and grab his shirt by the neck.

"Wills!" Annabelle screams. I turn back, and she's shaking her head.

"His whole family are judges, and you'll be fucked. Sadie will not be happy."

Shit.

I push him out the door and slam it in his face. She's right, I'm not wasting another second on this guy.

I have to pat my back for self-restraint. If that were even just a few years ago, Trey would be out cold, and I would probably be on my way to the police station.

I sit on the sofa, on the other side of Annabelle, she lays her head in Marco's lap and puts her feet in mine. We are both trying to comfort her, Marco is stroking her hair, and I rub her feet.

We let her cry it out for what seems like forever. I don't want to wake up Sadie, but I think Annabelle needs her best friend.

"I'll go get Sadie." She nods her head. So, I go to stand but the front door flies open and Jackson comes running in, right to Annabelle.

He kneels in front of her. "Are you okay, B?" he whispers. A bubble in her throat breaks when she goes to respond. He stands up, leans over, and picks up Annabelle. He looks over at Marco and me. "That dickhead came back to the pub and was gloating. If I didn't think I needed to come back for her, I would have killed him."

"Do you still want me to get Sadie?" She shakes her head no and puts her arms around Jackson's neck.

"She'll stay with me tonight, don't worry about it."

"Alright, wake us up if you guys need us."

Marco turns to me and raises his eyebrows. "What a fucking disaster."

"I know, mate, I know."

He points to Jackson and Annabelle as they ascend the stairs. "Is that a good idea?"

Nope, not even a little. "What do you think?"

We both shake our heads and go back upstairs. My body is crying for bed, I'm shot.

Poor Annabelle. Sadie has been distraught for the last two months over their relationship. She knew something was wrong the whole time.

I get in bed and pull her close to me. I need her as close as possible tonight. She's like the security blanket I never knew I needed.

I'm so happy we will never go through something like that.

One crazy incident in our lifetime is enough.

"Sadie, baby," I growl. I open my eyes, and what I see is a sight for sores eyes.

Sadie's head is thrown back, her chest is arched, and her hands are back leaning on my knees.

She's riding my cock, taking what she needs for her own pleasure, and It's fucking hot.

"There she is, my Sexy Sadie."

I maneuver myself to have a better view, run my hands up and down her thighs, and then slide them back to her arse. I squeeze and massage, getting lost in the feeling of Sadie.

I already feel like I could come. "How long have you been riding me, beautiful?"

Her eyes move to mine, her lids heavy with lust.

"You slept through the whole thing," she pants. "Because I'm about to come."

"I made a monster back in France, and it's the best thing I've ever done."

Watching her perky tits bounce up and down is a fucking turn-on. I thrust up hard as she grinds down on me, screaming my name in ecstasy.

I sit up at lightning speed, and her top half goes flying into the mattress.

"Wills! What…"

I silence her when I use every ab muscle possible to push up, land on my knees, and then jump to my feet—quickly pushing right back into her.

"What the hell, were you gymnast in a former life?" She screams as I continuously slam into her.

"Hell yeah, and I'm about to stretch you out real good."

She's practically upside down. Her head and shoulders are the only things touching the mattress. But I know this will feel fucking fantastic for her.

I bend and thrust right down into her. Dipping into that sweet pussy.

Sadie screams out my name while I hold her legs straight up towards the ceiling and maneuver my hips, hitting the exact spot she loves.

"Touch yourself, beautiful!" She doesn't wait for a second longer; her hand flies to her clit.

"Wills. Oh god, Wills!" she screams, and her orgasm rips through her as I slam down one last time. "Fuck!" I jerk and come in a rush. I couldn't even hold it if I wanted.

"That was the hottest fucking way ever to wake up."

I pull her up, and she slumps over on my chest and closes her eyes.

Her breathing is still labored, and her heart beats widely against my chest.

"Well, it was about time, I've been trying to get you up forever." Her voice rasps in the crook of my neck. I can't believe I slept through that, considering I'm a pretty light sleeper.

I must have been exhausted after last night.

A few moments pass, and I hear her breathing even out, falling back to sleep. I look over at the clock, and it's six in the morning. We have another two hours before Charlotte's up. So, I set my alarm, wrap us in the blankets and close my eyes, sleeping finding me right away.

"Sweetheart, wake up," I whisper into Sadie's ear and rub her back. She's still sprawled out on top of me. She slowly moves her head and narrows her eyes at me.

"What happened? Why are you calling me sweetheart?"

Oh, here we go again with that, I don't even freaking notice I'm doing it.

I grab her cheeks with both hands and give her a morning kiss, and she scrunches her face up against mine in concern.

"Wills," she warns.

"We had a little incident last night with Annabelle and Trey. I think she is going to need you today."

She jumps off me and rummages through her suitcase to find some clothes to put on.

"What kind of incident? I knew it, Wills. I told you, didn't I tell you that he was no good? So, what did that asshole do to her?"

"Sadie, relax. Jesus." I get up and maneuver her to the chair in the corner of the room. "Annabelle doesn't need you freaking out, she needs a stable friend to talk to. So, calm the hell down."

In frustration, she crosses her arms, making her push her tits together. Shit, I can feel my cock swelling, and her eyes nearly pop out of her head.

"Can you put that thing away, for God's sake!" She waves her hand dramatically in front of me. Probably not a good time to have my hard-on in front of her face. I put on some briefs and hand her a robe.

I go on and tell her about what transpired last night, and she does not look happy.

"He admitted to cheating on her, just came straight out and said it?"

"Yes, it was a nightmare. I think he might have been high and was probably just losing it." After I came to bed last night, I thought about the whole night, and I think I saw Trey doing coke in the bathroom.

I can't be sure because I wasn't exactly paying him that much attention. But now, his erratic behavior would make much more sense.

She takes a deep breath and gets back up to change, and I pull her back against me and take her back in the chair where I sit this time and maneuver her on my lap.

"They are probably still sleeping, and I just want a little more time with you, please." She softens against my body, and we don't talk, we just sit and relax for a while—both feeling sad for Annabelle and what comes next for her.

"Okay, I want to go see her now. Can you go make sure Charlie and Kathryn are okay downstairs?" I steal one kiss from her before she gets off my lap, and then I watch her get ready in the bathroom.

"Bye, I love you." She rises on her toes to try and reach me, and I wrap my arm around her waist and hoist her up to reach my lips.

"Wills." She giggles against my lips, kissing me back, and nibbles on my bottom lip a little before she slides down my body. Tease.

"Bye, baby. See you in a little."

Sadie

I slowly open Jackson's bedroom door, and what I see makes me smile. They look so lovely, cuddled up together. If Belle would just admit her feelings, maybe they could have been together the last few years instead of douchebag Trey.

I know Jackson says he doesn't ever want to settle down. But I know it would be different with Belle. They have a special spot in their hearts for each other, but both are too stubborn to acknowledge it.

When I walk closer, I see Jackson's hand is under Belle's shirt, palming her breast.

Oh god, I close my eyes for a second. I'm having a flashback of when I was a little kid, and I accidentally walked in on Jackson jerking off. It's not a memory I never wanted to think about again.

He definitely doesn't even realize he's doing it since they're sleeping. He's a boob guy, always has been, and it's probably second nature when he has a woman in bed with him.

"Guys, wake up," I say, loud enough for them to hear me but not startle them.

Belle stretches and inadvertently pushes her butt into Jackson's groin. He moans and presses back into her as he squeezes her boob.

"Oh god, guys!" I scrunch up my face in horror, and they both freeze and pull away from each other, and Jackson tries to adjust himself under the covers.

"Shit, sorry, B." She rolls her eyes and opens the blankets for me to crawl in next to her.

"Just move over, will you?" she says to Jackson. I get in the bed and instantly wrap my arms around her.

"Are you okay? Talk to me, please."

"I'm not, but I will be," she whispers against me.

"Of course, you will. You're so strong. But what can I do for you now?"

"Nothing, darling. Just lie with me for a while." And I do just that. I let her take comfort in my arms as I hold her against me and rub her back for what seems like hours.

Jackson leans over, kisses Belle, then me. "I'm going to go down to see the guys. Let me know if you need anything."

Belle grabs his hand as he's walking away, and he turns back toward her. "Thank you, Jack," she whispers, and he shoots her a wink and smiles, so his one dimple shows before he walks out. "Are you ready to talk?" I ask.

"There isn't much to say, I should have seen it coming. I know you did, so don't even bother."

"I didn't think he was cheating on you, Belle. I thought you just weren't compatible, and you could do better."

"He's just not been himself for the last year, and time got away from us. I should have left him a long time ago—we were too comfortable together and lived more like companions, not lovers." She sighs, then continues. "I'm not even sure I'm upset he's gone; I think I'm more upset someone can be so deceitful, and the way he was yelling at me was just outright scary and embarrassing. I can't believe Marco and Wills saw that last night."

"Don't be silly. Those two love you, and we're just happy they were there when they were."

Speak of the devil. Wills opens the door with Charlie in his arms.

"Charlotte Rose wanted to come make her Auntie Belle feel better."

"Yes, please, I need my lovely Charlotte right this instant." Charlie giggles and leans out of Wills's arms to jump on the bed and crawl between Belle and me.

Wills walks over to Belle's side of the bed and kisses her forehead without another word.

I smile up at him and he smirks before leaving us alone.

"Me and you, Belle. We will get through this. No more hiding stuff. Understand?"

"Yes, darling," she says, and she squeezes Charlie in her arms.

She looks back over at me, and I see a twinkle in her eyes. "Watch out, London, Annabelle Hughes is back." Isn't that the truth?

It's the way Belle is wired. Someone betrayed her, and she doesn't believe in second chances.

She will get over Trey fast and get under someone faster. "To get over is to get under," she once said to me about my ex, Colton. And I'm sure she will be following her advice sooner than later.

23

Sadie

"Wow, that was… amazing." I'm breathing heavily, lying lifeless like a starfish, unable to move a muscle.

"Merry Christmas, my love." I cast my eyes down at Wills smirking between my legs, his gray eyes sparkling with satisfaction.

"Was that my Christmas present?" I tease, and he playfully bites my inner thigh.

"If eating this delicious pussy of yours is a suitable Christmas present. I could have saved a lot of money." He leans over and pulls out a wrapped present from his nightstand. I sit up excitedly and clap my hands like a little kid.

I love Christmastime. Like, love, love, love it.

"Come on, Buddy," I hear a little whisper through the baby monitor. I glance over at Wills, and we're both off the bed within a second, throwing on our robes, just as the door flies open.

Excited blue eyes peer around the door. "Santa came?"

She's been asking if she's been a good girl every day for the last month. The poor kid has been driving herself crazy, making sure she would get the bike "with the extra wheels"—training wheels.

Little does she know; Wills has absolutely no limit with her and has bought all the toys London had to offer. I told him it would be unacceptable next year, but he was too excited this year, and I let him have it.

We can spoil her for one Christmas.

"Come here, princess. I have a present for you first." She runs as fast as her Christmas nightgown allows, reaching her arms up for Wills to help her up, and Buddy leaps on with ease to lie by Charlie's feet.

Wills hands the present he had in his hand over to me and then takes a smaller one out for Charlie.

I slowly unwrap it, it's jewelry. I can just feel it. I look over at Charlie, and she's trying to unwrap like a madwoman. I grab my phone and quickly take a few pictures of her sitting in Wills's lap as he tries to help her.

I open the box, and, oh my, I'm lost for words. I look up at Wills, but he's still concentrating on Charlie.

"Pwetty," she whispers and delicately takes her present out of the box, and my breath hitches.

"Wills." I place one hand on my chest, and I clasp his forearm with the other.

"After we bought Annabelle's present, I went back in the store and had her design them for the two of you."

Sitting in the velvet box is a stunning bracelet. It's a gold cuff lined with diamonds, and in the middle, sitting on top of the bracelet, is a beautiful gold abstract rose. This is something else. Just… out of this world. I put it on and snap a picture to send to Belle.

Charlie's is a dainty pearl bracelet with a smaller version of the gold flower in the middle.

"It's an English rose for you, princess." I smile at both of them. This is one of the most thoughtful gifts I've ever gotten. I stare over at my two loves.

I love my life, and I love the family we are building together.

My heart is whole.

"Charlotte Rose," she whispers. I'm surprised she understood the meaning of the rose. My baby is a smarty.

I lean over and put it on her tiny wrist. It's beautiful. She moves her wrist next to mine and looks at both of our bracelets. She's in awe.

Her ears are pierced with tiny studs. But other than that, this is her first piece of real jewelry, and I'm glad Wills was the one to give it to her.

"Otay, Santa time!" We both laugh, and I lean over to kiss Wills before we head downstairs.

I make sure he's looking right into my eyes, and I tell him how much I love my bracelet. I want him to feel the gratitude I have for him, for his thoughtfulness, of always thinking of both Charlie and me. For just loving us both unconditionally.

"I love it so much, thank you. I love you."

"I have one more present for you both, but I'll give it to you later." I shake my head. This is enough. But he won't listen.

"Okay, then we can give you your present too."

"Come on!" Charlie yells. Breaking our moment so we can all head downstairs to see what Santa brought.

"Let's go, girls!" a very impatient Wills yells from the front door. But, jeez, can he give us a second?

His good mood turned grumpy when he had to pack the G-Wagon up, with our luggage, Charlie's new pretty pink bike, and any other presents she said she wanted to bring. I think his New Year's resolution needs to be to say no to Charlie, making his life easier.

"What time is Jackson leaving?" I ask.

"I think he said he would give us a few hours head start to spend time with my family, so probably midafternoon."

We're on our way to the Cotswolds to spend Christmas with Wills's parents, and we plan to stay through the new year. I'm trying not to think about how nervous I am.

I've met them through face calls. But it's always quick and entirely informal.

Like when I'm in the kitchen cooking, and I wave to them from a distance.

Now both Charlie and I are staying at their house for a week, and I don't know what to expect. My only saving grace is Evelyn will be there with us the whole time.

They also kindly invited my brother to celebrate with all of us. I hadn't told Wills I wanted to spend Christmas with Jackson. I planned on it, but Wills beat me to it. He said Jackson is family, and it shouldn't even be a question.

When he says things like that, it makes me fall for him all over again.

"Did you have a nice time yesterday?" Wills asks.

I did. We hosted Christmas Eve with all our other family, our best friends. Marco even postponed his flight to Italy for this morning to spend time with us, which was the sweetest. Evelyn joined us, as well as two of Belle's brothers, who got along fabulously with everyone. They've already planned a whole guys' weekend to see some important rugby game, match? Whatever it's called.

Jackson used to be great friends with them when we were all young. I don't know why they ever lost touch, but I think this will spark their friendship back up.

We were lucky enough to hold it at the penthouse since there is way more room there. But we went back home once everyone left. I was happy to sleep there, but Wills insisted that the penthouse wasn't home anymore, and he wanted to wake up on Christmas morning in *our* bed.

"I had the best time. But I missed Declan. Why couldn't he make it?"

Wills shakes his head and lifts up his shoulder. "I really couldn't tell you, beautiful. He was kind of being shady, to be honest."

"Well, what did he say exactly?"

"After Ireland, he came to the office, tied some stuff up before he left again to head back to Ireland. He said he needed to get back for a family emergency and would stay through the new year."

"Weird. I feel like he would have at least called me. He took Charlie to the museum two weeks ago and even brought up Christmas Eve when he dropped her off."

"Yeah, something wasn't right. I felt like he was lying, but I couldn't exactly say that to him, just because I had a feeling. You know?"

Yeah, I get it. I even tried to call Dec last night when everyone was over, but he didn't answer. I hope everything is okay with him. Declan's a sensitive soul, and if something's up with him, I want to be there to help him.

We get each other and share a lot with one another, things he won't even share with Wills. So, if he won't even answer my calls, something must be up.

Oh! "Did you know John had grandkids, by the way? I didn't even know he had kids."

Wills chuckles from the driver's seat. "Of course. He's been my driver for a very long time."

Oh, now I feel dumb. Why didn't I know?

"Wow, Wills. This is beautiful!" We drive through small country roads, looking over beautiful rolling hills as we get closer to his parents' house. We have already driven through a few charming towns with storybook-style houses. He promised we could explore next week while we are here.

"I would love to come back here in the spring and summer when the flowers are in bloom," I say absentmindedly. Wills would bring me here whenever I wanted. He loves visiting his family, and he's told me his mom is a fantastic gardener.

"Horsies!" Charlie cries with excitement.

"Princess, you'll see horses, chickens, and another dog soon, and you'll get to play with them all week."

"Wow!" she says in excitement.

We pull down a long one-lane driveway lined with hedges and rose bushes that are obviously not in bloom, and then the land opens up, and a beautiful limestone house sits in front of us.

Wills places his hand on mine, making me realize I've been wringing my hands together. I'm all of a sudden racked with more nerves than before.

"Wills, this is not a small Cotswolds cottage. I thought you said your parents were teachers."

He laughs. "My grandfather, my namesake, was a very wealthy man. He left almost everything to my mum, they were extremely close. This was his weekend house, and he eventually retired here, like my parents. As a kid, I loved coming here." He pulls up his sleeve and shows me one of his watches that I love so much.

"This is actually his vintage Rolex. He left me his collection, it's where I get my love of watches from."

"How about your love for old cars?"

"Vintage, Sadie. And no, that would be my dad, he's a big car man. That's why I leave some of my cars here. He likes to take care of them, gives him something to do."

We park the car, and I can see the front door swing open in a rush, and a stunning regal woman walks out.

Eleanor is gorgeous. Wow.

And petite… I wasn't expecting that. She has long silver hair and is in incredible shape.

She's even more beautiful in person and looks just like Evelyn. I always thought Evelyn and Wills looked alike but not after seeing his mom. It's uncanny. The only thing the three of them share is their beautiful gray eyes.

But otherwise, Wills is the spitting image of his dad.

"William, Sadie!" She runs over and wraps her arms tightly around me. Oh… okay. This is the icebreaker I needed.

She pulls back and takes a good look at me. "You're just so beautiful, even more than Evelyn said." She leans in to give me another hug and kisses me on both cheeks. "I'm so happy you're here." She rubs her hands up and down my shoulders.

"It's so lovely to meet you, Mrs. Taylor. Merry Christmas. Thank you for welcoming Charlie and me into your beautiful home."

"Oh nonsense, call me Eleanor, and where is the infamous Charlie?"

"I'm still back here!" she yells from her car seat, and Wills's mom starts to laugh.

I lean in to take her, and when I pull her out, Eleanor's face drops, and it looks like she's seen a ghost. She coughs a few times, clearing her throat, and I look at Wills, wondering what that was all about, but he's oblivious. When I turn back, she's smiling at Charlie now.

That was weird.

I'm exhausted from cooking all day yesterday and getting up early this morning—maybe I imagined it? Because no one else seems to notice anything.

"Hello, my name is Charlotte Rose."

"Oh, hello lovely, you're just the cutest ever, aren't you? My name is Eleanor, but I'll think of something better for you to call me. How's that?"

"Otay!" she says and then runs yelling after Buddy, who found his friend, the family dog Petey, a beautiful collie.

"Come, come, let's get inside. It's quite chilly out here today, wouldn't you say?"

Eleanor guides me toward the house.

"Um, hello to you too, Mum."

"Oh, sorry dear." She laughs and hugs and kisses Wills.

"William, I will send your father out to help with the bags, and I'll give Sadie a quick tour."

I call for Charlie and Buddy, and then we head into the house.

"Your house is just beautiful, Eleanor. It should be in a magazine."

"It was." She winks at me. "It helps if your daughter is a brilliant interior designer."

Oh, well, that makes sense.

"This must be the woman who has stolen my boy's heart," a very attractive man says as he walks into the kitchen. He's even taller than Wills and so handsome, it's hard not to stare. This family won on the gene pool.

Wills's dad wraps me in a tight hug. His parents are both so warm and kind. I wonder where the heck Wills came from because warm is definitely not a word I would use to describe Wills.

"Oh, Eleanor, isn't she just gorgeous?" Wills's dad asks as he looks lovingly over to his wife, and I can feel the blush burning my cheeks. Now I know what Wills did get from him, his charm.

"Thomas, leave the girl alone. You're embarrassing her."

"Whose embarrassing who?" Wills asks as he walks into the kitchen

"Oh, you just mind your own business, will you?" I'm loving Eleanor already. She is unquestionably the boss around here. I like watching someone put Wills in his place.

You okay? Wills mouths to me, and I smile and nod. I am. I love his family already.

"Auntie Ev's here!" Charlie comes running into the house, holding Evelyn's hand. The other hand already has two barbies that she didn't get from us. Evelyn's in trouble.

"Oh, she calls her auntie?" Eleanor asks from beside me, and unease washes over me.

"Yeah. Well… I, we thought…" She laughs.

"No, sweetie, don't worry. I didn't mean it in a bad way. I think it's lovely. I can tell your daughter adores my son and daughter very much and vice versa." She gives me a genuine smile that puts me at ease. She rubs my arm and kisses my cheek before walking over to pick up Charlie and greet Evelyn.

"Let's all go in the other room and open presents before Sadie's brother gets here," Wills's dad says.

"More?" Charlie's eyes light up with excitement.

"No, sweet pea. Just for adults this time."

Her little face drops, and I instantly feel bad. I should have thought to save a few presents to have something to open here.

"Don't listen to that crazy mum of yours, Charlie sweets. Santa stopped at Auntie Ev's and left lots of presents for you."

"Us too!" Eleanor speaks up from behind me as we walk into the sitting room, and the number of presents is absurd.

"Oh no, you guys, this is too much! She doesn't need all this."

"Nonsense." And I can tell by Eleanor's tone that what she says is final, as I'm pushed farther into the room and told to take a seat.

"You're quiet." Wills scoots closer to put his arm around me, and I smile up at that handsome face of his. I trace my finger along his jaw and lean in to kiss him lightly on the lips.

"I'm just very happy, that's all." His smile widens, a full-on Wills Taylor smile that only comes out on occasion, so I don't take it for granted. He puts his arm around my shoulder and pulls me into his side.

"Look at them," I hear Eleanor whisper.

"Mum, enough," Wills groans, and his family laughs.

We all watch Charlie open all her presents; Evelyn must have bought every other toy that Wills didn't get in London. She also bought the two of them tickets to see *The Lion King* musical, which was so thoughtful. We didn't entirely graduate from *The Little Mermaid*, but we're onto *The Lion King* and *Aladdin* at the moment.

His parents assured us they only got gifts to stay at their house, so we would be forced to come back soon.

Their big gift was a bouncy house for the backyard that I'm sure Wills will be setting up tomorrow, and the rest were arts and crafts that Eleanor wants to do with Charlie since she was an art teacher for forty years.

Last night, Wills gifted Evelyn one of his Audemars Piguet watches he resized for her. I just learned that watch was also their grandfather's, and she has loved it since she was a little girl.

But that was her distraction gift. Wills said Evelyn has a hard time this time of year, and she deserves lots of extra love. He also told me she would explain the reason why, herself. The way he said it was pretty ominous, but something told me not to push him, so I'll wait for her to come to me.

"Are you insane?" Evelyn screams, and even Charlie pauses to look up at her. I knew she would freak out when she saw our gift, well, Wills's gift he insisted was from us.

"Holy hell, are you both nuts? I mean, I accept, but like… wow."

If I thought Jackson was generous, this is next level. Wills never sold his penthouse. Instead, he gifted it to Evelyn.

Wills's mom has that proud parent smile on her face, looking over at Wills with pure joy in her eyes.

After we all finish opening our gifts, I look around at everyone, and this is the family Christmas I've always wanted. Christmas music comes through the sound system, the fire is burning, while we all laugh as Charlie pretends to dance with Buddy.

It must have been so nice to grow up with parents like Eleanor and Thomas, you can just feel the love in this house. And it makes me remember how lucky I am to have had Jackson growing up because I'm not sure what I would have done otherwise.

Jackson arrived an hour ago and is downstairs with Wills and his dad, but I'm still getting ready with Evelyn while Charlie takes a nap.

"He did well, my brother. I would love to say I taught him well, but our age difference makes that impossible," she says, admiring my bracelet that I'm wearing for dinner tonight.

"It's beautiful, isn't it?" I sigh. I can't stop smiling every time I look at it, and Charlie refuses to take hers off.

"I can't wait for you to meet Poppy and Olivia tonight. You're just going to love them."

Evelyn has been trying to set up dinner with her best friends for the last month, but they own their own luxury travel company or something another and haven't been in London. But their parents have a house in the same town so we will see them later at the pub.

For years, a tradition all the "kids" in the town do. After all the family time is over, we will meet there for the actual party.

"Is she still sleeping?" Wills pops his head into the room.

"Uh-huh, she was exhausted. But I'm going to wake her soon."

"Okay, then, Evelyn, finish in your room. I want to give Sadie her last gift." Evelyn looks between the two of us, and her smile reaches her eyes. Clearly, she knows what my present is. Now, I'm really curious and excited because Evelyn looks ready to burst.

"Mine first." I hand him an envelope. "You are the man who has everything, so, yeah." Now a little unsure if he will be happy about it.

"Oh, my beautiful girl. What a great idea, all of us?"

"It's our special place, even if it didn't end well. I will never regret it, and I want to share it with Charlie too." I booked us a family holiday at the same hotel we met. I want to start new traditions—all three of us—and going back to where it all started seemed like the perfect idea. I spoke to my therapist about it before I booked it. Worried it may trigger my PTSD, she said it might, but we would work through it and figure it out together. So, I'm hopeful.

"This is going to be amazing; I can't wait. Thank you." He kisses me, then hands me an identical envelope.

What the hell is this? I look at him, then look back down, it's blueprints. It's blueprints to a house.

"What is this?" I ask stupidly. It's obvious what it is.

"Our new home. And, before you freak out—it's not ready, so we don't have to move Charlie for months or whenever you're ready. And it's still in Notting Hill like you love. It's just being refurbished and built out to be a little more modern on the inside. Evelyn designed the entire thing for us, but she hasn't ordered any tiles, furniture, or any of that good stuff until you okay it," he spits out fast, he's nervous I won't like it, and it makes me laugh.

It always surprises me when this big tough guy gets like this. I move to sit in his lap and put my arms around him.

"You're too good to us." I kiss him and go to pull away, but he coaxes my mouth open, and his tongue enters, deepening the kiss.

"What are you, like the real estate Santa this Christmas?" He's just gifting houses like it's no big deal. Must be nice to be Wills Taylor.

"No, I just want all my girls to be happy in beautiful, safe homes."

"Mommy?" Charlie breaks us out of our little love bubble, and she puts her hands out for a cuddle. Sleepy cuddles will never get old.

"You know you didn't have to get us that, right? Not that I'm not grateful, but I'm happy living anywhere with you. As long as we are all together." His one eyebrow lifts, calling me out on my lie.

"Fine, I would live anywhere but the penthouse." Which totally sounds like the snobbiest thing in the world, but I am not living near that woman. Over my dead body. He chuckles and walks over to kiss us both.

"I know, beautiful, and that's why I like buying things for you. Making you happy makes me happy. End of story."

Christmas turned out to be perfect. The food was divine, Eleanor is a fantastic cook, but the company made it all the more memorable for me.

Jackson was a hit with everyone, which isn't a shocker, he's a smooth talker and wins over both men and women wherever we are.

"Okay, pudding time!" Eleanor wheels out a legit cart you would see in a restaurant and every single person groans from fullness. How are we to fit one more bite of food in our bodies?

"So, Ev, any special guys in your life? I've never seen you dating anyone," Jackson asks.

Thomas's breath hitches and the whole table goes quiet. Jackson and I just look at each other, unsure what's going on.

"I'm married, so I don't need to date anyone," Evelyn deadpans, completely serious.

"What? What are you talking about?" I ask, laughing. She's joking.

Eleanor's eyes are filled with tears, and Wills grabs my leg under the table and shakes his head for me to be quiet. I don't understand. Silence fills the room for a while until Evelyn speaks up again.

"Two years ago, my husband was killed by a drunk driver. Next weekend is the anniversary."

My hand flies to my mouth, and Jackson bows his head in remorse.

"What?" I whisper.

"Evelyn, I'm so sorry. We didn't know." She smiles sadly and rubs Jackson's shoulder.

"You wouldn't have known, don't worry. I told Wills I wanted to tell you," she says and continues the story.

"He was killed the morning after our wedding. Some idiot woke up in his car still hammered and tried to drive home from the pub. We were to leave on our honeymoon that morning, so Andrew went out to grab breakfast, but he never made it home." Her shoulders sag as silent tears fall down her face.

"The day after?" I whisper in horror. They were only married for one day? I'm not sure what else to say, everyone is silent. I'm afraid if I say more, I'll lose it. I look over at Wills, and he gives me a sad smile.

"They had been together their whole life," Wills continues the story. "Since the day they were born, they have been inseparable, even if it wasn't their choice at first. Our mums are best friends and tried to get pregnant together, which, lucky for them, happened. Andrew was older, but only by two days. But not only are our mums close, but Andrew and his family lived next door to us in London. We saw them every day—they are family. When they were Charlie's age was when you started to see their inseparable bond. Then when they were about six, all of our neighbors came to their backyard wedding, and then again when they 'renewed their vows' at twelve. Eleanor chuckles at this memory, and I see a slight grin on Evelyn's face.

"Evelyn went through a goth stage and wanted a new dress. That's also when she made us all start calling her Ev. She thought it was edgier than Evelyn."

"I always wondered why you called her a nickname when you refuse to do so with anyone else," I reply.

"She wore this black tulle dress, combat boots, and heavy black makeup walking down her 'aisle,' that led to a smiling jumper-clad, Andrew. But it didn't matter what my sister wore. Nothing would get in the way of his feelings for Evelyn." He pauses, and we all look at

Evelyn, who's crying, but you can see the love and happiness in her eyes.

"I was twenty-two at the time and had to rush from a rugby match. Of course, no one would have ever guessed I was rushing for a twelve-year-old's wedding, the way I was acting. But I made it there right on time, and I, for some reason, can't get that moment out of my mind. It has stuck with me forever, more than their real wedding. The moment my sister walked down the aisle, even at twelve years old, I could see the pure love in Andrew's eyes. I just knew that he would make my sister a happy woman until the day he died. But, unfortunately, no one thought it would be at twenty-seven years old."

"I was lucky enough to be married to my great love for twenty-one years, from the day I was six years old."

"I'm so incredibly sorry for your loss, Evelyn. But that's a beautiful way to think of it." I get out of my chair to go kiss her, and she pulls me into her lap, hugging me to her.

"No more tears. Andrew loved Christmas and would hate us sitting around here sad. He may have lived a short life, but he was always so incredibly happy—we lived a beautiful, fulfilled life in the time we had together. I want to toast my husband." We all lift our glasses.

"Andrew, you are my life, my light, my eternal love. Your time on earth was up, but your time in my heart will last forever. Merry Christmas in heaven, hubby. To Andrew!"

"To Andrew." We cheers to Andrew and a beautifully tragic love story.

It's a few hours later, Wills's parents' friends are here for a Christmas nightcap, and we are waiting for Charlie to fall asleep.

She, of course, has been the center of attention the whole night, Wills's parents doting on every word she said. She's trying her hardest to stay up now. It's like she knows we are trying to leave. Wills is rocking her back and forth as he talks to a few other men in the corner, and she's fighting to keep her eyes open. There're too many people here, she doesn't want to miss out on the fun.

Evelyn settles up next to me. "You okay?" I ask.

"You know, for a long time, I was sad and depressed. But I want him to look down at me from heaven and see the woman he loves. Not a sad existence of her."

She is so strong, I envy her. Because if Wills died, I'm not sure I would be as resilient.

We're interrupted when a few ladies nearby start talking.

"Look how cute they are together. It's too bad she's not his real kid."

"You know he bought them a house. Eleanor told me all about it. Isn't that crazy? He can have anyone in the world, he's so handsome and rich, and now only after a few months, he's going to raise someone else's kid?" I frown. Is that what people think? I know people would think it was fast, but to bring Charlie into it, she's just a little kid who loves Wills unconditionally. It's not her fault he loves her back.

"If it were my son, I would be talking him out of it. She must have some motive, don't you think?"

"They aren't worth it, Sadie." My eyes well with tears, and Evelyn pulls me away.

"Excuse me?" someone interrupts the ladies. There is warning in the tone, which stops Evelyn and me in our tracks to listen.

"I think it's time you leave my home. Sadie is our family, and you do not disrespect her in this house. Wills will no doubt marry that girl one day soon, and it will be one of the happiest days of my life, to gain another daughter and granddaughter. I don't care whose DNA that little girl has because that's her dad right there," Eleanor spits out in anger.

"Goodbye, ladies." Her tone is threatening, and all the ladies huff and walk off to find their husbands and leave.

The tears are streaming down my face, I couldn't stop them if I wanted. Not because of the nasty women, but because I finally feel like I belong somewhere. Wills has been trying to tell me all along that we are a family, but right now, in this instant, I realize I have a *complete* family—it's not just Jackson and me anymore, or Wills and me. It's all of us.

"I love your mom," I choke out through my tears.

"I've never been prouder to call her my mum than I am right now," Evelyn says as we hug.

"Okay, I think we all deserve copious amounts of alcohol tonight. Let's go!"

24

Wills

WE'VE BEEN at the pub for over two hours, and I finally got my drunk sister to tell me why the girls were crying earlier. I had watched the two of them from across the room, wondering what was going on. It was killing me, and I couldn't get to Sadie. Charlotte was just falling asleep, and my lawyer Charles Whitmore was updating me on important business-related matters regarding the after-school program.

But what Evelyn told me had me speechless. I've known some of those ladies my whole life. Now it's too late to say anything, I wish I had known sooner. But at least Mum was there, sticking up for my girls.

I can tell she has a soft spot for Sadie and Charlie—I never told her about Sadie back then, it hurt too much. But, when I saw Sadie again a couple of months ago, I finally told her everything, and she was incredibly sad for both of us but happy we found our way back together.

But now, on top of all that happened, Evelyn got Sadie drunk, and they are dancing with Poppy and Olivia for every guy in the pub to see.

"Breathe… in and out, in and out," Jackson says from beside me.

"Oh, fuck off."

"Have another drink or something. You look like you're going to murder someone."

Because *I am* going to murder someone, I can't take my eyes off Sadie. I'm trying to have some restraint and not go all caveman on her, as she calls it, but I'm losing my patience very quickly.

"I'm going to go dance with the girls. You want to join?"

"Oh, come on, mate, don't encourage her." He walks away anyway, laughing his arse off, getting a kick out of me losing my plot.

Jackson makes it to the girls while Ev starts walking back toward me, her eyes are narrowed.

"Why are you all"—she waves her hands at me dramatically—"crazy looking?"

"Can everyone just shut the hell up? I'm not crazy. I am just standing here, drinking a scotch, minding my own business."

She rolls her eyes. "If you say so." I'm not even this overprotective with her, so I have no clue why it makes my blood boil if even one person looks at Sadie. It's been like this forever, since the day I met her before I even spoke to her.

Something deep down just makes me nuts over her.

I see a few guys in the corner get up, and I know they are going right for the girls still dancing.

And that's when I lose my patience. Over my dead body is she dancing with someone else. I stride right on the dance floor, making it to Sadie before they do.

"Oh! Hi, baby, are you here to dance with me?" She bats her eyelashes up at me dramatically. You can't help but smile. Sadie is a fun drunk, always has been. Unless Annabelle feeds her too much tequila, that's a whole other story.

"No, it's time to go home, beautiful. I'm going to call us a cab."

"Oh, boo-hoo! He's no fun, girls, right?" She looks at the other girls to confirm, and Jackson is in hysterics watching us, listening to Sadie's pretend baby voice.

"Please, one dance, please, oh please, Wills." Oh hell, I can't say no to her when she begs like that.

"Fine! One dance, Sadie. I'm warning you."

"Okay, one!" she says, winking at the girls or more like she tries, but her whole face scrunches up adorably.

"Come here, you." I grab her and pull her into my body. I need every part of her touching me right now.

"Hi," she whispers up at me. "Hi, beautiful, having a good time?" I leave down to give her a quick kiss and wipe her sweaty hair away from her forehead.

"The best time, these girls are fun." Yeah, single and wild too.

"I love dancing with you. You can really move for a big guy. You know that?"

"A big guy, huh?" We both laugh, and she looks around quickly, then says.

"I mean big everywhere!" She widens her eyes and looks down to get her point across, and my cock jumps to attention. But I'm ignoring that for now. My girl wants a dance, giving in, we somehow dance for thirty more minutes.

The tempos have changed, but we are still wrapped up, slow dancing, lost in our own world. Sadie and I don't always need to talk. Instead, we can communicate through silence and touch. Something I've never taken for granted.

"Oh, hey! Wait here for a second."

"Sadie, where are you going? Get back here!" I yell, and she puts her finger up to tell me one minute. I outwardly groan. Can she not just follow one thing I say?

She's running back to me now and trips right on the dance floor. Luckily, I'm standing here to catch her.

"Careful, you're going to break your freaking ankle," I warn. "Oops, sorry." She giggles.

God, give me strength.

"Where did you go?" She doesn't respond and just stands there listening to the music for a minute. Maybe she's drunker than I thought. It's that, or she's out of her mind and going completely insane.

The music changes and her face lights up as she puts her arms back over my shoulders.

"It's our song," she whispers. What song? I listen for a second and then it registers. It's the song from Ireland, last weekend.

We sway back and forth to the music, and I watch her closely, unable to take my eyes off her. I'm glad those women didn't upset her too much tonight because I love seeing her like this, just so utterly happy.

And when Sadie is happy, she has this energy that radiates off her, pulling everyone around her into happiness.

She takes a step back, her hips sexily moving to the beat, her head lolls back and forth, with her eyes closed, but she's still singing, and even though her eyes are shut, I can feel her singing to me. She stretches one of her arms toward me while still dancing, points a finger, and sings the chorus with the biggest and brightest smile I've ever seen.

"*You are the best thing*, Wills. You always will be. *Then, now and forever*. Right, baby?"

I love this woman. "Yes, beautiful. *Then, now and forever*," I choke, emotions getting the better of me.

Sadie

I feel little fingers playing with my hair, and I open my eyes to see Charlie and Wills smiling down at me.

"Good morning, Mommy!" She leans down and kisses me with her wet little lips.

"Good morning, my sweet pea. How did you sleep?"

"Great!"

"And you?" I look up to my love, who is huddling over us.

"Perfect, always perfect with you." Oh, swoony Wills is in the house today.

There's a knock at our door, and Eleanor peeks her head around, smiling when she sees the three of us lying down together.

"Sadie, when you're ready, would you fancy a cuppa downstairs in the sunroom?"

"Absolutely, let me just get changed, and I'll be right down," I tell her.

Jackson pops his head around her. "And I'm here to take my angel girl for breakfast and a walk around the property." Charlie jumps out of bed, and Wills kisses me goodbye and follows to join them.

"Hi," I greet Eleanor, who is already sitting with a cup in her hand.

"Good morning, sweetie. Come sit down with me, please." I take a seat and look around. This room is all glass, overlooking the grounds. It's breathtaking.

"It's just beautiful out here. I can imagine curling up with a good book and reading in this room."

"Well, you're more than welcome to come back and do that whenever you want. With or without William."

"Oh, thank you, Eleanor, I appreciate that." One thing I can tell you this whole family has in common is their generosity—easy to give and not to take. It's an admirable quality.

"I wanted to apologize for last night—"

I cut her off before she continues and shake my head.

"No, please don't. If anything, I need to be thanking you. I learned a long time ago not to take what others say about you to heart. I might have been upset, but I've learned to get over it. So please, thank you for sticking up for me and for the kind words you said about Charlie and me. You will never know how much that meant to me."

She takes my hand in hers. A move Wills often does.

"I don't mean to overstep, but William has told me about your history with your parents, and I just have to say that they must be selfish, stupid people if they don't want you, Charlie, or Jackson in their lives. They are missing out on three very special people." I have to close my eyes, to stop the tears. Wills already teases I'm an emotional crybaby. I don't need Eleanor thinking it too.

"If you don't want an apology, fine, but I never want you to feel uncomfortable or unwelcome in this home. And I can tell you now, if those ladies thought they heard the last of me, they are sorely mistaken. No one messes with my family."

I still can't speak, but I smile wide over at Eleanor to show her my appreciation.

"One more thing." Her face looks apprehensive, and I wonder what it could be.

"I know this is a little forward. But at my age, I don't really care anymore." We both laugh, and she grabs my hand again and squeezes.

"I know we are all just getting to know one another, but I feel as if you are already family. William sure thinks you are, so that makes you mine. I know I'm not Charlie's real grandmother, but if or when you're comfortable with it, I would love for her to call me Nan. I want to show her off as my granddaughter and spoil her rotten." Well, that does me in. I can't hold back the tears now.

This is everything I've ever wanted for my daughter. Unconditional love by all the people in her life.

Something I never had as a child.

"Oh, love, I'm sorry. I didn't mean to upset you." I wave my hand around because the words escape me. I take a deep breath to compose myself. *Alright, Sadie, get a hold of yourself.*

"I'm not upset, Eleanor, I'm… I don't know what I am. Shocked? Happy? In awe? I don't know the words, but how could I ever be upset with someone who cares for my daughter the way you do? Of course, she can call you Nan, it would be an honor. Truly."

"Well, good, that settles it then."

"Settles what?" I laugh. She all of a sudden has a look of resolution.

"Thomas thought I was crazy to ask you, even though he is desperate for her to call him Grandad. He said he would build Charlotte a pool in the back for the summer if you said yes. I've been begging him for the last ten years, but Charlie comes around, and he's already called the contractor." I start laughing along with her.

"Sadie, you should have heard him this morning. The poor contractor is still on holiday with his family, and Thomas said he would use someone else if he didn't listen up." She shakes her head but has love in her eyes for her husband. Last night, she told me she still looks at him like it's the first time they met. It's romantic and reassuring how their love is still so strong.

"Anyway, last thing. I thought maybe if you two wanted to spend some time together, we could watch Charlotte for a night or two, and you two can book somewhere special. Maybe for New Year's Eve?"

"Oh, that's so thoughtful of you." I wish we could take her up on her offer. But I'm not sure it would work with the way Charlie has been acting.

"But I think we will have to decline the offer, thank you anyway," I say with a heavy heart. I really could use some time alone with Wills.

"Oh, okay." Her face falls. "Oh! It's nothing to do with you, Eleanor," I assure her. "We are having some issues with Charlie at the moment. She has terrible attachment issues, especially with Wills. It's getting worse, actually, and Wills doesn't make it better because he never wants to leave her or say no. So as much as I would love a night away, just the two of us, I don't think it's in the cards for us. But I appreciate it."

"We have five more days until New Year's Eve. So go on and book something. I'm confident I can help, or at least make her want to stay with me as much as you two." Her face has such a look of determination on it, she probably could tell me anything, and I would believe her. So I guess it doesn't hurt to try.

I sip my tea, thinking how nice it would be to get away, just the two of us. We may live together, but we both work different hours, and when we're home, we want to spend time with Charlie. There is never time just for Sadie and Wills unless it's in the bedroom, but we need more than that.

I turn my head toward Eleanor because I can feel her eyes on me.

"You know, you're the only girl he has ever brought home?" *What?* How is that possible? He dated that one girl for like three years.

"What about that crazy girlfriend?" She rolls her eyes in disgust.

"Libby. Don't remind me of her. And no. They just lived a life in London, and he always came home alone. I only met her accidentally when I surprised Wills once."

Hmm, interesting.

"Why don't you go tell Wills the good news about your night away and send my granddaughter to me." She smiles proudly when she says granddaughter and points to Wills and Charlie in the paddock across the way, petting the horses.

I get up to walk across the field, and when I'm almost an earshot away, I hear Eleanor call my name, so I look back. "And when you're ready, Sadie, you'll call me Mum, yeah?" I swallow down the lump in my throat and nod my head. I'd love nothing more.

"Bye, Mommy and Wills!" Charlie says as we walk toward the garage that holds Wills's cars. Somehow, Eleanor did it. There wasn't a tear in sight today.

Charlie was actually pushing us out the door. She wanted "art and craft time with her nan."

"Wow, these are beautiful. Which one will we take? I'm excited. I have no idea about cars, but they look fun."

"Come on, baby, this way," he replies, pulling me along.

"Are these all yours?"

"Some are my dad's; we share the space. This car here is the one we will drive today." He stops next to a navy-blue Mercedes of some sort. I peer inside and see tan interior and an oversized brown leather steering wheel. Super chic.

"It's a 1954 SL300 Gullwing, and it was my first vintage car I invested in." He opens the door for me to get in. "Whoa! These are like Batmobile doors." Then I look inside, look at Wills, then look back inside.

"What's wrong?" Confusion crosses his face.

"Um, this car seems a little small for you." He narrows his eyes and gets in the car.

"I fit just fine, thank you." I get in and look over, not exactly calling it a fine fit. But if he wants to kid himself, I guess we will go with that.

We pull out, and Charlie is still outside, waiting to send us off.

Wills honks, and I think I hear a "woo-hoo!" in the distance. I'm so happy Charlie stayed with Eleanor and Evelyn. And I'm pretty sure Eleanor must be the Charlie whisperer.

Once we're on a straightaway, Wills shifts into gear and moves his hand to my lap.

"I'm so happy we have this time together. Of course, I'm sad not to bring in the new year with my princess. But we needed this, didn't we?"

"Ah, now you're seeing the light. Does that mean you'll start to tell her no?" He ignores me and turns the music louder. That's what I thought.

"How long is the ride to the hotel?"

"It's not far, but through the back roads, it will probably take thirty-five minutes or so."

"Okay, let's play a game!"

"That sounds terrible, Sadie. How about you just tell me a story, and I'll listen. Or better yet… use that mouth for something better." He winks over at me.

"Really?" I ask, looking down at him, watching his pants tent slowly. I've never done that before.

"Fuck. I was kidding. You'd do that for me, baby?"

I think for only a second, this is supposed to be a fun getaway. Why the heck not?

"Stop staring at it, Sadie," he hisses. He's completely hard now and is painfully pressed against his pants.

I answer by leaning over, unzipping his pants, and freeing him of his briefs. I barely touch him with my tongue, and he's cursing and quickly pulling the car over.

"Can't concentrate?" I mumble around him.

"It's been days since I've blown anywhere in your body, Sadie. So, wrap those pretty little lips around my cock already."

I open wide, and on my first pass, I take him to the back of my throat. I gag, and my eyes water. But I keep going, taking him in deep, over and over again. His breathing is ragged, and his legs are tense. He's freaking turning me on to the nth degree.

I hollow my cheeks and slowly suck him from bottom to top. My hand grips the bottom of his shaft, following my mouth in one long stroke.

"Fuck, fuck, fuck. Sadie." He groans deeply, and I close my eyes as arousal continuously runs through me. Getting him off always does it for me. "Eyes on me, beautiful."

I lift my eyes. His mouth is slack and his dark but almost pained eyes hold mine. I circle his head with my tongue. Small amounts of come drip out, and I suck it up like it's my last meal.

"You're one hot fuck, Sadie. Do you know that, baby?"

I slowly fist him and lean my head down to take his balls in my mouth. Licking and sucking them one by one. *This will be his undoing.*

"Sadie," he growls. "Get your mouth back up here and open wide, baby, because I'm about to blow the fucking house down."

I obey instantly, taking him deep and fast, but he can't resist. His hand comes to the back of my head, holding me in place, as he thrusts up into my mouth, hitting the back of my throat. I don't break eye contact as the tears run down my face.

"Yes, fuck. I knew you could take it. You're such a good girl, aren't you?"

One, two more thrusts.

"Sadie, goddamnit, fuck!" he roars, and hot liquid squirts into the back of my throat, not stopping and making me choke.

Shit.

He sardonically laughs at me. "I told you, it's been days." I narrow my eyes at him as I swallow down the rest, and he chuckles again.

"Jerk," I say as I wipe my mouth on his shirt.

He grabs my face, smashing his lips against mine. "You're always surprising me, beautiful," he says, then leans me back into my seat, reaching to put my seat belt on me before pulling back on the road to continue our trip.

But now I'm freaking turned on, and the rumbling of this old car is like a vibrator right on the perfect spot.

I close my eyes and press my legs together to ease the throb.

"Something wrong?"

"No," I snap.

"Good, because I won't touch you until we get to the hotel."

"Why?" I whine.

"Because while I didn't touch myself the last few days, you got yourself off, didn't you?"

"What, no!" I say a little too quickly.

"Are you lying to me?" he asks, eyebrows raised.

I cover my face. "How did you know?"

How embarrassing! I'm not someone who needs it, unless it's from Wills. But he kept touching me sexually, and I couldn't hold it anymore.

"All I had to do was take one look at your face after your shower. I know every square inch of your body, Sadie. Your looks, your taste, your sounds. Everything."

"Well, it was your fault for massaging me in bed!"

"How about when you were rubbing your arse on my cock yesterday?"

I huff. Is he kidding? "I was freaking sleeping!"

He ignores me and turns the music back on. Ugh!

After a while passes and I've calmed down, I finally speak and try again. "Come on, let's play a game. We can play the *get-to-know-you game*. Remember how we did in France, the night of my birthday?"

"You mean the night you left me alone in bed?" I groan. The second "my birthday" was out of my mouth, I knew it was a mistake. He loves to tease me about it.

"Plus, beautiful. I know everything I need to know about you."

"Don't you want to know things like who my first kiss was or…"

"What on earth would make you think I would want to hear about you kissing someone else?" He cuts me off, and I laugh and smile over at my jealous man. It wouldn't matter if I were only thirteen, he would still be crazy jealous.

"When we get back to London, let's take some time to do more things around the city. January will be slow for Marco and me, and I'd like to take advantage."

"Whatever you want, beautiful. As long as I don't have to do any guided tours, I'm yours."

"I also want to start running more in the park, so when I whine and complain, make me run more. Don't let me say no."

"Okay, I can do that. I'll bribe you if I have to." Wills chuckles.

"At least I usually get something out of a bribe. Oh! And I want to go to Borough Market, I've never been. And Charlie wants to see your office, so I should plan a day for that. Maybe we can get lunch? But I can't forget to bring her to the changing of the guards. You know the one with the horses? What's that one called? And she's been begging to ride in a 'big red bus,' so we have to do one of the double-decker ones, and…"

"Sadie." I look over at Wills, and he's smiling so wide. He takes my hand up and kisses the back of it, leaving it there a few seconds with his lips pressed against my skin. "You're very excited."

"I know, I'm sorry. Sometimes I get carried away when I think about how I actually moved and live in London now."

"Don't be sorry, beautiful. I love how happy you are. I think it's cute you're excited to explore London. And I'll do whatever makes you happy. It's my life goal always to see that smile on your face."

"Aren't you the romantic today, Mr. Taylor?"

"I try, Ms. Peters." He shrugs with a smirk, and we both laugh.

We continue driving in a comfortable silence, light jazz playing through the speakers as we coast through the beautiful English countryside.

I'm glad we came. Not only tonight, to the hotel, but the whole week to Wills's family estate.

It was a nice break from the hustle and bustle of London.

I landed there only two months ago and have been on the go ever since. But, this week in the country, let me sit back, appreciate, and take it all in.

Within two months, I moved to London to be closer to Belle and Jackson.

I started my own business and got two huge accounts. I made a few fantastic friends who quickly became family.

And most importantly, I reconnected with my love. After three and a half years, we somehow found our way back to each other. It's almost unbelievable. Something you would read about in a romance novel.

I think back to all the hardship we both endured because of that horrible misunderstanding and wonder… if that didn't happen… would we be here today? Were we supposed to separate and grow before we met again? Is our love so strong that the universe pulled us back together?

I genuinely believe we are soul mates—I'm not sure I believed in that word until I met Wills Taylor.

But, if our souls are one, then I think, yes, whatever way the road took us over the years must have been the path that was destined for us.

"We're here, baby." I peek out through the window, and I love what I see already. A mix of old and new. It is a limestone estate with an extension of all glass on the side that looks like it may be a restaurant looking over the rolling hills in the back.

"What's the name of this hotel again?" I ask.

"The Sage, after the herb. This hotel is known for its food and culinary classes. They grow almost everything on the property." Very cool.

After lunch, we were given a tour of the property. The main estate is more of a common area, for the bar, restaurant, and shopping. The accommodations are small cottages spread across the land, and I'm wondering now how we got one so last minute. The place seems five-star and pretty crowded for New Year's Eve.

I ask Wills about it, and he says, "There are very few times it pays to be a known sports player, but this is one of the times it does." I guess I won't complain because this place is breathtaking. We walk into the bedroom, and I plop right onto the massive bed.

Being a mom and business owner means I'm not stopping all day long, and it's not until you're away from it all that it hits you how worn out you can get. We only woke up a few hours ago, and I'm already ready for a nap.

Wills is in the bathroom, and I hear the water for the bathtub go on, and I sit right up. A relaxing bath is exactly what I need right now. I get up to walk toward the bathroom, and I realize the room is filled with beautiful winter-white flowers everywhere. I completely missed them when we walked in.

"Wills, baby, did you have these put in the room?" I point to some flowers that are sitting on the bathroom vanity.

"Some, yes, I thought you would be pleased with them. But most are from the hotel. It's one of their signature pieces in their rooms. I read it on their website, and it was one of the reasons I chose the hotel." That's so sweet, this is the side many people don't see of Wills. Of course, he wouldn't have even mentioned it to me either if I didn't ask him.

I walk over to kiss him. "Well, thank you. It was incredibly thoughtful. And is this bath for us, or just me?"

"Us. When have you ever seen a tub we both can fit in?" Although he laughs, it's true. Wills can't fit in most average-size tubs, let alone both of us.

He adds some of the oils and bubble bath the hotel has lined up next to the bathtub, and then he helps me in after stripping my clothes off.

"Scoot forward a little." Wills gets in behind me, then pulls me back into his chest, and my head rests against his shoulder.

"This is heaven, and I think we should ask Evelyn to incorporate this into the master bedroom somehow. I need to do this with you all the time."

"I agree. I never imagined I would be a bath guy, but this is nice with you in my arms."

"We should have taken a bath after our walkabout, not before." A little too late now, but we will be all muddy from yesterday's rain.

"We can take another one. I'm in no rush today. I just want to unwind and enjoy every second alone with you. I want to make no plans except to celebrate the new year together."

"That sounds so nice. No planning." I laugh. "You know you're really adulting in life when you are happy about not making plans." I feel him smile into the top of my head where his lips are pressed.

Wills is idly massaging my body, and I'm in a state of complete and utter relaxation. We've been in here a while, having to add more hot water a few times to keep us warm.

"Are you happy, Sadie?" Wills whispers.

"With what, today, this hotel?"

"No, with us, with life?" Why is he asking me this? Do I seem unhappy? I take a second to think about how I want to answer this. There is only one response. But I know how I say it will mean everything to him.

"Have you ever seen that movie *Sliding Doors* with Gwyneth Paltrow?" I ask.

"I don't think so. Why?"

"I was thinking about it earlier in the car. It's about how her life would be completely different if she missed her subway versus not missing the subway. I don't want to say what happened in the club years ago was supposed to happen because I wouldn't wish that on anyone." He squeezes me and takes a deep breath. I know he doesn't like to talk about that night, if not necessary.

"But what if that didn't happen? What path would I be on right now? I wouldn't have Charlie, and how do we know I would have definitely moved here? Or, if I did, can we guarantee it would have worked between us? Because I can guarantee it now. I know it deep down in my soul that this was our time to meet again, to become a family. So, to answer your question, yes. I am happier than words could ever describe. This is where I'm supposed to be in life right now, with you." I turn around to straddle him and look him in the eyes. "Now, who's the crybaby? I whisper against his soft lips." I love how Wills is always open with me, never afraid to show his emotions.

"I love you, my beautiful girl. I don't know what I did to ever deserve you, but I'm so happy you're mine. You make me so incredibly happy."

"I love you too, Wills." I lean in and press my lips against his, his arms circle my back, and mine go around his neck, and we stay pressed as one.

Slowly our mouths open, and we kiss tenderly like it's our first time exploring each other.

It's slow, deep, and meaningful. Our bodies naturally start to rock and glide against each other, and without a word, I lift slightly, and he moves himself to my entrance.

We stay still at first, continuing our passionate kiss until his hands move to my behind, and he slowly lifts me up and down, again and again. Eventually, on the downstroke, I stay there and grind back and forth, unhurried.

Wills's hands move around to my front, tracing my body. His large hands lightly cup my breasts, and with one finger, he traces around my nipples. He leans in, and with a barely there touch, he licks one by one. This is so sensual—my body is more aware of every touch and feeling than ever before.

Our mouths are slightly open, and our breathing is labored. Both of us close, I can feel it, and together we start to rock just a bit faster. I can feel the warm sensation taking over my body while Wills's eyes close, and he leans his head back on the ledge. My orgasm hits me, my body convulses around him, and then I feel his hot seed enter me. Neither of us made a sound besides our breathing. We just made love, completely silent, but so in tune with each other's bodies.

It's eleven p.m., and we are only just getting up to leave the room. We skipped our walk and dinner—Instead, we stayed in to make love over and over again. It wasn't rough or fast, we took our time and cherished each other's bodies, just loving on one another unconditionally.

It felt different today, like something clicked for both of us. I know Wills feels it too.

We contemplated staying in for the countdown, celebrating just the two of us, but after being in the room for the last twelve hours, we decided to join the party in the main house.

We walk into the room, and heads turn toward us. As usual, I don't know if it's because he's Wills Taylor rugby kicker extraordinaire or because he's a six-foot-four gorgeous man that just exudes dominance as he walks into a room.

Gold and silver streamers are hanging everywhere, there is a small live band playing, and champagne is flowing as people dance and laugh around the open space.

We're dancing, not on the dance floor, but off to the side in our own little bubble.

"Is this countryside, Wills?" I ask, looking down at his outfit.

"I'm embracing casual weekends again." For New Year's Eve? I doubt that he would choose to wear jeans and a sweater. "Fine, I ran out of clothes." He rolls his eyes, and I smile. That's what I thought. He probably hid a minor meltdown earlier from me when he didn't have proper attire for tonight.

I'm not particularly dressed up either, but I'm okay with that. I prefer it. The only thing I did make sure to pack was heels, so I had adequate height for a perfect New Year's Eve kiss.

We enjoy one more dance in each other's arms until we see it's almost time to start the countdown.

We grab another champagne from the bar as the band stops playing and the televisions turn on with a countdown.

It's almost time to start a new year. It's crazy to think how my life will be so different this time around. Last New Year's, I lay in my bed, holding a teething Charlie.

Now I'm in the countryside of England, with my long-lost London lover.

We are facing the big screen—Wills is standing behind me, his arms encase me, and my head is leaning back into his chest as I casually sip my champagne. The countdown is about to start.

"You know, you never told me if *you* were happy, Wills." He bends, turning his face to kiss my cheek but doesn't respond.

The crowd yells, "Ten!"

And Wills quickly spins me back toward him.

"Nine!"

"Marry me?" *What?* What did he just say? "Marry me, Sadie Marie Peters. I love you, my beautiful girl, and I don't want to start this year without you as my fiancée," he blurts out quickly.

"Eight!" … "Seven!" … "Six!"

I'm just staring in shock, and his eyes are wide, scared, but excited. He's waiting—for me.

Oh. My. God. Wills just proposed.

"Marry me, my love," he whispers as he pushes my hair from my face.

"Five!" … "Four!" … "Three!" …

"Sadie?"

"Two!"

"Yes, yes! Of course, I will marry you, Wills!" I cry.

"One! Happy New Year!" everyone yells, except us. We stare into one another's eyes, looking at each other with so much love.

"Happy New Year, Sadie."

"Happy New Year, Wills," I whisper.

We kiss and kiss some more. I'm kissing my fiancé for the first time in the new year.

I'm kissing my fiancé for the first time in my life.

25

Two Months Later

Sadie

"Hello?" Wills calls as he walks in the house, it's half past noon on Saturday, and he's just home from the office. Unfortunately, he got pulled in when a VIP client called, and I know he wasn't happy about it.

Besides, when I have an event, we don't like to be away from each other on the weekends, it's our time together no matter what.

"Hello, my princess. Where are you going?" I hear him ask Charlie.

"Naptime," she says with a yawn, and Wills chuckles.

"Okay, have a good sleep. I love you."

"I wove you." My heart swells. God, I love them and the love those two have for each other.

I would never admit this to anyone, but I may have been slightly jealous when we first moved here. My baby girl, who only ever relied on me, now had someone else—someone she usually chose over me.

But I quickly reeled those thoughts in because I couldn't be happier. Charlie has so many people who love her in her life, and it's truly a blessing. Trust me when I say Jackson and I prayed for a family like this our whole life.

"Sadie?"

"In the kitchen!"

He strides over and wraps his arms around my midsection, placing a lingering kiss on my neck. "God, I've missed my fiancée this morning." The F word is his new favorite.

Since New Year's Eve, he has to call me his fiancée three million times a day. And I freaking love it.

"Why didn't you wake me this morning?" I pout. I don't like him leaving without a goodbye.

"I'm sorry, beautiful, we were up so late, and I thought you needed rest," he teases.

Yeah… he's the one who kept me up all night long.

"Did my girls have a good morning?"

"We did. We went on a long walk in the park with Buddy and two new dogs that just came to the shelter."

"Is that why my other girl is putting herself to sleep?" he mumbles against my neck, goose bumps rising over my skin.

"I guess… she's never done that before. She must be exhausted."

"Oh, and get this. When we were walking in the park this morning, I saw Declan sitting on a bench by himself, deep in thought. It was bizarre. He didn't look himself. I didn't want to disturb him at first, but then I couldn't help myself, so I called his name, and he just walked the other way."

Wills steps back, looking concerned. "Are you sure he heard you?"

"No, yes. I don't know. I think he did. I'm almost positive I saw him freeze a second when I called him a second time. The whole thing was super strange."

"Hm, I can't figure out what's bothering him, and he won't talk to me either. So I think we will just have to leave this one, and he will come to us, or probably you, when he's ready."

He's probably right, but I want to help him now. I hate waiting.

"Have you heard from Annabelle?" he asks. I groan and throw my head back on his shoulder.

"No, what is wrong with all of our friends? She is just going out all night partying, then sleeps all day. Lola says when she's at work, she is a terror."

Wills laughs. "Opposed to when she's not a terror at work?" I smirk because Belle is a character. Lola says they are constantly calling her wild names behind her back. But Belle couldn't care less. She's killing it at her job, her company is top in the industry right now, and that's all she cares about.

"Did you speak to Alessia today?"

"Yes." I look back at him quick. "You have a lot of questions today, Mr. Taylor," I tease. "But she insists on me not paying the lease through the year. I couldn't convince her otherwise."

"Hmm, well, we will send her a very nice gift then." I was thinking the same thing. Our house will be done in a few weeks, and since Charlie seems very excited about it, we are moving in this April.

My lease is until October and I wanted to pay Alessia out, but she wouldn't hear anything about it. It wouldn't be right to just up and leave, but she said she wouldn't accept my money.

"When are you going out with Mum?"

Since Christmas, I've formed a great bond with Eleanor and an even better one with Evelyn. Of course, Belle will always be my soul sister and best friend. But Evelyn, my soon-to-be sister-in-law, and I have something equally as unique. I don't know how to explain it, but it's like we were born to be family.

We talk almost every day, and Eleanor comes to the city often to hang out with all of us. Wills's dad was even complaining about how Eleanor begs him to move back to the city—to be closer to Charlie. It's sweet really, we're fortunate to have them in our lives.

I know she's trying to make up for my parents, but I tell her I don't need that. I'm happy just to have her as she is.

I don't typically meet her on the weekends, or Wills comes along if I do, but today she insisted we meet for lunch without him.

And I wouldn't dare say no to her. She's a wonderful lady but also scares the crap out of me, so I'll try and stay on her good side.

"Soon-ish. I'm just making you lunch first." He looks over my shoulder at the sandwiches and then back to me. *I know that look.* There is no time for that look. I make a half attempt to wiggle myself free, but who am I kidding? I want this as much as he does.

"That's not what I want to eat for lunch, beautiful." He nips my neck as he presses his front into my back. He trails his hand down my stomach, under my dress, and into my panties, and we both groan.

"So wet and easy access," he breathes. He releases his hand, presses my panties aside, then pushes my front to the counter.

"We don't have time," I say, half serious. Wills's hand wraps around the back of my neck and squeezes with slight pressure as he whispers in my ear.

"There is always time. Now be a good girl and stay quiet, so Charlotte doesn't hear." I nod my head.

"Words, Sadie."

"Yes, Wills. I'll be quiet," I promise.

"Good girl." He drops to the floor, running his hands up and down the back of my thighs, then rests them on my backside, massaging both cheeks.

He hitches my hips up a bit, then leans over, sliding his tongue through my entrance, and I have to suppress a moan to stay quiet.

His tongue dashes out again, and in one long swipe, he starts at my clit and up to my backside. No matter how many times he licks or touches back there, I still tense.

"When can I have this?" he mumbles against me. He asks almost daily, now he's obsessed. I just shake my head. He's too big.

"It's too much, too intimate," I whisper as he pushes two fingers inside me.

"I'm your fiancé, we always do intimate. You said sex on your period was too intimate, and we did that."

"In the shower, and I was reluctant the whole time." He shrugs.

"So, we'll do anal in the shower too. I now pronounce the shower as our intimate sex location. I'll even build you a shower dedicated for it in the new house."

I burst out laughing.

He's an idiot. And the funny thing is, he's dead serious.

"How about when you're my wife? Will you give it to me then?" I don't know, will I ever give it to him? I don't give him an answer because I don't have one.

He pumps his fingers inside me a few more times before maneuvering his body against the cabinets, sliding down to the floor.

"Come here, baby," he rasps as he pulls me in front of him.

"Lay your chest back on the counter, stand over my face, squat down and take what you please, take what you *need*." Oh god, this is hot. *Shit*. I hesitate for a split second. "That wasn't a request. Come here now."

I rush closer and lean over the counter to hold myself up. There is no reason to squat. His mouth is at the perfect height.

Both his hands cup my butt as I press myself down right on his mouth—his tongue darts out with such precision. He knows exactly what I love. It happens fast, but I'm already there. I start to rock against his mouth as his tongue swipes through me continually. My legs are turning to mush, and I need him to practically hold me up, which he does with one hand. I look over my shoulder, and he's released himself and is pumping himself with his other. God, I love when he does that. My body starts rocking faster back and forth over his waiting tongue as he applies more pressure with each lick to my clit.

Knock, knock… we both freeze. Was that… *knock, knock*.

"Fuck!" Wills yells.

"You've got to be kidding me," I hiss at the same time.

"Do you want me to finish you off, baby?" He reaches up and swipes a finger through my wetness.

"Oh my god, stop it! Your mom is right on the other side of the door, you sicko." Or am I the sicko hoping he ignores me and keeps going?

But he gets up and puts himself back in his pants while my head falls forward. I should have told him to finish me off.

"I'll make sure to skip dessert tonight and have your sweetness later." I close my eyes. He can't say things like that right now, I'm so on edge. I'm going to get him back for this.

Wills walks to answer the door while I go in the bathroom to calm myself and freshen up. This is going to be a long freaking day.

"Ready to go, sweetie? Where's Charlotte?" Eleanor asks.

"Oh, sorry, she's napping. It's just us two today." Her face falls. "Um, I would love to see her today. We can wait," she says, taking a seat on the sofa. *Weird.*

I look over at Wills, and he shrugs, just as baffled as I am and unsure what to do.

Evelyn babysat Charlie just two days ago, and I know for a fact they had lunch with her mom. So why is she so insistent on seeing Charlie? And it doesn't look like I will be changing her mind anytime soon.

"I guess I can see if I can wake her up. Hold on." This can go one of two ways. Charlie will be ecstatic to see her nan, or the devil child will come out to play. Waking a sleeping child, especially mine, is never a good idea and a complete gamble.

Wills's eyes crease. "No, she was exhausted. Mum, just go out with Sadie this time."

She ignores Wills and looks right at me. "Thanks, Sadie, that would be lovely."

Okay then, I widen my eyes at Wills to say *what the hell*? And then walk upstairs to try and wake Charlie.

I walk into the room, and she's out like a light. Buddy doesn't move either, he's pressed against Charlie, snoring right in her face, and she's not in the least bit bothered. I snap a picture and send it to Wills. I send him daily pictures of them sleeping together, it's come to the point he asks where they are if I forgot.

Wills: Let her sleep. Mum is off her rocker today.

She is, but that's also why I want to take Charlie with us. Something is telling me she really needs to see her. I hope she's okay and not sick or something. She can't be. Wills would be devastated. *I would be devastated.*

I decide not to wake her but call up Wills to carry her straight out to the car. If she's as tired as we all think, she won't even wake up.

He's buckling her in her seat with a scowl. He is not happy we are disturbing her. He would much rather her stay home with him.

"I don't know what's up with that old bat, but she's going to be in big trouble if Charlotte isn't happy."

I swat at his chest. "Be nice." I smile.

He wraps me up in his arms. "I love you, baby. Have fun."

I'm feeling emotional all of a sudden. I don't want to go today. I want to stay with my man, but Eleanor loves this time with us, so I don't complain.

"I love you too, Wills." I kiss his lips softly, turn and get into Eleanor's car.

"Where are we going? This isn't the way to the restaurant."

"That's because we aren't going to a restaurant, Sadie." Eleanor has been super dodgy the whole car ride, and it's kind of unsettling. So where the heck are we going, if not lunch?

I watch as the city passes us by, and I'm starting to get a little freaked out.

Maybe Wills was right, and she is off her rocker. I look back at Charlie, and she's still out like a light.

"What's going on, Eleanor? You're kind of freaking me out." She doesn't answer but finally pulls off into an empty business center parking lot.

She turns off the car, and I see her close her eyes and take not one but two deep breaths.

She reaches in the back seat, pulling out a photo album with a pink rattle on the front. A baby album that looks old and worn.

"I need to tell you something, Sadie, and this is not going to be easy for either of us."

I'm all of a sudden on high alert, and I can feel my body tense. I am not getting a good feeling right now. Why did she bring me out here? What are we doing in an empty parking lot? I grab my phone, and I don't know why, in case I need to call Wills?

Eleanor reaches across and pats the hand that holds my phone. "Sweetie, I think I'm scaring you. I'm sorry. Don't be frightened, I must be saying this all wrong. What I need to tell you is good news, love. But it will come as a shock, so I wanted to tell you with no distractions. And the reason we are here." She sweeps her arm toward the building. "Will make sense once I'm done."

Okay, I'm still freaked out, but now I'm half intrigued to hear what she has to say.

"Forty-one years ago, I gave birth to a baby girl called Amelia. She would have been slightly older than William." What? She did? I look up into her eyes, and they are brimmed with tears. A look most probably wouldn't often see on a strong woman like Eleanor.

"She died of pneumonia when I was pregnant with William. She was very sick, in and out of the hospital. We blamed her doctor for sending us home. It was a complete and utter disaster. It was a very dark time in my life, as you can imagine, as a mom. After Amelia passed, I spiraled out of control. I couldn't even look at a picture of her or speak about her without going into a state of depression. I almost lost William, too, due to stress. Thomas finally stepped in and put all the pictures and albums in storage. He also informed friends and family that they were never to speak about her again." She takes a deep breath, and I sit here quietly in shock.

"I know that sounds horrible, but if he hadn't done that, I really might have lost William too."

"Eleanor, I'm so sorry." I take her hand in mine for some reassurance, and she smiles sadly at me.

"Over time, I got better, and we thought about taking her pictures out, but I think Thomas was afraid of how I would act. So, he put his foot down and decided against it. He said Amelia would always live in our hearts, but we had to move on for William's sake. Now, William and Evelyn only know about Amelia from our stories. But have never actually seen a picture of her." I feel her tense, and she takes a big gulp.

"If you look at my kids now, Evelyn looks like me and William looks like Thomas, but Amelia, Amelia looked like my Thomas's grandmother. I remember us laughing when she was born. I did all that work, and she looks like some cranky old lady." She laughs at the memory, and I can tell she's back there in her memories, right when Amelia was born.

"But she was so beautiful," she whispers. Her pain radiates from her, from one mother to another. I can feel her pain deep down within my soul.

She hands me the baby book that's in her lap, her hands are shaking wildly.

"The day I met you, on Christmas, I was shocked. I had to play it off quickly because I wasn't certain, but when Thomas confirmed it. After that, I knew it to be true with every fiber of my being."

"What to be true?" I asked, confused.

She nudges the book for me to open it. So I do, and then I instantly drop it to the ground.

"You see, my love, I believe Charlotte is Wills's baby." I scramble to pick it back up.

"I don't understand," I cry.

"Why, why do you have a picture of Charlie in here?"

"Sweetie," Eleanor whispers.

I look at her, I know this isn't a picture of Charlie, but my eyes and head are not working together right now.

"That's my Amelia, not Charlotte, love."

My head whips back to Charlie, then back to the picture. I am staring at her doppelgänger.

I try to speak… my mouth opens and shuts, but nothing comes out.

I deliberately blink my eyes over and over as if the picture would change. It doesn't, I knew it wouldn't.

Like my Charlotte, this little girl has crystal-blue eyes, dark hair, and porcelain skin.

Just like my attacker.

How is this possible? Could Wills be Charlie's dad, her real dad? This whole time, I thought I got pregnant from my rapist. My breathing picks up, getting deeper and faster, and I can't control it. I think I'm having a panic attack.

"Sadie?" I hear Eleanor's concerned voice, but it's muffled. I feel like I'm far, far away from reality right now.

I put my head between my legs and do the deep breathing exercises Dr. Esposito taught me.

I reach my hand up to open the window. I need air. God, what is happening right now?

I close my eyes and breathe in and out, in and out.

Eleanor is rubbing my back, and I can't hear what she says. But her touch calms me.

"Sadie, come back to me, sweetie. I'll help you through this," she whispers.

I slowly sit up and place my head back against the seat. She reaches over, gets some napkins out of the car console, and wipes my forehead. I didn't even realize I was sweating.

"Am I going crazy?"

She chuckles. "No, no, you're not. It's completely normal."

We sit in silence for a very, very long time. For almost three years, no, four, including pregnancy, I thought I had an evil man's baby. Wills and I always used condoms, always. And I know it's not one hundred percent. But, my rapist did not use anything, the hospital said. So what else was I to think, especially when she comes out with crystal-blue eyes and light skin? Neither Wills nor I have either of those two things. My attacker did.

"What are you thinking, sweetie?"

"I want to be happy. I do, I am, but I'm in shock. All these years, I thought my sweet baby came from that terrible person." I start to cry. It comes out of nowhere, but I'm racked with stress right now. I can't control anything.

"Shh, it's okay. It's okay to have all these feelings."

"Eleanor, why didn't you tell me with Wills? Do you not think he will be happy about this?" I can't imagine that to be true, though. He loves Charlotte like she's his own. *Well, she is.*

"Oh, no, he will be thrilled, Sadie! As a mother… as your mum." She smiles and leans over to kiss my cheek quickly. "I knew you would need time to process this, and Wills likes facts. So even though that picture proves she is, he will need to see it on paper. That's why we are here." She points to the building again.

"My friend is a doctor who deals with paternity. We have an appointment with her today. I know I'm overstepping, you can be mad, that's okay. But I wanted to do this for you because this is the hard part. If this were me, I would want just to rip off the bandage and get it over with. But, of course, we could be mistaken, and it's not his baby, another reason I thought we do this without him. But after your reaction, I think you agree with me."

I do, I really do. Charlie is Amelia's twin.

"One more question, Eleanor, why did you wait two months to tell me?"

She sighs. "Trust me, I went back and forth on this every day. But I wanted to gain your trust and get to know you before I broke the news to you. This is obviously not an easy conversation to have with someone." I understand, I guess.

"So, what now, if Wills isn't here?"

"Well, both Charlotte and I will get tested. A paternity test can also tell if a grandparent is related. If I come out a match, we know Wills is the father." She smiles, and I'm starting to feel the same way. The shock is slowly disappearing, and the joy is veering its head. Wills could be Charlie's freaking father! This will make my gift to him a lot easier now.

"Why are you smiling?" *Am I?*

"Well, as you know, next month is Charlie's third birthday."

She nods, of course she does. Eleanor calls every day about her party, driving me nuts. We are combining her birthday with our house-warming party, so it will most definitely be a stressful month.

Anyway…

"On her birthday, I had a whole presentation ready for Charlie to ask Wills if he would be her dad, for him to adopt her. I would have had a shirt made and had the whole party for Wills becoming her dad. But I guess he probably really is her dad already." This is going to take a lot to get used to.

I turn toward Eleanor, and she has her hand on her heart. "Oh, that would have just been so special. I almost wish that happened, then this." She laughs, obviously kidding.

"Well, maybe I can still do something?"

"Like what?" she asks.

"Let's get the results, and then we can chat."

"So that's it?" I ask the doctor. "Yes, I will call you both in a few hours, and you will have the results." Wow, okay. That was easy. A quick swab of both their cheeks and they were done.

"I hungy, Mommy."

I smile down at my baby. I hope I'm not excited for nothing; I really hope Wills is her dad.

"Okay, sweet pea, let's go eat."

"I can't eat," Eleanor whispers. I know, I know. Our nerves are both through the roof.

"Well, too bad you're driving because I'm having a glass of wine for lunch. I need something to calm me down." She huffs, annoyed, probably mad she didn't let me drive now.

We find a nearby restaurant and sit in a secluded booth in the back. I feel like we are on some type of covert mission.

I look down at Charlie, just living her best life eating a cheeseburger and fries, with not a care in the world.

"What now?"

"Why are you whispering?" I whisper. God, we are freaking idiots.

My phone rings from my bag. Oh god, it could be the doctor. "Answer it!" I take it out of my bag, and my heart drops. It's Wills, not the doctor. I can't answer this, I'm a shit liar. "It's Wills, I don't know what to say." Eleanor grabs my phone.

"William, it's Mum. She went to the loo. What do you mean, why are we so far outside the city? How do you know that?" Her eyes widen, and she looks around as if Wills can see us. I hit my head to my forehead. Why didn't I think of this earlier?

"You track Sadie's phone? That's an invasion of privacy, William. What is wrong with you?" She pauses, and I know Wills is telling her that it's for my protection. God forbid anything happens to me again, he would blame himself for the rest of his life.

I can see his location too, he insisted, "you can never be too careful" is what he said. And I couldn't agree more and love how he lives to protect me, even though he might be an overbearing lunatic half the time. I'd rather be safe than sorry.

"Oh, okay, I understand." She pauses and looks at me sadly, clearly thinking of my attack.

"But yes, we came out here on a whim. Charlie was still sleeping, so we drove around and just picked a random place. Okay, we will call you on our way home, love you too."

"He can be annoying and quite demanding, can't he?" I laugh. She has no idea. "That was nothing, Eleanor, but he means well."

"So, tell me, instead of the adoption, what were you thinking in the car? Or how are you thinking of telling him?"

"I'm not sure it will work anymore, I looked it up while you drove here." I blow out a breath. "I thought of having his name added to the birth certificate. The father part was obviously left blank. So, I wanted to send it away to have it fixed and then present it to him. With his name added, and Charlie's name changed officially to Taylor. And, since it takes a few weeks to process, I would have still done it on her birthday."

"Oh, that's a grand idea. My William would be so shocked. Why can't you do it?"

"Apparently, to add a father's name, I have to show proof of paternity and have it notarized that he acknowledges said paternity."

Eleanor's face lights up brighter than a Christmas tree.

"What's that look for?"

"This can work, and I'll help you. Tonight, you'll get a sample from William. Just tell him you're doing one of those DNA ancestry tests everyone is doing these days. And it just so happens to be your soon-to-be father-in-law is a notary and has identical handwriting and signature to William's."

"What! That's against the law or something." She is going to drive me to drink *more* today.

"Oh please, that's a stupid law. We would be doing this for the good of the people. How else would you tell him in a grand way?"

I think about it, and I don't have another way. I Imagine his face when he sees his name on the certificate. He would freak out; he probably would cry. I know he would.

"Okay, once the doctor confirms. Let's do it. I'm going to live on the edge a little."

She high-fives me from across the table.

"Hey!" Charlie scrunches up her face and puts up her little hand for us to high-five. Annoyed we didn't include her.

"Sorry, sweet pea."

We sit in silence for what feels like forever. My leg is bouncing a mile a minute. I don't know what else to do, and I almost feel like I could throw up; I'm so nervous.

Finally, my phone rings, and both Eleanor and I jump out of our seats. We stare down at it ringing and vibrating across the table. I lean over and press the button to answer the phone, instantly switching it to speaker. This is it, this could possibly be some of the best news I've found out in my life. My fingers are crossed. I need this to be what I think it is.

"Hello, Sadie speaking."

"Hello, Sadie. This is Dr. Werner. I am calling you with the test results. Are you with Mrs. Taylor?"

"Yes, she is with me right now. You're on speakerphone."

"Hello, Sarah, It's me, Eleanor."

"Hello. Okay, let's get to it. After conducting the test, I can say with great certainty that there is a 99.8% chance you are the paternal grandmother of Charlotte Peters."

"Oh my god, oh my god." I reach over and clutch Eleanor's arms, and our eyes mimic each other's. They are wide in delight. We both knew deep down these were the results, but not until we heard it for sure has it really hit us both.

I look at Charlie to make sure she's occupied with her coloring. "Eleanor... your son, the love of my life, is my daughter's father," I whisper in excitement.

"I'm so happy for you, Sadie. I'm so happy for my son and my granddaughter." She puts her hand on her chest.

"Oh my... Charlotte really is my granddaughter."

We both laugh. She sure is. Now the problem is—how the heck do I keep this a secret from Wills for a month? I will be busting at the seams; I hate secrets, and I'm terrible at keeping exciting ones. But this one, I think, will be worth the wait.

Then my Charlotte Rose will officially become *Charlotte Rose Taylor.*

26

Three Weeks Later

Wills

“What’s up your ass today? You’re acting crankier than normal,” Jackson asks.

When the hell did they get in here?

I’m starting to lose my mind. I think Sadie is driving me insane. It’s confirmed.

Jackson and Declan sit in the seats across from my desk, smirking like two arseholes.

“Don’t you two have anything else better to do than to bother me? You know, like maybe work since I pay you both more than I should.”

“He’s losing it, right?” Jackson asks Declan, shaking his head.

“Remind me never to get wifed up if I’m going to act like a moron.”

“What the hell are you talking about?” I ask.

“Umm, you’re the one who set the meeting, dickhead.” I look down at my new Rolex I gifted myself last week, that Sadie won’t know about, and shit, how the hell did it get so late? I need to leave soon to get home. I like putting Charlotte to bed if I can. I'd rather bring some work home than miss dinner and bedtime.

"I'm not in the mood for a meeting anymore. Let's just meet on Monday or talk over the weekend."

"Dude, seriously, what is going on with you?"

I huff out a breath. "Your sister is being weird as fuck. Has she mentioned anything to you?"

"No, nothing, just seems busy to me." Well, that's not fucking helpful.

"Just chill out, she has two new clients, and you guys are moving and throwing a party next weekend. She's just stressed."

"She threw up the other day, twice! She said she was nervous about all the changes. I made her take ten pregnancy tests because who throws up over a move to an already finished and furnished house?" Declan is biting his lip, suppressing a laugh. "What?" I snap.

"You were probably mad the lass wasn't pregnant, weren't you? You're like an animal, wanting her to birth twenty of your children."

I shrug… *so what*?

I can't wait for her to be pregnant with my baby. Charlotte will always be my princess, but I want to *see* Sadie grow a child, and I can't wait until I can touch her pregnant belly. She's going to look even more gorgeous than she does now.

"Aw, look at lover boy lost in thought."

I chuck my pen at Jackson. "Don't be a prick, I can't believe you're going to be my fucking brother… Sadie is lucky I love her." We all laugh because that's a lie. He's a good one and treats Sadie better than most brothers.

"Who are you texting? You look like you're about to lose your virginity for the first time," Jackson thinks he's living the life, but it's fucking exhausting even thinking about his social calendar.

"A girl I met last weekend. She was freaking wild, let me tell you, one of those shy on the outside but dirty AF in the bedroom. Every guy's wet dream. And she's a smokeshow—like fifteen out of ten." I wiggle my eyebrows. "Don't even fucking say it, Taylor, and I'm not kidding this time. I'll kill you."

It's too easy to rile him up. He can't stand if I even mention Sadie when anyone is talking about sex. Who am I kidding? He doesn't even like it when we kiss in front of him. He loses it.

"Wills, before you leave, I have some bad news and good news. Which one do you want first?"

These two are getting on my nerves today. "I don't care, spit it out."

"Mick didn't renew his contract, and I heard through the grapevine he's also signing with Acler."

"You've got to be fucking shitting me," I seethe.

"But we signed two new players, full package, using our lawyers and everything. One young girl who is a tennis player from Spain, who just moved to London. And an up-and-coming rugby player from Leeds."

"Well, that sounds promising, but what the hell is with Mick? He didn't even reach out to me."

Declan looks just as pissed. He was close with Mick when we still played together.

"You know what—no, I'm not doing this now. I need to get the hell home and end this shitty day. So, get the hell out of my office, lads… I need to go see my girls."

I walk up the steps to the house and hear the music blasting from the outside. *What in the world?*

I open the door or try because there are boxes everywhere, and I can barely walk into the damn house. I pinch the bridge of my nose to try and calm myself. I can't deal with anything else today.

Where is my crazy fiancée? Because it's official, she's lost her damn plot.

I maneuver around all the shit piled around the house and make it to the kitchen, where Charlotte is sitting on top of one of the boxes, swinging her feet back and forth.

"Off pwease." She puts her hands up with the grabby motion. Buddy is there, whimpering, concerned for a stuck Charlotte. I walk over, give him some pets, and pick her up, put her on my hip, and kiss her hello.

"Where is Mummy, Charlotte?" She scrunches up her little face and shrugs.

What the hell?

Why is she just leaving Charlotte alone on top of a box where she can't get off?

"Sadie?" I call, annoyed.

We walk around upstairs, and she's standing in her closet with her back to us, but I can see her staring at a piece of paper. It looks like she just opened some mail.

"What's that?"

She screams and jumps in fright. She throws her hand on her chest. "Are you insane, scaring me like that?!"

"Well, there was no way around it since you have the music blasting. What's that?" I ask again.

"This?" She looks down at the paper and frowns. "Oh nothing, it's for the trash." The red starts at her chest and creeps up her neck. She's nervous, or *she's lying*.

What the hell could it be that she's keeping it from me? She gathers all her belongings and walks out of the room, letter in hand. I narrow my eyes, trying to get a peek, but I can't see anything.

"Let's order dinner. I packed everything already."

"Sadie, I hired a moving company for a reason. And we don't move for almost a week." She doesn't even acknowledge me, walking down the stairs into the kitchen.

What the fuck?

I roll my neck and try to relax.

This day needs to end. It must be a full moon out or something because I can't get a freaking break.

We ordered dinner and would have eaten in complete silence if it weren't for Charlotte blabbering on about the music class Kathryn took her to.

Sadie barely said a word, even after asking her multiple times what was wrong. I saw her wringing her hands under the table, a telltale sign of when Sadie is nervous.

We finally put Charlotte and Buddy to sleep, and I honestly might just put myself to sleep too. I need today to end.

I head back downstairs, and Sadie is standing in the kitchen, looking like she's in another world. My annoyance turns to concern now. I've never seen her like this. I walk up to her and wrap my arms around her stomach, and she relaxes and melts into me instantly.

"Sadie, baby, please tell me what's wrong. I can't help you if you don't talk to me," I beg.

She turns in my arms and smiles up at me, and I'm seeing someone completely different now.

This is my girl.

"I'm just so tired and stressed. Let's just relax and watch a movie tonight, okay?" She leans in and kisses me softly, and I feel her stress radiating off of her. Maybe that's it? She's just having a bad few weeks.

I lie down on the couch, and Sadie scrambles to climb on top of me, resting her head under my chin, and I hold her tight to me. She smiles then presses small kisses into my chest.

"I love you, Wills. I'm so happy we're becoming a family. Things are only going to get better from here."

"I love you too, baby." She's right, things are perfect and will only get better when she becomes my wife. Something I never really thought about before Sadie.

I wake up and have to use the loo badly, but when I try to stand, I can't. There is deadweight on top of me, and I realize it's Sadie sleeping.

We must have fallen asleep during the movie, actually, I can't remember even turning the movie on. I think we both passed out right away.

I move her off my body and onto the couch, knowing she won't wake up, and make my way to the loo. In the corner of my eye, I see the clock only says eleven at night, and I can't help but laugh. Declan and Jackson are probably only just heading to **Charlotte's** now, and we've already been asleep for three hours. Times have definitely changed.

I'm about to go pick up Sadie and carry her up to the bedroom when I spot a pile of mail sticking out of her purse.

It's whatever she was looking at before, and I'm really trying to hold myself back from looking at what it is. I know it's a complete invasion of privacy to look, but we share everything. There are no secrets between us, so would it matter that much if I just snuck a peek?

Something is pulling me to see what it is. I don't know why, but I know I won't be able to sleep until I know what it is.

When Sadie was staring at it earlier, something just seemed off. So maybe whatever it is will help me understand what's been going on with her.

I pull out the one large envelope that she had in her hand earlier, and it has United States postage on it. The return address is listed as Department of Vital Records.

Huh? No clue what that is, maybe she needed information for her Visa? I mentioned something about it after I proposed. Perhaps she's just being proactive?

I stare at the envelope, fighting between my conscience and my need. *Fuck it.*

I pull out the thin piece of paper and realize it's Charlotte's birth certificate. It definitely has to do with their visas—I know how long this all takes. I'm glad she's on top of it all.

I'm just going to put it away, and she'll be none the wiser that I went into her purse.

I move my finger, where I was holding the document, to slip it back into the envelope.

What the fuck is that? Are my eyes deceiving me right now?

Father: William Thomas Taylor

Why is my name listed as the father of Charlotte? And that's when I realize Charlotte's surname is listed as Taylor and not Peters. I don't understand what's going on.

The room feels like it's closing in on me, and I don't know what to do.

This can't be happening to me *again*. No… no… no…

"Sadie!" My voice booms through the room, and she jumps, completely startled. I want to catch her off guard.

She looks around, confused about where she is and why I'm yelling.

"What's the matter? Is everything okay?" her groggy voice spits out.

"What the fuck is this?" Her eyes go wide and then narrow instantly.

"Where did you get that? Did you go in my bag?" Her voice rising. The fucking nerve.

"Answer. The. Fucking. Question. NOW!" My anger is on a level one million, and I can see I've scared her because she shuffles back a little on the couch and her eyes go wide.

But I can't seem to care right now.

"Can you please explain to me how my name is on Charlotte's birth certificate when I only just met her six months ago?"

"I-I was going to tell you. I swear!" she stammers.

"You were going to tell me you were a cunning liar, just like all the rest? You are no different than them, are you? What do you want, Sadie? Do you need money for Charlotte since mommy dearest cut you off? Was Jackson not paying for enough? Is that it? So, you had to come back into my life and lie to get everything you needed."

I've shocked her, I can see. And I don't give a shit right now.

Her eyes instantly fill with tears. As I thought, I hit the nail on the head.

"What… what are you talking about? I'm like the rest? Who is the rest? I don't understand. And I don't want your money. You know that!"

"I know nothing about you!" I spit, and she recoils.

I grab my keys and wallet. I need to get out of here. I can't even look at her lying face anymore. How do I keep getting this wrong, time and time again? I thought she was different than *her*. Everything I thought—when I left France—was true. Will I ever get a break in life?

"Where are you going?" she cries as she runs after me.

"I never want to see you again… do you understand me? I hate liars, but most of all, I hate users." I feel myself shaking from anger.

"I didn't lie, Wills, I swear it. I was going to surprise you!"

"I can't believe I let you in again, and I can't believe I thought you were a loving girlfriend. What a joke," I say as I leave the house.

"I'm your fiancée!" she yells after me.

I turn around and laugh, full on laugh in her face. This girl has some nerve.

"Not anymore, sweetheart. You… Sadie Peters are once again dead to me." *Fuck you, Sadie.*

"I think you've had enough, mate. Time to go home," the bartender tells me.

"One more." I slur.

"Wills, no more. You can't even sit on the stool. I'll call you a cab."

"You know my name?" Did I tell this man my name? I remember telling him I'm in love with a lying bitch, and that's about it. Sadie, my beautiful lying girl. I can't get over it. Why did she have to do this to us? I thought we were so happy. Declan was wrong all those years ago. She's not Slim Sadie, she's Shady Sadie.

"I think most of London knows who you are, Wills Taylor. But don't worry… you were never here. Oath of a bartender." He picks up his fingers and crosses them over his heart. Or I think he crosses them. I can't tell, the room is spinning. Shit, how many scotches did I have?

"Alright, your cab is here."

I look out the window. I don't really want to walk that far. I throw down a few hundred on the bar.

"No, it's too much," the bartender protests.

"Keep it—for letting me complain all night." I wave goodbye and get in the cab.

"Where to?" Yeah, where to is the question since I don't have a home anymore.

"Knightsbridge." I guess I'm crashing with my baby sis tonight.

I push the code over and over. Why would she change it? Finally, I walk or stumble over to the front desk.

"Mr. Taylor, are you okay?" Hell, what's his name again?

"Yes, sorry to bother you. But I think my sister changed the code. Can you let me up?"

"Not a problem, sir. Follow me."

"Look what the cat dragged in." I hear a voice I never wanted to hear again. I keep walking to ignore her.

"Too scared to even talk to me?" Scared? I turn around and look Victoria up and down. I hate her, but shit, why does she have to be so hot? It's fucking annoying when you're trying to ignore someone, especially when you're drunk.

I see her smile. I guess I wasn't subtle enough. *Shit.*

"Already problems at home? Crawling back to your old life so soon." She laughs. "No one thought you would last anyway." *What? What the hell's that supposed to mean?* "Wills Taylor, married with a kid," she spits out, laughing again. "Knew it wouldn't last!" she calls as she gets in her lift. "Call me." She winks as the doors close.

I will not fucking call her. Ugh, I'm disgusted with myself for even talking to her.

"Here you are, sir. I've called the lift." I nod my thanks and head to the penthouse.

My sister is in New York right now, so I'm not sure why I'm tiptoeing through my house. *Her house.*

Shit, where am I going to live now? I don't want to go to that house I bought for us.

I can't even think of that right now, it hurts my head. I just need to lie down and go to sleep, and I'll deal with everything in the morning. I will have to call Charles to make sure he is ready for any actions that legally need to be taken.

"Oh my god!" Evelyn screeches.

"I thought you were in New York," I say as I throw myself on the sofa. I can't even make it to the guest room.

"I came back early. What the hell Wills! It's three in the morning. I thought you were robbing me! What are you doing here?"

"Can you be quiet? Your screaming is hurting my head."

"Are you drunk?" She walks around and sniffs me. *What the hell*?

"You are drunk! What is wrong with you? Why are you here? I'm calling Sadie."

"Don't you dare call that lying sneaky bitch!" I slur.

Evelyn gasps. "Don't you dare talk about her like that. What has gotten into you?"

"Why don't you ask her since you two are best friends? She is a liar, and I hate her. I am too drunk to talk. I am going to sleep." I close my eyes and hear Evelyn rummaging around, then feel her put a blanket on top of me, which puts me right under. I need this night to end. I hope when I wake up, I realize it was all a nightmare.

I groan and stretch my arms over my head. I'm woken up by the sun shining in my face and the sound of the espresso machine going off in the kitchen. *Espresso machine?* We don't have an espresso machine.

"Good, you're up." The blankets get pulled back from me and thrown on the floor.

"Mum? Why are you at our house?"

"William, open your eyes and sit up. You are at the penthouse, you… you… just get up before I start hitting my kid for the first time at thirty-nine years old." Evelyn starts laughing.

"Sod off, Ev. You called Mum?" I shoot her an accusatory look.

"No, your fiancée, my other daughter, called me." Oh hell, I can't deal with this, I'm hungover and haven't even had water.

"She's not my fiancée anymore."

"I said sit up!" my mom screams, and I instantly sit up. Shit, Mum hasn't yelled at me like that since… I can't even remember.

I look over at her, and that's when I see her eyes are red brimmed with tears.

"Well, by the look of you, Sadie must have told you the truth."

"You stupid, stupid, stupid man. How could I have raised someone so arrogant and self-centered as you?"

"What the hell, Mum?"

She just shakes her head, and the tears come flowing down her face. I can't stand to see her cry. I go to move toward her, and she puts her hand up to stop me.

"Don't," she spits in disgust.

"What is going on? I don't understand. If you spoke to Sadie, how are you mad at me? She is doing what Libby did to us all over again!"

My mum's eyes shoot up to mine, and if looks could kill.

"Did you give Sadie a chance to talk?"

"For what? So she can make excuses? She probably had a whole lie planned out. Just. Like. Libby!" I yell. I'm getting really frustrated now. How are they not seeing the big picture here?

"If you weren't my son, I'd probably hate you right now." *What the hell is her problem, and why isn't Evelyn jumping in to say anything?*

"You think you know everything, William, don't you? Just because you're some hotshot rugby player doesn't mean you're winning at life. Because let me tell you, I'm about to tell Sadie to run far, far away."

"Mum," I whisper. *That hurt.*

"That girl is nothing like Libby, NOTHING! But you let your past dictate your future, so you can't see what's in front of you."

"What are you talking about, Mum? Just spit it out, please."

"Evelyn, darling, please get your brother some water and a mint. He smells like the pub."

I roll my eyes. Can she just get on with it already?

She closes her eyes and takes a deep breath. "I'm having trouble telling you because, after last night, you don't even deserve to know."

"Mum," I groan. She really knows how to drag on a story. She leans into a bag I now notice sitting next to her and pulls out what looks to be a baby book.

"William… Sadie was not being deceitful toward you, nor was she keeping secrets. On the contrary, she was trying to surprise you. Do you remember about three or four weeks ago, Sadie and I went to lunch? The day you called us asking why we had left the city?" I nod. Yes, of course, I remember her acting insane, insisting on seeing Charlotte.

"That day, I informed Sadie that I thought Charlotte was *your* daughter."

I scrunch up my face, a move I must have picked up from Sadie. What is she talking about?

"This picture here is of my daughter Amelia, your older sister," I remember Mum and Dad telling us about her a while back, but we don't really ever speak of her.

Mum moves closer, so I can see the picture she's pointing to, and my eyes almost pop out of my sockets.

"What? That's Amelia?"

"Yes, William. Charlotte, my granddaughter, takes after my sweet little angel." I'm in shock. I don't even know what to say.

"That day we went to lunch was the first Sadie heard about it as well. She was just as shocked since Charlotte doesn't look like either of you. Besides her dark hair."

"How do we know for sure?" My mum shakes her head again, annoyed.

"I knew you wouldn't believe it, and you would need proof. So, I surprised Sadie and took her for a paternity test. We used my DNA because if she's related to me obviously, she is related to you." My head is spinning a mile a minute, and I don't know what to say first.

"So, Charlotte is my daughter, as in my blood daughter?"

"Yes, William," she huffs.

"Why didn't Sadie just tell me? I don't understand all the secrecy. She had to have known I already love Charlotte."

"Well, maybe it was a good thing she didn't. Look how you reacted."

"That's because I found her hiding the paper from me!"

"I'm only telling you this because you already ruined it… but she didn't tell you because she was going to surprise you. She sent away to America to have Charlotte's surname and birth certificate changed and was going to present it to you when she got it back. But, since it was also going to be Charlotte's birthday party Saturday, she thought presenting it on the day of Charlotte's birth would be more significant for you."

"What?" I whisper, dropping my head in my hands. We are all then silent, and I'm trying to process what Mum just said. But I… I can't.

I can feel the tears welling up in my eyes. I fucked up. *Bad.*

"That girl has been killing herself over the last few weeks, and I had to keep her from ruining the surprise a hundred times."

"I have a daughter. Charlotte would have always been like a daughter to me. But she's my real daughter. This is why we just clicked so fast. It makes total sense."

Evelyn and Mum stand and walk toward the door, leaving me on the sofa.

"Where are you going?"

"Sadie's… I've already spent too much time here. That girl is wrecked. You messed her up last night, William. She told me some of the things you said to her." Mum's tears fill her eyes again. I don't know how I'll fix this. I'm scared she won't forgive me this time. I really, really screwed up.

"Can I come?" I ask, ashamed. I need to talk to my girl. I need to explain.

"Absolutely not. You do not come near those girls until you've figured yourself out, William. You don't get to just walk all over people and treat them like rubbish, then walk right back in. Make a plan for how you'll apologize and make it up to her. After everything she's been through in her life, I think she deserves better." With that, she turns and walks out.

She's right. I'm disgusted with myself. I also love my mum even more now for how she protected and defended Sadie.

Even from me, her own son.

Now I have to wrap my head around having a daughter, my princess, I already love so much.

And my beautiful girl, the things I said to her. Fuck! I told her she was dead to me. What type of person says that to someone they love so deeply? She's had to deal with so much in her life—I'm the one supposed to make it better, yet I'm making it worse.

For years, she had to deal with the fact Charlotte was from her attacker. It was one of the reasons she went to therapy early on. Now, she finds out it wasn't true, and I leave her and can't even ask how she is dealing with this.

How will she ever rely on me again if I'm not there now? I should be there, celebrating with my girls.

I hope I didn't fuck this up beyond repair, because I don't know what I would do without them. I promised Sadie forever, and I will do everything in my power to show her I mean it.

Victoria wasn't right last night. This will last, we will last. People make mistakes, right?

Or was this too big of one to ever forgive?

27

Sadie

"It's okay not to be okay. I learned that from the best." Marco smiles, throwing my words back at me. He's entirely correct. But easier said than done.

I hang my head low, embarrassed that I can't control my emotions. I'm still so torn up after Friday night that it's impossible for me to be okay. How much grief can one person go through? Because just when everything seems perfect, something happens to rip it again.

"It's only been a few days," Evelyn whispers as she lies on my pillow with me, rubbing my arm.

"I know, but now that we both know each other's truths, why hasn't he come home to apologize?"

I'm at the point I'm not sure what I would say to him, but I know I want to see him. I hate it, but I miss him even if I'm extremely hurt by how Wills acted and how he spoke to me. His words hurt and cut me deep.

It was like I was living with my mother all over again. Whether he meant it or not, I won't excuse it, and he owes me an apology. Yet, I haven't heard from him since Friday, and it is now Tuesday.

The only thing keeping me from losing it on him is some information I found out the morning after the whole diabolical shit show.

When Eleanor and Evelyn came to check on me, they told me about a terrible situation Wills went through and why the birth certificate triggered terrible memories from an incident with his long-term ex, Libby.

When Wills and Libby broke up, she slept with another guy and got pregnant. She told Wills it was his. Wills had a feeling she was lying, so he asked for a paternity test. Of course, Libby was not happy one bit.

So, what did Libby do? Libby went to the tabloids and told them she was pregnant with Wills Taylor's baby and that Wills was choosing not to support her.

She told anyone who would listen that he wasn't planning on paying child support and that he was cutting her and the baby out of his life.

None of that was true, of course, but Libby needed the money since Wills wasn't there to support her anymore once they broke up, and tabloids pay big bucks for gossip.

Wills sued anyone he could, and most took the stories down, but the damage was done. All people could see and remember was Wills Taylor, the deadbeat dad. Not Wills Taylor, one of London's best rugby players.

This, of course, didn't just affect Wills. It affected the whole family. Poor Eleanor and Thomas were even looked at differently in their community. Because what type of parents raise a son who abandons his unborn child? And with Wills being so protective of the ones he loves, he did not react well to this. He felt guilty that they were going through this because of him.

No one listened to the follow-up stories of how it was fake. The damage was already done.

Luckily, some other celebrity did something worse not long after, and Wills was old news.

He became obsessed with making sure he stayed out of the spotlight, so his family wouldn't be ashamed of him. Not that they were, but he didn't handle the situation well. And it clearly still affects him if he reacted the way he did.

So, this is the dilemma running through me. I'm angry and hurt Wills would speak to me the way he did and how he left me, *again*.

But I can't help but also feel sad for my love. He reacted because of a terrible incident he suffered through, leaving scars that unmistakably aren't healed. So much so he hasn't even been by to see Charlie when he knows now, he's her dad.

Kathryn says he's called her every day but through her. Not me.

I have tried to put myself in his shoes, and there is a good chance I would have acted similarly, and many people would have. I'm just sad, for me, for him, and I'm nervous if something terrible happens again, will he just up and leave?

"He'll figure it all out soon. I think Mum scared the shit out of him, and he's afraid to come around."

"Wills is my person, Evelyn. He should be here making it better between us. The longer we are apart, the longer it makes me think he doesn't care as much as I do. Because, when Wills wants something, he goes for it. So clearly, he doesn't want us."

I bury my head in the pillow, willing myself not to cry again. This is all wrong. We should be in this together.

"Sadie," Marco draws out. "You know that's not true at all, so don't play that game with us."

"You're supposed to be on my side, you jerk. And agree with anything I say. That's what friends do," I mumble into the pillow, and Marco laughs.

I turn my head, coming face-to-face with Evelyn. "Do you think he'll come home?" I whisper and finally let the tears fall.

"I don't think, I know. Wills was more hurt than you'll know when he found out the truth. I think he's ashamed of himself. So, if he's not barging in here like the madman he normally is, it's not because Wills doesn't want to be with you. It's because he needs some time to forgive himself before you forgive him. Give it time, and I promise everything will be okay between the two of you. If I don't have faith in the two of you, I will never have faith in a relationship again." She smiles sadly.

She's told me many times she will never be with someone ever again. I hope she changes her mind. She's just shy of thirty and has a whole life ahead of her. I didn't know Andrew, but I couldn't imagine him wanting her to be alone for the rest of her life.

"I spoke to Alessia," Marco cuts in. I had him call her in case Wills didn't come home since it's so close to the move-in date on the other house. I may need to stay here, and I was too embarrassed to call her myself.

What a joke she must think we are.

"She isn't renting it anymore. Or at least not for a while, so it's all yours. Don't you worry, but I doubt you'll need it."

"Mommy?" I hear Charlie's groggy nap voice from my bedroom door.

"Cuddles?" I ask, and she nods her head and comes over to lie between Evelyn and me. Her hair splayed out on the pillow, mixing with both mine and Evelyn's dark hair to seem like one. Something I wouldn't have noticed before the paternity.

"Did you have a nice nap, sweet pea?" She solemnly nods her head. She's been sad the last couple of days, and I know it's because Wills isn't here. She thinks he's away on business, and this is how she gets whenever he *actually* has a business trip.

"Mommy and Marco are going to go to work this afternoon. Do you want to go to the library with Miss Kathryn?"

"No!" She starts to cry. I knew this was coming, but I can't mope around in bed. Unfortunately, we need to go over a few things in the shop today.

"I won't be home late. Then we can color in the books Nan gave you."

"Wills too?" My heart breaks, and I can hear Evelyn sniffle.

"He's…"

"Actually, sorry to interrupt," Kathryn says as she walks into the bedroom. *Wills*—she mouths so Charlie won't see—"called and was wondering if he can come by and take her out for the rest of the day. I think he assumed you were at work."

Oh… okay. "Yeah, she should still be able to see him. Marco and I are leaving for the office anyway." She nods sympathetically. "Thanks, Kathryn, for this weekend. You were a lifesaver to my mental health."

"Of course, I love you guys. Any extra time with Charlie is fine by me."

"Okay, baby girl, go get ready. Wills is coming to pick you up soon."

"Wills!" she screams and jumps off the bed. Okay, well, bye then.

"Ready?" I ask Marco.

"Yes, love, let's go."

"What in the world!" I snap my head back to Marco who is walking into **Sweet Pea Blooms** behind me, and he gasps.

"I take it you didn't do this?"

"Sadie, no," he says with wide eyes, looking around the store, then points to the table in front of us, the one Jackson had gifted me. There is a notecard with my name on it, and it reads:

Apology Number One
Objective: Make Sadie Remember

My beautiful Sadie,
There are not enough words in the dictionary to write how sorry I am for hurting you, for hurting us. I will regret that for all my days.
As a start to my apology, I wanted to do something that will make you happy and remember the good times.
I've framed and hung all your flower photographs.
Three of my personal favorites hang right in the center.
The first one is one you took of an English rose for my Charlotte.
The second one is of the sunflowers from Pierre's Garden where we went on our first date.
The third one is of the beautiful flowers from the Tuileries when we spent the night in Paris.

That day confirmed you were the one for me, and I think you felt the same. Do you remember?
Because I'll never forget.

I love you,
Wills

"Oh my god!" Marco screeches from behind me, and I turn my head around the room, taking in all the pictures. These frames are beautiful and ornate. Something I would have picked for the floral shop, no doubt.

He's enlarged and printed my favorite photographs I've taken over the years. Besides his favorite, he also added ones like my cherry blossoms from Japan, tulips from Holland, and black-eyed Susans from my old garden in the Hamptons.

"This man acts all tough, but he truly is a romantic at heart," Marco swoons.

I say that all the time.

"Uh-huh, let's get to work." I take one last look around before heading to my office, unable to stop the smile creeping up my face.

Damnit, Wills, you're going to make it very hard for me to stay mad, aren't you?

The next night I get home late for dinner. We had a daytime event that ran a little later than expected. So, when I come home to an empty house, I'm a little surprised. Until I see an envelope on the kitchen counter.

Apology Number Two
Objective: To get in Sadie's good graces

Of course, my goal is always to make you happy, but I also need to get

on your good side. So, with apology number two, I hope it helps you forgive me faster.
Felix Black, the famous international florist, will be doing a private one-on-one class with you here at the house at eight o'clock. Have fun, baby.

I love you,
Wills x

PS Charlotte will sleep at the penthouse tonight. If you want her home, Ev will drop her off later.

Oh my freaking god! How did he make this happen? Felix Black… Felix Black!!

Okay, I need to slow down. I'm running around the kitchen like a chicken with its head cut off.

I need to change and eat, and I don't know what else! Felix Black, holy crap. This is going to be amazing. I love and hate Wills for making me love him even more right now!

I'm playing right into his hand. *His plan is working.*

"Sadie?" I hear Evelyn calling from downstairs. "Almost ready. Be down in a sec!"

"Hi, how was last night?"

"Evelyn, it was a night to remember. It's like a painter meeting Picasso. Felix Black *is* my Picasso. I don't know how your brother did it, but he undeniably earned some brownie points."

"Good, good! This is good." She spits and walks toward the front door in a rush.

"Um, where's my kid, and why are you being so creepy?" I ask, narrowing my eyes at her.

She huffs out a laugh. "She's still with Wills. He took her to the office and gave Kathryn the day off. And I'll stop acting weird, but I feel all tingly and nervous, and it's not even me apologizing. And because I'm supposed to give you this and drive you there."

She hands over another envelope.

"Why can't Wills bring her home so that we can talk? I love what he's doing, but we need to talk and make up. I miss him."

"I don't know. He has his plan. Just go with it." She shrugs, and I open the envelope.

Apology Number Three

Objective: To make Sadie forget

I had to remind you of the good times first.
Now, my love, I need you to forget the bad times. I hope we can move on after this because I miss you, and I miss our family.
There's the old saying "the third time's the charm," so I hope that holds true with my apologies as well.

I love you always and forever,
Wills xx

I look over at Evelyn, and she has tears in her eyes.

"How does Wills call me a crybaby, but he had you as a sister?"

"Probably because I was only eight when he moved out." Oh, duh. I always forget they are ten years apart.

"Okay, well, where are you driving me to 'make me forget?'"

"I may be a crybaby, but I'm an excellent secret keeper." And she pretends to zip her mouth closed and throw away the key.

"Well, can we talk about something else then?" I ask, and she lets out what sounds like a bunch of air she was holding.

"Yes, please. I'm not actually good at keeping secrets from you. Distract me," she says in a rush, and we both burst out laughing.

We chat about nothing in particular and make it to wherever we are in about forty-five minutes.

I look around at the building, and I have no clue what this place is.

Evelyn hands me one more card, and I rip it open to see what it says.

Apology Number Three *Addendum*
Objective: To make Sadie forget-ish

Don't forget the good, only forget the bad.

I love you for eternity,
Wills xxx

"What is he even talking about?" I turn to ask Evelyn, but she's already waiting, holding the front door open.

"Come on this way!" she chirps. What the hell turned her mood so bubbly?

We take the elevator to the tenth floor, walk down the corridor, and then I see the sign.

Miss Meyer's Hypnotist Extraordinaire

"What?!" I bend over, laughing my butt off. "Is he kidding? I'm not going in there, right? He's crazy if he thinks I'm doing that." I can't breathe. I'm laughing so freaking hard right now.

I look over where Evelyn has fallen to the ground, gasping for air.

"How the hell does he even come up with this shit?" she says through her laughter.

There is no doubt my mascara is just running down my face right now, but I can't even care because Wills has outdone himself this time. If he were here, I can imagine he wouldn't even crack a smile. Instead, he would probably really try to make me forget.

"Seriously, Evelyn. I don't have to actually go in there, right?"

"No, he won't know the difference." She still can barely get the words out.

"You know, your brother wasn't kidding. He wanted me to go in there, right?"

She shakes her head, this is too much.

"There is a covered rooftop restaurant, and our friends are up there already. Marco is filling in the girls on what's gone down."

"Oh, thank God, let's go. I need a drink now." Both of us continue to laugh the whole way to the rooftop. How did Wills find this hypnotist, and did he call them himself? I can't wait to make up and find out all the details because he's too serious to have had me come here as a joke, which makes it all that more hilarious that he thinks I would try and erase my memories.

Before we make it outside to our friends, I ask Evelyn one last question.

"So, Will's last note made it seem like this was the last of it. When do I get to see him?"

She just shrugs. "I think the party on Saturday. I'm not sure."

"So, what happens tomorrow? I just sit around thinking about everything again? What kind of game is he playing?" As much as I appreciate all the effort Wills has put into the last few days, I still wanted to talk, and he owes me a genuine apology.

"I don't have the answers, but I think he wanted you to have a day to take it all in. Then talk in person before the party. That's all I know. I'm sure you'll be busy with last-minute party details anyway."

She's right. Charlie asked for an under the sea party, and every time I think it's going to be perfect, she says something like, "Do I get to wear red hair like Ariel?" or "Can my cake have bubbles on it?" She's driving me insane.

"There you two are!" Annabelle yells, and I know that face. She's pretending to be happy, but she's mad at me.

I cut her off before she even says anything. "Don't be mad. I would have told you everything once you got back. But I was not interrupting your amazing trip for Wills and Sadie drama. So don't start," I warn.

"Well, it's bullshit. I want you always to call me. I would have been here for you in a minute."

"I know, and I love you for it. That's exactly why I didn't call, though. This account is too important to you."

I lean over and give Marco and Lola a kiss.

"I want to hear all about Italy." I haven't been in such a long time, it was one of Belle and I's first trips abroad. And from what she told me, this new deal sounds promising—it would be huge for her career.

"What did Jackson say?" Lola asks,

"Um, well, I didn't tell him." I didn't want to get him involved. There was no reason after I spoke to Eleanor and Evelyn, I knew we would eventually make up.

"He knows," I hear Evelyn whisper to the girls. I whip my head around. "What do you mean he knows? You told him?" I accuse, and she narrows her eyes at me.

"Nooo, Wills told him," she snaps back.

What is she talking about? Why would he willingly tell him something like that?

"And, before you ask, I don't know why," she says and looks away, but Evelyn forgets I know her telltale sign of lying. Wills likes to tell me I wring my hands when I'm nervous. Well, Evelyn puts her hair behind her right ear every time she lies.

The question is, why is she lying about Wills telling Jackson?

Today is my sweet pea's third birthday, and I couldn't be more excited to celebrate her with all our friends and family. So many people celebrate first birthdays in a big way, but we've never had that. Charlie's first two birthdays weren't quite that big. They were special for me because I was happy to celebrate her life in any way. But we didn't have anyone else in our lives at the time except Annabelle, Jackson, and Maria. So big parties didn't make sense.

So today, she will have a packed house of people who love her, including some friends from the library and music class. It seems like my girl is pretty popular among her peers, which doesn't shock me at all.

Although I'm nervous to see Wills, Charlie's birthday is a good distraction, and I think Wills and I would agree that she comes first, today and always.

To start her special day, I made her pancakes for breakfast as requested. We took Buddy for a walk in the park, where she got to ride her bike for hours, and then we both got ready together. And she's about to leave with Kathryn while Annabelle and I grab her cake from the baker.

"John's outside waiting for you guys. I should be like an hour, tops. We are going to leave right when Belle gets here." No problem.

"Charlie, time to go," Kathryn calls.

Charlie rounds the corner, holding Buddy's leash, ready for her party.

"Sweet pea, I thought we would leave Buddy home since we have a lot of people at the house."

"What!" she shrieks. "But… but…" Her little lip starts to quiver.

"Buddy's my best fwiend. He comes to my party."

Oh my heart, maybe I *should* be shocked she makes so many friends at her classes because she really only cares about Buddy and Buddy alone.

"Pwease, Mommy," she begs.

Well, how the hell do I deny the kid on her birthday?

"Okay, sweet pea, he can come."

"Woo-hoo!"

Ugh. Just when I thought the woo-hoos were over. I kiss her goodbye and walk out of the house with them when I see Belle pull up in a cab.

"Hello, darling, ready for today?" A double meaning surely. Throwing parties are stressful but seeing your fiancé for the first time in a week after *hopefully* one of the biggest fights you'll ever have, is a stressor on its own.

"As ready as I can be. We need to talk, but I miss him, you know?"

She smiles over at me. "I know, Sadie, trust me. You guys will work it out, I promise."

We pull up to the bakery, and the baker already has the cake on a cart to push out to the cab.

Belle's eyes go wide, and she looks back at me in question. And I shrug. I may have gone overboard.

"It's her first real party, and I wanted to make it extra special." I'm now a little embarrassed seeing how big it is. It could be some people's wedding cakes. But Belle knows.

"It's perfect, darling, perfect for my goddaughter." She grins. She loves calling her that, it's her special connection.

"Alright, to the party we go! Hopefully, traffic isn't that bad. You had to pick the baker that was all the way across town, didn't you?" I don't respond. I had a vision, and this was the baker for the job. What did she want me to do?

We pull up to the new house, and it's all starting to hit me.

I was so crazy about the party, I forgot that this is my house, or supposed to be my house, yet I feel like an outsider. So now I'm second-guessing waiting to talk to Wills. Maybe I should have pushed and reached out to talk to him yesterday.

"Come on, you, don't overthink it." Belle rubs my back and gives me a quick hug.

"Look, Lola and Marco are just pulling up. They can help with this monstrosity of a cake."

I step out of the cab, and in the corner of my eye, I see him.

"Beautiful." I take a deep breath and turn toward him, and Wills is staring at me with a pained expression on his face.

"Can I talk to you before you go in? Alone?" he asks, looking over at Belle and Lola.

"Sadie?" Belle asks, concern laced through her voice. "Yeah, I'm good. I'll meet you inside. You good with the cake?"

"Yeah, the three of us can handle it." I turn back toward Wills.

"You look terrible," I mumble. He doesn't, really. He hasn't been taking care of himself, but he's still so handsome with his beautiful hair and perfect face. I've missed him. It's been a week now, the longest I've gone without seeing him for six months. "Thank you for your apologies. They were thoughtful and unexpected."

"Sadie…" His voice cracks. He scrubs his hands over his face and takes a deep breath.

"Sadie, I owe you an in-person apology." I continue to stay quiet; I don't want to get upset, and I want to hear what he has to say.

"I am so ashamed of myself for the way I spoke to you. It was disgusting, and you deserve to be with someone better."

"What?" I snap. Is he saying… he shakes his head.

"But, you are my forever, remember? And I will do whatever it takes to be that someone better." He smiles sadly and takes a deep breath again. I can tell this is hard for him. "I'm not perfect, Sadie, and I can't promise I'll never get crazy mad again, especially since you love to push my buttons." He smirks.

"But I am going to try and not jump to the worse conclusion first. I will try my hardest to give you the benefit of the doubt, and I promise to never, ever walk away again without talking with you. I can only hope we never go through something like this again. I think we both have had enough hurt in our lives."

"But Wills, you caused a lot of that hurt for me this time. You broke my heart," I say through my tears.

"I know, baby, I know. I broke my own heart too. You never deserved any of this. I can't take it back, so I'm just going to try and make things better."

"But do you really understand? The way you spoke to me, it's unacceptable. I can forgive you for walking out, honestly. This time you had good reason because of your past. But you said things to hurt me purposely." I see the remorse in his eyes, and he's having a hard time holding his tears back.

"I did. I won't lie. I was so mad at the time that I was blinded by anger, and I was trying to say anything I knew that would cut deep. It was a shitty thing to do. Trust me. I'm just utterly disgusted with myself. I just pray you can forgive me because this week has been one of the worst in my life. It was worse than when I lost you three years ago."

"Was it?" I ask, shocked.

"Last time, I blamed you and didn't know the truth. This time I sat in the penthouse all day and all night, just replaying everything back, replaying the words I said to you. Replaying how I ruined a moment that should have been one of the best days of our lives. We should have celebrated with Charlotte as a family, and I ruined that," he says with a sob. "I ruined something I didn't even know I wanted… so bad." He can barely make out his words. He's crying so hard, and I can't take it anymore. I think he's suffered and punished himself enough, so I run closer to him, wrap my arms around him and press my head into his chest. "I am so happy I'm her dad," he whispers into the top of my head.

"I know you are."

"I would have had been her dad either way. But this makes it so real. We made her together. She's a part of me and you and… I ruined that." He starts to cry again—he's losing control.

"Stop Wills. You need to stop." I pull back to get a good look at him.

"What would people say if they saw the big tough, Wills Taylor blubbering on like a baby?" I say, trying to make him laugh.

No laugh, but it stopped his crying.

"I accept your apology, and you didn't ruin anything. Or maybe for a second you did," I smile, trying to keep the conversation light.

"But let's move forward from here, okay? We live, and we learn. And the moment will still be special because we haven't told Charlie yet—she's going to be so excited. She might not understand fully, but she will be thrilled to call you Dad. She already loves you so much." I can tell my words mean a lot to him because his gray eyes sparkle with pure happiness.

"I'm so sorry, Sadie."

"I know, baby." I lean in for a kiss to reassure him, and he instantly wraps his arms around me.

"So, we'll be okay, my beautiful girl?"

"Yes, yes, we will." People go through difficult times, which will only help us grow in our relationship. He made a promise to try and be better, and that's all I can ask for. I don't ask for perfection, I just ask for us to both put the same effort into our relationship through the good times and the bad.

I pull back from our embrace. "Felix Black, Wills, Felix freaking Black! How the heck did you make that happen?"

He smirks. "I can't reveal all my secrets," he replies, and I huff in annoyance. "Ready, baby?" he asks.

"Yes, let's go see our daughter and celebrate her birthday."

"Our daughter," he whispers and smiles to himself. I've had a month to get used to this, but it's all new to Wills.

"And our housewarming party, Sadie. You and Charlotte will move in tomorrow, and you're sleeping here tonight," he states, and just like that, Wills is back, and I wouldn't have it any other way. "But, before all that. You have one last stop on the apology tour." He pulls me toward the front door of the house.

"I thought you said, 'The third one's the charm'?"

He stops, turns, and he smashes his plump lips into mine, catching me by surprise, but holds them there for a few seconds.

He pulls away slightly, and his deep voice whispers, "And one for good luck." He then turns back toward the house, with me in tow.

28

Wills

"WHAT IS THIS?" Sadie draws in a sharp breath of shock and takes a step back.

The curtains are drawn, and the lights are off. The long hallway leading toward the living room is filled with candles and stringed lights. There are vases of sweet peas at every step, shades of white and purple… Sadie's favorite.

She cocks her head to the side and eyes me suspiciously. But when I don't reply, she looks back, taking it all in.

I've done this for her before, and they were both important times in our relationship. Our first date in the vineyards, and then again, the night I said I love you. I don't want a copy or redo of those nights, but I want to mark the significant times in our life, and this will just be a reminder.

"This is lovely, Wills." She whirls around a few times. "Remarkable, really."

I stand there looking at my girl, and I can't believe I almost ended us.

A part of me always knew that two people in crazy love, soul mates, could never end. But I came close to hurting us permanently.

I have already promised to try harder for her, but in this instance, I vow never to be that person again. We aren't perfect, I'm not perfect. We will fight and not get along. But this beautiful, kind woman deserves the world, and I intend on giving it to her.

"Come on, baby, this way." I take her hand in mine and try to lead her toward the main room. "No, Wills," she whispers, still in shock. "Tell me what this is." Her excitement is turning to nervousness, her hand in mine starts to tremble. Why is she so nervous over this?

"I told you, it's my good luck apology. I needed an extra one, in case you didn't forgive me." I wink, and I lean down to kiss her forehead.

"Well, where are Charlie and all our guests?"

"Beautiful," I sigh. "Can you just relax and follow me?" She eyes me apprehensively but then nods.

"Okay," she whispers.

I lead her down the hallway. Her eyes haven't blinked and are as wide as saucers.

"Close your eyes, Sadie." Her body is giving off so many emotions right now. She's shaking with nerves but bouncing with excitement. She has no idea what to think.

"I'll lead you, baby, trust me." Her bright-green eyes shine up to me with curiosity, but her need to trust takes over, and she slowly closes her eyes.

I walk her to the middle of the room, with her back toward the kitchen, where our friends and family hide in the background.

The candles and flowers follow into the room, and soft music plays through the speakers.

"Sadie, my love." She opens her eyes slowly, and her mouth falls open. Her fingers lift to cover her mouth as she finds me down on one knee.

She looks around the room, and her eyes widen more, if possible, when she sees that the candles and the abundance of flowers also fill up the living room.

Sadie's eyes travel back down at me. "What are you doing?" She grabs my hand and tries to pull me back up. I don't budge, so she drops to her knees in front of me, and I can't help but laugh.

"What are you doing?" she says again. "You've already proposed, get up."

"No beautiful… sshh, let me get out what I need to say." I can see she's holding back tears but lets me continue.

"Over the last week, I've used my time alone to reflect upon myself, on our relationship, and what it means to me. What it means to be loved by you, and what it means to love you unconditionally. How I failed, but vow to do better. But also acknowledge life is not perfect, and we can only try our best. And, in that time, I've also learned something important—the true meaning of love. Love is not just a feeling. It is communication, trust, and understanding. It is compassion and forgiveness. It is the bond and union we have between the two of us, heart, body, and soul, without any boundaries. So, I'm asking you to marry me again, because I love you.

But most importantly, because I respect you. I respect our love, and I promise to do anything in this world to keep it close to my heart." I take a breath while Sadie tries to control the sobs bubbling out of her.

"Sadie Marie Peters, will you marry me? Will you marry me, knowing that I have learned from my mistakes and vow to continue allowing myself to learn and grow? I vow to be the best version of myself, day and night, always and forever. For you, for myself, for Charlotte and our future." I choke out the last part, emotions getting the better of me. I look at Sadie for her response, and I can barely see her eyes through her tears.

"Sadie," I whisper. Her body flies forward, taking me by surprise, and we both laugh as we fall to the ground. She leans over and looks down at me. Her tear-filled eyes change right in front of me to a look of total conviction.

"Yes, Wills, of course, I will *still* marry you. I will want to marry you today, tomorrow, forever, and always. Anytime you ask me, I will say yes. I love you."

. . .

Sadie

I lean down and kiss Wills with all my might. But I'm quickly interrupted and startled by the loud clapping, laughing, and whistling.

I look back, and all the other people I love most in the world are standing over us. Jackson, Annabelle, Declan, Marco, Lola, Evelyn, Eleanor, Thomas, and even Kathryn and John. All with teary eyes and smiles on their faces.

When the heck did they arrive? And what must we look like, flat out on the floor?

Charlie comes from behind Jackson, running full speed toward us in her sparkly pink birthday dress, and jumps right on top of Wills and me.

"Hi, sweet pea." I pull her in, and Wills wraps his arms around the both of us.

I love you, he mouths and then closes his eyes for a second as he kisses the top of Charlie's head.

"You said all that stuff in front of them?" I whisper, and he grins.

"I was hoping they didn't catch most of it."

"Oh, we caught it," Jackson teases.

"My brother is quite the romantic, isn't he?" And they both burst out laughing.

Wills will not hear the end of this from Jackson or Evelyn. It's their life's duty to bust each other.

"Okay, up you get! Share the love," Eleanor announces.

I lean my hand on Wills's chest to push myself up, and I feel something cold. It's a ring. I look at Wills, and he smiles as he slides it on my finger.

"I know we said we would design one. But it's been months, and it's time people know you're mine."

I sit up and bring my hand to my face to inspect it.

"Wills, it's beautiful. I love it." It's a large, *too large,* oval diamond that has to be at least five carats. The band is whisper thin, and the setting is in an antique gold design. It's simple but unique. Exactly what I wanted.

I don't even have a second more to admire it because Annabelle's there, pulling me off of Wills, bringing me in for a hug. "I'm so incredibly happy for you, Sadie. I love you and Wills so much. I'm glad things are working out for the both of you. I knew from the beginning that you two were meant to be together." She sniffs, and I beam up at my best friend. She has been my best support system for nearly my whole life, and I'll never take that for granted.

I pull her into a hug and tell her, "I'm the luckiest girl on earth, most people don't meet their soul mate, but I've met both of mine." She hugs me tighter, and I can feel her tears soaking my shirt.

What a bunch of crybabies our group is, Wills included. The only one who didn't cry is the actual baby.

"Auntie Belle! Let's pway." Charlie breaks us out of the moment, and then I think, "Where the heck are all Charlie's friends?"

"I called all the parents to push the time up. We should probably blow out all these candles before a bunch of toddlers come over," Wills replies.

So that's what we do, and then for the next few hours, Wills and I watch our little girl have the best birthday with her new friends in her new home. With her life-size-ish mermaid cake and people that love her and loved celebrating her life.

"Finally, no more kids," Marco says as he plops down in my seat as I get off the sofa.

"Hey, one of those kids was mine," I call and sneak a peek at said kid.

She's lying on Declan's chest, both of them fast asleep. Apparently, kids like big men with tattoos because he was the life of the party. Uncle Dec for the win.

"Charlie is literally the best little person in the world, so she doesn't count," he yells back as I walk into the kitchen.

"Sades." I turn and find Jackson sitting at the kitchen counter. "Come sit for a minute."

I take a seat next to him, and he wraps his arm around me.

"Congrats again. I've said it before, but Wills is the exact guy I would have picked for you. Even if he's a little crazy at times, at least he's crazy in love with you, huh?" He smiles warmly at me.

"That means a lot, thank you. And thank you for helping set this all up." I wave my hand around to the flowers and decorations.

"Of course, and I want you to know that no matter what, you'll always be my priority. So even though you have a new man in your life, you can still always count on me, and I'll always be there."

"I know, honey, that's why you're the absolute best. And hey, that goes both ways." I kiss him and sneak a glance back to the living room, and happiness swirls around my stomach.

How did I get so lucky to be loved by so many amazing people?

"A toast!" Annabelle says, raising her glass of champagne. Jackson and I walk back toward them. I settle up next to Wills, and he wraps his arm around me, pulling me into his side.

"To catching the eyes of your soul mate across a hotel lobby, and to taking chances. Cheers to Sadie and Wills."

"Cheers to Sadie and Wills!" Our family cheers in unison, and we all clink glasses.

We drink champagne, laugh, cry, tell jokes, and funny stories the rest of the night.

A celebration I won't be forgetting anytime soon.

"Time for bed, beautiful." Wills picks me up, and I look at our friends, half sleeping, some still drinking.

"They can stay in the guest rooms or the couch if they want." He always knows exactly what I'm thinking. It's so late for them to go home now, and I don't want to interrupt their fun. I like having them in the new house. It feels right.

I nuzzle into his muscular chest and let him carry me to our room. A new room for a new start.

"Oh, Wills!" I squeal. My head turns wildly back and forth, taking it all in. What did he do? How did he do this? "This wasn't what we agreed upon with Evelyn." I look around the room again, and it's completely different from what we first chose. We went with something modern and fresh initially, so we wouldn't get tired of it. But… this is something else. This is so me.

"I wanted it to be a surprise, and I thought the bedroom could be your special place. We even built an area over in the corner for you to read." Wills points to a little nook with antique-looking bookshelves, filled with all my favorite romance novels.

The room is modeled after our suite at The Ritz in Paris. Nineteen twenties glamour.

Evelyn did an excellent job of modernizing it so it won't feel dated but would still have an old-world feel.

It's filled with beautiful jewel tones and art deco decor. I never thought Wills would go for something like this, but it's lovely. Everything Evelyn gets her hands on turns into a work of art.

"I love it, thank you, you spoil me. And thank you for getting this house for us. We are going to make amazing memories here."

"We are, Sadie. Starting in about one minute when I strip you out of these clothes because I haven't seen you in a week." I giggle. I would say he's addicted, but I need him just as he needs me. He playfully throws me on the bed.

"Mr. Taylor, I think I need a reminder of what this fiancé sex is all about. It's been too long."

"Clothes off now," he growls.

"Patience, baby." I smirk at my crazy man.

"Sadie, I don't have time for fucking patience. Clothes off now."

"I noticed you didn't add love is having patience in your vow earlier," I tease.

"A man can only hold himself accountable for so much, and I know patience will never be one of those things. Last time I'll repeat myself, clothes off."

"Sir, yes sir!" I slip out of my dress, panties, and bra as he takes off his pants, still in his dress shirt.

He's staring with one eyebrow raised. "How much champagne have you had, Sadie?"

"Enough." I shrug playfully.

His long muscular legs stride over to me fast. He flips me over and swipes his finger through my behind. Then applies pressure to the forbidden zone.

"Enough to let me have this?"

"Never!" I giggle and shimmy away from him up to the pillows, both of us laughing. He reaches up, grabs my ankles, and pulls me back down toward him.

"God, I missed you, beautiful," he whispers.

"Every inch of you, every single fucking inch of you, I've missed. It was like I was missing a limb. You are mine."

"I know, baby. I am yours, and you are mine." His eyes lock with mine, and he slowly unbuttons his shirt. Exposing his broad, muscular chest and perfectly formed abs.

My eyes greedily take him all in. He's perfect.

He crawls over me in what feels like slow motion until we come face-to-face.

Wills's gray eyes are shining bright tonight, and I can't help but reach up to trace his face.

I'm reminded of one of the first times I was face to face with him like this, when we had lain on the beach of the French Riviera, watching the spectacular sunrise.

He leans down to press his lips against mine, then eventually makes his way down, exploring my neck and the magic spot behind my ear.

"Wills," I choke out. I need him.

"Not yet, baby, let me…" His hand travels down my body and finds my sweet spot as his lips move back to mine, kissing me deeply. You can hear how aroused I am, my wetness on his fingers echoes through the room.

My legs naturally open wider. I need more. Why is he torturing both of us?

"Good girl, Sadie. Let me warm you up because I'm about to freaking lose control any second now."

I look down, and I see the pre-ejaculate dripping out of his tip. I try to reach for it, but he's too far down. *Ugh.* "Wills…" I groan. "Now, baby." He thought he lost me, but I don't just crave him, I crave our intimacy too. I could never live without this. "Please!" I beg, and he chuckles darkly as he crawls back up my body, rubbing himself against me in the same motion.

I throw my head back. I can't take it anymore. It's too much.

"Look at you, Sadie, my shy girl, truly doesn't exist anymore. Does she?"

"No, so put it in me already. For someone who doesn't believe in patience, you're really trying mine."

He throws his head back on a laugh, and I can't help but smirk.

I am feisty tonight.

When his eyes come back to mine, I can see them like it's night and day. They instantly darken as he presses himself against my opening.

The burn creeps through my body, a reminder he hasn't been inside of me in over a week.

He goes to pull back, giving me the time I need to adjust, *but not today.*

I bring my legs around, circling his body, and press down with all my might, so he slides back into me.

"Shit, Sadie," he moans.

My eyes close, and I take a deep breath through my nose to deal with the pain.

"You okay, baby?" he rasps, and I nod my head.

He pulls out and slides right back in. Moving his hips round and round, hitting all the right spots.

"Harder, Wills." He shakes his head.

"Go, now." He lifts his head to reach my eyes, and I nod, telling him to go.

I know he wants to go slow for me, but tonight I need it fast and hard.

Same as him.

He nuzzles in my neck, brings his hips back, then slams into me.

Over and over, unrelenting.

He leans up, takes my legs, and throws them over his shoulders, a move making him go so, so deep.

My eyes close for just a second.

"Eyes open," he demands.

His pace, if possible, goes faster. Pumping me harder and deeper. I won't last another minute and judging by his face, he won't either. The sounds of our bodies slamming together and our moans echoing throughout the room puts me over the edge, and I scream his name continuously as I come apart.

Wills' eyes glaze over, and he follows right behind me, biting my ankle as his cock jerks and fills me up. Collapsing on top of me.

Not a second later, he leans up to take my lips again. This time slow and loving.

"I'm so sorry, Sadie."

"Don't," I warn, maybe a little too forcefully. But it's over. We've moved past it. "Just, don't. Okay? I love you," I whisper and take his lips back with mine, needing that tender connection now.

"Sadie Marie Taylor," Wills whispers.

"Actually, I'm keeping my last name. I'll still be Sadie Peters," I deadpan.

"What!" he shrieks.

I start to laugh. God, I can't even keep up a lie for a second. "I'm kidding, I'm kidding."

"That's the worst joke on the face of the planet," he says through clenched teeth.

"I know, baby. I couldn't help it."

"Good, because I don't want to have to remind you that you're mine. In all aspects, including your name."

"Well, maybe I need another reminding," I tease as I wiggle against him.

"Sadie," he warns. And I smile up at my brooding man.

Of course, I will take Taylor. It will be a perfect day when I can share the last name of my best guy and my daughter.

Mrs. Sadie Taylor.

"Mommy?" I hear through the monitor, then little feet and little paws are on the move.

"Did you lock the door?" I ask Wills, and he's up, running into the bathroom before Charlie makes it to the bedroom. Luckily this house is much bigger, and it will take her longer to get here.

"Mommy?" I hear again, but her voice quivers. I get up, put on my robe, and look down the hall. My poor baby is confused. It's the first time sleeping here.

"Hi, sweet pea. Why aren't you in bed?"

"I scared and Buddy scared."

"He is, is he?"

"Mmhmm." She nods her head. "We sleep with you, Mommy? And Wills?"

"Of course, come on." I lean down, pick her up, and bring her back to our room.

Wills must have heard the whole thing because he's already changing the sheets. Smart man.

We all get in the bed, Charlie between us. It feels fitting for us to be all together tonight.

"I love you, my beautiful girl." Wills turns his head on his pillow to look over at me, reaching his hand to move the hair out of my eyes.

"I love you more."

"I promise you. You don't." He cups my cheek as he leans over Charlotte to kiss me good night.

"And I love you, princess." But she's already fast asleep, snuggled into Wills's side, as Buddy lays across her feet.

Today was a day for the books. Our first engagement was special between just us, something unexpected and marvelous—surprising and fast. But that's how we do things, always have, always will. We will have that memory between the two of us for the rest of our lives.

But today's engagement had a different meaning for me, not *more* meaningful or memorable. But it will be held in another special place in my heart because I could share it with all my family.

Something I wouldn't have been able to say just a few years ago.

I, especially, know how important it is to cherish your family… the people that are there to love and support you, blood or chosen.

Eventually, my eyes close, sad for today's end but excited for tomorrow and the future.

Tomorrow we get to tell Charlie she has a daddy who loves us both very much and completes us in every way.

Tomorrow officially changes the three of us. We go from making a family to becoming one.

And nothing will ever change for Wills and me… soul mates are for life.

Then, now, and forever.

EPILOGUE

Ten Months Later

Wills

"AND I SAVE the best for last. Thank you to my fiancée and biggest supporter, Sadie. The Taylor Foundation would not exist if it weren't for her, the true philanthropist in our family. Her altruistic ways have pushed me to be a better person, day in and day out. Sadie has volunteered in New York and now London at the World Animal Shelter for the last ten years, walking, feeding, and taking care of cats and dogs, come rain or shine. Her selfless ways have not only rubbed off on me but also on our daughter, Charlotte. Instead of begging to play with her friends in the park on Saturday mornings, she is asking how many dogs we can walk that day."

As some of the crowd quietly laughs, I glance over to find Sadie sitting with our friends and family.

She smiles softly at me and rubs her hand over her heavily pregnant stomach.

I can't keep my eyes off of her. She's more beautiful than ever.

"I'm not a betting man, but I would bet anything that next year, Sadie will be standing up here accepting this award. She has just announced she will be starting Amelia's Angels, a shelter for sick and elderly animals that normally get overlooked. What makes this foundation unique is that Amelia's Angels will also be a program for people with disabilities of any age to volunteer. A cause near and dear to our heart." I pause to look over at Declan, and he nods his head in appreciation.

"So, thank you Sadie, and thank you to the city of London for awarding The Taylor Foundation with such a prestigious award. Knowing we helped even one family and child was enough, but knowing we reached so many so quickly was the ultimate fantasy, and I'm proud that we made it come true. We hope that The Taylor Foundation will eventually help families throughout Great Britain over the next few years. Cheers!"

The room erupts in applause, and I exit the stage to make it over to our table.

"Stay put," I tell Sadie, who is struggling to stand up.

"Stop fussing and help me. I want to give you a proper kiss to congratulate you," she snarks.

I help her, and she leans up to kiss me. "I'm so incredibly proud of you and thank you for saying such kind words about me and Amelia's Angels," she says against my lips. I pull back and rub my hands over her stomach.

"How are you feeling?"

She shrugs. "Big, fat, swollen, tired. But happy." She smiles up at me. My beautiful girl is ready to give birth any day now.

When I was told I would be honored with an award for growing one of the fastest and most successful charities, I was thrilled. But then they told us it was today. I wanted Declan to accept on the foundation's behalf, but Sadie wouldn't have it.

I kid around that unplanned pregnancies must be our thing. But I quickly learned to shut my mouth because Sadie did *not* think it was funny.

In all seriousness, we couldn't be happier to add another little girl to our family.

Someone tonight asked me if I was upset that we weren't having a boy. And in all honesty, I have zero interest in having a boy.

Of course, I would have been thrilled either way, but I love taking care of my girls, so I couldn't imagine messing up what we have already.

"Congrats, Taylor. I'm proud of you." Jackson slaps my back and puts his arm around my shoulder.

"Yeah." Declan comes around to shake my hand. "I'm glad you asked me to be a part of this, mate. It's really good what the foundation is doing, congrats."

"Me too, although you're never around anymore, so who would know?" I eye him suspiciously. For a long time now, I've known something's been going on with him, and I want to know what the hell it is. And I'm pretty sure my fiancée knows something about it but is keeping quiet.

"Sadie!" Mum cries from the other side of the table, trying to push herself through the crowd.

"Oh sweetie, why didn't you tell me?" Sadie only made Amelia's Angels official this week and wanted to tell Mum about it in person, which I just remembered now. So, I'm sure I'll be hearing about it when we get home. And sure enough, Sadie turns quickly to give me a look.

"Mom, he was supposed to let me tell you about Amelia's foundation myself. But I hope it's okay we used her name."

"Are you kidding? It's an honor to have her name live on. I think it's time for her memory to be set free into the world." There was a weight lifted off of Mum when she met Charlotte, and I think it gave her the motivation to open up and get closure for herself.

"Slim," Declan groans. "Come on, Lass. Just sit down and relax."

"I'm going to kill you, my brother and Wills, if the three of you don't stop nagging me all the time. I'm fine!" Declan puts his hands up in defense. My girl has become a little feisty in her third trimester, I can't stand it. But I love watching the wrath of Sadie turned on someone else for once.

"Ready to go home to our girl?" I whisper in Sadie's ear.

Soon we will have a little baby to take care of, and I want as much time to ourselves as I can get.

Sadie looks back and smiles—I know that look.

That's the… I want to go home to have sex because my pregnancy hormones are out-of-control look.

"Behave, Sadie." I nip at her ear, and the goose bumps scatter up her arms.

"Yeah, let's go home to our girl," she says with a wink.

Eighteen Months Later

Sadie

I'm watching my husband, fast asleep, with both our girls on his lap, and Buddy at his feet.

Although a couple of years older now, Wills is still just as gorgeous as the day I met him. He works out harder than normal, making sure he never gets the dreaded *dad bod*.

I'm certainly not complaining about it.

Charlie is a real showstopper; she will be a knockout when she's older. She's five and a half now, and still, people stop to tell me how beautiful my daughter is. Her eyes are bluer than blue against her porcelain skin and long dark hair.

If she gets Wills's height, she'll blow Annabelle out of the water in the looks department. But of course, her strong outgoing personality is her greatest trait.

Chloe is a proper mix of Wills and me. She has Wills's light-brown hair, but my tanned skin and green eyes, and Will's dark eyelashes.

Belle and Lola like to say she's going to be the one to catch.

She'll be overlooked at first because she is shy and quiet, but whoever catches her will get the real surprise of a lifetime because she's a rare gem.

"Please prepare for landing," the captain says over the loudspeaker.

I get up to take one of the girls from Wills since he can't buckle them in at the same time.

"Hi, wife." His eyes are still closed, but he's smiling up at me.

"Hi, husband. I'm going to take Chloe so we can all be buckled in."

"Hey." He grabs my free hand, and I look back at him.

"This week was incredible. I love you."

"I love you, too, baby."

He looks down at Charlie then Chloe.

"Should we just buckle them in and go in the back quick, for old times' sake?"

"Wills!" I laugh. He's probably not kidding.

"The girls are not staying with us. We will have all the alone time in the world once we get to Paris." He wiggles his eyebrows in excitement, and to be honest, I can't freaking wait.

We've just left the South of France and we're now flying to our wedding in Paris. It's being held at The Ritz with all our friends and family.

But little does anyone know, we got married this past week in secret, at the same hotel we met: just me, Wills, our girls, and Buddy.

And, of course, we did it on a whim.

But that's us.

The best part was that Wills wore his linen suit, the one he wore all those years ago.

We would have liked to get married right away, instead Chloe was born, and it was pushed back. But it turned out perfect. I wouldn't have wanted it any other way.

That was our third year in a row going to the hotel.

I was worried the first time would trigger something in me, but it didn't, luckily. Having Wills and Charlie there the first time helped. They were the support I needed.

My phone pings in my hand as we land, finally getting service.

I pull my eyebrows in. "Who is that?" Wills asks, concerned. I pass him my phone, and I can practically hear the anger simmering off of him.

He passes me back my phone. "Deleted. You're a Taylor now and the only Peters you need in your life is Jackson."

It was from my mother.

This is the second time she's reached out since Charlie was born. Yes, *second.*

And only because she's a narcissist, only caring about her image.

News broke that Wills was Charlie's biological father.

So, my estranged mother sent me a text asking why I was keeping her grandchild away from her. The granddaughter she wanted nothing to do with when she thought she was 'illegitimate.'

Now, this being the second text. I didn't even look at it, but I know it's about the wedding. I got an alert that news broke about the location.

So, I'm sure she was vying for an invite. God forbid, her perfect image gets tarnished, having a daughter who would wed without her.

"Mrs. Taylor." Wills breaks me out of my thoughts. Thank God, because I don't want to ever think of her again.

"Mr. Taylor." I smile and give him my hand to hold while we exit the plane.

He's holding Chloe in his other arm, and I have Charlie's hand in mine while she holds on to Buddy's leash in her other.

One big family, literally always attached.

"Ready to get married again, beautiful?"

"Born ready, baby."

"Woo-hoo!" *Please, God, help me.*

Four Years Later

I'm lying on the sofa with Charlie, Buddy, and Clara. She's our third daughter, who is about six years younger than Charlie and two years younger than Chloe.

Clara and Chloe are very similar. Having an older sister like Charlie, who always wants to be the center of attention, can be intimidating.

Wills just walked in the room, and I can't even look at him. He's in a big time-out.

He sits on the other sofa, holding our two-month-old baby Claire.

She and Wills share a birthday, and I have a feeling our little girl is going to give us heaps of trouble with a strong personality, like Wills and Charlie.

We didn't mean to name all the girls with *C* names, it just kind of happened after Chloe. All four girls have middle names after flowers, of course, that was planned.

Charlotte Rose, Chloe Aster, Clara Violet, and Claire Ivy.

I told Wills, this is it. I can't have any more babies, four is my limit. But he's not convinced, he wants five or six.

Wills is the absolute best dad, and he worships the ground all of his girls walk on. He's hands-on, always there to help the girls and me, no matter what. So, I know I would have the support, but still. *Not happening*.

His response to me was, I always said no to anal, and that finally happened.

Yes… I finally gave in after years of him begging.

It wasn't bad, and we do it on occasion. It's just not my favorite—he's too big.

My phone dings with a message:

Apology Number One
Objective: To show Sadie how sorry I am

You know I didn't mean it. Please don't be mad at me, beautiful.
It was truly an accident.
Go upstairs. I've started a bath for you, and I'll put all the girls to sleep.

I love you, always and forever.
Wills xx

I look over at Wills. *I'm sorry*, he mouths, and I look away, back down at Charlie, who hasn't stopped crying all night, and it's breaking my heart.

I know he's sorry, and he didn't mean it. But I'm upset.

Charlie and Buddy's relationship hasn't changed in the last seven years. If anything, their bond has gotten stronger. They are the best of buds and completely inseparable.

The other girls love him, and he loves them but nothing like Charlie.

She even missed her best friend's tenth birthday because Buddy wasn't feeling well. She didn't want him to be lonely without her.

Buddy didn't feel well because he was diagnosed with an aggressive form of cancer and doesn't have much time to live.

I barely could breathe when the doctor told us, and keeping my emotions at bay in front of the girls has been the hardest.

Buddy is one of my children, and has been a part of our family for as long as I've been with Wills. So we're not taking it well.

But I just knew Charlie was going to be a freaking wreck when she found out.

This morning, Evelyn called from New York, where she is away for business, and Wills filled her in about Buddy.

Charlie overheard and went ballistic.

I heard the scream cries all the way from outside. I've never seen someone in so much pain before. It's something a mother never wants to see their kid go through.

My heart is just breaking for Charlie every second, and I don't really know what to do. I know it was an accident on Wills's part, but I'm just upset I wasn't there for her.

I look at Wills again. *Please go*, he mouths.

I kiss all the girls good night and give Buddy some extra love.

When I get to the bathroom, I realize maybe Wills was right. This is exactly what I needed to get my mind off of everything.

My favorite jazz station is on. He lit my favorite candles and even added my scented bubble bath he hates.

I close my eyes… this is relaxing.

I'm running myself ragged between the girls, a newborn baby, and work.

I'm supposed to be on maternity leave, but I can't help myself.

Marco is still my right-hand man. He runs **Sweet Pea Blooms** while I take care of the girls, but fashion week is in one month, which will include some of our biggest clients. So, it's all hands on deck.

I must have dozed off because I wake as Wills pushes me forward a bit to get in behind me. He tops off the bath with some hot water, and pulls me back to relax against his chest.

"I'm sorry, beautiful. It's killing me too, you know," he says with his lips pressed against the side of my head.

"I know, baby." I turn my head to catch his lips.

I will never tire of kissing this man while he holds me in his arms. All these years later, I wouldn't change one second of our life together. He is my everything, and now with our girls, life with Wills is nothing but perfection.

"Let me make you feel better. It's all part of my apology." He trails his hands down my body and through my sex.

I throw my head back in pleasure, going from sad to turned on instantly. I was only cleared last week to have sex, and it's safe to say I've missed this. I've missed Wills.

Wills is forty-six now, but his sex drive hasn't slowed even one bit. We can't get enough of each other, and I can't see that ever changing.

He picks me up and slowly brings me down onto him. Both of us release a loud moan.

"Can we stay like this forever?" I ask.

"Of course, my beautiful girl. It's my favorite place to be."

Me too, baby, me too.

THE END

ALSO BY J R GALE

The Taylored Men Series

London Lovers (Wills and Sadie)

Destined Lovers (Declan and Nora)

Secret Lovers (Jackson and Annabelle)

Novellas

Lilacs and Lovers (Lola and Matthew)

The Bonded Brother Series

Coming Soon

AFTERWORD

Thank you so much for reading my debut novel.
It means the world to me to have your support!
If you enjoyed reading London Lovers, please consider leaving a review.

Don't forget to check online for other releases and my website for my newsletter and updates.

ACKNOWLEDGMENTS

First and foremost, many thanks go out to the incredible and selfless T L Swan.
I've always had a creative mind, and after hearing your story, I knew this would be the next step for me. You're an inspiration.

Thank you to my fellow Cygnet Inkers for the continued support, wisdom, and encouragement.
Especially for those who I have constantly relied on.

To my betas, Katie, Vicki, Jaclyn, and Ali, thank you is not good enough to express my appreciation for the time and commitment you gave my characters. Your words and support over those few months made this book what it is today.

To my cousin, Katie, you have endured three-hour-long phone calls about two fictional people and analyzed every detail with me before I even started writing. Thank you for being the best sounding board.

To my family, Michael, Mom, and Dad. Thank you for always supporting my crazy ideas and ventures. And, Michael, for dealing with my very late nights and becoming a hermit for months at a time.

To my friends who had to hear about my book and nothing else for months. Thank you for being the best listeners and encouragers out there.

To Scooter, my golden retriever and first baby, who I sadly lost in 2021 to cancer. You were my inspiration for Buddy. Now you can live forever in my books.

Last but not least, to you, the reader. Thank you for believing in me and reading Sadie and Wills's story. I hope you love them as much as I do. They will always hold a special place in my heart as my debut novel. Remember, this is not possible without you!

J R Gale xx

ABOUT THE AUTHOR

J R Gale is a contemporary romance author obsessed with the happily ever after.
She is a native New Yorker, residing in New York City with her husband and dog Skipper.
When she's not thinking of your next alpha book boyfriend, you can find her traveling the world—romance book in hand.